MW00378392

Praise f

'A lovely, sunshiney story, bursting with wit and joy.'
Milly Johnson

'Has the Bella Osborne hallmark combination of wit,
wonderful characters and meaningful conflicts that never
fails to provide a fantastic read.'
Sue Moorcroft

'Sparkling and laugh out loud – Bella's books are
like a glass of the finest bubbly.'
Phillipa Ashley

'Bella's done it again, another gorgeous page turner of
a story. From the opening chapter I was completely
hooked by this fresh, funny tale full of Bella's
trademark wit and warmth.'
Jules Wake

'The summer invite you need to accept. It's a funny,
warm and gloriously uplifting romance with loveable
characters and, like all Bella's books, is the perfect blend
of hilarious and heart-warming.'
Cressida McLaughlin

'Pure, joyous escapism bursting with sunshine!
An absolute delight to read!'
Christie Barlow

'A gorgeous, feel-good summer read that will bring a smile to your face and joy to your heart.'
Kim Nash

'A perfect ray of sunshine. Packed full of love and laughter, this fun and funny read is
Bella Osborne at her best.'
Sarah Bennett

'Sparkling with warmth and wit, Bella's books are guaranteed to put a smile on my face.'
Cathy Lake

'I loved this book!'
Susan Mallery

Finding Love at Sunset Shore

Bella has been jotting down stories as far back as she can remember but decided that 2013 would be the year that she finished a full-length novel. Since then, she's written nine bestselling romantic comedies, two bestselling book club reads and won the RNA Romantic Comedy Novel of the Year Award.

Bella's stories are about friendship, love and coping with what life throws at you. She lives in Warwickshire, UK with her husband, daughter and a cat who thinks she's a dog. When not writing Bella is usually eating custard creams and planning holidays.

For more about Bella, visit her website at www.bellaosborne.com. You can follow Bella on Twitter @Osborne_Bella, Instagram @BellaOsborne Author, TikTok @BellaOsborneAuthor, or on Facebook – BellaOsborneAuthor.

Also by Bella Osborne:

It Started at Sunset Cottage
A Family Holiday
Escape to Willow Cottage
Coming Home to Ottercombe Bay
A Walk in Wildflower Park
Meet Me at Pebble Beach
One Family Christmas
The Promise of Summer
A Wedding at Sandy Cove
An Invitation to Seashell Bay

BELLA OSBORNE

Finding Love at Sunset Shore

avon.

Published by AVON
A division of HarperCollins*Publishers* Ltd
1 London Bridge Street
London SE1 9GF

www.harpercollins.co.uk

HarperCollins*Publishers*
Macken House 39/40 Mayor Street Upper
Dublin 1 D01 C9W8

A Paperback Original 2024

1

First published in Great Britain by HarperCollins*Publishers* 2024

Copyright © Bella Osborne 2024

Bella Osborne asserts the moral right to be identified as
the author of this work.

A catalogue copy of this book is available from the British Library.

ISBN: 9780008588045

This novel is entirely a work of fiction.
The names, characters and incidents portrayed in it are
the work of the author's imagination. Any resemblance to
actual persons, living or dead, events or localities is
entirely coincidental.

Set in Minion Pro by HarperCollins*Publishers* India

Printed and bound in the UK using 100% renewable electricity at
CPI Group (UK) Ltd

All rights reserved. No part of this text may be reproduced, transmitted, downloaded, decompiled, reverse engineered, or stored in or introduced into any
information storage and retrieval system, in any form or by any means, whether
electronic or mechanical, without the express written permission
of the publishers.

This book contains FSC™ certified paper and other controlled sources
to ensure responsible forest management.

For more information visit: www.harpercollins.co.uk/green

For my daughter, Grace. Here's to another chapter!
All my love, Mum x

Chapter One

Ros hated being late but if she needed a good excuse then taking a custard pie to the face was probably it.

'Seriously!' she snapped as she blinked gloop out of her eyes.

A group of student types in varying states of drunkenness fell about laughing.

'Here, let me help you,' said a kind male voice.

Ros looked up and was surprised to see someone quite a bit older than the others, with rainbow chalk-sprayed bushy hair and wearing a bright orange tutu. In any other situation she may have found him good-looking. 'Thanks, but I think you've done enough.'

'It wasn't me who threw it although it was meant for me and I did kind of duck out of the way. So, apologies.'

'Fine,' said Ros, scraping the worst of it off her face before realising it had all blobbed down her suit. 'Bloody hell.'

'It's just shaving foam – it'll wash out. I promise,' he said with a smile.

'Come on! Time for birthday shots!' shouted one of the other tutu-wearing gang and the rest broke into a chant of

'Shots! Shots! Shots!'

'Hang on!' he shouted at them before turning back to Ros. 'You sure you're okay?' he asked.

'Never better,' she said, as she marched away trying to ignore the sniggers of the people she passed. Southampton city centre was student party central on a Friday night and Ros berated herself for not picking somewhere quieter to meet her friend. She was thankful that it wasn't far to the little Italian restaurant and she was pleased to see Darla sitting at a table in the window, her highlighted hair in a ponytail and wearing her favourite 'going out' top. Ros went straight over, picked up the napkin and began wiping off the last of the mess.

'Blimey! Foam parties. That takes me back,' said Darla.

Ros gave her friend a long-suffering look. 'Some idiots chucked a plate in my face.'

'Shit. Sorry. Are you all right?' Darla was checking her over.

'A paper plate piled up with shaving foam,' elaborated Ros. 'Is there more on me anywhere?' she asked, feeling that she'd done a good job of tidying herself up.

Darla pointed to her head. Ros whipped out her phone, put it on camera and an image of her with an Elvis-style foam quiff appeared. 'Bloody students. They're a menace.'

'Shall I order you a white wine while you pop to the ladies?'

'Yes, please. A large Pinot Grigio. But only if it's been properly chilled,' said Ros, dashing off.

Ros felt better for sorting herself out in the ladies, and the damage was really only some unfortunately located damp patches in the boobs area of her jacket, although her fringe was now sticking to her forehead in that unattractive way it did when she got caught in the rain. She brushed out the rest of her dark shoulder-length hair to make herself more presentable. She returned to the table to find a large glass of wine waiting for her. She sat down and finally felt some of the tension ease in her shoulders.

'Bad day?' asked Darla.

'I don't understand why someone else's lack of planning instantly becomes my crisis.'

'Because you're good at sorting things out?' suggested Darla.

She wasn't wrong but Ros still found it incredibly frustrating and completely unfair that they called on her as the risk manager, expecting her to suddenly dive in to fix things and stop them contravening something they shouldn't just because they hadn't adhered to due process in a timely manner. She produced lengthy and meticulously detailed reports and yet they were rarely read by anyone other than herself. 'But if people just thought ahead it would make life so much less—'

'Fun, spontaneous, enjoyable?' offered Darla.

'I was going to say stressful.'

'That too. Talking of stressful, I tried the cruise ships again but no luck. Apparently my skill set isn't what they're looking for.'

'Sorry,' said Ros. 'But aren't you sorted jobwise with the house-sitting, cleaning and bar work?'

'Whilst I obviously love the glamour, I would ditch it all in a second for a chance to travel and get paid – a job on a cruise ship would be perfect. That's why I came to Southampton in the first place after The Wanker did what he did.'

Ros realised she didn't actually know the real name of Darla's ex; he'd always been referred to as The Wanker. A fitting title given he had squandered money on get-rich-quick schemes – all of which had come to nothing – whilst incurring debts along the way. What Darla hadn't fully comprehended until the bailiffs had turned up on her doorstep was that most of the debt was either in joint names or on her credit cards, and the minute he had disappeared she had become liable to repay it all. Her choice had been between finding a way to repay everything or declaring bankruptcy and forever having a terrible credit rating, but in either case she had to admit – to herself but certainly not to her parents – that they were right about her choice of boyfriend. She'd chosen the former and had planned to get a job on a cruise ship, which would pay her enough to make the monthly payments and eventually repay it all, only her plan hadn't gone to plan so to speak, so now she had got herself into a situation where her parents thought she was away travelling when in fact she was working her bum off in low-paid jobs in Southampton.

'I know,' said Ros. 'Maybe a job will come up soon.'

'It would be a lot easier to show my parents all the fabulous places I've told them I'm travelling to if I was actually there,' mused Darla.

'I can see that,' said Ros, trying to sound sympathetic. 'Do you not think it would be easier if you told the truth?' They had had this conversation before and Darla's grimace told her so. 'I know. I just think it would be easier.'

4

'I can't face the looks of disappointment on my parents' faces. Plus the "I told you he was no good" lecture. Although, to be fair, I still got a bit of that when I said I'd dumped him. But it would be awful to admit I was a gullible idiot. Pretending I'm off travelling the world is far more palatable for everyone. And I'm doing okay on my own.'

'Of course you are.' Ros could relate because she was also single and happily so. There had been boyfriends in her teens and a few at university and a couple since – they had sort of tailed off the older she'd become. Ros wasn't great at romantic relationships, mainly because she didn't really see the point of them. She could do everything for herself, with the exception of handling power tools – they were lethal and should be left to experts. And the same went for decorating – it was messy and time consuming. Also compromise wasn't one of her talents so going out with someone had always been a bit of a trial. To be able to please herself and keep her home neat and tidy far outweighed the few benefits of having a partner.

Darla waved a hand in front of Ros's face to let her know she'd zoned out. 'How's your dad?'

Even though Ros knew it was coming, the question still hit her like the pie to the face had. Her dad had recently been diagnosed with cancer and to say things looked gloomy was very much an understatement. 'I think he's still in denial. He looks okay and he's taking some tablets, having radiation therapy but . . .'

Darla reached across the table and squeezed Ros's hand, which made her smile despite the constant weight she felt she carried. 'You know I'm here. Any time, day or night.'

'Thanks. That means a lot. It's the feeling of helplessness

I hate. There's literally nothing I can do to fix this.'

'You're there for him and that's all you can do.'

Ros knew Darla was right but watching the man who had single-handedly brought her up fade away was her worst nightmare. Her mum had left when Ros had been in primary school, so Barry had been both parents to Ros for most of her life. They had a strong bond and the thought of him dying was a pain like no other. 'He won't admit it,' said Ros. 'But even walking the dog is tiring him out. I offered to walk him but he wouldn't let me.'

'The dog has a name.' Darla was smirking. Unlike Darla, Ros wasn't a big fan of dogs. She had absolutely nothing against them and she had to admit her father's one had kept him active and was great company for him. But to Ros they were dirty, made everything smelly and when they weren't doing that, they were sniffing things they shouldn't be sniffing and trying to lick you, and heaven only knew where that tongue had been. On top of that her dad had given his pet a silly name.

'I know it has a name but I really think there were plenty of better ones Dad could have come up with.'

'I think Gazza's an epic name.'

'This coming from someone who has named their car.'

Darla wagged a finger playfully at Ros. 'Hey! Don't diss Sunshine. She's ace.'

Chapter Two

Darla's day was going from bad to complete crap. She was moving again – the third time this month. It was an occupational hazard of being a house sitter. When she'd arrived in Southampton five months ago she'd been up to her ponytail in debt and desperate not to pile on any more. After one night in a hostel she'd desperately looked for an alternative and had seen an advert for a pet sitter. She'd got the gig, which meant she received free accommodation in exchange for looking after a yappy Pomeranian and fourteen rubber plants – sweet. Apart from a few nights at Ros's when she couldn't quite line things up, she had been living in other people's homes ever since.

Usually it went well. She'd had the odd hiccup like when a heron ate half the koi carp she was looking after, and the time she was feeding a chameleon and all the locusts escaped. The less said about that the better – she still occasionally had nightmares about that one – but otherwise things had gone smoothly. She now had a lot of repeat business, having built a reputation for herself and leaving each home immaculately clean even if that wasn't how she found them.

That morning Darla had packed her case and put the things in the car and was going back in the front door to do one last check and say goodbye to Spindle, the slightly incontinent whippet, when he shot out of the door. Darla went to grab the dog's collar but he was too fast. He was off like a greyhound out of a trap.

'Crap! Spindle!' she yelled but she knew it was pointless. Spindle had zero recall so couldn't be let off the lead, let alone set free in Southampton. Darla checked she had the house keys and dashed off in the same direction as the dog. She headed to the corner of Highfield Lane and as she approached she heard a car horn followed by a screech of brakes. Panic gripped her and she pelted around the corner already fearing what she would find. There was a Land Rover in the middle of the road and a man crouched in front of it. Darla scanned everywhere for any sign of Spindle as she dashed over.

'Are you hurt?' she asked, jogging up to the crouching man.

He stood up and in his arms he held a shaking whippet. 'Spindle!' she said, overjoyed to see he wasn't squished.

The man was about late twenties, with a shock of unruly fair hair, a Barbour jacket and handsome but cross features. 'Is this your dog?' he asked. His deep voice made him sound older than he looked.

'Er no, but I'm looking after him.'

'Then you're not doing a very good job,' said the man.

Darla didn't take criticism well. 'I do an excellent job. I have a five-star rating. This was a tiny blip. Is he hurt? Did you hit him?'

'I could have done and it wouldn't have been my fault if I had. When I beeped the horn he froze so I had to slam on my brakes. He should be on a lead.'

'Well, obviously he should be on a lead. But he decided to go out without one so . . . I'll take him.'

There was a moment where the man held on to the dog. 'Are you going to take proper care of him?' he asked.

'Bloody hell, who are you? The RSPCA?' He raised an eyebrow. 'Oh crap, you're not, are you?'

'No, but I could have been,' he said, handing Spindle over. 'You're lucky I don't report you.'

'Thanks for your help,' said Darla, through a forced smile; she was always keen to kill people with kindness rather than dwell on negativity. The man harrumphed and marched back to his car as people queuing behind had started to sound their horns in irritation at the delay. 'Bye, bye, now,' said Darla, giving him a cheery wave while he scowled back at her.

She almost danced back to the property with the whippet in her arms. That had been a near disaster and a lesson learned. She'd thought Spindle was asleep in the kitchen and that she'd shut the kitchen door; she would always double-check in future. The pup looked sorry for himself. 'It's okay, Spindle. Your folk will be back at lunchtime and I've got a treat for you before I leave.' The dog made a whimpering noise. She'd check him over when they were both safely inside, just in case he had injured himself. As they walked up the path Spindle gave her an odd look and then she felt it. A warmth that spread across her middle and down her legs as Spindle released the contents of his bladder. 'Great, that's all I need,' she said.

'You went to work smelling of wee?' asked Ros, horrified. She put her mobile on speakerphone while she put her breakfast things in the dishwasher.

'I didn't have time to get my case out of the car and change. But I changed when I got to work.'

'And you're staying here tonight?'

'If that's okay.'

'You know you can stay as long as you like.' Ros had offered for Darla to move in but Darla had her pride and she wasn't going to live there rent free but she also couldn't afford the going rate for an apartment overlooking the marina.

'Thanks but the agency has a job from Saturday and possibly something sooner if I'm lucky. I'll call them later to confirm what's happening. But either way I'll be out of your hair by the weekend at the latest.'

'It's up to you,' said Ros.

'You'd better go; you don't want to be late.'

'Today being late would actually be a blessing,' said Ros. 'We have a team-building event and it's in the marina.'

'Thant's handy. Just a hop, skip and a jump from your place.'

'I'll probably wish I'd jumped from the eighth floor rather than suffer whatever it is they have planned.'

'You never know. You might enjoy it,' said Darla. Her optimism was endless if somewhat misplaced.

'If it's anything like the team Monopoly they made us play last year I may throw myself in the path of the nearest yacht.'

Darla laughed. 'Try not to be your usual cynical self. Gotta go. Bye.'

Ros knew Darla was right. She decided she would give the event and its organisers the benefit of the doubt and her best positive attitude. Well, as much as she could muster. She locked up and left.

Ros was personally impressed with how long her positive attitude lasted: all the way through the initial gathering where they got their name stickers, which was completely unnecessary as they had all worked together for at least a year, through the first coffee of the day and right up until they were put into teams and given the icebreaker question: *What's the best prank you've ever played on someone?*

'I haven't,' said Ros, turning to the person next to her to have their turn.

'You must have pranked people when you were a kid or at university,' said the short lady from marketing, who Ros had recently found out was called Sonia.

'No. I was far too busy studying, both at school and at university. Especially at university.' She'd been quite baffled why intelligent people had worked hard to achieve the grades to get into a top university only to spend most of their time partying. It made no logical sense at all.

'Still. We all did pranks as kids, didn't we?' said someone else.

Ros shook her head.

'Not even knocking on doors and running away?' asked Sonia.

'Not something I could really see any point in,' said Ros.

'Whoopee cushion?' said Alastair, one of the legal assistants who was fast becoming her nemesis as he often talked over her in meetings and she was sure he was helping himself to her milk from the shared fridge. 'You must have had fun with a whoopee cushion. I know I did.'

'And that was only last Christmas,' said Ros, remembering the secret Santa debacle only too well. 'I'm afraid not, Alastair. But please tell us about your best prank.'

As Alastair's favourite subject was Alastair, he was fairly easy to manipulate. 'There are quite a few to choose from. Cling film on the loo was a favourite at uni.' He laughed. Everyone else looked mildly alarmed. 'And putting salt in with the sugar. That made someone throw up,' he said proudly. 'But my best gag was advertising a mate's car on the uni noticeboard. He had so many phone calls. It was hilarious.' Again only Alastair was laughing but at least things had moved on and the spotlight was no longer on Ros.

Ros decided there was a special circle of hell reserved for people who organised team awaydays. At least this year's event had a bigger budget than the previous one of playing a giant version of Monopoly, where they'd dressed up as the game pieces, at a sad-looking hotel near Southampton airport. This year when they'd said there was a surprise regarding the awayday, she'd very much hoped they were going to reveal it had been cancelled.

After the team icebreaker session, they were all called back together and the CEO, Clive, got up on a podium to announce that they were spending the day crewing yachts and would be going out as a flotilla. This was an actual nightmare of Ros's. Granted, this time it was unlikely that

Jaws would be steering the boat but still she could feel panic rising. She reached for her metaphorical safety net that rarely let her down.

'Can I ask a question?'

'Of course, Ros, go ahead,' said Clive although she could see a nerve twitching in his jaw.

'Has someone completed a full risk assessment? This is a lot of employees to have on one boat. I'd be happy to take a look at—'

'Thanks, Ros, but that won't be necessary. All the required forms have been completed and we are split across a number of vessels, all with experienced skippers from a company that are fully insured and do this very successfully, without incident.'

'Until now,' said Alastair in a half-cough.

'I can't swim!' blurted out Ros and someone spluttered a laugh. She suspected it was Alastair but she was too gripped by fear to admonish him.

'That's fine, everyone will have one of these,' said a friendly-looking man holding up a bright red life jacket.

'At least we'll be able to find the body,' said Alastair, laughing alone as usual.

The first fiasco was putting on the life jackets. They were all grouped on the pontoon next to their allocated yacht, individually trying to work out what went where. As one of the straps went between her legs, Ros was pleased she'd read the instructions and worn jeans, unlike Tiffany whose skirt was now bunched up around her backside. Life jackets were not the most comfortable garments. 'These are ridiculous,' said Ros to Sonia.

'Try wearing one over *my* chest,' said Sonia. 'One size

13

fits all? My arse,' she added, trying to do it up under her ample bust.

'Let me help,' said Ros, adjusting the buckles at the side and fiddling with the fastening at the front.

'Thanks,' said Sonia. 'I'm not keen on the water either. Got knocked over by a wave at Bognor Regis when I was a toddler.'

'Same but on the Isle of Wight. I didn't like the seaweed, pebbles, salty taste or the thought of crabs. Not a word, Alastair,' said Ros, wagging a finger in his direction.

'Don't worry, it'll be a walk in the park,' said Sonia with a smile.

'More like Jurassic Park,' said Ros, taking a deep breath and climbing aboard.

Ros had to admit, the experience wasn't entirely awful. When she was below deck or when she was sitting down, it wasn't too bad. She made a trip to the loo last as long as feasibly possible to avoid being on deck. Unfortunately poor Sonia discovered she suffered from seasickness so Ros had to vacate her safe place in the toilet. But she did keep going back down to check Sonia was okay.

Ros took hold of ropes when she was asked to but drew the line at dangling her legs over the side. Some of the men were finding it an adrenaline rush to stand on the bow of the boat and declare 'I'm the king of the world!'

Ros focused on the blue sky. It was a glorious spring day so that was something to be thankful for. The added insult of bad weather would have been too much.

Ros had been allocated the task of tying the mooring

rope around the cleat, a T-shaped piece of metal, on the pontoon. As she stood on the side of the yacht her hands were sweating with the stress and anticipation of getting the timing right and completing the only task solely allocated to her.

The vessel drew closer and closer as it came into the berth. 'Jump!' yelled someone and without checking Ros leapt off the boat. There was a moment where she landed with both feet on the wobbly pontoon but it was only for a second as her momentum propelled her across the narrow walkway and she flopped face first into the water on the other side. She wasn't expecting the life jacket to explode but that's exactly what happened. A load bang released the mechanism inside the jacket and as it instantly inflated she was unceremoniously tipped onto her back.

She bobbed there spitting water in all directions like an errant fountain, although she knew it wasn't just sea water; she'd seen the pictures of what was pumped into the sea.

'Man overboard,' yelled someone.

'Woman,' snapped Ros from the murky water below.

'Ros,' called their captain, leaning over the side of the boat. 'What happened?'

'You shouted jump,' she said with obvious frustration.

'No, I didn't.'

Sniggering from on deck answered some questions.

'I've still got hold of the rope,' said Ros, holding it up triumphantly. Surely that had to count for something.

'Let it go and we'll haul you out.'

Then, as if it couldn't get any worse, she saw something float towards her that was more alarming than seaweed or even Jaws – it was toilet paper!

Chapter Three

Darla juggled three jobs. It was the only way she could make enough money to keep to her plan of clearing the debts within a year. She had an early morning office cleaning job six mornings a week, and took a few evening shifts at a trendy cocktail bar. That left her the afternoons free to look after any pets in her care that invariably came as part of the house-sitting deal. In exchange for looking after the owner's animals and giving them the reassurance that their property was occupied and therefore less of a prime target for burglars, she got to stay there rent free. She was very grateful that there were so many cats and dogs that didn't fare well in kennels and catteries; without them she'd have been homeless for the last five months.

'So you're homeless again,' said Cameron, her colleague at the cocktail bar, when she'd got to the end of her sorry tale.

'Yep, but hopefully not for long. The agency are trying to sort me something out. Worst case I'll be spending a few days with a flatulent Frenchie.' Cameron gave her a look. 'I'm not being racist. A Frenchie is a French bulldog. He's a champion and cost thousands apparently, but he farts like there's no tomorrow. I mean seriously bad. If they had a canary it would have carked it.'

'I can't imagine spending that much money on a pet. Even one that is a champion trumper,' he said, checking the mixer stocks.

'Is this the start of another penniless student story?' she asked.

Cameron gave her a sideways glance. 'Do I do that a lot?'

She nodded.

'I don't mean to moan,' he said.

'You'll be minted next year when you graduate,' said Darla, trying to sound encouraging. 'Computer engineers, even the junior ones, get paid well.'

'And that's what I'm focusing on,' said Cameron, being his usual upbeat self. Darla liked Cameron but they were just friends. He was beefy with wild hair and whilst he was very sweet sometimes you just knew that mates was all you would ever be.

'Are you free tomorrow afternoon for a coffee? I want to pick your brains about some software I've seen on offer.' She didn't need to disclose that she was hoping it would enable her to make realistic-looking postcards from exotic locations. So far her parents had only received two postcards from people that Darla'd met in the bar and managed to persuade to post for her, from their holiday destinations. One had worked well, but the second one from Carla had confused her parents a bit until she'd explained she'd hurt her wrist skiing and someone had written it for her.

'Not tomorrow, sorry,' said Cameron, pulling an

17

apologetic face. 'Besides being skint, I've got course work to catch up on. I hardly did a thing yesterday because my housemates had an all-day party and the time I'd put aside this morning to study I had to spend tidying up.'

'You're not their dad. You should just leave it for those spoiled posh kids to sort out,' she said, moving past him to update the specials board.

'I can't. It drives me potty. The odd unwashed cup and a few scattered things I can cope with but the place looked like we'd been burgled. I actually wondered if someone had turned the place over when I went downstairs for breakfast. If we were ever robbed, we'd never know.'

'Then move out,' said Darla.

'I'm tied into the rental agreement until the end of July. I can't afford to pay for somewhere else as well as my share of this place.'

'Then you need a way of coping with them for the next four months. Earplugs?' she suggested.

'Are they expensive? Because I'm a—'

'Poor student, yeah I know. You've mentioned it once or twice.'

**

Late on Sunday morning Ros let herself into her dad's place on The Avenue. The double-fronted early Victorian property had been her home for her teenage years. Ros didn't need to announce her arrival as Gazza was already on it and was barking wildly as he cannoned into the hallway and proceeded to pogo around her, threatening to destroy her tights.

'Down,' she said to no effect at all. Her dad, Barry, had

18

done some training with Gazza, and the little black dog could present his paw on command, but Barry'd taught him nothing that appeared to be useful. Apparently, he was a purebred Patterdale terrier but that didn't mean anything to Ros.

'Hello?' called out Ros, shutting the front door.

'Cabbage! Gazza always knows when it's you,' said Barry. Ros very much doubted that this was the case. The little dog was barely in control of his bodily functions and didn't seem to be able to think beyond the next smell.

Ros went into the living room where her father was sitting in his favourite chair, looking a little paler and thinner than he used to. 'Hi, Dad.' She gave him a hug. 'How are you feeling?'

'Fair to middling,' he said with a wan smile. 'Always tired after radiotherapy. But we're nearly at the end of my sessions.'

Ros sat down and Gazza dutifully went to lie down at Barry's feet. 'What happens next?' she asked, mentally crossing her fingers, toes and anything else crossable.

Barry wobbled his head. 'From what they tell me, we wait for a bit. Keep taking the tablets. Do some more tests and see. There was talk of a trial, some experimental thing they've not tested on many people yet but—'

'I don't think in your state being a guinea pig would be a very good idea.' Ros was alarmed that the hospital had even discussed something like that with a terminally ill patient. The consultant she'd seen had told her all they could do was try to slow his demise and keep him comfortable and that she was to think in months not years. She had tried to press him for something more concrete but he'd not been keen to provide what he called an expiry date.

'I suppose,' said Barry, reaching for her. Ros gripped his hand and their sad smiles mirrored each other. 'Anyway, there's no point being all gloomy. How are things with you?'

Ros slapped on a more positive face. 'Good, thanks. Work is crazy. It's like trying to herd belligerent cats and nobody does as I ask until I've chased them umpteen times. But it keeps me out of mischief. The team event was a new level of hell and is thankfully over for another year. I'd best crack on with dinner.'

Sunday lunch was what anchored Ros's week. Her dad had made a roast dinner every week and as she'd grown up it had been the thing they always did together. His Yorkshire puddings were legendary and there was something very comforting about a home-cooked roast even if they made it together now. Barry got on with making the batter for the Yorkshires while Ros prepared everything else and Gazza pottered about looking up hopefully in case anything edible or otherwise was dropped. Ros updated her dad on her work issues in more detail and he nodded in all the right places, even if he didn't fully understand it. He had always been in her corner, her silent cheerleader, and she had no idea what she'd do without him.

Ros was a forward planner so it was hard not to think ahead, but sometimes she had to force herself not to and to focus on the now and the time they had left.

After their meal Ros tidied away and loaded up the dishwasher while Gazza tried to lick the gravy off the plates when she wasn't looking.

'What else can I do while I'm here?' she asked as she wiped down the surfaces.

'There's nothing that needs doing. Just a chat would be lovely.'

'I'll put the kettle on.'

Time with her dad had always been precious. Somehow work had leached into their plans, and until his diagnosis she'd only seen him for lunch on a Sunday, which she felt guilty about, but at least she was seizing all opportunities to spend time with him now. Ros made the drinks and they chatted. She pushed her mental to-do list to one side and enjoyed her father's company.

'I've been thinking,' said Barry.

'Sounds ominous,' said Ros.

'Hear me out before you say no.'

'Okay,' she said, but her father knew her well so she was already forewarned that she was not going to be in favour of whatever he was about to share.

He scratched an eyebrow before fixing her with a look. 'Life is short, Ros. Too short for grudges and regrets. I'd like you to contact your mother.'

At the very mention Ros felt her hackles rise. The thought of her mother always triggered resentment and hurt. 'Dad, please don't ask me to do that. How could that possibly end well?'

'Whatever has happened, she's still your mum and when I go . . . I don't like the idea of you being alone in the world. And I hear she's mellowed.' He passed her a scrap of paper. 'Here's her address and phone number.'

Ros didn't look at the details; she just shoved the note in her pocket. This was a very uncomfortable position to be in. She so wanted to please her dad and put his mind at rest but the thought of playing happy families with her

21

mother quite frankly made her a little bilious.

'Ros?' Her dad was looking at her. She could see this meant a lot to him.

'I'll think about it.' That was as much as she could promise. She had a lifetime of emotional damage that she laid at her mother's door so the thought of contacting her was as appealing as free climbing above hungry crocodiles.

'Don't take too long,' he said.

They talked about old times and happy memories until Barry looked a little tired. Ros picked up the mugs.

'I'll put these in the dishwasher. I'll call you tomorrow but ring if there's anything you need.'

'Will do,' he said but they both knew he wouldn't. As she stood up he added, 'Actually, could you put the recycling out please, Ros?'

'Sure.' She gave him a hug and a kiss and went to leave the room. The phone rang and Barry answered it as he waved her off. 'Hello, Pete, you okay? Yeah, about the same, fair to middling. She's well. She's been here for Sunday lunch—'

'Hi, Uncle Pete; bye, Uncle Pete,' called Ros from the hallway and she waved to her dad. She gathered up the recycling and could hear her dad's side of the conversation in the background. She took the rubbish to the bins and then came back to pick up her handbag.

'No, Ros doesn't change. She's still working too hard . . .' Ros smiled to herself and turned to leave. 'No, there's no room for anyone else in her life. Her job takes up all her time.' Ros paused for a second. She knew she shouldn't be listening but it was interesting to hear her dad's take on her single status. 'I agree, Pete. She's the classic strong independent woman. And I know she's content as she is, or at least she says she is, but I can't help feeling that she could be a little happier. Ros has always found it hard to make friends even as a kid. It's been just the two of us for so long that it breaks my heart to think of her on her own, and if I'm being honest it's the one thing that really worries me about dying.' Ros was reaching for the door handle but she froze. Her dad laughed as her Uncle Pete said something. 'I know,' he said. 'But if I could just see Ros settled in a relationship with someone decent, I'd rest easier knowing she wasn't going to face this by herself after I've gone. I could die happy.'

Ros felt the lone tear slide down her cheek and had to swallow down the emotions bubbling inside her. She'd heard enough. She'd probably heard too much. She quietly opened the back door and slipped out.

Chapter Four

Ros put her mother's contact details in a drawer and diarised a reminder to do something about it within the next two weeks. She figured that was enough time to have weighed up the pros and cons and completed a mental risk assessment. Although she knew her dad must be feeling desperate for her to not be alone if he had resorted to her mother. What with that and the eavesdropped conversation Ros had a lot going on and was feeling quite overwhelmed. Emotions weren't her strong suit so when they were triggered it seemed to take up a lot of energy and all her headspace.

She knew she was lucky to have a friend like Darla and it was lovely that she was staying with Ros for a few days as there was a gap in the house-sitting jobs. Within the hour Darla and Ros were curled up on Ros's sofa sipping glasses of well-chilled wine as Ros relayed the overheard conversation.

'Chuffing heck. I wasn't expecting that,' said Darla when Ros had finished. 'How are you feeling?'

Ros had to think for a moment. 'Is it bad that I'm a bit

cross?' She felt awful for feeling that way. 'I've lost count of the number of times I've explained that I don't need a blooming man to complete me and yet he still wants to see me in a relationship.'

'But that wasn't what he was saying. He even acknowledged that you're a strong independent woman.' They spontaneously clinked glasses at that. 'He's always been there for you unconditionally and he's worried that when he goes you won't have that anymore. I mean, you'll have me and whilst I am frigging marvellous, it's not the same,' said Darla.

'I'm frustrated that I can't say anything. I can't tell Dad that I'll be fine on my own because then he'll know I've been eavesdropping. But worst of all I feel so sad that with everything he's dealing with, that's what he's worrying about and I can't fix it.'

'Being a strong independent woman doesn't mean you can't be in a secure, supportive relationship too. They're not mutually exclusive. I mean they are about as easy to find as a dodo's tooth, but some people seem to manage it.'

Ros sighed heavily. 'I respect that but I think I'm better on my own. I don't have the time or the inclination to search out a mate. It's all a bit of an effort having someone else to constantly think about.'

Darla sipped her wine. 'At least you're not considering rushing into something just to put your dad's mind at rest.'

'And I feel bad about that too. It wouldn't take too much effort to hook up with someone so Dad could go to his grave at peace. Would a good daughter do that?'

'You'd hate yourself for it,' said Darla. 'And even if you could get past that, your dad is savvy enough to know if it was a casual fling, which is definitely not what he meant by wanting to see you settled.'

'Then we're agreed – there's nothing I can do and I just need to forget about it.' Ros nodded to herself as if in agreement. Although it was going to be very hard to stop her dad's words from repeating in her head like a bad TikTok video.

They'd drunk enough wine so Ros went to make two cups of vanilla and camomile tea as she found it was good for helping her to relax, especially before bed. When she returned to the sofa Darla was scrolling through her phone.

'Everything okay?' asked Ros, passing her a mug.

'I cleared another credit card this week. That's one down, one to go.'

'You're doing really well. I think your parents would be proud of you if you told them.'

'Maybe when it's all over and I've got enough money to get my own place back in Oxford.'

'You don't plan to stay in Southampton then? I thought you liked it here.' Ros didn't like to think of Darla moving away. She had very few friends. To be precise, Darla was the only one.

'I do, Southampton is great, but I feel I've got something to prove. Like I need to set everything straight so I can go home again. Not that I don't like the house-sitting.'

'But it's not the same as your own place,' added Ros.

'It's not. I'm still waiting on the agency to confirm my next job but don't worry, I'll definitely be out of your hair soon.'

'It's fine. You are welcome to stay as long as you like.'

'I know and I really do appreciate that but I can't pay you the going rate and that's not fair.'

'But we are friends. Which means you don't need to pay at all,' said Ros.

'Thank you. It's really kind of you but I also have my pride. I just don't want to feel that I owe anyone else a thing. Does that make sense?'

'I understand.'

'And anyway I quite like stopping for the odd night here and there; it feels like a sleepover, minus the sugary treats.'

'I have apples,' offered Ros.

'They're not Jaffa cakes now, are they?'

Ros and Darla had missed each other the next morning as Darla left for work before Ros's alarm went off. But even so Ros was a little surprised to get a phone call at work.

'What do you mean, you've solved my problem?' asked Ros, trying not to sound as harassed as she felt as she fired off another chaser email to a tardy colleague. If they worked for her, most of them would be on Performance Improvement plans.

'Meet me at the cocktail bar at half seven and I'll explain,' said Darla.

'Are you working?'

'Nope.'

'Cocktails? On a Monday?' Ros was dumbfounded.

'They do soft drinks too. Don't question it. Trust me.'

'Then why not meet at . . . Hello, Darla?' But she had hung up.

Ros spent the day firing off chaser emails, fielding Alastair's stupid comments and going over in her mind too many times what on earth Darla wanted to see her about that required her to go to the cocktail bar on a Monday. It wasn't exactly convenient and why couldn't they talk at the flat? Despite her irritation Ros was intrigued so after work she had a shower and a very quick stir-fry before putting on a jacket and walking the twenty minutes to the bar, even though it definitely wasn't a night of the week she would usually be drinking. She liked to keep a healthy eye on her alcohol intake. The risks of liver damage were to be avoided.

Darla was already sitting on one of the tall bar stools chatting to the barman when Ros arrived. They hugged and Ros ordered a lime and soda water with crushed ice and a slice.

'Are you okay, Darla? Because you weren't making a lot of sense on the phone.' Ros always felt it best to be honest.

'Feels a bit weird to be on this side of the bar but I am fine and so are you going to be. Now I know you can sometimes be a bit negative—' Ros wobbled her head but didn't completely disagree; if she was one thing it was that she was pretty self-aware and knew her own limitations '— but I need you to listen right to the end of what I'm about to say before making any comments. Okay?' Darla locked her with a serious gaze.

'Yep.'

'Right until the very end,' emphasised Darla.

'Yep. Got it,' said Ros, wriggling in her seat, aware that the barman was watching her. Bar stools were one of the most uncomfortable forms of seating; she put them in the same box as Marmite and Alastair.

Darla held up her palms as if playing charades. 'Your dad needs peace of mind. For that to happen he needs to see you with someone who is worthy of you, treats you well and doesn't put a foot wrong. Sadly it's literally only for a few weeks, a couple months tops.' Ros found herself swallowing hard at the thought of it. 'What you need is someone who will do a professional job for an agreed fee.'

Ros spat out her lime and soda, showering Darla. 'I'm so sorry,' she said through splutters. 'For a moment there, I thought you meant a gigolo.' Ros laughed.

Darla was twisting her lips. 'Not a gigolo, no. I'm thinking a professional arrangement, purely platonic, where they attend arranged meetings with your dad posing as your long-term boyfriend.' When there was no response from Ros, Darla did a ta-dah with her hands.

Ros sucked in a deep breath. She loved Darla, she really did, but boy did she have some hare-brained ideas. Now, to let her down gently. 'Whilst I really appreciate the time and thought that you've put into this, I'm afraid it most likely would be a complete fiasco, and also where on earth would I find someone to do that?'

'Hi,' said the barman, leaning on the bar.

'Excuse me, we're having a private conversation,' said Ros. Darla was off her stool and heading for the door. 'Hang on, Darla!'

'My work here is done,' called Darla. 'Sort out the fine details between yourselves and thank me later. Love you!'

Panic rushed through Ros's system. What sort of hell trap had Darla led her into? She was acutely aware that the barman was studying her. 'I'm really sorry um . . . what was your name?'

Someone was tapping a pint glass on the other end of the bar. 'Another pint in there, Ron. When you're ready.'

'Ron, is it?' she asked.

The barman nodded. 'Let me serve my mate and I'll be back. Don't go anywhere or Darla will kill the pair of us.'

An excruciating few minutes past where Ros swung between being glued to her seat and wanting to sprint for the door. Her manners got the better of her and she waited for the barman to return. 'Ros, I'm all yours,' he said.

'So it would appear,' said Ros. 'I'm afraid, Ron, I don't know what Darla has said but—'

'Pretty much what she just said to you. Your dad is sick. Really sorry about that by the way. Cancer sucks.'

'Indeed it does,' said Ros.

'And you need someone to pretend to be your partner until . . .' There was an awkward pause where the barman walked his fingers across the bar and then made wings and mimed them flying off over his shoulder. 'I'm short of cash and Darla thinks I'd fit the bill as your fake boyfriend. What do you think?'

'For a start . . .' There was so much wrong with Darla's suggestion she wasn't sure where to start. 'Ron? That wouldn't work. Ros and Ron sounds ridiculous.'

'I was thinking more Ron and Ros.' He grinned at her.

'I'm sorry. That's simply not believable.'

'Would you seriously not go out with someone because their name was too similar or didn't match perfectly with yours?'

'That's irrelevant. In this situation everything would have to work perfectly. It would have to in order to be completely believable. I'm sorry but Ron isn't going to work.'

The barman shrugged. 'Okay. How about Cameron?' he suggested.

Ros was amazed he had capitulated so quickly but she was grateful that he had. 'If you really don't mind, I think Cameron would be far better.'

'Cool,' he said, wiping down the bar top. The corners of his mouth were twitching.

Something was amiss. 'Cameron,' she said out loud. The barman instantly glanced up. 'Darla's friend from work.' Things were starting to make a little more sense although not to the level that would make Ros comfortable.

'Ahh rumbled,' he said, putting down a new coaster for her glass.

Oh great, thought Ros, *a comedian – that's all I need.* He leaned against the bar. 'Sorry, I couldn't resist. Ron is a nickname. One of the lads in halls misheard my name as Ron and it stuck. What happens next? Should we agree a price?'

'Oh no. I mean I appreciate what you are offering to do but it's completely bonkers.'

'Why? If it gives your old man peace of mind surely that's worth it.' Something was rocking her sensible core values and it was unsettling. 'I mean, is everything else all right with me? Anything else you want to change?' He splayed out his arms.

Ros took a moment to study the man in front of her closely – bushy hair, warm eyes and a disarming smile. Where had she seen him before? 'Do I know . . .' And then it dawned on her. 'You! You're the custard-pie-wielding, tutu-wearing stu—'

'Oh crap! That was you? I regret ducking that day. And

to show how sorry I am, here's another lime and soda on me.' He filled the glass and lined it up next to her current drink on another new coaster. 'I'm not usually like that. It was the birthday of one of the lads in my house share and they'd already bought me the tutu and it was quite hard to get one in my size apparently. I didn't like to let them down. That's what I'm like. I'm helpful and dependable and my student loans are spiralling out of control so I really need the cash. And I think you really want to put your dad's mind at rest so we could help each other out here. What do you say? Do we have a deal?'

Chapter Five

Darla was very pleased with herself. It was a genius plan introducing Ros and Cameron even if she did say so herself. Cameron was a completely lovely person who needed some cash and Ros was in need of a credible boyfriend stand-in. She was ignoring the many calls to her mobile from Ros. She'd known her for a while and had learned it was best to let her run out of steam before engaging. Right now Ros would be thinking of the many reasons why this wouldn't work. When she stopped to think, that was when Darla would step in and point out all the things that *would* work and how this solved everything perfectly.

Having sorted out Ros's problem Darla felt she was on a roll and was keen to sort out her own accommodation issues. For one thing she wasn't keen on staying the night at Ros's because Ros definitely needed longer to get her head around Darla's quite frankly genius fake boyfriend suggestion. She'd been calling the agency incessantly and nothing local enough was coming up. Her mum and dad had messaged and she had fobbed them off too many times so knew she would have to call them soon.

Darla went to the marina and strolled along the many rows of yachts. Some never left their moorings. People with more money than they knew what to do with, she supposed. As she walked past one with a large open section at the back she had an idea. Darla checked the coast was clear and climbed on board. She pulled out her phone and video-called her parents while also trying to remember where she had told them she was the last time she had spoken to them.

The kitchen ceiling in her parents' house came into view. 'Hello, Darla, let me find your father.' And the phone was left on the kitchen table.

Hurry up, thought Darla, glancing nervously around. She mentally went through the countries she'd told her parents she'd visited. Was it Egypt or Turkey last time? Eventually her mother returned and two familiar faces loomed close on the screen. She adored her parents and her heart squeezed with guilt that she was deceiving them, but when she saw how happy they looked, how could she tell them the truth? Reality would only hurt them.

'Where are you?'

'As you can see I'm on a yacht.'

'Have you left Turkey?'

'Yes, I'm in the sea near Greece,' she said. Thankfully her geography knowledge was pretty good and hopefully better than her mum and dad's.

'Ooh how exciting,' said her mum, peering closer. 'Let's have a tour.'

'We're about to set sail so I can't be moving about – it's not safe.'

'Whose yacht is it?' asked her dad.

Bugger. She'd not thought this through.

'I've got a job in another bar.' Her imaginary jobs hadn't been very imaginative, but then she wasn't qualified for a lot else. 'It belongs to the guy who owns the bar.'

'Where's he? Is it just the two of you there?' Her dad was looking concerned.

Yep, she really should have thought it through. 'Actually, I'm working. He's got some clients on board and I'm going to do some serving. Which is why it's just a quick call to say I'm having a great time and I just wanted to check that you're both okay.'

'Hey!' shouted someone from the pontoon.

Shit, thought Darla. 'That's my boss, I have to go,' she said quickly at the screen. Blew them a kiss and closed down the call.

'What are you doing?' asked an angry-looking man marching up to the boat.

'I'm looking for Terry. Is this not his boat?' She pretended to check it over. 'Goodness, silly me. This is far too small. Terry has a whopper. The boat, that is. Terry's yacht is much bigger than this. I'm so sorry. My mistake.' She held out a hand and the shocked gent helped her off the boat. 'Thank you. You're too kind.'

'My pleasure,' he said. Darla walked away. Yet another one charmed – she might have lost a lot but she still had that.

***

Ros was pacing up and down her living room carpet and it was leaving unattractive dents in the pile. Darla wasn't answering her calls and she literally had nobody else to discuss this with. The other person she always turned to when she had a dilemma was her dad, but for obvious reasons she couldn't talk this one through with him, and very soon, she realised she wouldn't be able to talk anything through with him at all. The thought hit her like a brick and she sat down hard on the sofa. Perhaps he was right that after he'd gone she would be alone. Very alone. Especially now she knew of Darla's plans to return to Oxford. Ros sucked in a breath. That was a worry for another day; she couldn't dwell on that right now. She needed to think through Darla's suggestion that she make a deal with Cameron.

She shook her head. She couldn't believe she was even considering the madcap idea for a nanosecond. It was all things ludicrous and then some. She'd already told Cameron that it definitely wasn't going to happen. He'd been completely reasonable about it and said she could get in touch through Darla if she changed her mind and wanted to go ahead with the simple business transaction. That's what he'd called it. It was none of those things. Running a bath was simple; ordering a coffee was simple (well, unless it was from the trendy new café on the waterfront; then you had to pick your roast, cup size, milk alternative et cetera but generally coffee was a much simpler thing than this.) And business – really? Business was a contracted transaction for money not a . . . *Hmm,* she wondered. Perhaps Cameron *had* got that part right.

What exactly was it that she would need him to do? He would have to meet her father at some point but perhaps that could be delayed and kept to a minimum of interactions. But then, how would she explain that away to her dad? Perhaps she could invent a job for Cameron where he was away a lot, that would make his absence more acceptable and hopefully avoid any awkward questioning. She could also say that they had been seeing each other for a while but he'd been away, which would make it seem less out of the blue. A sudden serious boyfriend would certainly raise alarm bells.

A business contract should also be documented, to ensure there was clarity on the deal – and that could only be a good thing. There would be an awful lot to map out and agree so that they both knew exactly what could and couldn't be said to avoid her dad discovering the truth. She came over in a cold sweat at the thought of it. No, she definitely couldn't do this. It was lying to her dad. They never ever lied to each other. They knew they could trust each other implicitly. She couldn't do it.

But then what was the alternative? Let him go to his grave worrying about her? That wasn't a great outcome either. She could spend whatever time he had left trying to convince him that she would be fine but, if she was being truthful, even she wasn't sure that she would be. Life without the one constant person in it already felt like a barren land she didn't want to explore. On that front she had no choice, but when it came to her father's peace of mind, Darla had presented her with another option. However ridiculous it was, the least she could do was to properly review the suggestion.

She was running out of steam and she checked her phone. A message from Darla popped up.

'At last,' said Ros, relieved, as she opened the message.

The farting French bulldog has come up trumps (no pun intended) lol. So I'm staying there for the next three days.

Please think seriously about my suggestion – you know it makes sense. Don't be mad – it's a waste of energy. Just call Cameron. That's all you have to do. Love D x

She would have to figure this one out for herself but first she needed to vacuum her foot marks out of the carpet.

Whenever Ros had a dilemma or needed to think she went to Sunset Shore. A thin strip of beach between where the cruise ships docked and the Isle of Wight ferry terminal which, to Ros's knowledge, didn't have a name. There was a bench and sometimes in summer an ice cream van but what Ros went for was the peace and quiet and to watch the sunset. It was only a fifteen-minute walk from her apartment building although she'd been coming since before she moved there. It had been a regular haunt of her confused teenage years.

Somehow the thirty minutes or so that it took the sun to sink was enough to help calm Ros's mind. She loved the vibrant colours that nature made but she liked the softer ones too. The sunset could be anything from a rich red to a soft pink depending on the time of year and weather conditions.

Occasionally her sunset viewing was interrupted by the ferry but it didn't really spoil the view. She'd bought her flat for a number of reasons but one of those had been that from the balcony she could catch a partial view of the sunset. And whilst she did like to sit out there and saviour the display she actually still preferred the short walk to Sunset Shore.

***

Tonight it was a stretch even for her happy place to sort through all the whirling thoughts; the pros, numerous cons and the many, many associated risks of a fake relationship. She watched the last of the sun disappear, leaving the merest glow behind and with a sigh she headed home.

Unsurprisingly Ros didn't sleep well that night. A hot shower and coffee did little to buck her up so she wasn't in the mood for any of the frequent interruptions she had to contend with at work. The offices were light, bright and open plan, which did cause Ros some issues especially in the late afternoon when other staff seemed to slack off and use the time for chatting to others at their desks, which was off-putting when she was trying to work. But the senior team pretty much left her to her own devices, which she liked. They'd brought her in as an expert and it was refreshing that they let her manage the risk and compliance agenda for the company. It was a lot of responsibility and took up all her time and some on top of that, but then Ros was possibly more thorough than most.

Ros had a desk in the corner of the office adjacent to the photocopiers. Previously she had been in the middle of the main office but when she'd complained about the constant chattering of her co-workers who seemed to congregate there, they'd given her a space of her own, and she liked it that way. She wasn't big on socialising. She wasn't rude but these were colleagues not friends, a common misconception of many.

'Hi, Ros, have you got a minute? Great,' said Alastair, pulling up a chair without waiting for a response. 'How are things with you?' His tone was friendly and she was immediately suspicious. She'd still not forgiven him for the awayday shenanigans.

'Fine. Was there something you wanted?' she asked.

'I got the document you sent round and asked me to sign.'

'Which I'm still waiting for you to do,' she pointed out.

'Yeah, about that. Could you give me an overview of the contents now to save me going through all of those pages as I'm a bit busy?'

'I'm busy too, and no, I'm sorry, I can't do that.' Ros turned her attention back to her emails but was well aware that Alastair hadn't gone away. He proceeded to make loud sucking noises with his lips until she spun in his direction, making him jolt back. 'Is there a problem?' she asked.

'I want to sign it but I kind of don't without knowing what it's about exactly.'

'Fine,' said Ros, reaching to take the folder.

'Cool. I didn't realise I didn't need to sign it. Great,' he said, getting to his feet.

'You don't have to, but if you don't sign it that will be detailed in my report to the directors where I spell out those who are in breach of company policy regarding risk and compliance.' Ros put the folder in her in-tray.

Alastair sat down again. 'Is there any option where I don't have to read it and also don't get ratted out to the senior team?'

Ros laughed. 'We're not at school. I'm not ratting you out. I'm reporting upwards on the status of compliance across the company. That's different.'

'Yeah, not from where I'm sitting. So you won't compromise at all?' Alastair's tone was no longer friendly.

'No,' said Ros. She lifted the folder out of her in-tray and held it up. Alastair snatched it and stomped off.

Chapter Six

Ros was at home in her slippers on Wednesday evening staring at the flip chart she'd just completed when there was a buzz on her apartment entry system. It was Darla so she let her in and a few moments later there was a tentative tap on the door.

'It's open,' called Ros.

'I bring gifts,' said Darla, waving a large bar of Cadbury's chocolate. 'Am I safe to come in or are you going to attack me with the egg whisk?'

'That happened one time and it was an accident,' said Ros.

'Jury's out,' said Darla, shutting the door and joining her at the flip chart. She pointed at the page titled 'Boyfriend Contract. Risk Assessment'. And the neat lists underneath. 'But Cameron said you've not been in touch.'

'Because this whole idea is a massive risk.'

'All boyfriends are, to be fair.'

'Not to the extent that they need a detailed control plan to reduce the risks. Although some of these are probably generic.' She scanned her lists. 'Anyway, I'm still ironing out key areas of the contract. And I've not completely decided if I'm going ahead with your quite frankly ridiculous idea.' She kissed the top of Darla's head. 'Thank you. You're a good friend. Completely nuts but a good friend.'

'Would you say you were leaning more on the "let's do this" side?'

'Possibly. I did want to ask, is Cameron my only option? I wondered, as I'd be paying, whether maybe there were any other candidates.'

Darla tilted her head at Ros. 'You should have said. I'm sure Ryan Reynolds would be up for it.'

For a moment Ros was buoyed until the penny dropped. 'You're joking.'

'You think?'

'Ryan Reynolds is happily married, so yes. I also know he's way out of my league but I did see myself with someone a bit more . . .' Ros couldn't think of anything that wasn't going to insult Darla's friend and colleague.

'I know Cameron's a bit scruffy,' Darla allowed. 'Although to be fair when he's working at the bar that is him at his smartest.'

Ros twitched slightly.

'But he has a nice smile and your dad would be suspicious if you turned up with Ryan Reynolds,' said Darla.

'I guess. As he is the only option then I have a flip chart for you with lots of questions about Cameron. I don't know anything about him. Is he trustworthy?'

'Totally. And anything detailed you want to know you need to ask him. I don't mean to be insensitive but . . .'

Darla scrunched her features up '. . . time isn't on your side.'

'I understand that but a business contract needs to be on a firm footing.' Ros tapped the flip chart with her marker pen.

'Firm footing yes. Clear mutual understanding of the requirements, agreed. But not a ninety-page countersigned document.' Darla flopped down on the sofa. 'Put the kettle on. I have crap to share.'

Ros did as Darla suggested and then moved to lean against the sofa and stare at the flip chart. 'I think I've covered all bases but I'll need to type it up.'

'No, you don't. You need to call Cameron and agree a price before he goes off the idea, and then . . . I don't know, get him to come over and go through your flip charts, then you can introduce him to Barry. Sooner rather than . . . well, later.' The way Darla said *later* had Ros's attention. Documented detail was her comfort blanket. But right now she didn't have time for that.

'Perhaps we could both sign the flip charts,' suggested Ros.

'There you go. Decaffeinated tea please and a sympathetic ear. If I ever sit for that dog again I will need a gas mask. It's good to breathe fart-free air for a couple of hours.'

'Tea coming right up,' said Ros, keen to hear about Darla's troubles and forget about her own.

Ros had almost cancelled her meeting with Cameron numerous times throughout Friday and had caught herself thinking about all the many things they would need to cover if they were to pull off the deception. There was easily enough to fill another flip chart. They had exchanged text messages and Cameron seemed very happy with the payment programme she had offered, which involved an initial sign-up fee, to make sure he was committed, and then weekly payments with an estimated duration of twelve weeks. Twelve weeks. On one hand she very much hoped her dad was going to be around a little longer; on the other, twelve weeks was a long time to fake being in a relationship.

Ros showered and changed into something casual and then thought that perhaps business attire might give a more formal feel; it was a meeting after all. She was putting on a shirt when the entry bell sounded. Cameron was early. She buzzed him in and hastily did up the buttons. Shirt and jeans would have to do.

'Hiya,' said Cameron shyly, slinking inside the apartment and closing the door before handing Ros a small bunch of yellow carnations. 'I got you these.'

'Thank you, that's kind of you but unnecessary. It has made me think of something else to add to the list . . . expenses.' She put the flowers down on the worktop and turned over three flip chart pages until she came to a free space. 'We'll need a process for you to claim back any valid expenditure.'

'They're just a gift,' said Cameron.

Ros wasn't sure what to say.

Cameron looked around. 'I figured if you lived in Ocean Village it would be a smart pad but wow this is a gorgeous place you have.'

Ros was happy to take compliments about her home. The modern top-floor apartment with wrap-around balcony and views over the marina was her pride and joy. 'Thank you.'

Cameron came to stand next to her and whistled through his teeth. 'That is some list. I know you said you wanted to go over a few details but this is a whole workshop. I bet you don't usually workshop your relationships.' He laughed.

Ros sidled over to the flip chart pad and tore off a couple of pages, hastily folded them on her way to the recycling box. He didn't need to know about the disastrous session with her last boyfriend.

'Anyway I'd best get these in some water,' she said, scanning Cameron as she picked up the flowers. He looked all studenty in his hoodie, ripped jeans and canvas pumps. 'Would you like a drink?'

'A beer would be great, thanks.'

'I meant tea or coffee,' said Ros.

'Gotcha. Builder's tea, two sugars please.' There was an awkward silence while Ros made the drinks. It was beyond weird to have this virtual stranger in her home. She wasn't blessed in the small-talk department as it was and this was stretching her skills.

'Did you come far?' she asked.

'Portswood. I'm in a house share there.'

'I remember my shared house. Awful, I don't envy you going back to university. Master's or PHD?'

'It's my first time at uni. I'm studying for a BSc in Computer Science.'

'Oh,' said Ros, not really knowing what else to say.

'Anyway, shall we crack on?' She passed him his tea.

'Sure. Can I ask about your dad? His diagnosis is really tough on both of you.'

'Thanks. It was a bit of a shock. Well, huge shock actually. He'd been fine. Just a bit tired. His GP sent him for a blood test and . . .' Ros didn't want to relive the series of appointments that had led them to the diagnosis.

'Sorry.'

'It's fine.' She lifted her chin. 'What did you want to know?'

'What's his name?'

'Barry.'

'Is he in hospital or . . .'

'He's at home for now.' She'd had some leaflets about care options but they were still in the kitchen drawer, although she knew she'd have to face them at some stage.

'That's good. And what's he like?'

Ros had a think. 'He's kind and generous. The sort of person you know will do everything they can for you. He retired early a couple of years ago but until then he worked hard. He ran his own business and he brought me up single-handed.' Ros had to take a moment to keep her emotions in check.

'He did a good job,' said Cameron. 'With you, I mean.'

'Thank you.'

'Anything else?' he asked.

'He makes the best Yorkshire puddings,' she said. 'Please can we turn our focus to you? We have a lot to cover.'

'Sure. You've probably checked if I've got a criminal record.' Ros let out a nervous laugh. 'Although I'm surprised you still invited me over.' *Oh heavens*, thought

46

Ros. What on earth had he done? She would berate Darla later for letting a criminal into her home. Cameron waved a hand in front of her to get her attention. 'I'm joking. I've never even had a speeding fine but that's because I don't have a car.' Cameron chuckled. Ros found she was staring at him. *Why would someone joke about being a criminal?* She was baffled by this man. 'Well, clearly I'm not as funny as I thought I was. What else do you want to know about me?'

'I've made a list,' said Ros, making a mental note to see how to find out about people's criminal records, just in case.

Cameron helped Ros move the flip chart stand nearer to the table in the dining area and she went back to the first page, which had a dividing line with areas of interest on the left and space on the right for Ros to fill in the answers. 'Your full name is Cameron . . .'

'Cameron Alfred DeFelice.'

Was it too much to ask that he had a simple name? 'DeFelice. Is that hyphenated?'

'Nope. Just plain old DeFelice. Gran did some digging on the internet and we have Italian roots.'

'How interesting,' said Ros, adding the names to the chart as well as his initials. 'C-A-D. Cad. Hmm. That doesn't bode well for a suitor. Maybe we should change your surname.' She said it more to herself than Cameron.

'I don't think we should overcomplicate things. Maybe not change things unless we really have to. It's more likely I'll forget and slip up.'

Ros spun around. 'Do you have memory issues?'

Cameron chuckled. 'No, but I've seen your list and I think there might be a lot to remember.'

They filled in some basic information about his family. 'Tell me about *your* family,' said Cameron, taking a sip from his mug. 'Nice tea by the way. You make a great cuppa.'

Ros was surprised by the compliment. 'Thank you. I don't think we need to go into any great detail about me. Dad will be interested in you.'

'Yeah, but I don't want to get caught out. If we're in a relationship there's stuff I should know like . . .' He looked to the ceiling as he thought. 'What was your first pet's name?'

'I'll let you know when I get one,' replied Ros.

His eyes widened in surprise. 'What? You've never had a pet?'

'No.'

Cameron remained shocked. 'Not even a goldfish or a hamster when you were a kid?'

'No. Dad was busy with the business and I don't really like to see animals in cages.'

'Fair enough. My first pet was a rabbit called Tango because it was an orangey colour . . . like the drink,' he explained.

'Yes, I understand.' She added the info at the bottom of the page, unsure it was of any use at all.

'What's Ros short for?'

Ros felt her shoulders tense. 'It's Rosanna but nobody calls me that.' *Not anymore,* she added in her head.

'Rosanna's a beautiful name.'

'Just Ros, please.'

'Sure thing. And your surname?'

There was such a lot they needed to know about each

other. Ros was beginning to realise that she needed to start another flip chart.

Two hours in and they were on their third round of drinks and as Cameron was hungry he'd opened a packet of Hula Hoops he had in his bag.

'Right. Let's move on to jobs. I'm a risk and compliance manager—'

'Tell me about that,' he said, leaning forwards and looking interested.

'I analyse any potential risks to the company. For example if a project is initiated I assess any risks of the change and work with the project manager to ensure they are properly managed, and there are a number of ways to do that, which I won't bore you with. And I also ensure that the company is compliant with any necessary business-as-usual regulations.'

'Sounds like a lot of responsibility,' he said, pulling his hand out of the crisp packet with a Hula Hoop on each finger.

Ros was transfixed as he ate them one at a time off his fingertips. 'Do you need to eat those like that?'

'What?'

'Children eat them like that.'

'Kids know where it's at. Way more fun to eat them off your fingers. Try,' he said, offering her the packet.

'No, thank you. Children are messy,' said Ros, failing to stop her feelings showing on her face.

Cameron looked shocked. 'You don't like kids?'

'Children can be lovely but they make so much mess.' Ros tried to keep her expression neutral.

'But that's a minor thing. Do you not want to have kids?'

That was a serious question she'd not been expecting. 'It's not that I don't want them. I just think you need to have a lot of other factors in place first. And they're a huge responsibility. They're a full-time thing. You can't take time off or change your mind on a whim. Children are a long-term commitment.' Something her mother didn't seem to have grasped.

'I agree and I'm well up for it,' said Cameron.

'But you're a student.'

'I won't always be a student and with the right person I'd love to be a dad. I was playing mummies and daddies with Gina, at preschool. I always assumed I'd have kids.'

'You seem very sure about that.'

'I am. I had a happy home. I can't imagine not building a family of my own. And anyway my mum would have something to say if I didn't make her a grandma.'

'Erm. We've gone off track. Where were we? Jobs. We've covered my job. Let's agree on a job for you.'

Cameron smiled. 'I'm a barman at the cocktail bar and I do some volunteering at a charity shop, which is great because I get first dibs on stuff.' He pulled at his Scooby-Doo T-shirt. 'One pound fifty. Let me know your size and I can look out for stuff for you.'

Ros couldn't hide her alarm at the thought of childish T-shirts. 'No, thank you. And what I meant by a job was what job we're we going to tell my dad that you do.'

'I don't follow.'

'I can hardly say you're a mature student.'

'Why not?' Cameron made a big show of sucking a Hula Hoop off his little finger.

'Because this has to be believable. I did cover that

50

at the start. He needs to be convinced that we are in a relationship.'

Cameron scrunched up the empty crisp packet, leaned back and considered her. She felt a little vulnerable under his gaze. 'And a student stroke part-time barman is below you?'

'No. Not exactly. But usually I'd not . . . It's just that I would normally be looking for someone who um . . .' She was running out of steam.

'It's okay, I'm not offended. I've been in this exact position before with me and Gina. Couples need to be equally balanced. But as I'm working towards a good career I think that goes in my favour and keeping it simple is better.'

'I'd be more comfortable if it was a role with a little more status. Is that all right? It's only that I don't want Dad to think I'm with someone who will sponge off me. Sorry, that sounded awful. No offence.'

'None taken. I'm hopefully going to be working in computing so you could say that if you like. I can field any questions about computers.'

'Great. Let's go with software engineer. That sounds credible and Dad won't ask any questions as he's not great with technology.' Ros merrily added this to the flip chart.

Cameron covered his mouth as he yawned. 'I'm sorry – I'm knackered. Any chance we can finish this off another time?'

'But I wanted to introduce you to Dad on Sunday.' Ros was feeling panicked they'd only covered half of page two.

'That's still cool. I'm free tomorrow morning. Let's catch up then, yeah?'

Ros could see he was tired as he stifled another yawn

so she reluctantly agreed. 'Okay. What sort of time? I can do early.'

He pulled a face. 'How about eleven o'clock? We could grab a coffee at Costa on the High Street.'

'I'm not sure about meeting in public,' said Ros. 'It feels a little premature.'

'Is coffee more of a third date thing?' he asked with a smile.

'I'm not sure what you mean but I'll meet you as arranged.'

Cameron got to his feet. 'It's been nice getting to know you, Ros.'

Could she say the same? It was merely a process she had to go through. 'Thank you, Cameron. I do appreciate what you're doing.'

'And I really appreciate the cash. And thanks for the tea. Take care. See you in the morning.' He stood in front of her as if waiting for something. 'Should we hug or kiss when we say goodbye?'

'No, I don't think so,' said Ros, heat rising up her neck at the discomfort.

'I meant when we're in couple mode,' he said.

'I see.' She was greatly relieved. 'I'll think about it and let you know.'

'Cool,' he said and he made for the door. 'Night, Ros. Take care.' As the door clicked shut Ros breathed a huge sigh of relief.

Chapter Seven

Darla was pleased to receive a phone call from the house-sitting agency and even happier to discover that they needed someone immediately. She was working at the cocktail bar that evening so wasn't able to go and check out the place until she'd finished her shift. She'd sailed through her shift feeling the most relaxed she had done in ages. The constant moving had not been easy so she was looking forward to being in one place for a while.

When Darla finished work it was after eleven at night but she merrily headed off to Netley Marsh. It was a bit further out of the city than she would have liked but this job came with a huge bonus: it was for five months! Up until now her longest stint had been four weeks in an apartment looking after a parrot for a chap who had to go away for work. That had made Darla a temporary neighbour to Ros and an instant friend. Although that wasn't how Ros had seen it. Ros had been standoffish at first but Darla was persistent, and in a strange city working as many jobs as she was physically able to, she was in need of some female company and Ros had fitted the bill.

Basically Darla had worn her down with invitations to watch TV, sip wine on the balcony, and to try out her famous brownies, which had been what had finally won Ros over. They had discovered that whilst they were quite different in personality they did share some common ground in that they both enjoyed musicals and bitching about incompetent colleagues. Ros reminded Darla of her friend back home in Oxford. Someone who was sadly no longer a friend. The longer she had stood by her con man boyfriend the more friends Darla had lost. Some of them had even put money into his stupid schemes. The shame had stopped her keeping in touch. She had found Ros at a key time and even though Darla had moved out of the swish apartment block they had stayed friends.

Darla couldn't stop grinning. She'd only had details by voice message but it sounded amazing. A four-bedroomed country house that was awaiting probate and needed someone to tend to the garden and the stock. She wasn't sure what the latter was but there were no incontinent whippets or trumping French bulldogs so things were definitely looking up. The agency offices weren't local and usually any handover was done by the homeowner, which obviously wasn't possible this time. But as Darla was an experienced and confident sitter she wasn't fazed by an empty house.

The property was just outside the village and surrounded by fields. She pulled onto the gravel drive and got out of the car. It was hard to see the house in the dark but from what she *could* see it was double-fronted and looked huge. Above the door was a well-worn sign that read *The Brambles*.

'Ahh, home for the next five months,' said Darla through a happy sigh.

She found the key hidden under a plant pot and unlocked the door, heaved in her case and felt around for a light switch. She touched something that might have been a switch but felt more like a cold brass nipple and she flicked it down. Light flooded the long hallway. Darla was struck by the beautiful tiled flooring in blue and white terracotta. Her eyes travelled up to the brass chandelier and the high ceiling – this place was something special. Darla had a little look around to get a feel for the layout. Usually she liked that the houses she stayed in had their owners' things scattered here and there. But as she knew the person who had lived here had died it felt a little strange being in their house without their permission.

A coat on the hall stand and wellies by the door reminded her this wasn't hers forever. She flicked the switch in another room and discovered the kitchen but it wasn't like any kitchen she'd seen before – or at least not like any she'd experienced in real life. It looked like something out of a history book. A chipped butler's sink was flanked by what she assumed were cupboards, but where there would normally be doors there were grubby floral curtains hanging desperately from bent wire. A battered wooden table sat in the middle and on top she saw a newspaper, a pair of glasses and a mug creeping with mould. She'd sort this out in the morning.

The living room looked lived in and the old leather sofas were comfortable but the lack of a television was alarming. There was a stool with a radio on top where you would have expected to have seen a TV. A quick hoover round and that room would be perfectly liveable.

Upstairs Darla found four good-sized bedrooms but only one of the beds had a mattress and enough space to get all the way around the bed. The other bedrooms were chock full of large pieces of old furniture. The main bedroom had been left as if someone had just got up and gone to get a cup of tea. She always carried her own bottom sheet and duvet cover just in case and this was one of those occasions. She sorted the bedding out and got ready for bed. She went to the last room on that floor: the bathroom. By this stage she hadn't been expecting a state-of-the-art rainfall shower like she had experienced at the last property she'd stayed in but she also wasn't fully prepared for the horror that met her.

A dark green toilet and a sink smeared with toothpaste stood next to a large bath – white on the inside and black on the outside. A constant drip tapped a rhythm as she took in the sorry-looking bathroom. She took a breath. It wasn't the end of the world and once it was clean it would seem a whole lot better. She needed to focus on the two most important aspects of the house – it was free and it was all hers for the next five months. Things were looking up.

**

On Saturday morning Ros was up early and going over the flip charts she'd completed with Cameron as well as jotting the unanswered questions into her notebook so they could carry on when they met. The discussion about children had stuck in her mind. She'd always assumed that she wasn't cut out to be a mother – her own mother certainly wasn't, so why would she be any different? No child deserved to experience what she had.

She'd just finished jotting down a few areas that Cameron needed to avoid when he met her dad – mainly Portsmouth FC, billionaires in space and roadworks. They always made him grumpy.

Her phone rang and it was her dad calling. 'Hi, you okay?'

'I am but I didn't sleep too well last night and when I did, I think I was in a funny position because my back is playing up this morning.'

'That's not good. Should I call someone?'

'No, it's nothing really, but Gazza it sitting staring at me because he wants to go for a W-A-L-K.' The fact her father had to spell it out to avoid the mutt going crackers made her roll her eyes. 'Do you think you could take him? Don't worry if you're busy.'

'Of course I can, Dad. It's not a problem,' she said, checking her watch. She'd be cutting it fine and Gazza would have to be happy with a short W-A-L-K.

Ros hadn't been expecting the wave of guilt that hit her on seeing her dad. The thought that she was about to lie her socks off to him didn't sit comfortably. She was keen to get on with her task so she wasn't late to meet Cameron. 'I'm not going to be out long with Gazza because I'm meeting someone for coffee at eleven.' Both Gazza and her dad stared at her and she felt like she was under a spotlight.

'Someone?' queried her dad. 'Not Darla then?'

'Err no. I'll grab his lead and we'll be off,' she said, quickly exiting the living room to avoid any further questioning. She almost tripped over Gazza as he dashed ahead of her and ran to sit in front of the cupboard where his lead and harness were kept. As soon as she took them out the dog began racing around in circles. She crouched down and made an attempt to put on the harness but he was moving so fast he was almost a blur. She had one more go at grabbing him before standing up again. 'This is ridiculous. Gazza, stop it.' He paused for a nanosecond but she wasn't quick enough to put on his harness so he set off again. She didn't have time for this.

'Bring his lead through here and I'll put it on. He gets a bit excited.'

'Yeah, just a bit,' said Ros, heading back to the living room with Gazza jumping up and trying to snatch the lead from her hand.

'Come here, boy,' said Barry and Gazza did as he was told. Ros handed Barry the harness. 'So is the someone for coffee a work thing?' Barry didn't look up.

'Err no.'

'Anyone I know?' he asked as he clicked the harness in place. This was her opportunity. Ros scratched her neck. Was this whole contrived boyfriend plan a good idea? She really didn't know. But when her dad looked up she saw something in his eyes. And oddly it felt like the right moment to lie through her teeth to him.

'Actually I did have something to ask you . . .' Her dad and Gazza stared at her expectantly. 'There's someone I'd like to bring to dinner tomorrow and his name is Cameron.' Oh my goodness, why did that feel like the hardest thing in the world to say?

Barry looked more stunned than if she'd slapped him in

the face with a pie. Gazza barked, which startled Ros and jolted Barry out of his speechlessness. 'Great. And is this Cameron a friend or . . .'

The hope and expectation in her father's eyes were quite something. Ros took a deep breath. 'He's my boyfriend.'

Chapter Eight

Ros couldn't get out of the house quick enough and thankfully Gazza felt the same. Her dad's face was something she would always remember. The smile that appeared – the likes of which had been something she'd not seen from him for a very long time. She'd dashed off before her dad could pass comment and had been hugely relieved to escape any questioning. She'd done it. She'd sown the first seed. This was happening. She felt breathless and then realised that she was almost jogging thanks to Gazza setting the pace. Why did he always pull? It couldn't be comfortable. For a small dog he had a lot of power. She tried to bring him to heel but he preferred to be semi-choking. Her phone rang and with some difficulty she answered it with one hand.

'Hiya, Ros, it's Cameron.'

'I've told him,' she blurted out. 'My dad. I've told him about us.'

'Okay. How did it go?'

'I left before he could ask me anything but he was pleased. He looked really happy.' Saying it out loud made something settle inside her. The lying wasn't going to be easy but if it put that kind of smile on his face then it was worth it.

'Well done. That's a great start. Any chance we could meet a bit earlier? I've been asked to do an extra shift at the charity shop because someone has phoned in sick and Saturday is a busy day for them.'

Ros looked at the dog dragging her along. 'I don't think I can. I'm having to walk my dad's dog because he's got trouble with his back. My dad, not the dog.'

Cameron laughed. 'I guessed that. Okay, how about we meet at a different café, one that's dog-friendly? Do you know the coffee house on London Road?'

'Yes, I'm not far from there.' *And at the speed Gazza is going I'll be there in ten minutes,* she thought.

'Great. I'll see you there in, say, fifteen minutes?'

It seemed like a good solution.

Ros took back that thought as she entered the little café. It was clearly a whole new experience for Gazza and one he was ill-equipped to handle. Being in an unfamiliar place where everyone was eating and there were new friends to meet under every table, Gazza wanted to meet them all immediately. He darted about until he'd tied himself and Ros to a table, a chair and a lady's walking frame. A kind waitress was clearing a table nearby and came to Ros's rescue.

'Here you go,' she said, leading Gazza away with a small treat and untangling his lead with the other hand. 'What can I get you?'

'Coconut latte with an extra shot please,' replied Ros.

The waitress attached the dog's lead to a loop on the solid-looking table before fussing Gazza who lapped up the attention. 'And what can I get for this little cutie?' she asked.

'Oh, he only drinks water,' replied Ros.

The waitress laughed. 'We have a doggy menu if he fancied anything to eat.' She pointed at a board.

Ros was wrong-footed so scanned it quickly. 'He likes sausage.'

'One hot diggity dog and a coconut latte extra shot coming right up.' The waitress left them and Gazza gazed adoringly after her. Ros hoped she wouldn't be long because she doubted that Gazza would behave himself for more than a moment.

The door opened and in came Cameron. Lots of furry faces all checked him out including a bearded man by the window. As he approached the table Gazza started to bark. 'Hiya,' said Cameron, kissing Ros on the cheek, which took her by surprise. She wasn't the sort of greeter who kissed people. She mourned the dying tradition of shaking hands. 'Oh would you look at you,' said Cameron, dropping to his knees to greet Gazza. He stopped barking and wagged his tail so hard Ros feared he might strain it. 'He's gorgeous. What's his name?'

She stopped her automatic need to apologise or explain and opted simply for the facts. 'It's Gazza.'

'Cool name for a cool doggo,' said Cameron.

Doggo? Ros let it go.

'Hang on.' Cameron had a huge grin on his face when he looked up at her. 'Does this mean your dad and his

dog have rhyming names? Barry and Gary. Imagine that –
names that are very similar,' he teased.

'I hate to disappoint you but he's not a Gary. Gazza was
some footballer when my dad was younger. And this dog
loves a ball.' Gazza's face spun in her direction at the word.
There was another one they'd have to spell out.

'Ahh okay. I'll let him off.' Cameron's voice changed as
he addressed the dog. 'Who's a good boy? You're a good
boy. Yes, you are. Gazza's a good boy.'

'I've ordered. Sorry, I didn't know what you wanted
to drink,' she said, interrupting the particularly one-
sided conversation. Although to be fair Gazza did seem
transfixed by Cameron's every word.

'I'm a large Americano with hot milk.'

'Okay. I'll remember that.'

The waitress appeared with Ros's drink and Gazza's
sausage, which the dog inhaled before the bowl was even
on the floor. Cameron gave his order and they settled
down to talk. Thankfully Gazza was happy to sit between
Cameron's feet in the hope of him dropping some pastry
crumbs from the pain au chocolat he'd ordered.

'There's something you need to know,' said Ros.

Cameron looked concerned. 'Okay, what's that?'

'I sort of panicked and now Dad is expecting you for
lunch tomorrow.'

'That's cool,' said Cameron. 'Who doesn't like a free
meal? And I love a roast dinner.' Ros instantly relaxed a
fraction.

'Right. Shall we pick up where we left off?' said Ros,
pulling her notebook from her bag.

'Okay,' he said, wiping the last crumbs from his lips and

surreptitiously letting Gazza lick his fingers. Ros took her hand sanitiser out of her bag and pushed it across the table to him. 'Cheers.'

Ros consulted her notes. 'Where did we meet?'

'At the cocktail bar.'

'Yes, I know that, but for the backstory when Dad asks.'

'But that works as good as anything we could make up. I work in the bar and you came in with Darla to pick up her paycheque and we got talking.'

'I don't know,' said Ros, making a note in her book.

'Why not?' Cameron sipped his drink but she knew he was still fussing the dog under the table. 'I think it's a very plausible story. What have you got that's better?'

Ros wasn't exactly blessed in the imagination department. Logic and facts were far more her cup of tea. She had a quick think and nothing of any use came to mind. 'Fine, we'll stick with the cocktail bar.' He probably did have a point.

'What happened?' asked Cameron.

'When?' Ros was lost.

Cameron smiled at her. He did that a lot. Why did people smile all the time? What did they have to be so cheerful about? 'When we met, what happened?' he asked. 'We need a better story than you came in and I asked you out.'

Ros straightened her spine. Her feminist spider sense had been triggered. 'I could have asked *you* out.'

'You could. I like that. Let's go with that. So why did you ask me out? What was it about me?' For once he looked serious as he turned his face first one way and then the other, lifting his chin and then doing a thoughtful look out of the window.

'I wouldn't have asked you out,' said Ros and then instantly regretted it. Sometimes her brain didn't have a softening feature.

Thankfully Cameron laughed. 'I don't think you would either. I'm guessing that's not your style. How about you ordered a . . .'

Belatedly Ros realised that was her cue to fill in. 'Oh . . . uh . . . Pinot Grigio. Properly chilled.'

'Okay, and I explained that we had a new-to-us wine in that I thought you might like. I gave you a taster. We got talking and we found that we had something in common, which was . . .'

Ros was too busy scribbling notes so she missed her cue again. 'Sorry. Um.' She shrugged.

Gazza made a whimper from under the table. 'I'm not sure this is working,' said Cameron.

Ros was disappointed because she was quite pleased with how far they had got. 'Perhaps we should keep to the list.' She tapped her notebook.

'It's not that I don't like your detailed flip chart questionnaire – very thorough. But I think what we really need to know, the sort of thing that could catch us out, are the little details that connect people. You know like when you have an all-nighter because one thing leads to something else and before you know it hours have gone by. Gina and I used to do that all the time.'

Ros had no idea what he was talking about. 'All-nighter? Like clubbing?'

Cameron frowned as if he wasn't sure if she was teasing him or not. 'I mean those nights when you first get together with someone and you stay up all night just talking and getting to know each other.' He beamed her a smile – or was he smiling at a memory? She couldn't be sure.

He made it sound like a common thing. Could she reveal that she'd never had this experience? 'How would that go exactly?' she asked.

Cameron pouted his full lips. 'We'd be lying down for a start.'

'Not really practical.' Ros indicated the coffee shop.

'I've an idea,' said Cameron, leaping to his feet, making Gazza jump up and bounce around. 'Come on,' he added, reaching for her hand.

Ros hastily paid the bill and they exited the coffee shop quickly with Gazza leading the way, even though he obviously was clueless as to where they were going. Cameron guided them down London Road to East Park. It was a place Ros hadn't been for many years. Scenes of picnics with her mother and father swam into her mind and then later ones where there was just her and her dad. Unhelpfully she now had an image of her picnicking alone – was that a glimpse at her future?

'This way,' said Cameron and a tug from Gazza's lead pulled Ros back to the present. They walked under the wisteria-clad walkway. The sweet scent of the pretty purple flowers was delightful. They left the path that Gazza seemed particularly excited about and followed Cameron until he plonked himself down on the grass in the sunshine. 'Here'll do,' he said, lying down.

Gazza saw this as an open invitation to jump on Cameron

and try to lick his face. 'I'm so sorry,' said Ros, trying to restrain the overexcited hound.

'He's fine,' said Cameron, lifting up the wriggling creature and setting him down on the grass where he sniffed about wildly.

'What now?' asked Ros.

Cameron smiled at her. 'You need to lie down.'

'But it might be dirty or wet.'

Cameron pulled off his hoodie and laid it on the ground next to him and kept Gazza away by fussing him. 'Here you go.'

Ros wasn't sure. But then she reasoned that she wasn't sure about any of it and she'd come this far so she carefully sat on the top and Cameron kindly kept Gazza's advances at bay by hugging him.

'Give me the lead and lie down,' said Cameron.

'Is that really necessary?' asked Ros, starting to feel rather silly, and she had a quick check to make sure nobody was watching them.

'I'm afraid it is,' said Cameron, slowly lying back down.

Reluctantly Ros joined him and was immediately struck by how blue and cloud-free the sky was.

'Take a moment,' said Cameron.

Ros took a deep breath and Gazza walked over her solar plexus, making her emit an 'oomph' sound.

'Sorry,' said Cameron, guiding Gazza back to lie between the two of them. When the dog finally settled down then so did Ros.

The sun was warm, the ground beneath her was soft and there was a faint smell of grass and flowers in the air. She felt surprisingly calm. Especially given there was a hairy black dog panting away near her shoulder.

'What are you thinking about right now?' he asked.

'Literally nothing. Except possibly what my head is lying on.'

'Okay. Try not to think about that. We're trying to find something we have in common so focus on that. What do you like?'

'My job.'

'Risk management. See, I remembered.' He seemed to be thinking for a moment. 'Probably nothing that we have in common there. What else do you like?'

There was an embarrassingly long pause while Ros tried to think of things that weren't work that she liked and was struggling to find anything. 'Sorry.'

'It's fine. Shall I go through things I like and you can jump in when there's something you can relate to? Anything, however small a connection.'

'Okay.' Ros nodded and closed her eyes so she could concentrate.

'I'm into hiking and hill walking. I've only been a few times but I had a blast skiing and learning to snowboard. I love the outdoors in pretty much any weather. I like it when you've gotten really cold and wet and then you come inside to warm up.'

He left a little pause as if willing her to agree but she couldn't. Skiing seemed very high risk and Ros didn't take risks. She also loathed being cold or wet. Being cold *and* wet was the worst.

He continued. 'I read a lot. I have to for uni so my novel reading time is reduced but I still enjoy a good thriller.

Something twisty. I like watching those sorts of things on TV too.'

'I only read non-fiction.'

'Okay. Don't worry, we'll find something. What else? I enjoy comedy, stuff that makes me laugh. I've been to a few comedy club nights; they're always fun. Um . . .' She got the feeling he was running out of things. 'Music!' he said a bit louder as if discovering it lurking at the back of his mind.

'Yes, I like music.'

'Excellent,' he said, sounding relieved. 'I like anything from Eighties pop to indie rock. Who do you like to listen to?'

'Bach mainly,' said Ros and she heard the gush of air as Cameron let out an exasperated sigh. 'But I like classic musicals like *The King and I*. Do you like musicals?' she asked.

'Nah, I'm afraid I'm more into club classics,' he said. He was quiet for a bit and she missed the sound of his voice. It had a lovely timbre to it.

They lay there in silence for a couple of minutes. Ros listened to the birds in the trees, the sound of nearby traffic and then footsteps as someone was walking the nearby path. They were listening to the radio and Ros almost tutted that they didn't have headphones plugged in. She did not like those people. As they grew closer she could hear it was sports commentary and she tuned in.

'Cricket!' they both said at the same time.

Chapter Nine

Ros had been hoping to offload Gazza at her dad's quite quickly but while she and Cameron had been chatting about cricket the dog had slunk over to a flowerbed and managed to dig a sizeable hole before they'd realised. Thankfully Cameron had tidied up the flowerbed but Gazza was caked in dirt and she couldn't let him loose in her dad's home in that state.

She scooped him up and carried him inside, the whole time keeping her head as far away from his tongue as possible because she was pretty sure she'd seen him eat a worm earlier. 'Hi, Dad, we're back,' she called.

'That was a long walk. Gazza will be your best friend for evermore.'

Ros briefly appeared in the living room with the wriggling canine under her arm. 'He's covered in dirt. I'm going to bathe him.' Gazza's tail immediately stopped wagging.

'Shhh, we try not to use the B word.'

'Dad, he's not a toddler and he needs a . . .' Her father pleaded with his eyes. 'To be clean. I'll sort him out and then I'll be off. Okay?'

'If you're sure you don't mind. I'll give you a hand.' Barry got to his feet and followed her.

'You don't need to and it does rather defeat the object,' said Ros, trying to sound cheery as she took Gazza upstairs. She also wanted to avoid the Spanish Inquisition if she possibly could.

Ros put a forlorn-looking Gazza into the bath and got down the showerhead. 'It's no good going all pitiful – it's your own fault.' She switched on the shower and the dog flinched.

'Ooh those stairs'll be death of me,' said Barry, puffing out a breath as he came into the bathroom.

'Dad!' She didn't like it when he talked like that. It would have been fine a few months ago but now it was no joke. 'Do you think we should get a stairlift?' she asked, checking the water temperature as Gazza shuffled backwards away from the jet of water.

'Don't be daft. Waste of money.'

'Not if it would be useful and save you getting tired.'

'They cost thousands and for just a few . . . Nah, not worth it.' Ros's heart clenched. 'Hey, Cabbage. Don't look like that. It's fine.'

'But it's not fine, Dad.' She swallowed hard. It felt like nothing was ever going to be fine again. She was worried about him because he seemed to still be in denial.

Barry turned his attention to Gazza. 'I'll hold him; you dowse him. And then you can tell me all about this new fella of yours.' At least for a few minutes that took her mind off her father's health.

***

71

Ros had managed to sidestep the interrogation by saying that it was best if he waited and met Cameron tomorrow. She wasn't ready to fly solo on the questions and answers just yet. Thankfully her dad didn't push it and they had bathed the reluctant Gazza together in companionable silence. It gave her time to think about her morning with Cameron and the revelation that they both liked cricket. She was still thinking about it that evening.

If she was being honest Ros was surprised that she and Cameron had anything in common. She wasn't being unkind, they were just vastly different people, as their long list of differences had shown. But at least they both liked cricket. Whilst Ros didn't play, she had watched hundreds of matches and helped make the sandwiches on many occasions. Barry was and had always been into cricket and the fact that he'd had a daughter instead of a son did not stop him from sharing his love of the sport.

Now Ros thought about it, her dad had never restricted her to what might be termed girls' activities; he'd always encouraged her to go for what she wanted in life. Thanks to him she'd never felt any of the limitations or desire to submit to the gender norms other women frequently were burdened by. He probably didn't know it but Barry Foster was quite the feminist. Barry would still have been playing cricket for the Hampshire seniors over fifties had it not been for his diagnosis, but thanks to a friend he was still making it to watch some of the matches. At least there was one topic of conversation they could all join in with tomorrow.

Tomorrow! Ros hadn't been so apprehensive about a Sunday lunch since her dad had had a go at making vegan Yorkshire puddings. Bugger. A thought struck her. What if Cameron was a vegan? That was something she'd not thought to ask. Then she remembered the pain au chocolat and hot milk he'd had with his coffee and relaxed. He wasn't a vegan. But he could still be a vegetarian so she pulled out her phone and composed a message. While she was doing so she double-checked her list and added in a few last-minute questions. She was feeling ill-prepared and Cameron was slow to reply, which did not help her stress levels.

Ros tidied up her already neat apartment but at least it gave her something to do even if it only killed the best part of half an hour. Saturday nights were always a bit defunct but tonight she wished she had something to take her mind off Sunday. She had a strict rule of not working at weekends. She knew Darla thought she was a workaholic and it was true that she gave the company more hours than she was paid for during the week, but her dad had instilled in her that it was important to have weekends off. He saw them as time with his daughter but also as a chance to recharge his batteries and said he worked better in the week because he'd had a break.

For once in her life she wished she had hobbies, something to keep her busy. Quite a few of the women at work did crochet or knitting on their lunch break. Ros struggled to see the point of taking hours to produce something she could easily buy in a shop. She switched the television on and scrolled through the channels. There was no news on and everything else appeared pointless. She sat in silence, which gave her thinking time, which wasn't helpful. Perhaps they were rushing into this. They hardly knew anything about each other. She'd never done anything like this in her life and it went against her sensible approach to everything. If Cameron didn't reply soon she would have to seriously consider cancelling lunch.

He finally texted back:

Answers: Carnivore, size 11, bees, cuddles, sharks and ghosts tied. Stop worrying about tomorrow. Your dad's gonna love me ☺

She wished she shared his confidence.

***

Darla slept surprisingly well. The mattress was remarkably comfortable and she felt the fact that she knew she was here for a while had aided her sleep. Usually she was automatically on countdown until she had to pack up again and move, but not here. Also there had been no restless pets to interrupt her slumber. Or so she thought.

She was dragged abruptly from a lovely dream about Tom Holland by the most awful sound. Like something crossed between screeching brakes and a rooster crowing. She sat up in bed. The noise went again: it was an actual cockerel doing his level best to say cock-a-doodle-doo. It was not the nicest wake-up alarm she'd ever had but she was now definitely living in the countryside. Hopefully whoever owned it would be able to switch it off or whatever you did to chickens to keep them quiet.

Darla put on some clothes and headed downstairs. She'd make a cup of tea and then she'd explore the garden. She wasn't a gardener but she could run a lawnmower up and down and hopefully that was all they meant by her having to tend to the garden and stock. She yawned as she filled the kettle and gazed through a dirty net curtain. She blinked a few times and then realised that she'd overfilled the kettle. The neighbouring farm seemed very close to this house. Darla put down the kettle and went to investigate. There was a room off the kitchen with some sacks and a key in the back door.

Outside there was a big garden and an ornate low red-brick wall with a rounded top that ran all around it but there were a number of wire enclosures on the other side. The first of which she could see contained chickens. She walked to the wall and looked across at the hens. Her presence seemed to set off a cacophony of noise. The cockerel started up again, as did some nearby ducks and geese in the pen behind. Darla could see a gate in the wall so she went to investigate further. A new noise joined the birdlife as she discovered a small pen of weird-looking sheep with little horns in the last enclosure.

'Hello,' she said. Two of them jumped in the air and the others continued to bleat at her through the wire. Who did this lot belong to? She looked around and that was when she spotted an even higher wall that went further down past a large green space and then right around all the animals to join to the garage. Darla had another look. This was all part of the property, not a neighbouring farm. The low wall was there to separate the normal garden from the menagerie. All these noisy creatures must have been the stock that the agent was talking about. This was suddenly a very different job to her usual problematic canines, and the responsibility hit her like a speeding bull.

Darla checked the sacks by the back door and sure enough

they contained pellets and grain, which she assumed was animal feed. There was also a small, untidy pile of hay. The only problem was, she had no idea who was meant to get what. She found a bucket and decided to start with refilling their water because she had no idea how long these poor things had been left alone. She got mobbed in each enclosure but after a few squeals from herself she managed to refresh all the water dispensers. She returned with some food from each of the sacks she'd found and the chickens came to peck her feet so she threw down a selection and backed away which distracted them.

Hopefully they'd recognise what they usually ate and leave the rest. They had a little wooden hut in the pen so she had a peep in there and found some eggs. She carefully put a couple in her pocket and feeling like a burglar she crept out, being sure to shut up properly afterwards. She did the same with the ducks and the geese. The ducks were quite friendly and she'd fed ducks before so they felt like the least of her worries. The geese were the opposite of friendly and seemed most put out that she was in their pen even if she was bringing food and water. With a squeal she dropped the food and ran.

Once she was safely on the outside of the enclosure Darla had a good hard look at the sheep. That was when she realised they were goats. She tried the same plan with them and chucked in a bit from both sacks but they seemed to hoover up anything she put down at warp speed and then wanted to devour her jeans. Getting out unscathed was a victory. She felt overwhelmed as she stared at all the creatures in the pens – this was like a petting zoo. She was out of her depth. Darla knew nothing about farm animals and she'd never had this many creatures of any sort to look after before.

'Not as alone as I'd thought,' she said to herself.

'Meow,' came a reply. She turned around to find a large grey cat sitting on the low wall watching her.

'Hello, are you another inmate I haven't been told about?'

The cat walked along the wall, following Darla to the gate where it hopped down and trotted at her heels. 'Another one for breakfast then. I hope you know where your food is kept.'

When Darla opened the door the cat trotted inside, leapt onto the kitchen table and recoiled at the mouldy mug. The cat gave an accusatory look at Darla.

'Hey, this is not my mess. Your owner left it like this.' The cat flicked its tail. 'But I guess dying is a good excuse.' The cat mewed pitifully. 'I'm sorry for your loss,' added Darla, taking the eggs carefully from her pocket and placing them on the table.

She put out her fingers for the cat to sniff and they began rubbing around them. 'I'm glad you're friendly. Have you missed a fuss?'

This time a long meow. 'And you're hungry.' A quick scan of the floor told her there was a distinct lack of any food or water bowls. While she was pondering where to look there was an ominous sound next to her as the cat patted the eggs off the table and they smashed on the stone floor. It peered over the edge of the table at the mess. 'I don't suppose you eat those do you?' Darla tentatively

77

picked the cat up. There was no sign of claws, which was good. Darla knew from bitter experience how cats could be and had gone through many boxes of sticking plasters as proof. But this one seemed nice. Now it was on the floor the cat turned up its nose at the broken eggs and ran to the fridge. 'You're not meant to have milk but maybe there's something else in here that you like.' Darla opened the fridge door and she and the cat looked inside. There was milk past its sell-by date and lots and lots of grated cheese, most of which was still in date although only just. Darla offered her new furry friend some grated cheese. The cat licked a bit and then spat it out. 'I'll take that as a no then.'

Darla went on the hunt for cat food. The weird curtain-strewn cupboards held lots of tins but they were all for human consumption. No sign of cat food anywhere.

'I have to go to work but I'll be back in three and a half hours with some food. Okay?' she said, putting down a cereal bowl filled with water.

The cat purred deeply and snaked around her legs. She'd take that as a yes.

A phone call to the agency filled in a few blanks. They clarified that the message they had received had said garden and *livestock* but that had got amended somewhere in the message chain. They confirmed that more food was being delivered and checked that she was okay to continue with the job. There had been a brief moment when she'd wondered if she should take the get-out option she was being offered. Yet the thought of leaving The Brambles and a place to stay for five months was enough for Darla to banish it from her mind. The menagerie did worry Darla but she liked a challenge and was actually really pleased that there was a cute cat. The house had seemed large so the thought of another heartbeat living inside with her was comforting. And at least that was one animal she knew how to look after. The others would take some googling because she'd have to gen up on them and fast.

After her cleaning job Darla went to the supermarket and got a couple of tins of cat food and some tuna to tide her over until the delivery, as well as some of her favoured cleaning products. There was little she liked more than making her mark on a grubby home; the pleasure of getting it spotless was immensely satisfying. As there was a queue at the supermarket she also had a chance to watch a few farming videos on her phone but none of them were particularly helpful, although she had enjoyed watching lambs and goat kids skittishly bounce around.

When Darla returned to The Brambles there was no sign of the cat but the other animals were all hollering for more food. She found a couple of glass jugs in the kitchen, filled them from the sacks and ventured out. She was met by the same racket she'd experienced that morning. 'Shhh, I bring food.' There was a brief lull in volume. 'Now who wants what?' she asked, opening the mesh door into the geese enclosure. They all ran at her with wings spread wide and honking loudly. Darla chucked the jug's contents on the floor and fled back the way she'd come. She repeated it for the ducks and then went to the chickens. Unfortunately the cockerel was marching up and down like a beady-eyed sentry. Every time Darla went to step inside, he about-turned and flew at her with wings flapping and a particularly menacing screech.

'Okay, I get it. This is your home and I'm an intruder,' she told him – perhaps empathy was the best approach. 'But if you and your um . . . Girlfriends? Lady friends? Wives? Ooh, is this where the phrase birds comes from?' The rooster cocked his head at her. 'Anyway, whatever. If you want some food then you need to back off.' He came closer and pecked menacingly at the mesh. 'Fine. Let's try something else.' Darla walked around the side of the enclosure and flicked a little bit of grain into the top corner. After a moment or so curiosity got the better of one of the hens and she came over and started hoovering it up. The cockerel was there in a flash. Darla dashed back to the entrance, quickly went inside, deposited the food and was about to escape when the rooster looked up. They made eye contact.

'Bugger it!' said Darla and she pelted back out with the sound of flapping and screeching close behind her. She slammed the door shut just in time and took a moment to compose herself. Her heart was racing. The cockerel strutted up and down with his feathers extra puffy, looking mightily proud of himself. 'Yeah, well I made it out alive so who's the real winner?' He squawked and flapped triumphantly. 'And same to you,' she said before going back inside to clean as much of the house as she could before her shift at the bar.

Darla was cleaning glasses when Cameron arrived. 'Hiya. I hear tomorrow's the big day,' she said, feeling quite sorry that she wasn't going to be there to witness the encounter with Barry. She was secretly very proud of her bright idea and how far it had come.

'You know what? I'm kind of looking forward to it.'

'Really?' Darla couldn't hide her surprise.

'Yeah. I mean I love my folks but what Ros is doing for her dad is something else, and I really want this to work mainly because . . . of how Ros is. She's kind of . . . unusual. Is she always like that?'

'Like what exactly?'

'I don't want you to think I'm bad-mouthing your best friend . . .'

'You're not. Tell me some specifics and I'll tell you if it's normal for Ros or if it's because she's a bit wound up about my fake-dating idea.' Darla was keen that nobody should forget the origins of the whole scheme.

'Okay. Well, for starters she's not exactly the friendliest person. I mean she's not rude. At least I don't think she means to be. She's obsessed with work and I get the feeling she doesn't know how to relax. I'd describe her as quite repressed and she has to plan everything to the nth degree. I mean, like, she has lists all over the show. She's even brought a flip chart stand home from work. Who does that?'

'That's her own stand,' said Darla.

'Blimey. Didn't see that one coming.' Cameron pushed a hand through his hair, making it stick up and stay there. 'I guess it might be handy for . . . nope, I've no idea why you'd buy one.'

'She got it a while ago so she could apportion chores with her boyfriend at the time,' explained Darla. 'Actually the day before they broke up as it turned out. She's nice when you get to know her.'

Cameron raised an eyebrow.

'Not warm and fuzzy nice, but what you are struggling with are things I like about her. She's consistent, never moody and she always has a pen and paper on her. Sometimes even sticky notes,' she said.

'You're right, she has lots of good points and she's being really generous over how much she's paying me. Although she did ask if I could get my hair cut and have a shave before tomorrow.' He widened his eyes.

'Actually, she does have a point there,' said Darla.

'Hey,' said Cameron, rubbing his hand over his chin. 'It's stubble. That's trendy.'

'It's a scraggy beard. That's lazy. I agree with Ros on that one.'

'You're going to tell me everything else is normal for Ros, aren't you?' asked Cameron.

'Pretty much. Watch out tomorrow though because she will be hyper stressed.'

'What happens then?' Cameron looked alarmed.

'It's best you don't know in advance,' said Darla, slapping him manfully on the shoulder.

Chapter Ten

Darla was exhausted by the end of the day. She'd been up extra early, thanks to the noisy cockerel. She'd worked her cleaning job only to come back to The Brambles and clean the kitchen although despite all her efforts it still looked only marginally less grubby. She'd had better results in the bathroom where the bath now gleamed, the taps shone and she no longer needed to hover her bum over the toilet seat. She'd not managed to fix the dripping tap so the constant noise made her feel like she was on *Countdown* and had to hurry up. She'd vacuumed and dusted throughout. The bedroom windows had been open most of the day and it now looked and felt fresher. She'd endured a long and busy shift at the cocktail bar thanks to a hen night and now she was ready for her bed.

She pulled onto the drive and cut the engine. She let herself in and walked through the house. She went to get herself a glass of water and through the kitchen window she could see a light bouncing around outside. Her breath caught in her throat – she had an intruder.

Darla picked up the nearest thing there was that might

pass as a weapon and crept outside with the soup ladle. She clutched her phone in her other hand. She could video the intruder as evidence or perhaps she should go back in and call the police. It dawned on her how vulnerable she was with just a soup ladle to protect her and she froze by the gate. The intruder was bending down on the other side of the bird pens but there was no sign of the animals as they'd probably gone into their little wooden huts to sleep, which was what she'd hoped she'd be doing around about now.

Suddenly the intruder stood up and started to head her way. In her panic to get back inside unnoticed Darla tripped over her own feet, stumbled into the low wall and tipped right over the top of it, landing in a heap on the other side and losing the ladle.

Big thudding footsteps approached her as she felt around for her weaponised utensil and scrambled to her feet without it. 'Stop! I'll call the police!' she yelled.

For a moment she was blinded by torchlight. Her heart was thumping hard and blood was rushing through her system. 'Is this yours?' asked a gruff voice, shining the light on the soup ladle lying on the grass. It looked quite menacing as the torchlight glinted off it. She wished she'd kept hold of it now.

'Yes, thank you,' she said, reaching for it.

He stepped in her way. 'Who are you?' asked the gruff voice.

'I live here. More importantly, who are you, creeping about the place in the dead of night?' she countered, wishing she hadn't used the word 'dead' in case it gave him any ideas. 'Get that torch out of my face and explain yourself,' she said, trying to make herself as tall as possible.

The light swung to one side and a face loomed in front of her out of the darkness. 'Heavens, not you again,' he said.

Darla was baffled. She didn't know this bloke, did she? She blinked a number of times but still, all she could see was the bright white blob the torch had left on her vision, but the face in front of her was vaguely familiar. Then it all clicked into place. He was the guy who had stopped the day Spindle had run into the road and if she remembered correctly he'd been quite rude to her. 'You!' At that moment she also noticed he was holding the pretty grey cat. 'Hey! You can't steal my cat.' Darla went to take the feline but the man stepped back.

'Definitely not your cat.'

'Erm, I think you'll find it comes with the house.'

He shook his head. 'I'm confused. There's no way you've bought this already. Horace only died a few days ago and I'm pretty sure he didn't have any family.'

'There's a distant relative in New Zealand apparently. Everything is being dealt with through a solicitor. I'm house-sitting. And I'm looking after all the animals including the cat.' Darla held her hands out.

'The cat doesn't live here. He's mine but he is a cheeky bugger who would come up here to stare at the chickens and try and cadge some tuna off of Horace.'

Darla wasn't sure whether to believe him or not. 'How do I know you're telling the truth?'

'You don't. Just like I don't know if you're lying or not. You might be a squatter for all I know. But this cat won't let just anyone pick him up.'

'He let me,' said Darla.

'Huh. Well, usually he's picky.'

85

'Rude! If he's yours what's his name?'

'Winston,' he said, and Darla noted the cat look up at the sound of the name. Perhaps this bloke was telling the truth.

'I don't suppose the birds and goats are yours by any chance, are they? That would save me a job.'

'Nope, they're all Horace's, along with about two hundred sheep over the way.' He tipped his head behind him.

'What?!' Darla's mind was racing. How on earth was she going to look after sheep? 'B . . . but . . .'

'I'm joking; the sheep are mine.' He freed up a hand for her to shake. 'I'm Elliott. I live over there at Nettle Bank Farm.' He gave another nod behind him. 'My land joins Horace's.'

'That makes us neighbours,' she said with a big grin. She was feeling hugely relieved she wasn't looking after umpteen sheep and was always happy to make a new friend.

He frowned at her. 'I suppose it does,' he said.

**

On Sunday morning Ros decided it was best that she and Cameron arrived separately at her dad's. Mainly because she usually got there just after ten so they could have coffees and a chat while making the dinner at a leisurely pace. That was far too much time for questioning so she'd told Cameron to get there between half twelve and one ready for a one o'clock lunch. She wasn't so sure that had been the best plan because now she was worrying about what time he would arrive. Too early and she would be busy in the kitchen, which would allow her dad an opportunity to interrogate Cameron alone. Too late and her dad would likely judge him for his tardiness. Or worse still, what if he was a no-show?

'That's a lot of pepper you're putting in the gravy,' commented Barry, leaning over her shoulder.

Ros stopped grinding. 'I wasn't concentrating,' she said, throwing the dry gravy mix in the bin and starting again with the *Bisto* tin.

'You seem out of sorts. Is there anything about this Cameron I should know beforehand?' asked her dad as he whisked his Yorkshire pudding mix.

'No. It's best that you just meet him.' Ros nodded more to herself than her father. She needed to stay focused and keep calm. They had done all the prep work, and they were going to keep the duration as short as possible by offering to walk Gazza after lunch, which would tick the job off Ros's to-do list as well as give them an opportunity to debrief and regroup.

'He's not got two heads then?' asked Barry with a smile. 'Or worse still a Portsmouth fan?' The smile changed to a flat line.

'No to both. And I thought we agreed you wouldn't turn this into an interrogation.' The timer went off for Ros to turn the roast potatoes over.

'I'll be on my best behaviour. I promise.'

Gazza barked and ran to the front door a moment before the doorbell sounded.

'I'll go,' said Barry, moving faster than Ros had seen him do in a while. As she already had the oven gloves on she had to concede and turn the roasties as quick as humanly possible whilst trying to keep an eye on the hallway.

Barry opened the front door. 'You must be Cameron.'

'Hello, Mr Foster. It's lovely to meet you.'

'Come in, lad. Mind the dog – he can be a bit funny with strangers.'

Cameron crouched down and the little dog went bananas. 'You must be Gazza. Hello, mate. Aren't you a handsome fella?'

'Bugger!' said Ros as she went to grab a potato with the tongs and missed because she wasn't paying full attention and the potato shot off the tray and bounced across the kitchen floor.

'Everything okay?' called Barry.

'Errant roast potato,' said Ros, slinging the tray back in the oven, shutting the door and binning the escapee roastie as she dashed to join them in the hallway still wearing the oven gloves.

Cameron stood up from greeting the dog and for the first time that day Ros got a good look at him. He was wearing a white polo shirt and jeans, thankfully without any holes in them, but the most noticeable thing about him was that he'd had a haircut and a shave, which made him look quite different. He appeared far less studenty and more than presentable.

'Hi, hon,' said Cameron casually, leaning in and kissing her cheek.

Ros froze. And then realised her dad was watching them both closely. 'Hello, Cameron.'

'This is for you,' said Cameron, handing Barry a bottle of white wine. 'I'm hoping you drink the same as your daughter.'

Barry admired the bottle. 'Pinot Grigio. Nice. Thank

you, Cameron. You didn't have to do that. Ros has got dinner under control so how about you come through to the living room?'

'Actually I could do with a hand in here,' said Ros in a panic, raising her oven-gloved hand.

'What with?' asked Barry.

'Err . . . gravy boat. I don't know where the gravy boat is.' Ros headed back to the kitchen, checking over her shoulder that they were following her.

Barry started looking in cupboards, which gave Cameron a chance to mouth *'Are you okay?'* to Ros.

Ros mimed her head exploding and he grinned. He looked very different. So much smarter than he usually did. *'I like your hair,'* she mouthed. *'Thank you for . . .'* She mimed scissors in the air.

'You're welcome,' he mouthed back. They smiled at each other.

'Here it is!' said Barry triumphantly, recovering the gravy boat from the back of a cupboard. He looked at Cameron and then at Ros. 'What did I miss?'

'Something smells good,' said Cameron, taking two strides to stand next to Ros.

'It's just chicken.'

'My favourite,' he said.

Barry opened the bottle of wine as Ros got out three glasses.

'Did you drive here, Cameron?' asked Barry.

'I cycled over so I'll only have one small glass please.'

'Very wise. That's not a local accent. North somewhere, is it?'

'Midlands. I'm from Derbyshire.'

'What brings you to Southampton?' asked Barry, pouring the wine.

'University,' said Cameron.

'And you settled here.' Barry handed out the glasses of wine.

'It's a lovely part of the world,' said Cameron.

'Cheers to that,' said Barry and they all raised their glasses.

Ros had to admit she was impressed with how Cameron had handled the initial grilling. He'd answered everything confidently and whilst he may have withheld some facts, he hadn't out-and-out lied to her father, who so far was smiling. Gazza trotted in and went to have a sniff around Cameron's feet. He pawed at his leg until he gave him a fuss.

'I have to say I've not known Gazza react to someone like that. He usually does a lot more barking and is quite standoffish. But he certainly likes you.'

'Gazza likes everyone, Dad,' said Ros, realising that the dog had met Cameron the previous day and already associated him with getting a lot of fuss.

'Not when they come to the door. He's fine when he's out meeting new people but when they come here he's quite territorial. Remember that charity collector a couple of weeks ago? I think the poor bloke thought Gazza here was going to savage him.' Barry laughed at the memory. He watched Cameron scratch the dog behind his ears. 'He's a good judge of character is Gazza.' He nodded at Ros before taking a sip of wine, making Ros feel like they'd cleared the first hurdle.

Ros served up while the men discussed the weather, a safe topic she was comfortable to not be included in. 'These must be the legendary Yorkshire puddings I've heard all about,' said Cameron, pointing at his plate. 'Impressive.'

'Thanks,' said Barry, looking proud. 'The secret's in the amount of warm water I add. Also, not too much mixture and an extra hot oven.'

'I'll remember that,' said Cameron and they all started to eat. At last Ros felt she could relax a little.

Barry took a pause to drink some wine. 'You know you're a bit of a surprise,' he said to Cameron.

'Am I?'

'Ros only mentioned you yesterday. How long have you two been dating? You do still call it dating, don't you?'

Ros was instantly uncomfortable. Had they covered this? She was pretty sure they hadn't. 'Err . . .' Too short an amount of time would make it weird that she'd brought him home. Too long would look like she'd been hiding him.

Barry was waiting for a response. Cameron stepped in. 'We met just before Christmas and started seeing each other in early January.'

'Not long then,' said Barry.

'Long enough,' said Cameron, giving Ros a lingering look that made her concentrate on cutting up a piece of carrot that didn't need cutting.

'How did you meet?' asked Barry before loading up his fork.

Ros could take this one. 'In a cocktail bar in town.'

'We had a new wine that we were trying to upsell and I persuaded her to try it,' said Cameron.

'You work there?' asked Barry.

'Yes,' said Cameron.

Ros's stomach felt like it had turned to ice. 'Only part-time,' she said whilst trying to signal to Cameron with her eyes that he'd made a major blooper. This was not the fake career they had agreed for him.

'What do you do the rest of the time?' asked Barry, focusing on Cameron.

'Computers,' said Ros quickly.

'Computer science,' said Cameron. 'I'm studying it at university.'

Ros would have banged her head on the table had she not had a gravy-filled plate in front of her.

'You're a student?' Barry looked confused.

Cameron chuckled. 'I know I look a bit older than most. I'm a mature student. I missed uni the first time around. No one in my family went to university so getting a job was the normal thing to do. But however hard I worked I just couldn't seem to progress. I found it was a stumbling block in a number of things. People looked down on me. So I decided to retrain as a computer engineer.'

'Right,' said Barry. Ros was holding her breath. 'Well, good on you for wanting to better yourself.'

'Thank you,' said Cameron with a wink at Ros, who was growing increasingly uncomfortable with his maverick approach of telling the truth.

'But I'm guessing that means Ros here pays when you go out.'

'Sometimes,' said Cameron. 'But we don't go anywhere

expensive. Yesterday we went to the park.'

'Hmm.' Barry didn't look convinced. 'Are you living in student digs?'

'A house in Portswood. There's six of us sharing.'

'Ros's penthouse flat must make a nice change then.'

'Dad!' said Ros. 'That's really unfair. He's only been to my apartment once.' At least that was true. 'Cameron will likely get an excellent job when he graduates and until then what does it matter who pays for stuff? And it's not a penthouse just because it's on the top floor.'

'You're already thinking long-term then,' said Barry, seeming surprised.

'Yes,' said Ros firmly.

'I'm sorry, Cameron, if I was rude,' said Barry. 'But Ros here is very special to me. I think dads and daughters have a unique bond and her being an only one just intensifies my protective nature.'

'I understand. No apology needed. I hope I'm the same when I'm a dad.'

Ros could not believe it. Cameron had walked straight into the children conversation. Had he not paid any attention during their flip chart session?

'You want kids?' asked Barry with a quizzical look on his face.

'Definitely,' said Cameron.

Barry gave Ros the side-eye. 'Before you say anything, Dad. Yes, we've discussed this and Cameron knows how I feel about children. I think it's time for pudding.'

Cameron hastily replaced his cutlery as Ros whisked his plate away and stormed out. This was not going well. Ros plonked the plates down on the worktop and was startled when Cameron appeared with the gravy boat. 'What's the matter?' he asked in hushed tones.

'What's the matter?' Ros was incredulous and struggled to keep her voice to a whisper. 'You went off piste. Like not even a little bit off into fresh snow. This was skiing with abandon through loads of trees and into a car park.'

'What?'

'I took the skiing analogy too far. My point is Dad now thinks you're a gold digger so he's going to be worried about who I'm with instead of happy I'm not alone. This was a bad idea. I might have to murder Darla.'

'Calm down,' said Cameron. 'I think you're overreacting,' he added as she started to pace around the kitchen.

'Do you not see that we've made the situation worse?'

'How?'

'Either we carry on with this charade in which case he thinks I've hooked up with Amber Rose—'

'Who?' asked Cameron.

'Famous gold digger. Dated Kanye West,' said Ros. Cameron shook his head.

'Anyway, if we split up then he'll die thinking I've had my heart broken.'

Cameron was looking over her shoulder. 'But that's not going to happen because we're rock solid.'

'What are you t—' Ros didn't get to finish the sentence because Cameron swooped in and kissed her.

Chapter Eleven

Darla usually had to be up early for her cleaning job that started at six thirty in the middle of Southampton but she did object to a five o'clock wake-up call on a rare day off midweek. She pulled the duvet over her head but the rooster was in full voice. A grumpy Darla stomped downstairs and put the kettle on. She moved the pile of library books she'd picked up to one side and put *Keeping Chickens For Dummies* on the bottom just in case Elliott stopped by. After a coffee and a long hot bath in the biggest bath she'd ever been in she felt slightly more human. She filled her jugs and went out to feed the animals. She did her usual trick of chucking the food and running. As she bolted from the goat pen and only narrowly missed a pair of horns up her bum she almost ran straight into Elliott.

'Blimey, you gave me a start. Good morning,' she said.

'What are you doing?' Elliott pointed at the goats who were merrily munching through the food.

'Feeding the animals.'

'They don't eat that,' said Elliott.

Darla waved a jug at the greedy goats. 'I think that proves that they do.'

'I mean they're not *meant* to be eating wheat.'

Darla was puzzled. She figured they'd only eat what they liked. 'Who eats the wheat then?'

'The geese, but you have to put it in the bucket of water?'

Was he winding her up? This was all sounding a bit complicated and she'd not read any of this in her library books although she had mainly been looking at the pictures and trying to skim-read them. They weren't the most riveting reads. 'Why would I put their food in water?'

'It stops the rats and mice eating it.'

'Ahh that's clever. Eek, rats?' Darla hopped from one foot to the other whilst scanning the ground for any sign of vermin.

Elliott exhaled heavily. She got the feeling he was despairing with her. 'They mainly emerge at dusk and they move about most at night-time.'

Darla gave an elaborate shudder. 'Are there many of them?' But she immediately held up her palm, making Elliott pull his head back. 'Don't tell me – I don't want to know.' She took a moment to calm herself. 'Okay. I put the wheat in the water for the geese. What should I feed the ducks?'

'They eat the pellets.'

'Yay, I got something right.' She carried on quickly before Elliott pointed out that she'd actually given all the animals some of the pellets. 'And the goats. What should I feed them?'

Elliott was scratching his head. 'Do you know anything about animals?'

'Rude. And yes, I am well versed in many types of animals but mainly the domesticated kind.'

Elliott smirked. 'These are domesticated.'

Darla threw up her arms. 'I know you're winding me up. I won't be letting them inside the house. I'm not that daft.' She lifted her chin. 'Back to the goats, what do they eat?'

'Hay,' he said and he strolled away.

Hay? 'Hang on!' she called and she bounded after him. 'I don't have much hay.' She'd used most of it for beds for the chickens. How was she to know it was goat food? 'I'm expecting a food delivery sometime next week but those guys are going to need some to tide them over.'

Elliott stopped walking. 'And?'

'And . . . as my lovely new neighbour I thought you might be able to help me out.' Darla beamed him her best smile.

Elliott harrumphed. 'Hay doesn't come free you know.'

'I'm sure we can come to an arrangement.'

Elliott looked shocked and then Darla realised her mistake. 'Oh no, no, no. I wasn't offering sex in exchange for hay.' Elliott's eyebrows shot up even higher. 'I wasn't meaning to offer sex at all. I meant eggs. I have lots of eggs. Not my eggs. Chickens' eggs! The hens are like machines. I'll swap eggs for hay. Deal?' She held her hand out and he glared at it.

'Fine.' He shook her hand briskly and stomped off.

'Bye, Elliott. Lovely to see you again,' she called after him but she got no reply. She'd wear him down eventually; she always did.

* * *

97

The kiss had thrown Ros far more than she liked to admit. Although it made more sense when she realised her dad had walked into the kitchen behind her and if Cameron hadn't stopped her talking she could well have given the game away. With hindsight she felt there may have been a number of other options available to Cameron rather than resorting to close personal contact. However, what she hadn't banked on was her whole body reacting to his kiss. It hadn't lasted long but wow, had it made a big impression. But then, she'd not kissed anyone for over a year so it was to be expected. Kissing was a very intimate thing and an area they had not fully thought through. There was only one way to solve it: get Cameron over for another workshop. They had to work around his shifts and university studies so they had agreed that Thursday evening was best for them both.

First, she had to get through the follow-up to the team awayday. Ros put on a smile and joined her team in one of the company breakout rooms where their yacht captain from the awayday was already waiting.

'Welcome, Ros, nice to see you've fully dried out,' he said.

'Yes, thank you.' Ros had heard most of the jokes since they'd returned to work.

Alastair strode in and broke into a grin as soon as he spotted Ros, which was not something she was used to. Rarely did he smile in her presence. 'How's the little mermaid today?'

'Fine thanks. And you are hilarious as always, Alastair.' Ros checked her watch. There was still two minutes until the meeting officially started.

The captain did some more unnecessary introductions before revealing a flip chart. She liked that he was prepared; it instantly settled Ros. She scanned the flip chart; it bore no resemblance to what she'd experienced. She raised her hand. 'Yes, Ros.'

'Sorry, is that the right list?' she asked.

It made the captain have a quick look at the sheet. 'Yep. Let's quickly run through it. This is everything we covered on the awayday and what I'm sure you've all been applying in the office.' There were a few shared guilty looks. Ros remained utterly confused. The captain read out the list. 'Connecting on a personal level which we did on the day as part of the initial icebreaker. Uniting around a common purpose.' Ros must have been frowning because the captain looked straight at her. 'Which was when we came together to crew the yacht.'

'Oh I see. Yes,' said Ros.

'Gaining new skills,' he continued.

'Like walking on water,' said Alistair. This time everyone laughed.

Ros acknowledged the joke with a smile and a nod. She could see it was funny from their perspective.

'Improved communication,' said the captain. 'Coming together as a cohesive team and celebrating success.'

Sonia was scribbling feverishly in her notebook.

'Sorry,' said Ros, holding up a finger. 'Did I miss the last three things?'

'Err.' The captain seemed unsure as to whether Ros was being serious or not. 'I only think you missed a little of the celebrations because you were getting dry.'

'Oh.' Ros didn't feel she could press him further; there

was clearly something she was missing because she didn't feel they had achieved very much at all – not on the awayday or since.

'This is our opportunity to give some feedback to each other about what we think individuals do well, where we feel they have improved and where we've identified opportunities for growth in the future. Who wants to go first?'

Ros had to fight hard not to let her disdain show. Sadly the company was probably paying a lot of money for this sort of rubbish.

'I'll go first,' said Alistair. 'Mike, I thought your knot work was excellent. Sonia, you got better once I'd explained which rope did what. And, Ros, maybe learn to swim.'

'I didn't mean on the awayday so that's not exactly—' began the captain but Ros was already responding.

'Fine,' said Ros. 'Sonia, you were positive even when facing a day of mansplaining. Mike, things got much better once you'd stopped posing like a Bond girl. And, Alastair, why don't you try not being a complete arse for once?' She turned to the captain. 'How did I do?' But as the man had his head in his hands she felt that communicated his answer quite well.

Even Ros wasn't in the mood for another flip chart session but needs must. The first outing for Cameron and Ros as a pretend couple had not been great. She wouldn't go as far as to say it'd been a complete disaster but, in the captain's words, there was room for growth. She opened the door on Thursday evening to a yawning Cameron.

'I won't keep you late,' she said.

'Sorry. I didn't mean to be rude. It's just last night they had games night at my digs.'

'Ooh what sort of games?'

'Drinking ones mainly,' said Cameron. 'Which rapidly got out of hand, ending in a food fight just after three this morning. So I'm a bit done in.'

'That's not on.'

'Tell me about it,' he said, flopping onto the sofa. 'But do I gather you like games?'

'Bridge. Do you play?'

'Nah. I'm more of an Uno fan but I'm a demon at strip Jack naked.'

Ros pulled her chin in. 'I definitely don't play strip poker or the like.'

Cameron laughed. 'No clothes are removed. It's just a card game. Maybe I'll show you one day.'

'Maybe. Anyway, can I get you a drink? I did get some beer in if you'd like one but as I don't drink it myself I have no clue if it's any good, but I have seen Darla drink this brand.'

'That's really kind of you, Ros. Yeah, I'd love a beer.'

'Excellent.' She was delighted that he seemed genuinely pleased.

She popped the cap off and brought it to him on the sofa. 'Scrabble,' she said.

'Thanks, and what now?'

'I like a game of Scrabble. I don't have a board here but Dad has one. We play at Christmas and Easter sometimes.'

'Cool. I like Scrabble too.' They smiled at each other.

'I'll add it to the list,' said Ros. She turned over a new

flip chart with the header 'Things We Have In Common or Both Like'. Currently all that was listed was cricket.

'I know you're going to disagree but I think there was a lot about Sunday that went well.'

Ros stared at him. 'For example?' she prompted.

Cameron leaned forward. 'Barry bought the fact that we were a couple. I know I'm currently not his ideal son-in-law but he didn't suspect a scam.'

'Please don't call it a scam,' said Ros, feeling the punch of guilt to her gut. 'He may have accepted that we were a couple but if he can't understand what I see in you then he's going to get suspicious. Which is why . . .' Ros tapped the flip chart; she needed to keep them on track.

'I've had an idea,' he said. 'What if I took your dad out for a beer? Have a man-to-man chat. Say that I get that I might not be his first choice but I want to do whatever I can to make him like me.' Cameron grinned at her, clearly pleased with his suggestion.

'Then he'd definitely know you have something to hide,' said Ros. 'How about we have a list of subjects that we feel are safe to discuss and agree exactly what we can and can't say about them?'

Cameron swigged his beer. 'Sounds like a bundle of fun.'

'Sarcasm is not helpful,' said Ros.

They were interrupted by a buzz on the entry system. Ros paused for a moment; she wasn't expecting anyone. It buzzed again. 'Shall I get that?' asked Cameron. Already reaching for the phone. 'Hallo,' he said.

Ros strode across the room but Cameron stood up, making it difficult for her to grab it off him. 'Barry! We were just talking about you,' said Cameron. Then completely unnecessarily he mouthed to Ros that it was her dad. 'Come on up,' he said into the receiver as he pressed the entry button.

'Buggeration,' said Ros. 'Hide the flip chart. I'll stall him.'

'On it,' said Cameron.

Ros was sweating. She did not need this level of stress. There was a tap on her door. She took a deep breath and checked over her shoulder. The flip chart was gone and so was Cameron. Ros opened the door and was immediately assaulted by Gazza who was over the moon to find Ros on the other side of the door. He yelped his excitement as his claws trashed her tights in one easy move.

'Dad, hello. This is a nice surprise,' she said, kissing him on the cheek.

'I'm not interrupting anything, am I?' asked Barry.

'Of course not,' said Ros, shutting the door and turning around to find Cameron walking in whilst pulling his T-shirt over his head as if he was getting dressed. She felt like she was intruding as she was suddenly presented with his bare torso but she couldn't look away. Horror was keeping her fixed in position. What on earth would her dad think? This was a nightmare.

'No worries, Barry,' said Cameron, checking his flies were done up. 'It's great to see you again.' He put his hand out to shake and belatedly Barry shook it. 'Hey, buddy, how are you?' said Cameron, addressing Gazza.

'What's wrong?' asked Ros, now realising that this was an unplanned visit and Barry had brought the dog.

'Nothing's wrong. I just need a favour as something has come up last minute.'

'What is it?' asked Ros.

'Did you want a beer?' asked Cameron, picking up his bottle.

'Er no thanks. I wasn't going to stop. The hospital want me to pop in first thing tomorrow and stay overnight. I know it's short notice but I wondered if you could have Gazza?'

'Of course,' said Cameron before Ros had had a chance to process the information. 'We'd love to have him.'

'Why do you need to go to hospital all day and overnight?' asked Ros, instantly concerned by what appeared to be an unplanned appointment.

'It's routine. They're just double-checking and monitoring a few things. Absolutely nothing to worry about. Well, nothing more to worry about,' said Barry with a weak smile. He glanced at Cameron. 'I take it he knows.'

'He does,' said Ros.

'And I was very sorry to hear about your condition,' said Cameron, snaking an arm around Ros's waist and making her freeze. 'And I'm here to support both of you in any way I can.'

'Thanks,' said Barry. 'That means a lot.' He turned his attention back to Ros. 'So is it okay to leave Gazza with you until Saturday?'

Ros knew she'd failed to stop the alarm showing on her face. 'Er, well, he'll need food and bowls and—'

Barry held up a carrier bag. 'I brought all he needs. His blanket is in here. He'll sleep on that wherever you put it. And I put a toy in but not a ball.'

Gazza spun around to stare at Barry. 'Great,' said Cameron, taking the lead and bag from Barry. 'He'll be

104

fine with us,. You've nothing to worry about.'

'Shall I pick him up sometime on Saturday?' asked Barry.

'Let me know when you're home and settled and I'll bring him back then. You might be tired if the hospital have been poking and prodding you.'

'Don't worry. I'll be fine,' said Barry, giving her a hug. 'Thanks, I really appreciate it.' He patted Gazza. 'You be a good boy, won't you?'

'He'll be just fine,' said Cameron. 'You leave it to us.'

Ros got herself a glass of water while she counted in her head how long she thought it would take for her dad to leave the building. She'd not felt this out of control since her mother left. Ros wasn't good at trusting people or letting them take the lead. She'd found it hard to make friends at school. She was always the serious and slightly sad little girl who questioned others' motives. The truth was she couldn't understand why anyone would want to be friends with her if even her own mother couldn't be bothered to stick around long enough to build a relationship. And now here she was, thrown into one that had to look on the surface like it was perfect and she had no yardstick to measure that by.

'What the hell was that, Cameron? You can't just improvise.'

He seemed wrong-footed. 'Surely you weren't going to say no to having the dog?'

'What? Of course I wasn't. Although . . .' She watched as the little dog jumped across her expensive sofa and skidded

105

on her highly polished wooden floor. 'No, of course not. I meant the stripper routine.'

Cameron grinned. 'You see now, *that* made it believable.'

'Believable. Now he thinks we're having sex.' Ros was mortified and feared her dad would be feeling the same way.

'Yeah. That would be kind of normal if we'd been dating for over two months.'

'Would it? I suppose so. But still.' She shuddered. 'Eeew!' she said with feeling.

'Jeez, thanks. You know how to massage a guy's ego.'

'Oh, no offence. It's the idea of my dad thinking about us . . .' There was the shudder again. 'Not the thought of sex with you. Not that I have thought about sex with you because I obviously haven't. But I'm sure it's very nice.'

'Nice?' Cameron tipped his head.

'Are you after a greater compliment than nice for imagined sex?'

'Er yes, I am.'

'Really, this is silly,' said Ros.

Cameron folded his arms.

Ros could feel her cheeks heating up as an image of Cameron's torso flashed into her mind. 'I'm sure you're stupendous.'

Cameron stuck out his lip and nodded. 'Stupendous I will accept.' His phone beeped. 'Arse,' he said. 'Sorry, that's a reminder about some uni work I need to do. It's a group thing and I've not chased the others. I'd better shoot.' He downed his beer.

'Hang on,' said Ros. 'You're not leaving me with him.' She pointed at Gazza who groaned and trotted after

Cameron as if repeating Ros's sentiments.

'Were you expecting me to stay the night? Because I don't think we've covered that on the flip charts.'

'Stop being silly. I just thought you'd maybe entertain him for a bit.'

'Ros, you're a grown woman. You can handle anything and anyone. Including Gazza.' He went to kiss her cheek and she froze. 'We need to normalise this. Okay?'

She closed her eyes and took a breath. 'I'm sorry. You're right. Go ahead.'

He leaned forward and Ros tried very hard not to pull her chin into her chest. Cameron kissed her briefly on the cheek. 'See, not so bad. Some might even say stupendous.'

Ros smiled despite herself. 'We need to fill in some blanks.'

'Leave it with me, I'll think of something.' He crouched down at the door as Gazza ran to him. 'Now you need to be nice and try to bond. That means no barking, no chewing and no farting. Got it? You too, Gazza,' he said with a wink at Ros as he left.

Gazza spun around and stared at Ros. 'I know, but we'll just have to make the best of it. Okay?' Gazza barked and Ros jumped. 'I very much hope that was a yes.'

Chapter Twelve

It was a sunny Friday afternoon and Darla decided to take a wander down to Nettle Bank Farm and pick up the hay to save Elliott a job. It was partly that she was trying to be helpful but mainly that she was being nosy. She'd never lived in the countryside before let alone next to an actual working farm and she was interested to see what it was like. She was a city kid and whilst she was grateful for the loving family home she'd been brought up in she was excited to explore what was on her doorstep.

If she'd had the money she would have been travelling a lot further afield. That was what The Wanker had promised. He'd painted enticing pictures of exotic locations, told her stories of deserted beaches and stunning lagoons. She'd been utterly bamboozled. Just the thought of it filled her with shame. That she'd been so easily hoodwinked made her feel such a fool. He'd charmed her. Told her how amazing she was and she'd believed him. Her parents had had their doubts and tried to warn her but she'd thought she knew best. Because how could someone who made her feel so very special be anything but a good guy? How wrong she'd been.

It was hard to move on emotionally when she was still paying off the debts, which were going to take longer than she'd hoped to clear but she was getting there slowly. It was like The Wanker still had a hold over her and she hated that. She felt sad if she spent too much time thinking about her situation and how she'd got there.

All she could do now was focus on the positives and house-sitting at The Brambles was definitely one of them. There was the slightly daunting responsibility of a multitude of animals that was weighing on her but she was trying hard not to stress about that. It was a beautiful sunny afternoon with a sky full of lazy clouds. She followed the hedgerow with a basket of eggs in the crook of her arm, and walked past fields of sheep until she reached a turning and a rickety sign for the farm. She made her way along the dirt track until she saw a large house, not dissimilar to The Brambles – only bigger and flanked by large barns. She knocked on the door and waited. There was no response. She looked about her. It was very quiet. Did farmers have Fridays off? she wondered.

A meow made her turn around to see Winston trotting up to greet her. Darla put down the basket and gave the cat some fuss. He rubbed happily around the basket and Darla's legs.

'Where's your daddy?' she asked. 'Is he busy being grumpy somewhere?'

'Hello, can I help?' said someone behind her, making her start.

Darla stood up to find a man with a shaved head wearing green overalls. 'Hi. I was after Elliott?'

'He's gone fixing fences on the north border. Phone signal is a bit wobbly down there but I could try giving him a call. Unless I can help you?'

'I'm sure you can. I'm Darla.'

He wiped his hands on his overalls and then glanced over them. 'Actually I won't shake hands because they're still a bit grubby. I'm Lee, senior farm hand at your service.'

'Nice to meet you, Lee. Elliott said he could let me have a small supply of hay for the goats at The Brambles.'

'Right.' He pointed at her. 'You're the one he was having a rant about.' Darla pulled her chin in, making him shake his head. 'I say rant. What I mean is obviously not a rant – more a one-way conversation. Sort of a chat with himself. Nothing bad. Not really . . . Anyway, hay! I can sort that out. I'll bring it down to The Brambles when I finish, if that works for you?'

'Any charge for delivery?' she asked. She didn't want to get lumbered with an unexpected bill. She'd definitely learned her lesson the hard way.

'No, course not.'

'Brilliant. Here's the eggs I agreed with Elliott as payment,' she said, handing over the basket. 'I might be out at work so would it be okay for you to leave it by the back door please?'

'No trouble. It's nice to meet you, Darla. Please don't think I'm being rude but I've got a sheep with scald that I need to treat. I'd better get on.'

'Don't let me keep you. You get back to your scalded sheep. And thanks for your help.'

'Pleasure,' said Lee, walking away.

Darla set off back to The Brambles wondering if there

was a local course in animal management she could do. The library books were a bit dry and long-winded. She'd never been the sort of person who learned from books; she did much better if someone showed her how to do something. When she'd made it to the end of the track she had a sense that she wasn't alone. A quick look over her shoulder revealed Winston was trotting along behind her. He looked up at her. He was a handsome chap and she had liked the idea of there being a cat on the premises. It didn't look like Elliott had much time to spend with Winston in the day; perhaps she could borrow him. She glanced about. There was no one there. She crouched down and Winston saw that as an invitation to rub round her legs.

'I've got cat food and tuna at my place but you mustn't rat me out,' she told the cat. Winston ran on ahead. He was clearly a smart feline.

Darla liked her job at the cocktail bar. She'd learned lots about bar work and it was a skill she could utilise if she ever got the chance to travel the world. Her shifts with Cameron were the more fun ones but today he was updating her on Ros, which was making her laugh so much she had to put down the bottle of vodka she'd been about to replace on the optic.

'I mean it, Darla. Ros makes control freaks look easy-going. I am really struggling to figure her out. I have never come across anyone like her. And before you say anything, I am trying. Really I am,' said Cameron.

'I know Ros can be . . .' Darla had to search for the right word '. . . a bit difficult sometimes but she's a good person.

And I'm proud to call her my friend. She was there for me when I first came to Southampton and had nobody.' He didn't need to know that it had taken a lot of knocks on Ros's door, multiple failed attempts at small talk and a couple of batches of her famous brownies before Ros had accepted defeat and let Darla into her life. But even Ros had admitted that she was glad she had done.

'I agree. I think under all the stiffness and armour she's probably a lovely woman, but I don't know if I'll get under all that in twelve weeks or however long we have.'

'So what could you do?' asked Darla.

Cameron tilted his head as if thinking the question over. 'Stick it out, I suppose,' he said at last.

'Up to you.' Darla shrugged.

'You think I should do more don't you?' said Cameron.

'She is paying you well for doing this. And it's so far out of her comfort zone she may as well be on another planet. There is no blueprint for what you two are doing and that's why she's going overboard with the flip charts. They're her comfort blanket. And until she feels back in control of the situation she's going to have you workshopping the shit out of things. So yeah, I think maybe you could help her a bit more, and I think you'd benefit from it too. Ros is a good person to have in your life, so if you're lucky, after the sad bit is over, you might have made a friend.'

'Hmm, you could have something there.' He seemed to be thinking again but then he snapped out of it. 'Anyway, how are things with you?' he asked.

'Well, the good part is that my new house-sitting job is in this gorgeous old house, next to a farm. The not so great bit is that there's ducks, geese, goats and chickens, all of which I have no idea how to look after and they seem to want to attack me every time I go anywhere near them.'

'That sounds a lot like me and Ros.'

'But the only way is up right?' Darla touched the wooden counter three times so as not to jinx things.

As usual Darla was tired when she pulled up outside The Brambles. Early starts at the cleaning job and late nights at the cocktail bar weren't the ideal combination but it was all work and slowly the debts were going down. She reminded herself it wouldn't be like this forever as she let herself in. She definitely felt different now, and knowing she was staying put for the next few months made things feel less manic. She planned to ask the agency if she could change a few things around seeing as poor Horace wouldn't be coming home and that whoever did own it would want it looking its best if they were planning on selling.

She went through to the kitchen and switched on the kettle. While that was boiling she went to check outside on the hay delivery so that she could feed the goats something they were actually meant to be eating before she turned in for the night.

She opened the back door and almost walked into a wall of hay. 'What the heck?'

Darla stepped back, got out her phone and put it on torch. There must have been a dozen bales of hay stacked three high in the back garden. She'd not been expecting that. Was Lee having a laugh with her? That was not a small amount of hay – it was more like a year's supply! Although she had to admit the goats did seem to have big appetites despite their size.

With a yawn she got a bag from the kitchen, tugged enough hay from one of the bales to fill the bag and went to feed the goats. They were excited and began chomping on the hay. One of them also tried to eat the bag but Darla was getting wise to their antics and she managed to snatch it out of reach just in time.

Chapter Thirteen

Ros was surprised by Cameron being proactive in making contact and wanting to arrange for them to meet up Saturday afternoon. She was less impressed when he said the flip chart would not be involved and that he felt it was a third wheel in their relationship. What exactly his plan was had been unclear but he had pitched it as a live learning session to help them communicate better and be more relaxed in each other's company. She'd immediately done some googling and come across some very unsavoury things. He had clarified, upon request, that they would not need to remove any clothing, which had made her feel a little calmer.

Cameron buzzed the entry bell early on Saturday afternoon and she came down to greet him with Gazza almost tripping her up in his haste to get to Cameron first. It wasn't as warm as it had been and they both wore jackets to keep off the sea air chill.

'Hiya,' said Cameron, hesitating before he kissed her cheek. She had prepared herself for the encounter and didn't noticeably flinch although it still gave her an odd sensation. 'Definitely looking less repelled by me,' he said. 'I'll take that as a win.'

'Where are we going?' asked Ros. She liked to know what was happening and what to expect. Spontaneity unnerved her.

'It's a surprise,' he said proudly and Ros had to quell the urge to groan. Why did people assume surprises were a good thing? It just meant one person was in control and the other powerless and at sea – something she found unsettling.

'Could you not share your plans?' she asked as they walked out of the building.

'I think you'll like it. It's a nice thing. It's a bit of a walk but we have plenty of time so tell me how you're getting on with Gazza. Are you two bonding?'

'It's hard to bond with someone when they're pissing on your curtains,' said Ros and Cameron belly-laughed.

'I can understand that. He was in a strange place and probably felt the need to mark his territory.'

'It wasn't *his* territory to mark. And imagine if we all did that every time we stayed in a hotel room.'

'If we did that they'd have to change the name of Ibis to the Ipiss,' said Cameron.

'Very droll.'

'Was it just the curtains or . . . ?'

'No, he didn't like where I put his water bowl so he moved that onto my rug, so that was soggy but thankfully that was only water. Dad said he sleeps wherever his blanket is but failed to point out that it would be Gazza who decided where that would be and not me. I had to remove it from my bedroom three times before I put him

116

in the kitchen area where he proceeded to make the most ungodly noise and scratch my paintwork. At which point I relented and then we had a battle of where in the bedroom his blanket would reside. I initially won with on the floor in the corner but I woke up in the small hours fearing I had developed asthma as I couldn't breathe properly, to find he was sleeping on my chest and had left his saliva-covered chew toy on my pillow.'

'Oh well now, that's a gift. I'd say that's definitely progress.'

'And then he destroyed my favourite cushion.'

'Hmm.'

'Obviously I won't tell Dad any of this because he'd feel bad and he'd want to pay for the damage. And he'd also not bring him to stay again.'

'You're up for that are you? Another Gazza sleepover?'

'I'd rather not but as Dad declines, I can't see any other choice.'

'You're doing really well, you know. I'd be a mess if this was one of my parents but you're really practical and keeping it together, which is way more helpful than I'd be.'

'Thank you.'

'You're welcome.'

Outside it was a bright, crisp day as they made their way through Ocean Village. They walked for a bit in silence until Cameron turned to her. 'Here's a question. Do you think we're hand holders?' he asked, holding his out for her to take.

She glanced at his outstretched palm. She wasn't big on physical contact. It wasn't something she'd done with any legitimate boyfriends. 'Sorry, I don't think we are. It's more that I'm not great with anything like that.'

'That's okay. I'm a big hugger. I'm sure if we take it slow we'll find some middle ground.'

Ros wasn't so sure. 'Are we any closer to you revealing where we're going?' she asked.

'Nope.'

'Shame,' said Ros and they carried on walking in step.

They turned onto St Mary's Place, which was a fairly ordinary street with a variety of trees on one side of the road as that was the edge of Hoglands Park. Ros was intrigued as to where they were heading. She was pleasantly surprised when they entered Hoglands Park and she saw a crowd of people in cricket whites. They headed in that direction. 'We both like cricket and whilst it's only a local match it's dog-friendly,' said Cameron, his eyes conveying his trepidation as to whether or not he'd done the right thing. Ros couldn't help but be touched by his thoughtfulness and planning.

'It's a lovely idea. Thank you. It might be dog-friendly but I'm not sure he's cricket-friendly,' said Ros, holding on to Gazza's lead with two hands as he strained to get to a man who was polishing a cricket ball on his trousers.

'He'll be good, won't you, boy?' asked Cameron and Gazza gave him a worried look.

'I used to go to the cricket with my dad. It's my earliest memory, just him and I watching the cricket. Mum would never go with him, so as soon as I was old enough to sit still he took me along.'

'What happened to your mum?' asked Cameron.

This wasn't something Ros usually discussed. It was one of the subjects she sidestepped. Usually she found a way to avoid talking about it if she could but something about Cameron's expectant face made her feel she should say something, even if it was only part of the story. 'She left when I was young. I was seven.'

'And she's never contacted you?'

Ros clenched her teeth together. This was harder than she'd thought it would be. That familiar feeling of abandonment always much closer at hand than she liked. 'She used to call each week but I would ask her to come home and she'd say she couldn't and I'd get upset. And I think she got fed up of repeating herself so she stopped calling. There have been a number of points in my life – landmark birthdays, exam results, graduation – when she has shown up out of duty but I've not seen her for five years.' Cameron's look of pity was hard to take. 'But it has taught me an important lesson.'

'That grown-ups are twats sometimes?'

'I was thinking more that you can't rely on anyone in this life but yourself.'

'Wow,' said Cameron, his eyes wide.

'Sorry, what do you mean by wow?'

'That's either really deep or the saddest thing I've ever heard.'

She didn't need his pity. 'It's a simple fact.'

'But you can't go through life being closed off to opportunities. They come from opening yourself up. By helping others and letting other people help you. Life is a team sport – we all get much more out of it if we work together.'

What he was saying sounded familiar. 'Have you recently been on a training course?'

He laughed. 'No. It's what I believe. Maybe you can't always rely on others but that doesn't mean you shouldn't give people the benefit of the doubt; they might surprise you. Anyway, let's get some lemonade,' he said, offering her the crook of his arm. She hesitated for a moment but the old-fashioned gesture did appeal to her so she took his arm and they went to find somewhere to sit.

Cameron took off his backpack and, like a hairy Mary Poppins, he proceeded to pull a multitude of things from it including a picnic rug, plastic cups and a Tupperware box. It took Gazza a while to settle as he was immensely keen to join in with the match, but thankfully he stopped barking during the second over – thanks to the lure of a sausage roll. The sun came out and they were able to take off their jackets and despite it only being a local match the cricket was of a good standard. Cameron had made cheese and pickle sandwiches and brought a pig's ear for Gazza, which he was thrilled with. Cameron handed Ros a packet of Hula Hoops and refilled her lemonade. She was having an unexpectedly nice time.

That evening Ros let herself into her dad's house to return Gazza as planned. The little black dog was excited to be reunited with his owner but Ros didn't want him dashing off and alarming her dad. She worried daily about how much longer they had together. She wanted more time and yet the thought of watching him slowly fade away broke her heart. She put her head around the living room door to find him asleep in his chair. It wasn't like him to nap. It made her sad to see him looking so tired and drawn. His skin had a dull hue and his sparkle was definitely fading. She knew she had to get used to this and that things would only become increasingly worse over the coming weeks, but it was still hard to accept.

'Gently now,' she told Gazza as she let him off his lead and he dashed to his master.

'Oh, hello, fella,' said Barry, coming to. Gazza and Barry were overjoyed to be reunited. 'Thanks for having him, Ros. How was he?' he asked before turning to Gazza. 'Were you a good boy for Ros? Were you?'

'He was fine,' she said. It almost felt like Gazza gave her a look of thanks that she'd lied about how he had behaved at the sleepover. The litany of offences was still fresh in her mind. She feared her dog-sitting would become a more regular thing so she'd just have to get used to that too.

Chapter Fourteen

Sunday lunch at her dad's was marginally less daunting than the previous week. They'd decided that whilst Cameron wouldn't go along every week they needed to try to put things straight and upsell the relationship to Barry. Once the welcomes were out of the way and Gazza had brought Cameron his chew toy and half a plant pot he'd discovered in the garden, they congregated in the kitchen where Ros was keeping an eye on the dinner.

'Any update from the hospital?' asked Ros.

Barry appeared bemused for a moment before he spoke. 'I'm not expecting one.'

'No news is good news,' said Cameron.

'Let's hope,' said Ros, getting out the carving knife. 'Cameron took me to the cricket at Hoglands Park yesterday.' They had both really enjoyed themselves. But best of all it gave them something they could confidently talk about in front of her dad.

'It was cricket or a musical,' said Cameron.

'I've never liked musicals,' said Barry. That was a much shorter conversation about their cricket trip than she'd been hoping for. 'How's work?' he asked. Ros couldn't be sure but she felt he darted a stern look in Cameron's direction, or she could have been imagining that look being his thinly veiled disapproval at Cameron being a student and not having a full-time job – although she may have read far too much into one simple glance.

'Work was the usual bunfight. They say we have to work collaboratively but that only works if everyone is at the same competency level. They're not, so I end up checking what they've done so I might as well just do it myself in the first place.'

'But if you show them how to do it to your standards, they will become competent and you'll have less to do,' said Cameron.

Ros was shocked by what she felt was a challenge and she could see Barry was watching them closely. 'But it would still need to be checked,' she said.

'Maybe to start with but eventually you'd be able to trust them. Might be worth a go. A little time invested now might save you in the longer term. Life's a team sport – that's all I'm saying.' Cameron turned his attention back to Gazza.

'I suppose,' said Ros. That was as much as she would concede. 'And as if it wasn't bad enough to spend all day with these people there's the annual social on Friday night that I have to attend.'

'What's this?' asked Cameron, popping back up.

'It's the annual Easter barbecue at the CEO's place that Ros complains about every year,' said Barry. 'But at least this time she won't be going on her own. Will it be the first time you've met her colleagues, Cameron?' asked Barry.

'He's not coming,' said Ros.

'Why not?' asked Barry. 'You always say it's worse than going to a wedding alone because even though everyone brings partners to a wedding at least the food is edible.'

Ros needed a good excuse and quickly. 'He can't come because he's busy with his thing,' she said very unconvincingly.

'I'm not anymore. My thing is off,' said Cameron, with his trademark grin in place. He clearly found this amusing. 'And who doesn't have fun at a barbecue?'

'Ros,' said Barry, tipping his glass in her direction.

'I simply don't understand why they are so popular,' said Ros. 'You have a perfectly good oven inside so why burn things over charcoal in what is inevitably inclement weather, especially around Easter? Usually the person cooking only does barbecues and is therefore without any competent cooking skills resulting in frequently undercooked meat, leaving you vulnerable to salmonella, E. coli, yersinia, and other bacteria.'

'Really not a fan then,' said Cameron, and Barry chuckled.

'I wouldn't attend at all, but apparently the CEO takes it personally if people cry off. I go along for an hour, make a point of talking to the CEO, his wife and my boss, and once people have had a few drinks they don't notice when I leave.'

'It won't be as bad this year,' said Cameron. 'I'll be there.'

Ros forced a smile. 'Right. If you're sure.' There was an awkward moment and Ros busied herself with getting out plates ready for serving.

'I was speaking to your Uncle Pete,' said Barry. Ros's mind flashed back to the overheard conversation.

'That's nice. How is he?'

'He's fine. Touch of sciatica, but it's not stopped him golfing so it can't be that bad. He said you've not changed your relationship status on Facebook.'

'What now?' said Ros, starting to get food out of the oven.

'Pete says you've not put up any pictures of you and Cameron and that you're down as single on the internet.' He leaned towards Cameron. 'I don't understand it myself but Pete's into that sort of thing. He said it's the first thing you youngsters change.'

'I've changed mine,' said Cameron. 'I'll try not to be offended that she's not said we're in a relationship but she has been super busy with work.' He picked up a tea towel and took the hot tray off her. 'I'm sure she'll get around to changing it soon.'

'Er, yes. I will. I don't really like social media. I rarely post any updates. I don't see the point. It was Darla who made me join.'

'I said it would be something like that,' said Barry, inspecting his magnificent Yorkshire puddings as Cameron carefully put down the tray. 'Let's eat.'

Thankfully the rest of the meal went without anything contentious popping up. Ros gave Cameron a lift back to his digs as he'd got the bus over to avoid the rain that had been forecast but never materialised.

'I think that went well. Definitely better than last week,' he said.

'I agree. It was a shame we didn't get to say more about the cricket, but I don't think we needed it in the end. Once you got him talking how he got Gazza, there was no shutting him up. Great call by the way.'

'Thanks. It wasn't a ploy to get him talking, I was genuinely interested.' He pointed ahead. 'Next left and then it's the third house on the right.'

'Oh.' She'd not realised Cameron was actually interested in her dad's story. 'And thanks for saying you'd come to my boss's barbecue but you really don't have to. That's definitely above and beyond our contract.'

'I think I'd quite like to go. If you don't mind. I don't want to cause you issues at work but if I don't go it might make Barry suspicious unless we lie about me going and I think the less we lie about the better.'

That was unexpected. Ros had a think about how that would look to her boss and colleagues. Given that the feedback she'd had was that she didn't get on well with anyone in the office, perhaps showing them that she was capable of getting on with someone would be a bonus. 'It's up to you,' said Ros, pulling up outside the house.

'Great, I'll see you Friday.'

'Do we not need to have a flip cha—'

'Ros, you need to relax. We are doing great. Your dad suspects nothing and neither will your work mates. Call me if anything comes up. Bye.' And he got out of the car.

***

It was Monday afternoon when Darla had a chance to walk down to the farm and ask Lee about the hay bales. It was either a joke or a mistake and either way she wanted to check she wasn't going to receive an unexpected charge for them all. She probably did need all the hay because the goats were eating it at a startling rate but then in their defence they had been living off duck pellets for a few days. She was going to ask if he could somehow bill the owners of The Brambles although she wasn't sure who that would be. Obviously it wasn't poor Horace but she assumed someone somewhere was inheriting the lovely property and its assorted menagerie.

She wandered up the farm track and into the yard. There was the sound of a radio in one of the barns so she followed the sound of Harry Styles. As she got closer she could hear someone singing along to 'As It Was' and she spotted a green overall sticking out from behind a muddy tractor. When he missed the high note she spluttered a laugh but quickly changed it into a greeting. 'Hiya,' she called, expecting it to be Lee.

Elliott's scowl appeared.

'Oh, Elliott. I didn't have you down as a Harry Styles fan.'

'It's just the radio,' he said, breaking eye contact as he wiped his hands on a cloth and walked around to the front of the tractor. He constantly had a look on his face as if he was waiting for bad news. 'Are you taking care of Horace's animals?' he asked as if keen to change the subject.

'They're all still alive and very vocal so I think that means they're all fine. And I'm really enjoying living there. It's a bit of a juggling act as I'm a cleaner and a bar worker as well as doing the house-sitting.' He hadn't asked about her but that wasn't going to stop Darla giving him an update. He nodded and she continued. 'I'd like to make a few changes but I need the okay before I can do that. There's a lot of furniture in a small space so I was thinking maybe—'

'Sorry,' he said, cutting her off. 'Is there something I can help you with?' he asked.

'Yes. I came to ask about the hay.'

'Is there a problem with it?'

'Not a problem as such. I asked Lee for a small supply and he built a wall with it in the back garden. There's like twelve great big cubes of the stuff.'

She could see Elliott was trying to hide a smirk. 'Twelve bales would be a small supply to Lee. We go through a lot here with the sheep.'

'Okay. It's just that that's probably quite expensive and more than a basket of eggs, so I was wondering if you could bill it back to whoever owns The Brambles now. Is that okay?'

'Don't worry about payment for those. Horace can have them on me. He's been a good neighbour over the years.'

Darla saw a chink in Elliott's armour and dived in. 'What was he like?'

'Horace?' A hint of a smile briefly appeared. 'He loved his animals and nature. He was a belligerent old bugger but he knew all there was to know about farming. His advice got me out of a few problems more than once.'

'I bet you miss him.'

'Yeah.' Elliott looked sad but then as if he remembered who he was talking to his head snapped up and he frowned at Darla. 'Was there anything else because I've got things to be getting on with?'

'Um . . .' But while she was thinking of something else to say he disappeared behind the tractor. 'Take care, Elliott. Hopefully see you again soon,' she said but the radio went back on and she was drowned out by Ed Sheeran.

Chapter Fifteen

Darla had been looking forward to a midweek catch-up with Ros mainly because, for a change, she was hosting it. With her usual house-sitting jobs she didn't bring anyone back because it never seemed appropriate, but this time things were a bit different. Although she hadn't heard back about whether or not it would be all right to make some changes, Darla decided to take matters into her own hands. It wasn't like she was redecorating; she was just moving a few things around.

'I didn't realise I'd be working for my cuppa,' said Ros with a puff as they lugged the giant sofa up the hallway. Getting it out of the living room hadn't been too bad as there were double doors but it was still very heavy and they had to keep stopping.

'Did I not mention that?' said Darla, with a shrug.

'You know you didn't,' said Ros.

'Only a couple more things and we'll be done.' That was mainly because the old garage already had quite a bit of junk in it and what they were moving in there now properly filled it up.

They put the sofa down by the front door. 'This might need some thought,' said Ros, studying the doorway. 'I think we have to put it on its end and then turn it. There's a risk that you might damage the leather.'

'It should be fine if we take it easy,' said Darla. 'Let's tip it up at an angle and see if it will go through.'

'Hang on,' said Ros, dashing off. She returned moments later with a blanket, which she threw over the side of the sofa nearest the doorframe. 'Just in case,' she said.

'Good call,' said Darla. 'When you're ready, lift.'

They heaved the settee into their arms and, with Darla waddling backwards, tried to get it through the doorway. It was more than tricky.

'Tilt it a fraction to the left,' said Ros.

'Maybe you go up and I'll bring my end down.' Darla tried to twist the sofa as Ros lifted it higher. The settee was once more horizontal. There was a squeak as it wedged in the doorway.

'I'm going to have to put it down,' said Darla. She let go but the sofa didn't move. Darla looked at it. 'I think it's stuck,' she said, half aware of a car going by on the road outside. The car stopped and made a whirring noise as it sped back in reverse, making Darla look. Elliott's Land Rover came into view as it bumped up onto the kerb and swung into the driveway. 'Ooh look out, you're about to meet the grouchy farmer,' she whispered to Ros before turning around and going to greet Elliott. 'To what do we owe this honour?' she asked as he got out of the car.

'What are you doing with Horace's belongings?' He pointed at the crammed garage and the sofa in the doorway.

'I'm having a go at a bit of feng shui and moving a few things out so it feels less cramped in there.'

'They're not your possessions. You can't turf them out.' His tone was starting to annoy her and it took quite a lot to annoy Darla.

'I'm not turfing them out. Simply redistributing.'

Elliott stabbed a finger towards the garage. 'They're in a damp garage not inside the house where they should be. How is that not turfing them out?'

'Okay, let's look at it from a different perspective,' said Darla. 'Once probate and everything else that happens after someone dies is sorted out, it's most likely The Brambles will go up for sale. At that point there will be photographs and the owners are going to want the house to look its best. Decluttered will definitely look better. Come in and see for yourself how much bigger the rooms look already.'

'No, thank you. Have you got permission to do this?'

'It's not that I haven't tried but the agency's only contact is a solicitor who is very busy so it's kind of a long chain to get to whoever it is we would need to ask.'

'I think you should keep trying,' he said.

'I will and if it's an issue we'll move it all back.' There was a groan from the other end of the settee.

'Anyway,' said Elliott, seeming mollified. 'You did say you were a cleaner didn't you?'

'I did and I am,' said Darla proudly.

Elliott pulled a business card from his pocket. 'A friend of mine needs someone to clean his boat. I don't know if you do that sort of thing but I said I'd pass on his details.' He handed her the card.

'I'll take on pretty much anything. I'll give him a call and thanks for recommending me.'

'I didn't exactly recommend you but anyway, I need to get off.' Elliott made a bit of a harrumph noise before heading back to the car.

'Hang on,' called Ros from the other side of the sofa. Elliott turned around. 'Any chance you could give us a hand?' Elliott shook his head, got in the car and drove off.

'I think that was a no,' said Darla. 'Never mind, we are strong independent women and we can do this ourselves.'

'Agreed,' said Ros.

Darla stared at the sofa stuck in the doorway. 'Perhaps after a cup of tea?'

'Definitely,' agreed Ros.

Darla had climbed over the stuck sofa and while the kettle boiled she and Ros spread out the remaining furniture in the living room. Darla went to get the cushions she'd found at a charity shop in town and placed them on the remaining sofa and chair, which instantly added a shock of colour and brightened the place up.

'It does look much better,' said Ros as they surveyed the room. 'I'd probably get rid of a few more things if it was me.'

'You've seen the garage,' said Darla, giving the last cushion a plump. 'And all the bedrooms upstairs are the same. The place is overflowing with old furniture.'

'Some of the things in here looked like antiques,' said Ros. 'But I don't know anything about antiques. I like things clean and new.'

'I like the idea of things having their own history. A story to tell.' Darla ran a hand along an old dark wood writing bureau. 'Take this for example. Think of all the people who have sat here and written letters or perhaps even a book. I wonder what exciting times this little thing has seen.'

'Probably a lot of bills and not a lot else,' said Ros.

Darla gave her a look.

'What? I'm just being realistic. People don't write letters anymore,' added Ros.

'But they used to. When this was first made, I bet it was the must-have piece of furniture. Ladies in crinolines with fountain pens—'

'Now there's a disastrous combination for start,' said Ros. 'And you've watched too much *Bridgerton*. It's probably a good thing there's no telly.'

'Don't!' said Darla, leaving the room and going through to the kitchen with Ros following her. 'I thought I would embrace it but it's a lot harder than you'd think. I thought I didn't watch much TV but it turns out I was watching it every night. And if I had a good gig I was on all the extra channels: Sky, NOW TV, Netflix. You name it. I was halfway through a number of series and now nothing. Complete cold turkey. It's been very hard. A lot like giving up smoking.'

'You used to smoke?' asked Ros.

'No. Yuk, horrid habit. But I bet it's very similar to giving up television.'

'Hmm.' Ros looked doubtful. 'So that was the infamous Elliott.'

'What did you think?' asked Darla.

'I think it's nice to find someone who comes across as more standoffish and grumpier than me. He makes me look sociable.'

'You're not grumpy,' protested Darla. Ros tipped her head on one side as if questioning her. 'Okay, maybe a little bit, but you're lovely underneath. I bet Elliott's the same.'

'Are you planning on investigating his underneath?' asked Ros.

It was Darla's turn to tilt her head.

'Okay, that came out wrong but you know what I mean,' said Ros. 'Are you liking the look of him?'

'Goodness, no! I am sworn off men thanks to The Wanker. And you've seen how Elliott is. If I can get him to the point of talking to me without frowning, I will consider that a great success.'

Darla made the drinks and they settled down at the kitchen table. 'How are you feeling about the work do with Cameron?'

'I'm still not sure that he should come,' said Ros, lining her mug handle up with the corner of her coaster.

'Why not? It's got to be better than going on your own.'

'You would not believe the inappropriate comments I've had this week because I said I was bringing a plus-one to the barbecue. They're like children. Only worse,' said Ros, gripping her mug unnecessarily hard.

'I think it's really nice that he's coming with you.'

'I wish I wasn't going at all. Although I am interested to see the reactions when I turn up with Cameron. But I find it quite stressful when we're at Dad's together. Cameron is far more natural and relaxed. I tense up every time he comes near me.'

'Are you usually like that with men or is it just Cameron?' Darla blew on her tea to cool it down.

'I think I'm out of practice and I'm not naturally a touchy-feely person.' Ros shuddered as she spoke.

'Really? I'd not noticed,' said Darla with a grin. 'My mum and dad are very cuddly people. We used to snuggle on the sofa together on a Saturday night and watch game shows. Sometimes we'd all be under the same blanket. I kind of miss that. I miss them. I wonder if perhaps saying I was going to be away for a whole year was too long. I could do with a week back home with them just to top up my snuggle meter.'

'You're weird,' said Ros, with a dry smile.

'I think we're all perfect in our own way. We all like and loathe different things and that's how it should be. But you are definitely missing out on cuddles and affection. A hug is the best thing if you're having a bad day, and I am not ashamed to admit I have had some nice hugs from Cameron when I've been feeling a bit down. I can't believe you don't like his cuddles.'

'I can't help it,' said Ros. 'I'm not making an excuse but it might be because Mum wasn't good at showing affection. Dad gave me plenty of cuddles growing up and we always greet each other with a hug, but I'm not like that with anyone else. I never have been. Perhaps I needed someone more like me to be in a pretend relationship with,' mused Ros.

'Yeah, because someone like you would have been well up for it,' said Darla.

'Your sarcasm levels are very high today,' said Ros.

'Sorry. Hurry up and drink your tea. I need to show you the animals.'

136

'You don't have to,' said Ros, looking quite alarmed at the thought. 'Anyway, moving that sofa is the number-one priority because it looks like there's a more than average chance of rain.'

Chapter Sixteen

As arranged Cameron came to hers so that they could go to the barbecue together. Arriving separately would look weird. 'Hiya,' he said, giving her the now expected kiss on the cheek. 'You look . . .' He was scanning her up and down.

'What? Out with it. Remember we're not actually in a relationship so I'll not be offended.'

He wobbled his head. 'You look smart. But you look like you're going to work.'

'I am,' said Ros.

'No, you're not. This is a social engagement with colleagues. That's different.'

'Only in that I'm not being paid. It will still feel the same. I'll have to behave the same.'

'Maybe, but I'm thinking casual would be better.' He checked the clock. 'We've got plenty of time if you want to change.'

'Fine,' said Ros and she went in search of something less formal, which was more of a challenge than expected. She came back into the main room and did a curtsey in a white fitted T-shirt and cropped jeans. 'Will I do?'

He gave her a look that made her feel a little exposed. 'Perfect,' he said. 'Now what do I need to know about your colleagues? Who are the good guys and who should I avoid?'

'Avoid all of them but especially Alastair.'

'Why?'

'Because he's my nemesis,' she said, picking up a grey cardigan, just in case it turned chilly.

Cameron laughed. 'What makes him your archenemy?'

'He makes jokes all the time, and I'm the butt of them.'

'People like that are trying to distract from their own flaws. Play him at his own game.'

'How exactly?' Ros picked up her bag and keys and headed for the door.

'You need to flip things around. Make him the joke. He'll hate it.' She wasn't sure if she could do it, but she did like the idea.

As Ros had anticipated there were a number of people who did a double take with surprise at her not being alone. What she hadn't anticipated was the level of intrigue and questioning it generated. When Cameron went to get them drinks, people who avoided her in the lunch room or, when she thought about it, avoided her pretty much all the time were now queuing up to chat to her.

'Ooh you're a dark horse,' said Sonia.

She'd been called worse. 'Not really – why would I discuss my personal life at work?'

The woman chuckled heartily. 'That's the only reason

I go to work: to live vicariously through everyone else. I love a good gossip me.' She took a sip of her drink. 'So tell me all about him?'

Ros was amazed that the self-declared office gossip thought her stupid enough to divulge anything. 'He pines if I leave him alone too long so I'd better find him.' Ros made good her escape but loads more people had arrived and now Cameron was lost to the throng. An unwelcome face popped up in front of her and stopped her search.

'Are you looking for me?' said Alastair.

'Funnily enough . . . no.'

'I heard you were bringing a plus-one. My source must have got that wrong,' he said, knocking back the free beer. Ros tried to scan the crowd behind him for Cameron. 'I'd been looking forward to meeting your plus-one. I had a fiver on it being a woman.' He chortled at himself.

Now he had her full attention. Cameron's advice came back to her. 'Alastair, that's where you and I are exactly alike.'

Alastair stopped laughing. 'How?'

'Women don't fancy either of us.' Alastair's face looked like he'd been slapped with a large wet fish and Ros was about to dart off when she felt a strong arm around her middle and a kiss on her cheek.

'Hi, I'm Cameron,' he said, stretching out a hand, which Alastair belatedly took whilst still agog at Ros's retort.

'Alastair.'

'I have heard an awful lot about you,' said Cameron, his smile shifting into a stern line.

'All good I'm sure,' said Alastair.

'No,' said Cameron flatly as he took Ros's hand and led her away.

Ros felt a mixture of flustered and elated at having matched Alastair and was pleased to see him looking bewildered when she glanced over her shoulder. Perhaps a bit of his own medicine was exactly what he needed.

Clive, the CEO, introduced himself and Cameron engaged him in talk about computational fluid dynamics. Cameron was confident, disarming and he knew his stuff. Ros had to admit she was impressed. Clive was called away by his wife to check on the spatchcock chicken.

'These people seem nice,' said Cameron.

'Hmm, you don't have to work with them.'

'Maybe try getting to know a few on a social level? They might surprise you. Right, let's get these drinks topped up. I'll be back in a mo,' he said, striding off.

Before Ros could object he'd disappeared into the crowd. Ros was very unsure about socialising. She faced these people on a daily basis and found them awkward, uncooperative and frequently inadequate. She decided she'd get some food and perhaps then they could sneak away.

She joined the queue near a gazebo and picked up a shiny porcelain plate.

'Hi, Ros,' said a tall woman in a flowery top.

'Hello,' said Ros, who had no idea who this was. 'I'm sorry, your name escapes me.'

'Berlinda Macey,' she said. 'So how long have you been with Cameron?'

Ros was slightly wrong-footed. 'Er since . . . actually, why do you want to know?'

'I'm just interested. I wouldn't have put you two together.'

'Do you know him?' Ros was on red alert. The thought of being outed as a fake relationship here wasn't something she'd considered but the shame of it made her cheeks heat up.

'I was chatting to him while I got a drink. He's a lovely guy; smart, funny and sexy – the perfect combination. He seems like a nice, kind person. I suppose it's true what they say that opposites attract.'

Ouch, thought Ros. Should she counter this with a comic response like she had Alastair? She went for it anyway. 'They also say those who are busy discussing someone else's life are probably not happy about theirs.'

Berlinda gasped. 'There's no need to be rude. I was complimenting your boyfriend for goodness' sake. What's wrong with you?' Before Ros could answer Berlinda knocked the plate from her hand and as it smashed on the patio Berlinda flounced off. All heads turned in Ros's direction.

In a heartbeat Cameron was there picking up the pieces of the broken plate. 'Are you okay?'

'Yeah, I'm fine.' If she was honest, she was a bit shaken by Berlinda, both her comments and her actions. This social interaction lark was a minefield.

Cameron stayed with her while they got some food and found somewhere to sit and eat it, which was slightly away from the masses and near a pretty flowering bush. Ros relaxed a little while they ate their food in silence. At least this barbecue food was edible.

Other people congregated on the other side of the bush and started to natter.

'Did you see Ros chuck that plate at Berlinda?' said one.

'After she called her a bitch apparently. Berlinda's in bits,' said another.

'Much like the plate,' said the first one and they all laughed.

Cameron stood up and leaned over the bush. 'Ladies.' There were giggles and hellos when then saw him appear. 'It was Berlinda who smashed the plate, not Ros. And nobody swore at anyone. You might want to think about who might be listening before you spread lies about people.' Cameron sat back down and the women on the other side of the hedge were silent.

***

Darla had managed to keep her parents happy with a few phone calls. She was particularly pleased with the one where she pretended to be in Florence, Italy, for the dramatic spectacle of the Scoppio del Carro, which translated to the explosion of the cart. Darla found some suitable music to stand in for the parade, followed by a montage of fireworks. Her parents were suitably impressed, meaning Darla could relax for a few days. It hurt her that they were so proud of her travelling Europe on her own and so excited by all the experiences she claimed to be having. Perhaps one day she would be able to see all these amazing countries for real. In the meantime she had to work out how to clean out the goats without getting butted in the legs.

Darla came out of the back door to find Elliott on the other side of her hay bale wall. 'Hiya,' she said brightly although the sight of him did now have her on her guard. 'How are you?'

'Fine apart from Winston being missing again.' He gave her a look and it took a moment for her to work out the accusation.

'And you think I'm holding him prisoner here. Is that right?' She folded her arms and stared him down.

'I simply wondered if you'd seen him,' said Elliott.

'I saw him day before yesterday but not since.' Darla unfolded her arms. 'Does that mean he's lost?'

'Nah, he does this from time to time. He's a farm cat so he's outside a lot and he wanders. He'll come back.'

'I can help you look for him, if you like?' Darla didn't like the idea of Winston being away from home for too long.

'It's okay. If you see him, maybe give me a call?'

Darla unlocked her phone and passed it to Elliott. 'Of course. Pop your number in my phone.'

Elliott did as she asked. He handed back the phone over the bales. 'Did you know there's rain forecast for tonight?'

'I did not know that,' said Darla, unsure as to where to go with this but it was small talk and she felt that was progress for her and Elliott.

He pointed at the bales. 'They should be under cover. You don't want them getting wet.'

'Right. I see.' Darla looked around. She knew the garage was full.

'Horace kept the hay in the shed.'

'It's got a padlock on it so I figured I wasn't meant to go in there.'

'Key should be on the main set. It'll be smaller than the others.'

Darla pulled the keys out of the back door and sure

144

enough there was a tiny key. 'Umm, I don't suppose you'd like to give me a hand?' She gave him her best smile.

'Sure,' said Elliott, picking up the nearest bale and lifting it onto his shoulder.

'Oh,' said Darla, who had been expecting them to get one end each of a bale. She scooted around the other bales to get to the shed ahead of him. By the time she had jiggled the key and got the rusty old padlock to open, Elliott had already stacked up four bales outside the shed. Darla had a quick look inside. There was a large, well-worn workbench, some rusting tools and a large pile of wood in all shapes and sizes. When Elliott lumped another bale on the growing pile she decided she had better get to work. She opened the door right up and dragged the top hay bale down and reversed into the shed. Working together they soon had them all inside.

'How are you getting on with the animals?' asked Elliott.

'Good question,' said Darla. 'The cockerel, the boy chicken—'

'I know which one a cockerel is,' said Elliott. At least he looked amused for once.

'Sorry, of course you do. Well, he does not like me one little bit. He's quite aggressive towards me. I've noticed him interacting with the hens and he's fine with them so it's definitely directed at me. The hens and I get on a treat apart from the occasional peck at my laces. I think maybe they think they're worms. Now the geese were very vocal but they do seem to be calmer around me. I don't know if you'd call that getting on but it is an improvement.' Darla was bewildered by the full-blown smile Elliott now displayed. 'What?!'

'I meant were you managing okay. Not, are you best buddies?'

Darla wobbled her head. 'It's basically the same thing. We are all creatures and being in balance with each other is an important part of getting on.' He was looking at her like she was trying to sign him up to a cult. 'To answer your question – I get who eats what now so we're good.'

'I still don't understand how you got this job if you have zero experience of farm animals.'

'It was a mistake on the—'

'Oh, that explains it,' said Elliott a little too quickly for Darla's liking. She'd show him how good she was. She just needed a bit of time.

Chapter Seventeen

There wasn't much of a chance for a chat on a Saturday night at the cocktail bar and even less chance on Easter Saturday – it was heaving. But it did mean the shift went fast and there were quite a few tips, which were always appreciated. Cameron and Darla left together and stepped outside into a downpour.

'Do you want a lift or have you got your bike?' asked Darla.

'My bike has a flat tyre but I didn't have time to sort it and nobody in the house was willing to give me a lift.'

'Why's that?' asked Darla.

'I had a go at them. They are driving me nuts. The place is a constant tip; however much tidying and loading and unloading of the dishwasher I do it's never enough. So I walked to work. The short answer would be: "Yes please, can I have a lift?"'

'Great, this way,' said Darla, whipping out a brolly and then realising that if she held it she would keep stabbing Cameron in the chin with it. 'Here, you can be in charge of this.' She handed it over. 'This is brilliant. Now you can tell me all about the barbecue because I've not had a chance to hear it from Ros.' Darla also thought it might be interesting to see if the two perspectives differed. 'Did it go okay?'

Cameron opened the brolly with a flourish and gallantly kept it mainly over Darla. 'You know, I thought it went really well.'

'That's terrific.'

'Until the drive home and Ros was super quiet and not engaging.'

'That sounds fairly normal for Ros, especially if she was tired,' said Darla.

'Nah, this was something else. I asked her if she was okay and she said fine and—'

'Oh hell! What happened? I mean either something kicked off or you did something majorly wrong.'

Cameron seemed baffled. 'How on earth do you work that out from Ros saying she's fine?'

'Dear Cameron, you have so much to learn. This isn't just Ros; this is most of womankind. Let me tell you with absolute certainty that the woman who says she is "fine" is anything but.'

***

Ros was feeling quite conflicted about Cameron defending her at the work barbecue. On one hand she could appreciate that he had been standing up for her but on the other she could, and always had, look after herself. There had been an awkward silence in the car on the way home, which had been broken only by Cameron asking if she was okay and Ros replying 'fine'.

Ros opened the door to him on Sunday morning at her

dad's to be met by a bunch of flowers. The bouquet lowered and Cameron's sheepish face appeared over the top. 'I think I may need to say sorry although I'm not entirely sure what I did wrong,' he said, offering her the flowers.

As he tried to come in she shooed him back outside and pulled the door to – to stop Gazza escaping. 'I appreciate that you were coming to my defence, I really do.'

'Great, because those women were mean and you were quiet in the car so I thought perhaps I'd pissed you off, but if we're good . . .'

'I hadn't quite finished,' said Ros. 'I would say I was a little put out, rather than pissed off. Maybe I didn't need you to come to my rescue like that. Perhaps I could have handled it myself seeing as I'm an adult.'

'Okay. And how would you have handled it?' he asked with a tilt of his head.

'Well, I would . . .' Ros replayed the situation in her mind. 'It probably didn't need any intervention so—'

'You would have done nothing?'

'Possibly.'

Cameron raised an eyebrow.

'Okay fine,' said Ros. 'I wouldn't have said anything. It's easier that way. They are not my friends so it doesn't really matter.'

'Which means they would have got away with it and would continue to be unkind to you and possibly other people. I think I did the right thing because maybe now they'll think before they speak. But if I upset you then I'm sorry.'

'Again, I'm not upset. But another time perhaps you could ask me first?'

'Sure, thing.' He offered the flowers again. 'Friends?'

'What's going on here?' asked Barry, pulling the door fully open. 'Oh I know what this is. That's a man in trouble right there,' he said, pointing at Cameron with a chuckle. 'What did you do? One too many beers? Forgot something?'

'Dad, it's fine and it's all sorted now.'

Barry looked questioningly at Cameron. 'I stuck up for her at the barbecue and I should have asked first.'

'Ah, she's a feminist, lad. You'll get used to it. Come in.' Barry ushered him inside. 'Was there a row?' he asked, looking keen to get the gossip.

Ros shook her head at both of them and brought the bouquet inside.

Cameron regaled Barry with a blow-by-blow account of the barbecue, making it sound like an enjoyable affair apart from the women's comments. Ros's recollections were slightly different but then she had had to endure far more of them than he had. Ros kept the flowers in their cellophane but put them in some water to keep them fresh until she took them home.

When she joined them in the living room Barry was literally sitting on the edge of his seat, enwrapped, and Gazza was lying on his back on Cameron's lap having his tummy rubbed – they both looked exceptionally happy.

Barry leaned back and patted the arms of his chair. 'Well, I think you did the right thing, Cameron.'

'Are we taking sides?' asked Ros, feeling slightly put out.

'No. I'm only saying that I think Cameron acted as any caring partner would and he stood up for you. I think that's to be admired.' He held up his palms before she could put him straight. 'But what do I know? I'm not PC, or "woke" is it these days?'

Cameron was grinning but when he saw Ros's expression he reverted to neutral. 'Anyway, I think overall it went well.'

'At least it's over for another year,' said Ros.

'Your Uncle Pete sends his love. And he wants a photo of you and Cameron. He says you've updated your status but still no pictures. I said you're bound to have some of the two of you together that you can share.' Barry looked from Cameron to Ros.

'Err, I don't tend to take many photographs.' Ros was not a fan of everything being recorded on social media and felt the people who posted pictures of their breakfast probably needed specialist help – had they not seen food before? And why on earth would they think others would be interested? She found it bizarre.

'I've got some,' said Cameron, making Ros frown at him. She would have had to be present so she knew he hadn't taken any. 'I'll send you them later and we can post them on Facebook.'

Ros was confused. 'Could you help me with the beef please?' she asked and Cameron moved Gazza onto the sofa and followed her out.

Once in the kitchen Ros swivelled around to address Cameron, startling him a little. 'What are you doing?'

'Hey, it's okay. We'll take a few after dinner, upload them and then Uncle Pete will back off. It's all cool.'

'Please can you run things like this by me before confirming them to other people? That's all I'm asking. And don't go ganging up against me with my own father.'

'Whoa! There was no ganging up. He just agreed with me.'

'Same thing.'

'Gotcha. Again, I'm sorry.' Cameron pointed at the flowers. 'It's a good job I got a big bunch.'

'You didn't need to get flowers and I don't think I said thank you, which was rude.'

'It was.' Cameron watched her and waited.

'Thank you, they are lovely, but as this is a business arrangement you don't need to buy apology flowers.'

'Maybe not but I do what I think is right.' Gazza trotted into the kitchen, which distracted them, and Ros got on with serving the dinner.

After dinner her dad looked like he needed a nap so Cameron suggested they take Gazza for a walk. He made the mistake of saying the word 'walk', which meant there was no getting out of it as the dog was now dancing around their ankles like the trip hazard he was. Barry put on Gazza's harness and handed the lead to Cameron, which Cameron looked very pleased about. Gazza led them out and in the direction of the park.

'That meal was stunning. The beef was excellent. You're a very good cook.'

'It's just a roast. I don't have a wide repertoire I'm afraid.'

'I liked it. Obviously the Yorkshires make it.'

'Obviously.' Ros and Cameron walked in step with Gazza in the front like he was on a mission. He was a little dog but he was quite strong. She wondered how long it would be before it was too much for her dad to walk him. 'Thanks for offering to walk the dog. That was thoughtful. Dad is looking more tired each time I see him.'

'I have to confess I was thinking it was a good opportunity to get some photographs for Uncle Pete.'

'Ah, I see. Now explain to me your idea about these photos.'

'I think a few selfies in the park will do it.'

'I don't like that he's stalking me online,' said Ros.

Cameron laughed. 'He's your uncle, and I'm not being rude but I get the impression it's been a while since you had a boyfriend.'

Ros turned to look at him. 'Depends on what you'd call a while. I suppose it's been almost two years. But it's not any of his business.'

'I agree, but if he's like your dad he's got time on his hands, probably not many people he interacts with and he's curious. That's normal.'

'Is it? He has a job. You'd think that would keep him busy enough.'

'Totally. It's the right side of normal. We could not do what we're doing with my mum. Let me tell you. She'd be in your sock drawer after the first date.'

'That's rather intrusive.'

'She doesn't mean to be like that, but she's intense. I'm her baby boy and she's always going to look out for me.'

'But you're a grown man. Don't you find that undermining?' she asked.

'Nope. In her eyes I'll always be her baby. It's the power of maternal love. It's intense. Plus she's done so much for me – I can let her get away with a little overprotectiveness.'

Ros wasn't sure. It sounded like a violation of privacy to her but she wasn't going to argue. What did she know about maternal anything?

They reached the park and walked down to where the wisteria covered the arch that went across the path. 'This is very Instagrammable,' said Cameron, swapping Gazza's lead to his other hand so he could get his phone out.

'Is that even a word?'

'It'll keep Uncle Pete happy. Look like you love me.' Cameron held up his phone to snap a selfie.

'And how would that look?' Ros was genuinely curious. Would her uncle read anything into these photos?

Cameron was grinning and Ros was frowning. 'It doesn't look like that. Just smile and it'll be fine.'

'Will it though?' Ros was getting concerned. 'I'm not great in photos at the best of times. Even Dad said my passport photo looked like a police mug shot.'

Cameron nodded. 'I've got an idea.' He passed Gazza's lead to Ros and she wondered what he was doing. He manoeuvred her a little so the purple backdrop of the wisteria was in shot. 'Ready?'

'No, because I have no idea—' She didn't get to finish her sentence because Cameron lifted Gazza into her arms and the overexcited pup began trying to lick both their faces. Despite the unwelcome doggy kisses it did make Ros laugh and Cameron snapped away.

'You had better have got a good one,' she said, wiping her chin, but she wasn't cross. She felt a bit giggly, which wasn't like her.

'Yeah I think I did,' he said, scanning the reams of shots of her laughing.

Chapter Eighteen

Wednesday was Darla's night off from the cocktail bar. It was a great opportunity to have a catch-up with Ros. She was itching to hear her side of the barbecue story.

Ros had already chilled the wine and they sat on the sofa and shared their updates. Ros went first and gave a detailed account of the event as only Ros could. Darla was surprised that Ros didn't use the flip chart. 'In conclusion I asked that in future he run things like that by me before taking action, and he brought me those flowers.'

Darla glanced at the beautiful bunch of blooms in a vase on the table. 'Wow, they must have cost him a bit.'

Ros seemed to look at them afresh. 'I suppose they must. They are lovely.'

'I get where you're coming from completely, but I'm more traditional and a little less militant than you so I actually think it was a nice thing that he did. Women like that would never listen even if you challenged them; they'd put that down to you overreacting but when someone else calls them out they might take notice.'

Ros gave her a knowing look. 'They've left the break

room every time I've gone in there this week. One of them even walked out with her half-eaten sandwich in her hand.'

'You should speak to Human Resources.'

'And say what? The mean girls are being mean again? We're not in primary school. No, I'm going over their project with a fine-tooth comb and I'm hoping to find a number of areas for improvement.'

'Be careful. Don't give them any reason to get you into trouble.' Darla sipped her wine. Ros was smart but she wasn't that streetwise and whilst she did everything by the book, many people didn't. Darla feared Ros could be outwitted by underhand tactics.

'They won't because I'm implementing a new policy. Cameron thinks things will improve if I make an effort to be more approachable and find common ground with others. I'm picking one person a day and I'm engaging them in superficial conversation whilst attempting to look friendly. I'm avoiding the mean girls but that still leaves plenty of people.'

'Blimey, that is a big change. Well done you. You might even make some friends,' said Darla.

'It's fine. I don't want to be friends with these people. Talking of friends, have you lured Elliott yet?'

'I'm not trying to lure him. I just think we got off on the wrong foot . . . a number of times. I want to show him that I'm capable.'

'How's that going?' asked Ros with a hint of a smile.

'Don't you start. I've borrowed a few more books from the library on rearing livestock and keeping chickens. But oh my days they are the dullest books ever written.' Darla flopped her head back on the sofa for emphasis.

'I actually fell asleep reading one of them. I thought it would be helpful on two fronts. One, it would increase my knowledge so I'd look less of an amateur in front of Elliott, and two, it would stop me missing a television.'

'Did it work?'

'No! I need a television. I really do. I've spoken to every charity shop in the city and none of them take in electrical items. I think I might have to buy one.'

'Don't do that. You can take the one out of my spare bedroom.'

'I couldn't. Could I?'

'My ex put it in there for reasons unknown but it never gets used. Apart from when you stay.'

'You are a lifesaver. I cannot tell you how much I have missed it. At least now I know I could never be on *Love Island*. And before you say anything, yes, that would be the only thing stopping me from getting on that show.'

'I'll take it off the wall at some point and you can have it.'

'Could we do that now? I know that sounds desperate but I am.'

Ros good-naturedly found a screwdriver and they headed to the bedroom. It was easy to get it off the wall but Ros couldn't find the stand it would have come with, although Darla didn't care. 'I'll find some way to prop it up,' she said, placing it reverently by the door so she didn't go without it.'

'You'll need to get a television licence,' said Ros.

'I'll sort it out first thing tomorrow. I promise. It'll be worth every penny. Thanks again. I really appreciate it.'

'You're welcome. Those holes in the walls will give me an incentive to get it redecorated,' said Ros.

157

They topped up their drinks. 'I didn't see much of Elliott from the other side of that giant sofa last week, but I did see how you interacted with him. Are you moving on from The Wanker?'

'I'm not after Elliott if that's what you mean. He thinks I'm incompetent for a start. But I do think I've moved on from The Wanker in that I feel I could date someone if I wanted to. I probably won't ever trust anyone enough to be in a relationship with them but that's a different issue. I get men flirting with me in the bar all the time so I have the opportunity, but . . . I don't know.'

'Too much effort?' asked Ros.

'It's more that I don't want to take the risk.'

'I can relate to that,' said Ros.

'Not in a risk-management way. But I couldn't bear to get into a situation where it affects my parents again.'

'But I thought they didn't know about everything The Wanker did?'

'They don't. And I thought telling them I was going travelling was sparing them from any upset as well as saving me the embarrassment, but being away from them for such a long time is hard for all of us. I figured it would be fine. I'm an adult but I miss them. And the thought of being a let-down after all they have done for me weighs heavy.' Darla's shoulders sagged as she spoke.

'Why are we so programmed to please our parents? Surely back when we lived in caves it wouldn't have been like that.'

'We'd have been too busy trying to stay alive to worry about what our parents thought. Ahh,' said Darla wistfully. 'Simpler times.'

158

'I'm not entirely sure that's true but I do think we worry far too much what other people think. We pass judgement on ourselves based on others' standards. I suspect we didn't overthink things as much when we lived in caves.'

'That's because you'd have been eaten by a sabre-toothed cat or squashed by a woolly mammoth long before thirty,' said Darla.

'I'm not sure which I'd prefer,' said Ros, looking like she was actually weighing up the pros and cons.

'Difficult choice. Disappointed parents or a herd of marauding mammoths? Parents, who'd have 'em,' said Darla and they clinked glasses.

The rest of the evening flew by and Darla ordered an Uber. They hugged and Darla left with the television in her arms. What the Uber driver would think she didn't know but she didn't care because now she had a telly. All she had to do was track down Winston and she was sorted for lovely afternoons in front of her favourite programmes with a cat on her lap – bliss.

***

A few minutes later the entry door buzzer sounded as Ros was getting changed for bed. She pressed the button. 'What did you forget?' she asked, expecting it to be Darla although after a cursory sweep of the living room she didn't spot anything she'd left behind.

There was a brief pause before anyone spoke. 'It's me,' said Cameron in a forlorn voice.

'Oh. Hi.' This was unexpected. 'Come up,' said Ros, hitting the button. She was instantly worried. Why had he come round rather than calling? Surely there could be only one reason. Someone had found them out and blabbed to her dad. Her heart clenched at the thought and she felt a bit queasy. She'd dreaded this happening. Her logical brain was already telling her 'I told you so'. She realised she was pacing when there was a tap on the door. She took a deep breath and opened it.

A damp and dishevelled Cameron was standing there with a bicycle hanging off one shoulder and holding a rucksack and bin bag in the other.

'Whatever's happened?' she asked, feeling a little exposed in her PJs.

He took a deep breath. 'My housemates had a vote and they've kicked me out.'

For a moment she was relieved – at least they hadn't been rumbled. But instantly she realised Cameron was in distress. 'Come in,' she said, stepping back as the bicycle wheel tilted in her direction. 'I don't think your housemates can do that.'

'Well, they have.' Cameron lifted the bicycle off his shoulder and looked around for somewhere to put it down. He propped it against a kitchen cupboard. 'I got home to find all my stuff outside with a note saying they would let me off the rent as they didn't need my contribution but they couldn't live with my moaning anymore.'

Ros hadn't seen him look down before. His usual smile no longer etched in place, he was a sad sight. She got him a beer from the fridge and joined him on the sofa. She grabbed a cushion and hugged that in an attempt to cover up her pyjamas. 'Darla said you were tidying up after them a lot.'

'Cheers. I was. I suppose I did grumble about it though.'

'That's understandable. I expect they'll miss you when they realise they've got to tidy up themselves.'

'They won't bother.' He took a swig of his drink and sighed.

'So what now?' asked Ros.

Cameron slowly turned to look at her. 'I was kinda hoping I could stay here for a bit.'

Chapter Nineteen

It had been a long while since Ros had had a man stay in her apartment. She'd felt put on the spot the previous evening but she could hardly turn him away, especially as it was raining and he had a flat tyre. He'd helped her make up the spare bed and had thanked her a number of times.

There had been no sign of him when she'd got ready for work so she began writing a note but everything she put made it sound like she was asking when he was leaving. It was something they hadn't discussed. She screwed up her third attempt and decided she would text him during the day to ask how everything was going.

As soon as she was outside, she called Darla. It was early but Darla would already be coming to the end of her shift as a cleaner.

Thankfully she picked up straightaway. Unfortunately she also started speaking. 'Hiya,' said Darla. 'If you've found the stand for the telly, I'll love you forever. I can't get the bloody thing to stand up on anything. At the moment it's on the floor propped up against the chimney breast at such an odd angle I have to kneel on the sofa to see the screen properly.'

'Darla, that is a minor issue.'

'Not to me it's not. Don't get me wrong, I am hugely grateful. Even viewing daytime telly like a meerkat will be a bonus. But I'm not sure it's worth the TV licence. You see—'

Ros was struggling to find a gap. 'Darla! Please listen.'

'Sorry. What's up?'

'Cameron turned up at mine last night with all his worldly goods. His housemates have evicted him and now he's staying at mine.'

'Poor Cameron. They were a right bunch of Hurray Henrys. That's good of you to put him up.'

'Little choice really. I felt obliged. But it was also the right thing to do.' Conflicted didn't really cover how she felt.

'I guess he doesn't have anyone else in the city apart from me,' mused Darla.

'He did say he'd considered asking you but seeing as Netley Marsh is quite a way out when he only has a bicycle with a flat tyre as transport, it wasn't feasible last night.'

'Also I only have one actual bed. You have two. So definitely the right choice.'

Ros wobbled her head; she wasn't convinced. 'You do have three spare bedrooms, even if they're lacking beds, and you have a large sofa,' said Ros, thinking out loud.

'It's frowned upon to sublet properties while you're house-sitting,' said Darla.

'It would hardly be subletting. A friend sofa surfing wouldn't get you into trouble, would it?'

163

'Are you trying to dump your boyfriend on me?' Darla laughed.

'He's not my boyfriend. He's a stand-in, as well you know. And not *dump* exactly. It just feels awkward him being here.' Although she had to admit she even felt a little like that when Darla stayed. Perhaps Ros had just spent too long living alone.

'Ahh come on, it's Cameron. He's a sweetie. And we know he's tidy. That's what's got him booted out by the rich kids.'

'But still – sharing your home with a virtual stranger feels weird. I'm hoping he isn't planning on staying long.' And by long she meant more than a couple of nights.

'Don't be hasty,' said Darla. 'He's not a stranger and the more time you spend together can only help make you seem more authentic as a couple. I reckon he'll be a great housemate.'

'But for how long?' Ros was aware her voice was a few octaves higher than usual.

She heard a noise that sounded like Darla was sucking her teeth. 'Students usually go home June or July time so he'll probably get a new house share around then.'

'But that's months away!' Ros's voice had reached a whole new pitch.

Her dilemma was on Ros's mind all day and she was aware that she had been a little abrupt with a couple of people, which was against her new policy. As soon as it was noon she fired off a well-composed text to Cameron:

Good afternoon, Cameron. Hope you slept well. How has

164

your day been so far? I hope you are managing to resolve your issues. Ros

There was no immediate response so she went to get her lunch from the office fridge. Berlinda was stirring a Pot Noodle.

'Hello, Berlinda,' said Ros, before rummaging in the fridge. 'I was thinking of getting out a plate, or should I stick with my Tupperware?'

Berlinda snorted a laugh. 'I don't know how that happened. But no hard feelings. Yeah?'

'Indeed,' said Ros, thinking murderous thoughts, which was technically different.

'How's that cute boyfriend of yours?' asked Berlinda.

'Very well, thank you for asking.'

'Does he have any brothers?' Berlinda made an unattractive snorting noise.

Ros liked straightforward questions especially the ones she knew the answer to. 'No, he has an older sister.'

'Shame. He was quite the star of the barbecue.'

'Was he?' Ros wasn't sure how she felt about that comment. A little pride perhaps?

'Yeah. Most of the admin team were drooling over him.' She leaned closer, and Ros had to stifle the urge to move the same distance away. 'The thing none of us can figure out is how you landed him. I mean no offence or anything.'

How could you not take offence at that? Berlinda and her coven obviously had discussed them as a couple and decided that Cameron was out of Ros's league. Annoyingly it now made Ros consider it too. They were the same age. She currently had a more lucrative job although he would hopefully secure something of a similar calibre when he graduated. Ros realised Berlinda was most likely more focused on looks – they were a shallow bunch. Cameron wasn't classically good-looking but he certainly couldn't be described as ugly. She didn't know where she would class herself in the looks department – it wasn't something she thought about. Cameron had certainly tidied himself up since their first meeting. He had a strong jawline and an almost constant smile. A little off-putting at first but she was getting used to it. Ros rarely smiled.

Right at that moment she made a point of pasting on a smile. Now to answer the question. She took Cameron's advice of being comical so as not to be in conflict or cause offence. 'He offered me a screaming orgasm. How could I resist?' she said.

Berlinda looked like she'd been hit in the face with a spanner and Ros resisted the urge to wave a hand in front of her eyes to check if she was still functioning.

'It's a cocktail,' clarified Ros when there was no response other than the shock on Berlinda's face. 'He works in a bar,' added Ros. It definitely lost something when you had to explain it.

Ros's phone pinged. A timely response from Cameron. 'That's him messaging me now,' she said.

Berlinda seemed to recover. 'Oh right. I see . . . still doesn't really explain it. But then it takes all sorts.' She forked up a heap of noodles and chewed thoughtfully.

'There you go then,' said Ros, now keen to escape. She grabbed her Tupperware box from the fridge, waved it at Berlinda as if it were evidence and exited the break room. On her way back to her desk she read the message from Cameron.

Good, thanks. I got my tyre fixed and some uni work done. Loving the peace and quiet here. Hope you're having a good day. See you later.

Ros read it a number of times. There was definitely no mention of him moving out. In fact he seemed quite settled. After mulling over a number of possible responses she went with:

OK

Ros unlocked the apartment door and was immediately met by a delicious aroma. She scanned the kitchen area and was pleased to see the bike had gone. Cameron was standing over the hob, stirring with one hand and his mobile in the other. 'Okay, Gina. I've gotta go. Yeah, you too.'

Cameron turned in her direction. 'Hiya,' he said, shoving his phone in his pocket. 'Your timing is perfect.' He left the cooker, took a bottle of white wine from the fridge and poured a glass for Ros. 'Dinner will be ten minutes. Kick off your shoes and relax – or whatever it is you usually do.'

'I usually make dinner,' said Ros, feeling quite thrown by the change in routine.

'Not tonight. I thought I would cook you my speciality – paella – to say thanks for letting me stay.'

'That's very nice of you and really not necessary. But now you've brought it up I—'

'This is such a great apartment. I am so grateful for you letting me crash here but we need to agree on rent. Would it be too weird to say take it off what you're paying me?'

167

He pulled an awkward face.

'To calculate that we would need to know how long you will be staying.' There, she'd broached it.

The kitchen timer sounded and Cameron raised a finger. 'Hold that thought. I need to serve up.'

Ros sipped her wine. It was perfectly chilled and she noted he must have bought it specially even when she had bottles in the rack. She glanced around. There wasn't anything out of place. Even when Darla stayed some of her things migrated into the main living area – odd things like her hair straightener and socks. She watched him plating up the meal he'd clearly cooked from scratch. She was frequently tired when she got in from work, but the pre frozen batches of lasagne and chilli had become a little humdrum. What was it Darla had said? *Don't be hasty.* Maybe she had a point.

They sat down to eat.

'How was your day?' asked Cameron.

Ros was surprised by how much the question threw her. She couldn't remember ever having this sort of domestic chat. Her last boyfriend had been keen to tell her all about his day, the highs and lows and how brilliant he'd been, but showed zero interest in her job. 'It was okay. Berlinda seems to think you're out of my league.'

'Blimey, she's blunt. And I disagree; I'd be punching well above my weight with you. How's the meal? Is it okay?' He was watching her carefully.

Ros was impressed. 'This is really good.'

'Special family recipe,' he said.

'Paella is Spanish. I thought you said your family has Italian ancestral roots?' she asked.

'I did but this is nothing to do with that. Nan picked up one of those recipe cards in Sainsburys but over the years we've tweaked it a little. I'm glad you like it. There's more where this came from.'

Ros eyed the pile on her plate. 'Oh I have more than enough, thank you.'

'I meant I have a few other DeFelice dishes I am a dab hand at that I'll rustle up while I'm here.'

'You're thinking of staying for a while then?' The prospect was seeming less daunting somehow.

'Only until I sort out a new house share. I put some feelers out today so hopefully someone will have a spare room when they take up their new rental agreements at the end of term. Shouldn't be more than a few weeks. End of July tops. If that's okay with you.' He paused to judge her reaction.

'I think that will be fine,' she said, having another mouthful of paella.

Chapter Twenty

Darla was having an altercation with the rooster. When she'd finished cleaning out the animals there was a cupcake with her name on waiting for her in the kitchen. The cockerel was getting more bolshy and despite Darla trying to stand her ground he was quite intimidating when he came at you beak first with feathers flapping. 'Eek!' she squealed, darting behind the henhouse.

'Ahh . . . the master at work,' said Elliott. She wondered how long he'd been lurking there. Darla stood up straight and pulled her shoulders back but at the same time kept a close eye on the chickens and one in particular.

'Mistress would be more accurate.' Although as soon as she'd said it, it conjured up thoughts of adultery, which was not the image she wanted to portray. 'Anyway how can I – whoa!' The cockerel was on the attack again. Darla dashed for the exit and took a few pecks to her calves as she fumbled her escape. Once out of the chicken run she was faced with Elliott's smirking face. 'And you could do better could you?'

'I did all right until you arrived,' he said with a certain

smug lift of his chin.

Darla had wondered who had been looking after the animals in between Horace dying and her moving in. 'Any top tips?'

'You can let the chickens out from time to time.'

'Nice try. Are you trying to get me fired?'

'No. I'm serious. They like to stretch their legs and they'll find a variety of bugs and things to eat, which are good diet supplements.'

'But they'll fly away and then I'll be in deep . . .'

Elliott was proper belly-laughing and Darla was lost as to why.

'What's so funny?'

'Chickens can't fly,' said Elliott, clutching his side as he was gripped by a fresh wave of hysteria.

'Yeah they can. The big boy one definitely can.'

'The rooster,' he said as the laughter faded to a broad grin.

'Yes, I know. Him. He flies at me all the time. Did you not just see him do that?'

'Okay. But a couple of feet is literally as high as they can get. They can't take off, so they won't fly away. And if you want another tip, you need to stand your ground with The Captain.'

'With who?' asked Darla.

But Elliott was already pointing at the strutting rooster.

'I didn't know they had names,' she said.

'Horace only named him and the goats. He didn't like to get too attached to something he would later be eating.'

Darla grimaced. 'He ate his pets?'

Elliott laughed. 'They're not pets. They're livestock. Your

chicken korma looks a bit different when it's on your plate, but this is how it starts. You knew that right?'

'Yes. And I'm not a big fan of Indian curry by the way.'

'Nor me. I prefer Thai.'

'Me too,' said Darla. 'Tell me what the goats are called.' She walked around to their pen and he followed.

'Dusty, Panda and Nibbles,' said Elliott as he pointed first at the white one that looked like it had grubby knees, next to the black and white one and then the brown one with a white line down its face. 'And these . . .' he pointed at the three predominantly black ones '. . . are Curly, Larry and Moe.'

'Sorry I missed which was which.'

'I don't know exactly. And if I'm honest, I don't think Horace did either. But it's okay because they're not like dogs – they don't respond to names.'

'Good, then at least I won't offend anyone. Any sign of Winston?'

'I was coming to ask you the same thing.'

'Elliott, I'm sorry. You must be so worried about him.'

Elliott gave a quick shrug but Darla could see the concern on his face. 'He is a wanderer but he's never been away this long before. He has a favourite food, maybe I could drop some down to you in case he's hanging around here somewhere.'

'Sure.'

Elliott checked his watch. 'I'd best get back.'

'Of course,' she said.

Elliott turned to leave.

'Oh and Elliott, thanks for the advice,' she added.

He nodded before walking away.

***

It wasn't warm but for early April it was sunny and in between fluffy clouds, the sky was an unexpectedly brilliant shade of blue. It gave Darla an idea. If she could set up her phone to film her with an upstairs window behind her, she could pretend to be literally anywhere. As she hadn't video-called her parents for a while she decided it was worth the effort of rigging something up. A phone call with them was nice but she missed them. It would be good to see them even if it was only on a screen, and they were always keen to see her too and worryingly they were increasingly interested in her surroundings.

It took her quite a while to work out what she could stand her phone on. She could have held it but that wasn't ideal as she was prone to gesturing with her hands and she needed to be careful not to reveal too much, so a carefully angled shot was safest. Also she had decided to elaborate on her genius idea and go for a full costume change to aid the deception. She'd been lugging around her beachwear for six months. She'd packed a few nice bikinis and some colourful sarongs, none of which had seen light of day, thanks to her not getting any further than Southampton docks.

Darla got changed into a pretty purple bikini and a floral sarong. It was a bit chilly in the upstairs back bedroom but she could tough it out for ten minutes to reassure her parents that she was somewhere sunny and having the time of her life. She dug out her sunglasses and popped those on her head so it looked like she'd just come in from the pool.

She checked the angle was right. They would get a good

173

view of most of Darla plus a good splash of blue sky behind her – perfect. She pressed the button to dial her parents.

There were excited shouts and a blurred view of her parents' kitchen before the image settled and her parents' smiling faces appeared in front of her. It squeezed at her heart, she missed them so much. Of course they irritated her, as all parents do, but she loved them and as an adult she'd also realised that she actually liked them as people, which was an added bonus.

'Hiya,' she said and they both waved as they greeted her.

'Where are you?' asked her mum, bobbing from side to side as if trying to see around Darla. 'Are you still in Italy?'

She'd thought this through and she'd checked the map so she could sound authentic. 'No, I'm done with eating pizza. I'm now in Corsica. It's a beautiful little island between Italy and France. They speak French here. It has some stunning beaches and is quite mountainous in places so I've been doing some hiking. Look it up on Google after this call.'

'What do they eat there then?' asked her mum.

Bugger, she'd not looked that up. 'It's a bit French and a bit Italian. I've been eating salads, which are basically the same wherever you go.' She made the last bit up but her parents had only been as far as Jersey so they nodded in agreement.

'Must be warm if you've got your bikini on,' said her mum. 'Have you got sunscreen on?'

'No need,' said her dad, waving his phone. 'It says it's twelve degrees there today.'

Oh great, *now* they decided to get smart and start checking up on her. The last time she'd checked temperatures it had

174

been for Turkey and that had definitely been warm enough for sunbathing. She'd not expected such a temperature change with such a short jump on the map. Darla tinkled a laugh. 'It definitely feels warmer than that and can you see that blue sky?' She leaned to one side and pointed over her shoulder. Her parents both squinted. Darla had a glance out of the window and it was looking a lot cloudier than it had five minutes ago. The British weather was really unhelpful sometimes.

'Are you okay for money?' asked her dad.

'I'm fine. I've got a job as a cleaner.' At least that bit was true.

'That's good honest work,' said her mum. 'Where are you staying?'

'I'm—' But Darla didn't get to tell them because all hell broke loose outside. It was as if all the animals had decided to kick off at once. She could see from her dad's expression that they'd heard it too. 'Sorry. Gotta go,' she said with a forced smile and she dashed to end the call. She puffed out a breath – that was a close one. Darla's sigh of relief was premature because when she looked out of the window all she could see was flapping feathers. She had no idea what was going on. She dashed downstairs and out the back door. She'd have to conjure up an explanation for her parents later. Now she had to see what had unsettled the animals so much.

As she ran outside she felt the first spots of rain on her skin and the chill breeze whipped up across her bare shoulders and up her sarong, but the noise the animals were making was her priority. They definitely looked and sounded in distress. As she went through the gate the door to the chicken pen burst open and the chickens poured out. 'Shit!' she said, running too late to close it. That was when she saw what was causing the problem. There was a weird-looking brown and white creature racing around the coop and now it was heading her way. It had a long body and she'd not seen anything like it before. When it saw her it darted in the opposite direction, making the ducks increase their noise and flapping.

Darla wasn't sure what to do but getting the chickens back inside seemed like a priority and she opened the hen enclosure door fully. What Elliott had said about them not flying flashed through her mind. But she'd been pretty sure he'd been joking. She turned around to begin coaxing the chickens back inside but they had all disappeared. 'What the hell?' She spun around full circle as the rain started to fall harder. 'Chickens can't fly, my arse,' she said to herself as she looked skywards, but there was no sign of them.

While she was searching everywhere for the chickens she did spot the strange brown and white furry creature scurry past, which signalled calm in the other animals. The goats were still a bit skittish but she figured they'd been set off by the birds because whatever the invader was the goats could easily have stomped on it. To be fair, she couldn't see it was that big of a threat to any of them. It was no longer than a ruler. But then there was a reason that people used the phrase *bird brain*. Not that she was feeling particularly clever as she peered into bushes, with the rain now lashing down making her sarong stick to her thighs and legs. She looked around. This was hopeless.

She decided to go inside and quickly get into dry clothes and a coat and then resume the search. As soon as she stepped in through the open back door things became clearer. The chickens had invaded the house.

There was one on the kitchen table pecking at the cupcake and three on the floor pecking up the resulting crumbs. 'Hey!' said Darla but to no avail. It seemed the chickens were scared of the small furry brown creature but not of her. At least that was four hens accounted for. But where were the others? She raced through the kitchen, dripping water as she went, and into the hall, shutting the door behind her. She found three more in the living room; one scratching at the rug, one pecking at its reflection in the television screen and The Captain pooing on the windowsill. She reopened the kitchen door and shooed them from the living room into the kitchen. She'd deal with the poo situation later.

She ran upstairs where she found one chicken pecking at her phone where she could see she had a number of missed video calls from her parents. At least the chicken hadn't managed to answer one. She had no idea how she would have explained that. She ushered the hen out. She had one more chicken to find. The last hen was one of the fluffy ones that looked like it was wearing trousers and she found it snuggled up on her bed between the pillows.

'Come on,' she said, pointing at the door. The chicken didn't move. Darla walked over and picked it up and escorted it downstairs. In the kitchen her cupcake was no more than a pecked paper case. She shooed all eight chickens but now they seemed to realise they had the numbers advantage and they looked at her quizzically, jerking their heads about. Elliott had said she had to stand up to them. 'I mean it.' She put her hands on her hips. They ignored her.

She had another idea. She went to the sacks in the cupboard by the back door, filled up a jug and returned to the kitchen. She sprinkled a little grain on the floor and that got their attention. She laid a sparse trail as she reversed outside into torrential rain. She was bent over with the rain hammering on her backside and the sarong sticking to her when she heard someone burst out laughing. Elliott.

'I see you decided to let the hens out then?' He grinned at her. But in her bedraggled state she found it hard to see anything amusing.

***

Ros didn't adjust well to change. She knew this about herself. Having Cameron living in the apartment was proving to be a bit of a test. He'd found a home for his bike in the underground car park but other items of his kept popping up. They weren't out of context like Darla and her odd socks on the sofa or mugs in the bathroom but it was still a big reminder that Ros was sharing her space with someone she knew little about. She quite liked the pot plants he'd introduced and she'd overlooked the Hula Hoops appearing in the tinned food cupboard and the tube of squeezy garlic in the fridge but when she walked in on Saturday afternoon to face a life-size cardboard cut-out of a *Doctor Who* Cyberman she felt a line had been crossed.

'Cameron?' she called.

He appeared a few moments later. 'Hiya.' He pointed at the Cyberman. 'I see you've already met Cyril.'

'Please tell me he's only a temporary guest.'

'I won it,' he said proudly. 'Are you not a *Doctor Who* fan?' He looked shocked.

178

'I watched it occasionally as a child but quite frankly it creeped me out. Especially things like this.' She jabbed a finger at the Cyberman.

'Cyril's not creepy.'

'He is a bit,' said Ros. 'I can't believe you're scared of sharks and ghosts but not this.'

'He's not real. Sharks definitely are and they can take a big chunk out of you, which is definitely something to be scared of.'

'Not likely in Southampton though. And ghosts aren't real.'

Cameron wobbled his head. 'I'm in two minds on that one. My gran swears she saw her old PE teacher walk through the wall of Aldi, which was built on the old school playground.'

Ros wasn't sure how to respond to that. 'Not a particularly scary encounter. Unlike me bumping into this chap in the dark.'

'He won't come to life you know.' Ros was alarmed at the prospect, which likely showed on her face. 'I can put him in my room if you'd prefer,' added Cameron.

'Yes please.'

Cameron picked up the cut-out. 'Perhaps I should have chosen the Ant and Dec one instead. Although it was smaller.'

'Goodness, no. That would be far more terrifying,' said Ros with a smile. Cameron grinned at her and took Cyril to his room.

Ros put the kettle on and Cameron joined her in the kitchen area. 'What did you get up to today?' he asked, getting out two mugs.

'I went to look for a new bedside lamp because mine appears to be faulty but I couldn't find any I liked.'

'I could see if I could fix it for you,' he said. 'No promises though.'

'Thanks. How was your day?'

'Good,' he said, nodding. 'I spent some time in the uni library mapping out some ideas I have for my dissertation and I walked Gazza.'

Ros was instantly concerned. 'Why did you walk the dog? Did Dad call? Is he okay?'

'He's fine. It was a nice day and I thought it would save your dad taking him.'

'That was thoughtful of you,' said Ros. 'How was Dad?'

'He seemed good. He did suggest he come with me until I pointed out that that defeated the object. We had a cuppa when I got back and a chat.'

Ros's jaw tightened. She busied herself with making the drinks. 'Anything in particular or just small talk?'

'You're okay; we didn't talk about you,' he said, passing her the milk from the fridge.

'As long as you've not gone off script.'

'It's all good. Don't worry.' She handed him his tea. 'Although at some point we're going to need to tell him that I've moved in.'

The situation was playing on Ros's mind as she got ready for bed and she decided to have a chat to Cameron about it. He was one of only two people she could discuss her concerns with although he was increasingly becoming her go-to for other things too. She found Cameron in the kitchen.

'Are you hungry?' she asked, watching him load bowls with popcorn, mixed nuts and crisps before putting them onto a tray.

'No, this is vital preparation. There's a rundown of the best *Doctor Who* episodes as chosen by the public and I'm here for it.' He raised the tray. 'Hang on, no dips.' He put the tray down and went to the fridge.

'Right. I can see you're busy. I'll speak to you in the morning. Goodnight,' said Ros, feeling that she'd now be mulling over her worries into the small hours but that couldn't be helped.

'Hang on. Is everything okay?'

'Er it was just . . . actually it's nothing. Don't miss your programme,' said Ros and she went to leave.

'Come on, Rosanna. I know you well enough now. There's something bugging you. Here,' he said, handing her a bottle of milkshake and picking up the laden tray. Ros ferried the milkshake to the sofa and waited for Cameron to get settled before handing it to him. 'Sit down.' He indicated the space next to him.

'I was going to bed.'

'But you wanted to talk. You know you won't sleep so you might as well join me. We'll watch a bit of *Doctor Who* and we'll solve whatever it is that's bothering you too. I mean it can't be as bad as being caught in the middle of a Dalek and Cyborg altercation now, can it?'

'I do feel like I'm torn between competing forces,' said Ros as Cameron waved her into the space next to him. She sat down and he pulled the throw off the back of the sofa and laid it over both of them, making her feel quite cosy.

'You're worrying about our situation, am I right?' he

asked, wriggling about so that his body was against hers, not an altogether unpleasant sensation, Ros noted.

'It's more the development that we now appear to have taken quite an important step forward in our relationship by moving in together.'

He tucked the throw around them and balanced the tray on top of their blanket-covered laps. 'I get it. It's a big commitment and not one you would make lightly.'

'Exactly.'

'But then,' he said, offering her a tortilla chip. She hesitated. She'd need to redo her teeth. He waved the bowl a second time and she took one. 'Circumstance has presented us with the opportunity to live together. Me moving in now could be a chance to see how we manage because dating and living with someone are two very different set-ups.'

'That is true.'

He thoughtfully munched on a tortilla chip. 'I think we're the sort of couple who would seize the opportunity and view it as a test bed. I'd still be moving into new student digs come July because I've made a commitment, but we would have a fun few weeks living here and we'd know each other better at the end of it. Both the pluses and minuses. What do you think?'

It did make a lot of sense. 'I think it's actually far more sensible than moving in with no end date,' she said. 'That's always very awkward. There's implications that it is indefinite and relationships rarely are. Also as you say seeing each other casually is very different to sharing a home.' She dipped her tortilla in the proffered dip.

'Shall we tell Barry that?' he asked, snuggling under the

blanket. 'Then we'll be sound.'

'Yes, I think we will be.'

They watched the lengthy *Doctor Who* programme and chatted. Cameron had a wealth of *Doctor Who* knowledge and was able to answer all of Ros's questions. After too many snacks she found she was dozing off and missing bits of the programme but as the plot of each episode was basically the same – land in a strange time or place, fight a baddie or right a wrong and go on to the next location – she was able to keep abreast of proceedings.

'Damn near broke my heart when Rose went,' said Cameron, shaking his head at the screen.

It had become apparent that the tenth Doctor's sidekick was his favourite. 'They do have a very strong connection,' she said, watching Billie Piper cry on a beach. As the actress told the Doctor she loved him, Cameron reached for Ros's hand and squeezed it. It was nice to feel that for a change she was there for him, even if it was only a fleeting moment brought on by a fictional TV programme.

They debated the merits of the number-one voted episode 'Blink', whilst a gripping and slightly troubling episode it did appear, to Ros, to be rather lacking on the key component of the popular series as there were few scenes with Doctor Who in them. The programme ended and the credits rolled.

'Goodness,' said Ros, astonished to see it was gone 4 a.m. 'I'd better get to bed.' She tried to free herself from the blanket that bound her to Cameron's side.

'That was a great night though, wasn't it?'

Ros smiled. 'I had a very pleasant time. Thank you.'

'And now you can say you've had an all-nighter.'

'Can I?' Ros hadn't really understood the concept but if this was it she could see the appeal.

'Apart from the lack of sex,' added Cameron. 'But I think I like this better. Added *Doctor Who* and no pressure to perform.' He got to his feet and kissed Ros gently on the cheek. She paused, unsure how to react, or more importantly in a quandary over how her body wanted her to respond. 'Night, Ros.'

She pulled away. 'Good night, Cameron.' She went to bed alone but feeling very much part of something special.

On Sunday morning Ros was woken by a tapping sound. It took a few blinks to realise someone was knocking at her bedroom door. She quickly wiped sleep from her eyes and checked her hair wasn't sticking up like a pineapple top before answering. 'What is it?'

The door opened and Cameron peeped in. 'Sorry, did I wake you? I did, didn't I?'

'Kind of but it's fine.'

'Sorry. I went for an early run and I got you a coffee on the way back.' He came in and deposited the cup on the bedside cabinet.

'Thanks, that's really kind. I usually head over to Dad's about half ten. Does that work for you?'

Cameron pulled a face. 'Yeah, about that. A friend of mine messaged to say they're in Southampton just for the day today and I'd really like to have a catch-up. But it means I'll miss Sunday roast at your dad's. Is that okay?'

Ros tried hard not to look as disappointed as she felt. 'Sure. Not a problem. It's not like couples are joined at the hip.'

'Exactly. Thanks for understanding.'

'I'll tell Dad the truth that you're catching up with a mate,' she said, feeling that was what Cameron would want her to say.

'Cool. I'd better get showered and get my swank on. Well, my best jeans anyway.'

'Ooh best jeans,' said Ros, having a sip of coffee. 'Where are you off to then?'

'I'm going to give Gina a mini tour of the sights of Southampton,' he said with his trademark grin and Ros felt something unpleasant burble in her gut, but before she could ask questions he was heading out the door. Who exactly was Gina? Although the name did ring a bell and she had a feeling Cameron had mentioned her, she couldn't recall any details. 'Give Barry my best,' said Cameron. 'And tell him I'll thrash him at Scrabble next week. Don't wait up – it'll probably be a late one. See ya.'

'Will do, bye. Have a lovely time. With um . . . Gina.' But she didn't mean it one bit.

On her way to her father's, Ros decided that she needed to have a firm word with herself. There was nothing in the contract about Cameron seeing other people. Not that he'd said he was seeing Gina but the mention of another female had kicked Ros's risk brain into overdrive. There was a risk that Cameron could be seen out with Gina by someone who would report back to her dad. Although she wasn't sure who might do this. Mrs Pemberly next door was a possible but then as long as Cameron didn't show any obvious signs of affection with Gina, like kissing, then they were fine. If questioned he was out with a friend. The fact that friend was female was irrelevant. Although it didn't feel irrelevant to Ros. This was a level of risk she was considerably unhappy about.

She was mulling over other possible lines of enquiry her father may take if Cameron was spotted out with another woman, when she walked up the steps to his house and pulled her key out. However, there was no need to let herself in today because the door was already being opened. Ros smiled in anticipation of her dad's greeting only to be met by someone altogether unexpected.

'Mother? What on earth are you doing here?'

Chapter Twenty-One

'I'm visiting,' said Amanda, Ros's mum. 'Are you coming in?'

Ros was fixed to the top step. The sight of her mother after five years was more than a shock. A shock was when the lift at work suddenly stopped working. This was on more of a lift plummeting at high speed to certain death level.

'Good morning, Cabbage,' called out her father and she finally stepped inside.

Ros lowered her voice. 'Why are you here?'

'I presume you're aware of your father's condition?'

'Please keep your voice down.' Ros feared she may spontaneously combust from outrage. 'Obviously I'm aware as it was me who took him the day he found out and—'

'Excellent. That short-circuits the discussion somewhat.' Her mother's lips went taut and Ros wasn't sure if she was trying to smile or not. 'He will need additional support and—'

'No, I won't,' called Barry from the living room.

'I told you to keep your voice down,' whispered Ros to her mother.

'I can hear you too, Ros,' called Barry. 'Come in here both of you.'

Like scolded children the two women joined Barry in the living room. Ros took her usual place on the sofa but was instantly uncomfortable when her mother sat down next to her. There were so many emotions vying for attention, it was quite overwhelming. Many times Ros had thought about seeing her mother again, but not recently, although her dad had mentioned that he felt she should get in touch. The note he'd given her was still residing in her drawer at home. Ros realised that her dad had taken things into his own hands. She was not happy that he had but if she was being logical she could understand why. She wouldn't have contacted her mother voluntarily, and Barry knew Ros well enough to know that.

Barry looked at the empty doorway. 'Where's C—'

'An impromptu day out with a friend,' said Ros, keen to not go into any detail about Cameron's whereabouts or to have to explain who he was to her mother. Ros noticed something or rather someone else was missing. 'Where's Gazza?'

'I put him outside,' said Amanda. 'I can't be around canines.'

'Are you allergic?' asked Ros, realising that she knew next to nothing about her mother.

Amanda seemed surprised by the question. 'No. I find dogs irritating. They're so dumb and needy.'

For the first time ever, Ros felt for poor Gazza. He wasn't blessed with intelligence but he was completely devoted to her dad and in some strange way he was supporting him through this difficult time. 'Perhaps if you bothered to get to know them better you'd realise they are loyal and capable of understanding commands.' Not that Gazza was very good at the latter but she'd seen others who were able to sit when asked.

'He can be a bit excitable with new people,' said Barry. Was he defending her mother? Being in the same room as the woman was triggering something inside of Ros that she wasn't sure she could control. She was struggling to stay calm as all the questions she'd held on to for so long were begging to be asked. But she knew she'd not be able to ask them without getting emotional. Ros was usually very good at keeping her emotions under wraps but today that skill was being tested. She needed to take control before she went down a road she definitely didn't want to go down.

'Please can someone update me on what's happening here?' said Ros, pointing at her mother but looking at Barry.

'Your mother is staying here—'

'Staying?' Ros's voice had hit a rather high pitch.

'Just for a few days,' said Barry, adding a calming motion with his hands.

'B-b-but why?'

'Have you developed a speech impediment?' asked Amanda.

'N-no,' spluttered out Ros. She took a breath. 'I'm trying to understand why you are getting involved when Dad has my support. I could stay here and nurse him if that's what he needs.'

'I'm not nursing him,' said Amanda, looking disgusted

at the thought. 'But I can assess his needs and put strategies in place.'

'I can do that,' said Ros. 'In fact I have done *exactly* that. For example, I'm here to make dinner.'

Amanda checked her watch. 'What are we having and what time will it be served?'

Ros took a moment. 'You turn up after five years and expect me to cook for you?'

'Can you cook?'

'Yes, I had to learn at a very young age,' said Ros, trying to stop her jaw from clenching.

'That's a useful life skill.'

'It does at least mean I can wield a rolling pin, so watch out!' said Ros and she stomped off to the kitchen.

***

Darla had been avoiding Elliott since yesterday's great chicken escape. She'd thought getting them back in the coop would be easy but a gust of wind had whipped the flimsy door out of her hand and while she'd been struggling with that the first few chickens had escaped again. They'd then all darted off in different directions and it had taken her and Elliott a while to usher them inside, by which point it was hammering down with rain and she feared Elliott would rupture something from laughing so hard.

She had shut the chickens up, gruffly thanked Elliott and stomped back inside, her feet emitting a squelch with every step. She'd vowed to avoid Elliott for as long as possible.

She'd had a hot bath where she'd focused on the smell of her bath bomb and the gloomy colour of the bathroom and she was warmed and a bit more relaxed afterwards.

She pulled on her sweats, settled herself on the sofa and messaged her parents to say that the reason for her rapid departure from the video call was that some chickens had escaped from a nearby market. Thankfully they had bought her story.

There was no lie-in for her on Sunday. The Captain was nothing if not consistent. Darla had barely dragged herself downstairs and made a cuppa when her phone beeped and she picked it up to find a message from Elliott.

You miscounted the chickens. Please collect the last one.

Darla knew she'd got them all out of the house; surely she'd managed to get them all back in the coop. Hadn't she? She grabbed her coat and stomped outside to find it drizzling and she went to count the chickens, who were either huddled up in the corner having a nap or scratching about happily as if nothing had happened. She counted them up.

'Bugger it,' she said and The Captain tipped his head at her. Somehow she had lost a hen. Darla looked at her outfit – she was still in her pyjamas. It wasn't exactly glamourous but at least she would be wearing more than the last time Elliott'd seen her. She fired back a quick *OK*, turned up the collar on her coat and huffily headed off towards the farm.

She had her head down and was striding up to the house when Elliott shouted. 'Stop! Stay where you are!'

She'd had enough of him for one weekend but she did slow her pace and look up just in time to notice that the surface she was about to step on looked different to the rest of the track up to the farmhouse.

'Wet cement. Wait there!' called Elliott and he came over holding a chicken.

'Everything's wet – it's been raining!' she yelled back.

'Newly laid cement. She's made a right mess of my new driveway.' Elliott pointed at the myriad of chicken footprints scattered all over the damp surface.

'I hope you're not after compensation,' said Darla, trying to hide her concerns.

'No, but it is irritating.'

'I quite like it,' said Darla, following the swirly design with her eyes. 'It's a pretty pattern and it makes your farm look authentic.'

'Look authentic? It *is* authentic. Here, take the culprit.' He held out the hen but as Darla went to take it from him he pulled it back out of reach. 'Did you not bring a basket or a crate?'

'Why would I do that?'

'To put the hen in.' Elliott was looking exasperated.

This man really did think she was incapable. 'You're carrying her in your arms so why can't I?'

'You can but I'm wearing overalls so if she poops it doesn't matter.'

'Oh, then a crate does make sense. I'll just have to be quick and hope she doesn't need the loo between here and The Brambles.' She went to take the chicken but Elliott wasn't about to hand her over just yet.

'What if she's spooked by something? Like a dog.'

'Hmm,' said Darla, thinking it through. 'Or if the little brown and white creature is about. That thing really put the wind up the animals.'

'How big was it?'

'About the size of a long ruler – maybe a bit shorter.' She showed him with her hands. The action pulled her

192

coat open to reveal her pyjamas and they both froze for a moment before Darla hastily did up her coat and Elliott scratched his head.

'Probably a stoat or a weasel. If there was no black on it then it was most likely a weasel. Anyway, you need to get a crate from The Brambles.'

'But I don't think there are any at the house. Although there were some mesh boxes at the back of the garage. Would that be . . .' Elliott was already nodding. 'There's no way I could get to them anyway with the sofa in there. Have you got something you could put her in?'

Elliott frowned and she assumed he was having a think. 'I don't know.'

'Cardboard box? Nappy? Rain hat?'

Elliott's eyebrows rose with each suggestion. 'Do I look like someone who would own a rain hat?' From his tone she could tell he was getting grumpy now.

'All right, how about a carrier bag or an old piece of clothing?'

'Come inside,' said Elliott, turning his back on her and marching off. 'Mind the cement!' he yelled just in time as Darla was about to take the shortcut across the newly laid drive. She tiptoed around it and followed him inside.

The house had a similar feel to The Brambles but with the benefit of more recent decoration and an expensive-looking fitted kitchen. Elliott had the hen tucked under his arm while he opened and closed cupboards with his free hand.

'Here, this'll do,' said Darla, picking up an Isle of Wight tea towel.

'That was my mother's.'

'I'll wash it,' offered Darla.

Elliott took it from her and reverently placed it on the back of a chair. 'It was from the last holiday she went on before she died.'

'Sorry for your loss,' said Darla, feeling a bit awkward.

'Thank you,' said Elliott, adjusting his grip on the chicken.

'Was it recent? Her dying?' Why did asking sound so crass?

'Four months ago.'

'That's tough. Did she live with you?'

Elliott looked uncomfortable. 'This is my childhood home. Since Dad died last year it's been just me and Mum running the place. With Lee's help and a lot of sound advice from Horace we've muddled through.'

'Geez, that's tough, losing your mum and dad so close together; that's really harsh.'

There was a moment where Elliott looked like grief was weighing him down. His eyes were full of sadness and his lips pressed into a hard line. 'Thanks. It has been tough.' He swallowed hard and Darla thought he was going to open up some more but he seemed to perk up and returned to methodically checking everywhere for something to put the chicken in. 'How about this?' he asked, pulling a string bag from a drawer.

'Perfect,' said Darla.

She quite liked the odd looks she received from some hikers as they bounded past her with a jolly 'Good morning!' and did a double take at the head of a chicken sticking out of the string bag as it swung at Darla's side.

'And to you,' she said with a smile.

194

Chapter Twenty-Two

Ros had had the Sunday from hell. When she got home she decided to have a long soak in the bath in the hope of it easing the tension gripping her shoulders and the troubles that were occupying her mind. She tuned the radio to the classical channel, turned it down low and eased herself into the water. If a little Debussy and Jo Malone couldn't help her unwind then nothing could.

She let her mind drift off and every time a picture of her mother popped up she mentally rubbed her out like an error on a whiteboard. Ros was almost dropping off when she thought she heard something. She listened but there was nothing. It was probably time she got out anyway.

She wrapped her hair in one towel and another around her body. What she needed now was a cup of camomile tea to finish the calming process. She was drying her ear with the corner of her towel as she exited the bathroom and headed towards the kitchen. After a few strides across the living room, something made her stop and look up.

'Ros!' Cameron's alarmed voice made Ros jump and drop the edge of the towel she'd been holding around herself. Cameron was sitting rather close to a pretty woman. His eyes widened. 'Towel. Australian outback on show!' he garbled.

'Outback?' queried the woman, turning to Cameron, which gave Ros a chance to cover herself.

'The bush,' explained Cameron.

'Oh, that's funny,' said the woman with a giggle. She got to her feet and embraced Ros while she was still trying to get the towel properly around herself. 'You must be Ros. I'm Gina. I've heard so much about you.'

Ros was fixed to the spot. 'Have you?' She'd never really cared what people said about her but right at that very moment it seemed incredibly important. She would have liked to find out what Gina had heard but she had the more pressing matter of her virtual nakedness. She hastily readjusted the towel. 'Pleased to meet you, Gina. I'm afraid I need to get some clothes on.'

'Of course. Then you must join us. We're ordering a takeaway.'

Ros realised what they were intently studying was the local Indian menu.

'Ros will have had a full roast dinner at lunchtime,' said Cameron. 'So she probably doesn't want anything.'

'I bet you can squeeze in a bhaji though,' said Gina.

'Um.' Ros gripped her towel. It was hard to think about food when there were so many thoughts vying for her attention.

'Can I get you a drink while you put something on?' asked Cameron.

Too many questions. 'I just need to get some underwear on,' said Ros and she made a dash for the bedroom, very aware that her bottom was in view as she exited. She raced into her room only to walk straight into someone. She squealed in alarm. Cyril toppled backwards and forwards before settling on Ros's forehead.

'Are you okay?' asked a concerned-sounding Cameron from behind her.

'Why has Cyril taken up residence in my bedroom?' she asked with the cardboard cyborg still leaning against her forehead because she had no free hands as she was still gripping the towel tightly to her, although she was now even more aware that it only covered her front.

'Let me just . . . um . . . excuse me . . .' Cameron inched past her with his face turned away. He took hold of Cyril and uttering more apologies he sidestepped out of the room and shut the door.

Ros threw on her most casual clothes and gave her hair a quick blast with the hairdryer. She reached for the doorknob and then paused. Was she intruding by joining them? But then it was her apartment and the invitation had seemed genuine. Although perhaps three was a crowd. What was she about to walk in on? She imagined Cameron and Gina in a steamy embrace. Instead of being cautious she was now keen to intervene and stop any such interaction without thinking too hard about what her motivation was.

Ros flew out of her bedroom to see Gina curled up on the sofa alone and Cameron carrying three mugs. 'Heavens, Ros. You made me jump,' he said, nodding at the drinks sloshing violently. 'Are you okay?'

Her mother had cannoned into her life unexpectedly, she was utterly confused about how she felt about Cameron and she'd just exposed herself to a complete stranger. 'Fine,' she said in a small voice.

'Sit next to me,' said Gina, unfurling her legs and patting the space beside her. Ros was happy to oblige as it put her between Gina and Cameron. 'We've ordered an Indian banquet so there'll be plenty for all of us and you can just have whatever you fancy.'

'Thank you – what do I owe you?' asked Ros.

'You're good,' said Cameron, putting down the mug and taking a seat in the chair opposite. 'My treat.'

'You seem to be doing okay for a student,' said Gina. 'I didn't know any student who lived in a pad like this one. When I was at uni, I lived in a dump with mouldy ceilings and mice who lived in the kitchen wall and used to pilfer my Weetabix.'

'Don't worry, it's only a stopgap until July, then I'll be in some suitably scabby dump,' said Cameron.

'I wouldn't be in a hurry to move out of here,' said Gina, turning to face Ros. 'Your place is really lovely,' she added.

'Thanks,' said Ros. She wasn't very good at small talk but that was usually because she wasn't that interested in the mundane minutiae of other people's lives, but Gina was different. She'd not known she existed until a few hours ago but now she was compelled to know everything about her. She looked at the woman sitting next to her – short dark hair framed petite features, pretty light eyes with a warm smile and of slim build but with an ample bust. She was quite the package. 'Tell me about yourself, Gina,' said Ros.

'I'm from up north. Bolton,' she said in a forced northern accent. 'I studied business marketing at De Montfort and now I'm a brand manager for a pharmaceutical company in Derbyshire.'

'She's being modest,' said Cameron. 'She's flying up the corporate ladder.'

'Impressive,' said Ros, with a tight smile. 'And how do you know Cameron?' Ros asked.

Gina wriggled a bit as if settling herself in for a long story. 'Cam and I go way back.' Ros noted her use of a name abbreviation. 'We were like what? Eight or nine when I moved onto your street?'

'Eight. She had roller boots,' said Cameron, 'and I was determined to get to know her so I could have a go on them. She saw this as an opportunity to boss me about. I basically became her bitch for a whole summer.'

'Hardly the best start to a relationship,' noted Ros.

'Nah, I wasn't that bad,' said Gina, tucking her hair behind her ear.

'Huh! I was at her beck and call 24/7, had to give her backies on my bike and I even had to let her have daily cuddles with my hamster.'

Gina started to giggle, which pulled Ros's attention back to her. 'Only thing was when I finally let him have a go on my roller boots his feet were way too big to fit in them.' Both Gina and Cameron burst into laughter and Ros did her best to join in but it was hard when she was feeling tense and hadn't gleaned much information of any importance.

'You've been friends a long time then. You must be close?' Ros tried to look at both of them but they were too far apart and it was probably beginning to look like she was shaking her head so she focused on Gina. Sweet perfect girlfriend material Gina.

'Yeah, we've dated off and on for years. He'll always have a special place in my heart,' said Gina, getting up and kissing Cameron on the temple as she passed. 'Loo this way, is it?'

'Yes, third door.' Ros pointed but Gina was already on her way.

As soon as she heard the bathroom door lock click, Ros turned her full attention to Cameron. 'And do you feel the same?'

Cameron leaned closer. 'Gina is the reason I'm here.' He kept his voice low.

'Sorry, I don't follow.'

'Her dad is high up in some consulting agency and he made a few remarks when Gina graduated. He's always been a bit scary and protective like most dads are, but these comments were pointed and about me not amounting to much and sponging off Gina. And that's when I realised I needed to better myself. I was working my socks off but in jobs that were going nowhere. It was Gina and her dad that made me want to get a degree and focus on a career.'

'So that you were worthy of Gina and her achievements.'

'Exactly,' said Cameron. 'But—' There was the flush of the toilet and Cameron shot over to the chair opposite, leaving Ros with a lot to think about.

***

Darla found she was going over what Elliott had said. She couldn't imagine how hard it must have been for him to lose both his parents so quickly. She loved her mum and dad and didn't doubt Elliott had felt the same about his. The worrying thought that one day she would lose them both tugged at her heart. Being away from them had been hard but she hadn't missed them as much as she did in that moment. She pulled out her phone and called her mum.

'Hello, Darla, my lovely. How are you? Any more escaping chickens? That did make your dad and me laugh.' It was comforting to hear her mother's voice.

'No, Mum, they're back where they should be.' It made her think. Was *she* where she was meant to be?

'You must have a sixth sense. Your dad was just this minute saying how amazed he is that his little girl has turned into this big adventurer.'

Darla snorted a derisory laugh. 'I'm hardly that.'

'But you are to us. We are so proud of the experiences you're having and the confidence you're building. There's nothing you can't do if you put your mind to it,' said her mum.

'She'll be the CEO of Tesco when she gets back,' chipped in her father and it made Darla smile.

'I doubt it,' she said.

'That's what I said,' said her mum. 'I'd said you wouldn't be working for someone else after all this. You'll probably be setting up your own business, become your own boss. Aren't I right?'

Darla hadn't considered anything past clearing her debts but now she definitely needed to think a little further into the future.

Chapter Twenty-Three

Ros couldn't say she hadn't enjoyed the evening with Cameron and Gina because that wouldn't have been true. They were perfectly good company, they included her in the conversation and the few nibbles of food she had were delicious, but she couldn't help feeling that she'd lost something. Something she had been so close to working out and now it had been pulled from her grasp. Cameron and Gina were easy in each other's company; there was an obvious connection.

It was nine o'clock when Gina clapped her hands together. 'Right,' she said. 'I need to make like a banana.'

'And split,' said Cameron, finishing her sentence. 'Do you have to?' He gave her those puppy dog eyes of his and pouted his full lips.

'I sure do. Some of us have to get a train to London so they are ready for big important corporate shizzle first thing tomorrow.' Gina stood up and engulfed Ros in a tight hug, which caught her off guard. 'Aww, Ros, it's been so nice to meet you and to know my Cam is being looked after. Hope to see you again.'

'Err yes. You too,' said Ros.

'Bye you,' said Cameron, wrapping Gina in a hug, and Ros took that as her cue to move the last of the takeaway cartons into the kitchen and busy herself with tidying up. She could hear kissing noises behind her so to drown them out she turned on the tap full pelt, which splashed water all over her. She was wiping herself down when Gina called, 'Bye, Ros. Thanks for a lovely evening.'

'My pleasure,' said Ros, looking away as she really didn't want to see them kissing.

'Call me,' said Cameron.

'You're so needy,' said Gina with laughter in her voice. There was one last kissing sound, followed by the door closing and Ros's shoulders slumped in despondency.

'Isn't she the best?' said Cameron, joining Ros in the kitchen area and sounding quite giddy.

'Indeed. She is a very nice person.' It pained Ros but she really couldn't find fault with the woman.

'I'm glad you two got on. After you'd flashed your . . . well lots of you at her.' Cameron chuckled.

'Heavens, don't remind me,' said Ros, feeling her cheeks burn at the memory. 'What Gina must have thought I don't know.'

'She blamed me for not checking if you were home.'

'I blame you too,' said Ros with a smile. Whatever this was, she still liked Cameron and while she now knew there couldn't be any romantic involvement she would be happy to settle for whatever it was that they had.

'Hey, you were the one who—' He was interrupted by the intercom. 'What's she forgotten?' he said, scanning the room. He hit the answer button. 'Hallo?'

'Ah, Cameron, can I come up please?' asked Barry.

At the sound of Barry's voice, Ros and Cameron exchanged wide eyes at each other. 'Sure,' said Cameron, hitting the entry button.

'OhMyGoodness. They must have passed each other on the stairs,' said Ros. 'What if Gina had still been here?'

'Stay cool, Ros. It's all fine,' said Cameron, making calming motions with his hands. That was all very well for him to say but it felt like a close call to Ros.

There was a knock on the door. Cameron looked at Ros. 'You okay?'

She took a deep breath. 'Let him in.'

Cameron opened the door. 'Hi, Barry. This is a nice surprise. And Gazza, me old mucker.' The dog greeted Cameron with his usual display of pawing, jumping up and enthusiastic licking.

'Is everything all right?' asked Ros, coming over to greet her father with a kiss on the cheek and a brief pat for the dog.

His expression was grave. 'I'm all right. I've been worried about you.'

'I'm fine,' said Ros, feeling her shoulders tense up again. Perhaps she needed to see someone about that.

'Can I let him off the lead?' asked Barry. Gazza looked over at her with big innocent eyes.

Ros eyed her curtains. Darla's instructions of soaking them overnight in a mix of white vinegar and cold water before sprinkling with baking soda and washing on a hot cycle had worked but the curtains didn't quite look as perfect as they once had. 'It's probably best not to.'

Barry and Gazza looked disappointed. 'Okay. But you're

sure you're all right?'

'Why wouldn't Ros be okay?' asked Cameron, taking Barry's coat.

'Didn't she say?' asked Barry, fixing his gaze on Ros.

'No,' said Cameron. 'What am I missing?' He glued his eyes on Ros.

She felt like she was being interrogated and realised that if she ever was, she would cave a lot quicker than she'd ever imagined she would. 'My mother.'

Cameron looked to Barry for an explanation. 'Amanda, Ros's mum, is staying at mine for a bit.'

'And she was there when you went over for lunch?' asked Cameron.

'Yep. First time I've seen her in five years.'

Cameron was at her side. 'That must have been a shock.'

'Total ambush,' said Ros.

'I'm sorry,' said Barry from the sofa. 'I don't suppose there was any easy way for you two to meet after all this time.'

'I should have come,' said Cameron.

'I did assume you'd be there to give Ros some support,' said Barry.

'If I'd known of course I would have been there.'

'You've been a regular for the last few weeks. I just assumed,' said Barry. 'Did you have a good time with your friend?' he asked.

'Er yeah. We had a nice day, thanks, Barry.' Cameron looked furtively at Ros. This was awkward.

'We all had a takeaway together,' said Ros, holding up a tray as if presenting evidence.

Barry nodded. 'Your mum is worried that she's upset

205

you,' he said.

'Thanks, Dad. But I doubt that very much.'

'Ros?' Cameron looked embarrassed.

'Actually it's okay,' said Barry, twisting his lips. 'Amanda can be . . .' he wobbled his head as if trying to conjure up the rest of the sentence '. . . a bit of a trial.'

'Thank you!' said Ros with feeling; perhaps finally her dad was on the same page.

'Tea?' asked Cameron, putting down a bowl of water for Gazza, which he immediately started lapping up before dribbling most of it off the whiskers on his chin and all over the rug.

'Please, lad,' said Barry, putting his palms on his knees and looking around the apartment while Cameron and Ros had a hushed conversation in the kitchen.

'You should have said something,' said Cameron. 'I knew there was something up. The whole time G—' Ros willed him not to say her name with her eyes. 'They were here, I knew there was something wrong.'

She couldn't really explain that the problems she'd been wrestling with while Gina was there had nothing to do with her mother. 'There's nothing you can do.'

'I can be here for you and listen to how you feel about it,' he said.

Ros tipped her head.

'Okay, I can listen to you rant about her then. All I'm saying is, if you need me, I'm here,' he added, resting his hand on her shoulder. The unexpected contact was confusing. He was being friendly; she needed to get her head around that. All the things she'd started to think were possibly signals of something more developing between them were just a nice person showing that they cared.

'I know that's not yours,' said Barry, pointing at Cyril when Ros and Cameron came back into the living area. And then scanning the throw on the back of the sofa and the cactus on the windowsill: 'Did you two have something you wanted to tell me?'

***

Darla switched on the telly, moved herself up and down the sofa and into various positions until she could see the screen and then decided that she couldn't concentrate on the property programme anyway. She switched it off. What her parents had said was filling up her brain so much that there wasn't even any room for Fred and Gloria from Bolton who were never going to find a place with three bedrooms and a pool, walking distance to the beach for the ridiculously small budget they had. A caravan in Slough would probably have been a stretch. She swallowed hard; right now she couldn't even afford a caravan in Slough either.

Darla had been so focused on clearing the debt that she hadn't been able to think beyond that. If she repaid all the money she would be able to return home but then what? Was the plan to pick up where she'd left off? She'd assumed she would move back in with her parents for a while but now she wasn't so sure. They clearly weren't expecting her to, because now in their eyes she was this strong independent woman who went on multiple adventures and took on the world. Not a cleaner, bar worker and house sitter who spent her free time cleaning things with a toothbrush or watching daytime programmes on a borrowed telly. She wasn't the person they thought she was. What Darla needed to work out was how she was going to bridge that gap. But first she needed to feed the animals and make herself some dinner. She walked into the kitchen just in time to see a furry grey bum jump off the windowsill. 'Winston!'

She dashed outside and continued to call the cat's name but there was no sign of him, just an empty bowl where the tuna had been.

Chapter Twenty-Four

The silence where either Ros or Cameron were meant to respond to her father's question had been going on far too long. 'Erm . . .' said Ros at last. A blind panic had taken hold inside her head. She had no idea what to say. She glanced at Cameron expecting to see how she felt reflected in his features, but he was his usual smiling chilled-out self.

'Shall I take this one?' he asked. Ros could think of a million reasons why that might be a bad idea but at that moment she had no better suggestion so she nodded. 'Barry, you're no fool so I'll not lie to you,' began Cameron, and Ros had to swallow down a lump that had formed in her throat. 'I have moved in.' Barry looked at Ros. His expression was unreadable. 'But only because I got kicked out of my student digs and it seemed like the most logical place to stay. It's only until I get my next house arranged, which should be July. However, we thought it would be a great opportunity to see how we got on. Didn't we?' he said, putting his arm around Ros and giving her a reassuring squeeze. She had to admit it was very close to the truth.

At last she took a breath and could find enough words to make a sentence. 'It's like a test bed to see if we can live under the same roof, temporarily.'

'Sorry we didn't mention it but we didn't want to make a big thing of it because it's not permanent,' said Cameron.

'I was going to let you know at dinner today but with everything, I forgot. And by *everything*, I mean Mother.'

'Yeah, I guessed that bit,' said Barry. He pursed his lips and Ros held her breath. He looked like he was mulling things over and that made her uncomfortable. 'Loving someone and living with them can be two quite distinctly different things. How's it going so far?'

'Really good. Cyril and I feel right at home,' said Cameron, nodding at the cardboard cyborg.

'He's a very good cook. Cameron, not Cyril,' said Ros.

Barry smiled. 'I figured that was who you meant.'

'We've not had a row yet,' said Cameron.

'That's better than me and Amanda,' said Barry with a wince.

'Why is she staying with you?' asked Ros.

'I've got the space, and hotels around here cost the earth so—'

'But why is she here at all?' asked Ros, hearing the tension in her voice.

'She wants to help and I don't want to be a burden to you.'

'You're not,' said Ros. 'I hope I've never made you feel that way.'

'No, but I know you're busy and you two have a life and I don't want to get in the way of that. And on that note . . .' He stood up and Gazza trotted over to have a sniff of Cyril but thankfully Barry pulled him away before he had a chance to think about cocking his leg. 'I'd best be getting back.'

They said their goodbyes and both Cameron and Ros were relieved when the door finally closed behind Barry.

'Thank you,' said Ros.

'It's all part of the service.'

'I suppose it is,' said Ros. It was an unwelcome reminder that she was paying for his support.

Ros and Darla decided to meet at the café in Mayflower Park for their usual Wednesday meet-up and take a stroll along the waterfront with their takeaway cups. This was the place Ros called Sunset Shore, it was simply the area along the waterfront with a funny little scrap of beach where she often came to watch the sun go down. There was a breeze but the weather was mild, and Ros always felt April was an unpredictable month so was happy to seize the opportunity to go out in an evening without getting rained on. She unburdened herself to Darla and instantly felt a sense of release. She was beginning to see the value in friendship.

'He's never mentioned this Gina to me,' said Darla. 'Or any relationship to think of it.'

'But you're work colleagues – why would he?'

'I'm dead nice me,' said Darla, looking affronted. 'People like to tell me stuff.'

'But still, who would discuss things of a personal nature with people they work with?'

'Most people, Ros.' Darla gave her one of her looks that made Ros feel like she lived on a different planet.

'Really? It seems most unprofessional.'

'It's quite normal. I think I need to talk to him and get an absolute confirmation of what's going on with this Gina.'

'Goodness, no,' said Ros, her words coming out as quite a high-pitched squeak. 'He'll know we've been talking. He'll probably think I've asked you to interrogate him. That's a very bad idea. And I think it's quite unnecessary, as you only had to look at them to see their connection.'

'We've got a connection,' said Darla, waving her coffee cup in Ros's direction.

'Definitely not the same. Gina said they'd been dating for years and he had a special place in her heart. There was also kissing when she left but I only heard that as I obviously turned away.'

'Blimey, sounds like they are a thing then.'

They walked in silence and sipped their drinks. Although the silence didn't last long as Darla had quite a bit to update Ros on. Her download came with violent gesticulations and virtual re-enactment, which made Ros fear for Darla's coffee. Darla appeared spent by the time she got to the end of her update. She was looking at Ros. 'This is the bit where you give me the benefit of your insight and wisdom,' she prompted. 'Like I did for you.'

Ros supposed she must have missed that part of their earlier conversation but was keen to fulfil her side of the friendship. 'Well, in summary. Winston is a cat and they are notoriously nomadic and fickle, so it's likely he will use you and Elliott as he wants and still receive your undying devotion. The chicken coop needs some additional reinforcement to stop the weasel coming back and it probably needs a new latch if they were able to escape. I think there's something called scree that Elliott might be able to put over the top of the chicken footprints to—'

Darla waved her hands and Ros stopped talking. 'What about what happens when I go home to Oxford? When my fake year of travelling is done and I go back to normal life. What do I do then?'

'You mean when you've paid off The Wanker's debts?'

'Exactly.'

'I have no idea because you've not told me,' said Ros.

'Because I don't know and I want you to help me work it out.' Ros was sensing a level of irritation in Darla's words.

'Then I'm assuming that you would like to return home ready to accomplish something in addition to the debt repayment as your parents won't be aware of that.'

'Yes, but what?' asked Darla.

'These are two different things. Your primary aim is for a zero balance, which you are on track to achieve. Secondly you need a longer term goal to present to your parents and that will fulfil you as an individual.'

'Exactly. I've been asked to clean a yacht in the marina on a weekly basis and it pays well so I should be able to build a small amount of savings.'

'Would that be enough to secure a rental property in Oxford?'

'Possibly not.' Darla puffed out a breath. 'I'm going back to square one. All this work and effort has just been to get me back to zero.' She looked forlorn.

'But that is a considerably better position than you were in. And you have gained a wealth of experience that I'm sure will be useful going forward.' Although Ros couldn't think specifically how it would be useful.

'How is it useful?'

Ros had been hoping she wouldn't ask. She took a moment to think as she looked out to sea at the fading sun. The sky changing from bright blue to burnished orange nearest the sea. The colours all perfectly reflected in the water. 'You have acquired skills as a cleaner, bar worker, house sitter and animal carer. Should you wish to work in those fields again you would have references. Or perhaps if your finances improve you could consider self-employment.'

'Self-employed?'

'Starting your own business.'

Darla's hand gestures hit a new high and as Ros feared her coffee cup went sailing through the air. Darla threw her arms around Ros, making her stiffen. 'You are a complete genius.'

'Thank you,' said Ros although she had no idea why she had been given such an accolade.

As Ros opened the door to her apartment she was feeling more settled in herself, having had a good chat to Darla about the Gina situation and also alighted on a strong secondary life goal for Darla. There had followed an excited discussion, on Darla's part, about what setting up a business would entail. Ros hoped she had summarised the key steps adequately although Darla had appeared somewhat daunted by the time Ros had got to the end of the list. With hindsight perhaps Ros should not have focused on the many risks associated with being a sole trader and the perils of running a start-up business.

Ros wasn't sure if she was alone as she closed the door behind her. 'Cameron?' she called.

His bedroom door opened, and he appeared topless holding aloft a paint roller. He looked a lot like one of the pages from the Hot Men calendar she had received in last year's secret Santa draw. It took a high level of self-control to focus her eyes on his face and not his exposed torso. 'What are you doing?' she asked.

'Painting.' He waved the paint roller and grinned at her.

'And why?' She was trying to manage her inner control freak who was going berserk at the thought of him redecorating without discussing it with her first.

'I noticed the holes in the wall so I thought I'd make myself useful. I've filled them and now I'm painting that wall so you'll never know the holes were ever there.'

Ros was pleasantly surprised by the explanation. 'The holes were from a television set that was mounted there, which I've now given to Darla. May I enquire as to the colour of the paint you are using?' She didn't want to seem ungrateful but before she steeped him in praise she needed clarification as she was already mentally reviewing her last decorating bill and the thought of getting the decorator back again was an inconvenience she could do without. Ros didn't do painting and decorating; it was messy, fiddly and time-consuming, hence her need to get a workman in for such tasks.

'I zapped the wall with this app I downloaded so I got an exact match. It's Strong White by Farrow and Ball.'

'It is indeed,' said Ros, going past him and into the bedroom. She surveyed his workmanship.

'I masked up and put down some bin bags to protect the

215

carpet. I just have that last bit to finish and it's all done.'

Ros was impressed. She knew she had a critical eye – for one thing the last decorator had told her something similar. Although she seemed to recall he had termed it obsessively nit-picky. 'You've done an excellent job. Very professional. In fact possibly better than the average self-styled professional. Thank you. Please let me know what I owe you for both your time and materials.'

'Nothing, Ros. I've fixed your bedside lamp too. I wanted to make myself useful.'

'You definitely have,' she said, inadvertently scanning his stomach and almost giving herself whiplash as she snatched her head up to a more decent level.

'You okay?' he asked.

'I may have strained my neck.'

'I meant with me painting,' he said with a chuckle. 'Sorry if I should have checked first.'

'Oh, yes. I'm very happy with that. With everything really. But why are you half naked?'

'Because I don't want to get paint on my clothes. These shorts are already knackered so they don't matter, but I wouldn't want paint splatters on my Danger Mouse T-shirt.'

'Of course not.'

'Want to join me?' asked Cameron.

Ros wasn't sure if she was experiencing a bout of angina, but her heart rate had increased dramatically.

'I meant painting, not in taking your top off,' said Cameron with a laugh.

'Of course you did. No, I'll give that a miss if it's all the same to you.' And with that Ros made a hasty exit.

Chapter Twenty-Five

Darla came home from a busy shift at the cocktail bar. An evening of wall-to-wall hen nights would wear anyone down. Cameron had garnered a lot of attention from the women and Darla had noticed how he was polite but always ignored any flirting. It wasn't something new but she'd not really spotted it before. Perhaps Ros was right that he was devoted to Gina. She still wanted to find out more from him but tonight had been too busy and, even if she'd wanted to, there was no chance of a chat. Which was probably for the best because she needed to think through her approach so that it wasn't obvious otherwise Ros would not be happy with her.

Darla was glad to get back to The Brambles and gave the animals one last inspection just to be on the safe side, especially after the weasel encounter. A couple of the goats came to check she didn't have any food as they had one-track minds. The little white one with the grubby knees came to the fence but he was limping. 'Oh, Dusty, what have you done?' The goat replied with a pathetic bleat. Darla got out her phone and rang the only person she could.

'You know it's . . .' There was a slight pause. 'It's quarter past one in the morning!' said a rather annoyed Elliott.

'Yes, and I am very sorry about that, but I didn't know who else to call.'

'How about a vet?'

'I figured if I called them in the middle of the night they'd be horribly expensive.' She'd also assumed that she'd have to pay and then claim back from someone and her bank account balance currently didn't have a surplus.

'I'm lambing,' he said through a yawn.

'I'm very sorry to hear that but can we focus on the goat first? Why would he be limping?' She sucked in a breath with shock. 'OMG, has the weasel bitten him?' She crouched down to Dusty's level. 'Did the nasty beastie bite you?'

'That's unlikely,' said a tired-sounding Elliott. 'He probably has something stuck in his hoof. Have a look and if there's nothing obvious, I'll come up in the morning.' He huffed. 'Later this morning. Okay. Bye.'

'No, hang on. When you say have a look . . .' As she was talking she twisted her neck to try to have a look at Dusty's feet but it was dark and he was standing on them.

'I mean get hold of him and look at the bottom of each of his feet . . . I mean hooves.'

'Right. It's just that that's going to be quite tricky on my own.'

'I suppose I'm awake now anyway. Give me a chance to throw on some clothes and I'll come down.'

'Aww you don't have to but I would be very grateful. I'll even make you a coffee.'

'Thanks . . . I think.'

Ten minutes later Darla heard the sound of wheels on gravel and looked out the front to see Elliott getting out of his big car. She went to let him in the front door. 'I can't believe you drove here from next door.' She tilted her head in mock disapproval.

He scowled at her. 'I can't believe you got me out of bed in the middle of the night.'

'Sorry. Come through and I'll make you a coffee after you've looked at Dusty.'

'Slave driver,' he muttered as he followed her through the house. 'How are you so bright and chipper at this time of the night? It's unnatural.'

'I just got in from work. I'm always a bit buzzy after a shift. I expect you're the same after a day farming.'

'Nope. Buzzing is the last thing I am; I'm knackered most days. Anyway, let's have a look at Dusty.'

Outside Darla opened the pen and stood back for Elliott to come in, but he stayed put. 'You need to learn,' he said. 'I'm here in an advisory capacity only. In you go.'

'Oh, okay.' Darla went into the goat pen and Elliott followed her.

All the goats came over to check if there was food and when they found there wasn't, one of the black ones had a chew on Elliott's overalls. 'Get hold of Dusty,' he said as the little goat limped past Darla.

'Right.' Darla followed behind him, trying to grab him around his middle and pick him up. When she heard Elliott laughing she stopped. 'Problem?'

'You two look like you're doing the conga.' At least Elliott was smiling.

'Funny. How do you suggest I pick him up then?'

'Come at her side on . . .'

'Wait, Dusty's a girl?' Darla was trying to have a look underneath the goat but they were all quite hairy so it was hard to see.

'Yep, she's a nanny goat.'

'But she's got horns.'

'Yeah, goats generally do have. Can we get on with this?'

'Of course. Sorry.' Darla had been thrown by the revelation that Dusty was a girl. She turned her attention back to the task. 'What do I need to do?'

'Ideally get her by the fence, stand at her side, reach underneath her and take a firm hold of the legs furthest away from you and pull them towards you. She'll have no choice but to go down on her back. The ground is soft so she'll not hurt herself.'

That was a lot of information to take in. Darla sidled up to Dusty. Maybe because of her limp she was looking weary, but as soon as Darla leaned down Dusty bolted for the other side of the pen. She might have been limping but she could still move pretty fast. Elliott cornered Dusty and held her gently while he beckoned Darla over.

Darla stooped and tried to grab Dusty's legs but she tried to bolt again. Elliott wrapped his arms around the goat and lifted her up. She bleated her frustration. 'Back right, have a look at it.'

Darla lifted the hoof. 'Eurgh! It's dirty.'

'I've got a tool,' he said and Darla couldn't help grinning. Elliott shook his head. 'In my pocket there's a tool you can use.' It took a moment before Darla realised he had his hands full with Dusty so she would need to get the tool out of his pocket. Darla moved her hand towards the side of his overalls. This was all oddly intimate. 'Other side,' said Elliott, tilting his other hip at her.

'Right. Got it,' she said. She couldn't look at him as she slipped her hand into the overalls pocket. She could feel the heat of his body. She didn't want to rummage around too much but was pleased when her fingers touched something and she victoriously pulled out a metal prong.

'Get the muck out from between her toes with that. Be gentle in case there's a wound.'

'Right.' Darla gingerly held the tool and was pleased it was blunt with no blade. She held Dusty's foot firmly and gently ran the tool down where the hoof split into two toes. Dirt and a small sharp stone pinged out from between the toes.

'Well done,' said Elliott, putting Dusty down, who happily trotted off to join the others.

'Is that it? Did I do it? Did I fix a goat?'

Elliott laughed. 'Yeah, you fixed the goat.'

Darla punched the air. She was feeling elated. 'I think maybe we should celebrate with wine rather than coffee.'

'Not for me.' He yawned deeply. 'In fact I think I'll skip the coffee thanks and go straight back to bed.' He checked his watch. 'I need to be up in three hours anyway. Unless a ewe has me up before then.'

'Oh, I won't bother you again.'

'No, a ewe. Not you.' Darla wasn't sure what he was on about and it probably showed on her face. 'Never mind. I'm off to bed. Night, Darla. Night, Dusty.'

'Okay. Thanks,' she said.

'You coming?' he asked, holding the pen door for her.

'I think I'll just get her some food to say well done.' She

was far too excited to sleep now anyway. She felt like she'd made a breakthrough by helping Dusty albeit with a lot of assistance from Elliott.

'Please yourself,' he said and with another mammoth yawn he left.

***

Ros opened her front door at the end of a long day to the smell of herbs and spices. She loved that Cameron cooked sometimes, especially as it was always a little surprise as to what he was making. There was no sign of him but her lidded casserole dish was in the oven. She put down her bag and went to have a nose. She reached for the oven door but was interrupted.

'Caught you!' he said, coming out of his bedroom.

'Hi, something smells amazing.'

'Good. It's lamb tagine. It's been cooking most of the day so it should be . . .' He kissed his fingers. 'How was your day?'

'Tiring.'

'Are you still really busy?' he asked as he flicked the switch on the kettle.

The obvious thing to have done at this point was to simply say yes but it wasn't the truth. And despite the mountain of lies they had told her father and a variety of other people who had got caught up in their deception, she really wasn't one for lying. 'I'm trying to interact with my colleagues more. And it's exhausting.'

Cameron laughed easily as he leaned back against the worktop. 'They can't be that bad.'

Ros tipped her head at him. 'Today I have listened to

Jeff tell me in detail about his clematis.' Cameron chuckled. 'No, it's not funny. Jeff is very serious about his clematis. Especially the timing of pruning. But that wasn't the most taxing conversation I had today. I am trying hard to be civil to Alastair.'

Cameron grimaced. 'I bet that's a stretch.'

'Thank you for noticing. It is rather. Apparently he's one of those people who are into conspiracy theories.' She paused for a moment. 'Please tell me you don't subscribe to them.'

'No, you're good. What does Alastair believe then?'

Ros shook her head. 'Amongst a great many other things, he believes that man did not land on the moon, lip balm contains an ingredient that actually dries out your lips rather than moistening them and that the king is part alien.' She could hardly believe she was repeating Alastair's ridiculous suggestions.

Cameron laughed. 'Although those ears aren't human.' He mimed pulling his out for comic effect.

'Stop it,' said Ros. 'I couldn't challenge him for fear of undoing any progress I've made by small talk. Which meant I had to listen and nod. I have never been so grateful to hear a fire alarm in my life.'

'Did you set it off?

'Tempting but no. Although, I might if I get trapped like that again.'

'I'm really proud of you,' said Cameron, making the tea. Ros tried to shrug off the compliment but he shook his head. 'Credit where it's due. I know this doesn't come naturally to you so I'm well impressed that you're persevering. It'll pay dividends in the end.'

'I hope so. I'm also working on how I can make risk management more accessible and fun. Although I think the latter is a step too far.'

'Maybe I can help with that. We can go over it after dinner if you like? I've got no other plans.'

She really couldn't think of anything she'd rather do.

Chapter Twenty-Six

It was Darla's turn to get an unexpected call in the wee small hours when her phone went off at four o'clock on a rare day off. 'Oh come on!' she grumbled as she tried to grab the phone but instead knocked it off the bedside cabinet and onto the floor. Darla hung almost upside down as she tried to reach it without actually getting out of bed because that would definitely wake her up fully. With any luck she'd be able to fob off whoever it was calling so ridiculously early and go back to sleep. She hit the answer button, with her head still hanging over the side of the bed. 'Hallo?'

'Darla, great, you're up. I need your help,' said Elliott.

'No, I'm not up,' she said, scrunching her eyes up in a feeble attempt to stay sleepy. 'It's my day off and—'

'Brilliant, I was worried you'd be dashing off to work. Can you come straight up to the farm?'

'What, now?'

'Great. Thanks, see you in about five minutes then.'

'Hang on, wh—' But it was pointless because the phone had gone dead. Darla huffed as she threw herself back onto her pillow. It was no good. However much she wanted to have a lie-in, there was no way she would be able to go back to sleep now, mainly because she was curious as to what on earth Elliott needed *her* help with. And after he'd coached her through helping Dusty the other night she could hardly let him down.

She had a quick wash, got dressed and headed off to the farm. She figured it must be urgent if he was asking her for help. She couldn't imagine she was high on his list of people to rely on. An image of her trying to catch Dusty shot into her mind, closely followed by her chasing chickens in a soggy sarong. It seemed unlikely that it would be animal-related; she knew Elliott's feelings on her failings in that department. Perhaps it was a cleaning emergency. Whilst she wouldn't be impressed if he'd woken her up for that, she did know that was something she could handle. What she didn't want was to be useless at whatever it was he needed help with. She wasn't sure why it mattered but she cared what he thought of her and an opportunity to prove that she wasn't a complete idiot would be good. It was cold and still quite dark as she walked the lane, making her zip her jacket right up and bury her hands in the pockets.

The farmhouse was in darkness but as she approached she could see a light from one of the barns. She walked across the now dry concrete and smiled to herself at the just visible chicken footprints. She wasn't sure what she'd been expecting as she walked into the barn but she definitely wasn't prepared for the sight that met her; rows and rows of pens all full of sheep and lambs, most of which were sleeping. At the far end she could see someone bending over, who looked like they were graffitiing a sheep with a paint aerosol.

'Is this the farming equivalent of Banksy?' she quipped.

'Bloody hell!' said Elliott, jumping in fright. 'You shouldn't creep up on people.'

'Good morning to you too. No, please don't thank me for coming to your aid at a moment's notice in the middle of the night. It's my absolute pleasure.' She fixed him with a sarcastic smile.

'Yeah, well. Thanks for coming and all that. I figured I helped you so it's . . . tit for tat.'

'And which one does that make me?' asked Darla, putting her hands on her hips in mock disapproval.

'I don't know,' said Elliott with a frown. It was clearly too early for frivolity. 'I'm swamped here and Lee's girlfriend has gone into labour as have three ewes. I can't manage and that puts lambs' lives at risk. And that's where you come in.' He pointed at her with the aerosol. 'You, not a female sheep.'

'I know I'm not a female sheep.' Darla felt on edge. 'I'm also no midwife. You know that right?' Darla had quite a phobia when it came to blood and gore.

'I thought as much, so I'll handle the deliveries,' said Elliott. 'But what I really need is someone to feed the cade lambs.'

'Whose lambs?' asked Darla, scanning the many cute new arrivals; adorable fluffy lambs were skittering about, whilst others fed from their mothers. It was a lovely scene to witness and reminded her of the farming videos she'd binge-watched on her mobile when she'd first moved in at The Brambles.

'Cade lambs are the orphans or like in my case where the ewe has given birth to three and can only really cope with two. They're all next door under a heat lamp but they're going to want feeding again in about half an hour and I'm already multitasking.'

Feeding lambs sounded like something she could do. 'Okay, point me in the right direction.'

'Great,' said Elliott, who then proceeded to give her fast and lengthy instructions of how to make up milk from a powdered feed and how much to give them and how to make sure they all got enough.

'Can I just recap?' she asked. 'Powder and bottles in the kitchen. Make up one litre of mixture and split into four bottles, one per lamb.'

Elliott looked surprised. 'Spot on.'

She wasn't sure if she was pleased or slightly insulted.

'I need to get on. Shout if you need anything,' he said, pointing to a very fat sheep lying on its side.

Darla went into the farmhouse and switched on the kitchen lights, which was when she was met by another surprise. What Elliott had failed to mention was that his kitchen looked like a dairy had exploded in there. The sink was full of used bottles – there must have been a couple of dozen, all with a dribble of milk in the bottom. The kitchen table looked like something very similar to a crack house in a crime drama she'd recently watched as there were two sets of scales, a few spoons and lots of white powder scattered all over it. Darla set about tidying up because that was something she was good at and she'd be able to work better if everything was clean and uncluttered.

Once the kitchen was sorted she realised she was

missing one key piece of information: how many lambs she needed to feed. She left the bottles to drain and went to investigate. The barn creaked as she slipped inside. Under a glowing lamp was what she could only describe as a pile of lambs, like a sloping pyramid. As she came closer sleepy eyes opened and regarded her with interest. They were the cutest things she'd ever seen and it made her heart squeeze that these poor little mites couldn't be cared for by their mums. She was suddenly very keen to do a good job.

A white one with a black head scrambled out of the pile and ran to the mesh bleating. Apparently this was like a battle cry as they all then woke up and joined in the noise, which was quite something as there were a lot of them. Darla tried to count them but they wouldn't keep still. Clearly they were all very hungry so she made an estimate and went to make up some bottles.

Darla filled up all the available bottles and left the ones she couldn't carry standing in a sink of warm water to keep them at temperature while she ferried the eight she could manage into the barn. As soon as she opened the door the bleating started up again and only got worse as she squeezed into their pen with a wiggle, keen not to let any of them escape. She made sure the gate was closed and sat herself down on a hay bale. Big mistake. All the lambs tried to join her as they desperately clamoured to get to the milk.

'Whoa!' she cried as they overpowered her and she toppled off the hay bale backwards still clutching the bottles, some of which leaked over her. There was a moment where the assembled lambs stared at her but it was only fleeting before they all jumped on top of her. 'Oof!' That was when she knew she needed some help. 'Elliott!'

she yelled.

As she daren't let go of the bottles, she couldn't defend herself against the multitude of little lamb feet parading all over her in their frantic attempt to get fed. She didn't hear Elliott appear until she heard his laugh. Not really the supportive response she'd been hoping for.

'Did you get ambushed?' he said through his laughter.

'Something like that. They're monsters.'

'Yeah, the whole wolves in sheep's clothing thing is true. You okay?'

'Absolutely fantastic, thanks. I needed a lie-down, so where better?' She glared at him.

'Here, let me show you,' he said, striding through the gate to join her. He took two bottles from her arms, popped them in his pockets and picked up two lambs; one under each arm. He nudged open a gate between where they were and the empty pen next door. Darla tilted herself up so she could see better. It was a bit like watching telly at The Brambles. She and the other lambs watched as Elliott sat down on another hay bale, put down the lambs, pulled the bottles from his pocket and they both immediately began to tug on the teats. Despite her uncomfortable position she couldn't help but smile at the sight of their little tails whirling around as they downed the milk mixture in record time.

'See. Easy,' he said, getting to his feet. 'If you feed them in there you'll know who's had what.'

'Okay,' said Darla, still lying on her back.

Elliott came over and with strong arms he helped her to her feet. 'Are you sure you'll be all right?'

'Absolutely,' she said with as much confidence as she

could muster. But she soon discovered that was far easier said than done.

Darla tried her best, she really did, but all the lambs wanted the bottles regardless of whether they'd been fed or not. The lambs were all variations of black and white so it was difficult to tell them apart, a fact she discovered when she carried two into the end pen, put them down and then had to concentrate very hard on which were the two already fed and which were the ones she'd just brought in. It was like they'd been cloned.

They had no idea about manners and happily pushed each other out of the way. One grabbed a bottle by the teat and wrenched it from her hand and ran off with it, quickly becoming frustrated when they couldn't get the milk to come out properly. And when she did manage to get the right lamb on the right end of a bottle she had to hang on tight with both hands because they had more suction than the best industrial vacuum cleaner on the market. It wasn't long before she was exhausted, splattered with milk and getting grumpy.

'How's it going?' asked Elliott, popping his surprisingly cheery face over the split barn door.

'Rubbish. I'm rubbish at this. I can't keep track of who's who or who's had what. I'm worried someone will not get fed and die. Could we swap jobs? Is there much blood involved with delivering lambs?'

Elliott didn't bother to hide his glee and held up his bloodied palms, making Darla's stomach churn. 'I think birthing difficult lambs on your own is tough even for me,' he said. 'You'd probably be better off sticking with these guys.' A little black lamb bleated his frustration at

231

not having had his breakfast yet. 'Let me get cleaned up and I'll give you a hand.'

'Thank you,' said Darla and the little black lamb bleated as if in agreement.

A few minutes later Elliott returned with a bale of straw on his shoulder. 'Mind out,' he said as he plonked it over the mesh. 'I've had an idea.' Darla waited while Elliott brought in more bales and built up a wall around Darla.

'I used to love making forts when I was a kid,' she said, as he placed another bale in place.

'Me too. Hours of fun. But we're not playing forts today. Right, here's the plan. I'll pass you a lamb to feed in there so the others can't get to you and that one can't escape until it's fed.'

'Brilliant,' said Darla, impressed with the solution.

Elliott grinned. He went into the neighbouring pen, picked up two lambs and came back. He then climbed over the bales and plonked himself down next to Darla. They were now sitting thigh to thigh in a small straw fort. The warmth against her leg was reassuring. 'Pick your lamb,' he said.

She went for the smallest in the hope it was less vigorous with the sucking than the one under his other arm. She handed him a bottle and he swapped her for the lamb. One on one it was a lot easier and as the others couldn't see what was happening their bleating had reduced. 'Hold the bottle a little higher, so they don't take on too much air. There you go. Good job,' he said with a smile and she felt like she was finally being useful.

232

Chapter Twenty-Seven

Ros usually liked Sundays but the thought of her mother still being at her dad's made her feel tense. The fact that Cameron was going with her this time was both good and bad. She was pleased to have his support, even though she knew she was paying for it. But she feared their façade may not withstand her mother's scrutiny. Ros hadn't slept much, desperately thinking through all possible scenarios and even more desperately looking for ways to mitigate them. The problem with that was that the scenarios she was able to conjure up appeared infinite and none of them good.

The other issue was that Ros really didn't know her mother at all, so trying to predict how she would react to Cameron was almost impossible. Would she even care that he'd moved in with Ros only a few months into a relationship? She had no idea because the bottom line was her mother was a stranger to her. How could she not be, having walked out on Ros when she was seven years old? Ros huffed into her healthy muesli mix that Cameron had made for them both.

'Let me guess,' he said, pointing a loaded spoon at her across the table. 'You're worrying about your mum?'

'Very astute.'

He shrugged one shoulder. 'I think you're overthinking it. Barry was cool about me moving in. And when your mum gets to know me she'll love me too.' He beamed a smile at her.

'I admire your optimism but I don't think it will be that easy this time. And whilst she is my mother, it feels odd to call someone I feel I barely know "Mum".'

'Then just call her Amanda. Can I offer some advice?'

'Of course.'

There was more spoon waving. 'Don't let her wind you up. Or at least don't let it show.'

'Again very easy to say but—'

'Yeah, I know. Look at it this way. All of this was for Barry, not your mum. If she disapproves, so what? Making Barry feel that you won't be alone after his demise is all that matters. It's all about Barry's peace of mind and that's still what we're focused on. Okay?'

'I guess you're right. I wish I knew how long she was planning on staying around for.'

'Probably until . . . you know,' said Cameron, finally eating the muesli on his spoon.

It made her realise that Cameron would be the same. 'I suppose that's the end point to our arrangement. Well, it actually is the end point because we wrote it into the contract.' Ros concentrated on her cereal bowl. The weeks were disappearing, which meant time with her father was too.

Cameron put down his spoon. 'I've been thinking

about that and I'm here for you as long as you need me, and before you say anything about money you don't need to pay me anything more. You've been brilliant about me moving in here and picking up the food bills and stuff. And anyway, I've grown fond of Barry. I feel I owe it to him to make sure that you really are okay. So I'm here for the funeral and for as long as you need a friend.' He fixed her with sincere eyes. 'I mean it.'

'I know you do and it's very kind of you. Thank you,' she said.

How come something so lovely made her feel so sad?

For once Ros was pleased to be greeted at the door by Gazza. Although he bypassed her quite quickly in favour of Cameron. 'Hello,' she called tentatively into the hallway.

'Hello, come in. I'm in the kitchen,' called Barry.

Ros was surprised to see her father on his feet whisking something. 'You're at the Yorkshires early.'

'I had a few eggs that needed eating so I thought I'd made a bread and butter pudding.'

'Top idea,' said Cameron, greeting Barry warmly.

'You probably should be sitting down,' said Ros. She'd not seen him this active for a while.

'I'm fine. While I'm feeling good I figure I should get on with things.'

'Good approach,' said Cameron. 'But you'll still be doing your Yorkshire puds right?' He seemed to freeze while he awaited Barry's response.

'Of course.'

'Phew. That's a relief.'

'Where's Amanda?' asked Ros.

Barry stopped whisking. 'Your mum popped out for a coffee maker. She's not keen on instant.'

'She's making herself at home then.' There was discomfort in her words.

'She's just trying to help, Ros. You don't need to be so wary of her.'

'I'll get the potatoes started,' she said.

'Come on. Let me finish preparing the bread and butter pudding and then we can have a coffee and a chat like always.'

Cameron gave her a look that said she was being unreasonable. She remembered what he'd said about this all being about Barry and to not get distracted by her mother. Ros took a breath and slapped on a smile. 'Sure, I'll put the kettle on.'

Ros was feeling easier once they were all settled in the living room, with Gazza lying by Cameron's feet with his legs in the air, and them all chatting about who the next Doctor Who might be. The moment burst like a balloon as a key went in the front door. The chatter stopped and everyone waited. The front door closed and Amanda appeared in the doorway holding a large box.

'Here, let me take that,' said Cameron, getting up quickly. Gazza looked on with disappointment that his tummy rub had been interrupted.

'Oh, you must be the boyfriend,' said Amanda.

'Yes, I'm Cameron. Lovely to meet you, Mrs Foster.'

Ros and Barry winced at the same time. 'I am not,

nor have I ever been, Mrs Foster,' said Amanda, fixing Cameron with an irritated look.

'Oh sorry. My mistake I just assumed you and Barry were married. My apologies. Hello and pleased to meet you . . .'

He left a pause that Amanda didn't fill. Barry cleared his throat. 'We were married but she didn't take my surname. Maybe just call her Amanda.' He was looking to his ex-wife for her agreement.

'I've never been keen on complying with social norms or bowing to the patriarchy,' said Amanda. 'I was also establishing myself in my profession at the time so a change of name would have been detrimental.'

'Right,' said Cameron, for once appearing as if maintaining his smile was a little tricky. 'I'm very pleased to meet you, Amanda. Let me help you with that.' He went to take the box from her.

'I am quite capable of carrying it into the kitchen. I managed to get it from the car to here. Is your assumption that I'm not capable as a mere woman or that you would like to be seen as a knight in shining armour by coming to my aid?'

'Err, well. I was just trying to help. But if you're good, I'll leave you to it.' Cameron shoved his hands in his pockets. Amanda went off to the kitchen. Cameron hovered awkwardly in the doorway looking confused by the rebuff.

Ros was incensed by her mother's rudeness and stormed out after her.

'Ah, Ros, can you move whatever that is?' she asked, nodding at Barry's bread and butter pudding. 'I need to put this box down.'

'I thought you didn't need anyone's help. Or was it just Cameron you were being rude to?'

Amada seemed taken aback. 'I wasn't being rude. Simply asking what his motivation was. Are you going to move that?'

'If you ask politely I might.'

'Fine.' Amanda put the box on the edge of the worktop and used it to shove the pudding out of the way.

'Everything okay?' asked Cameron, joining them and placing a reassuring hand on the small of Ros's back.

Ros could feel emotion bubbling in her gut. It was anger mainly and she wasn't sure how to deal with it. 'Barry tells me you've moved into Ros's apartment and that you're a student on a low income,' said Amanda as she stared Cameron down.

'I didn't say that exactly!' called Barry from the other room.

'It's fine – that's all accurate,' said Cameron. 'But once I graduate, hopefully I'll secure a good job and that will put things on a more even keel.'

'Hang on,' said Ros to Cameron. 'It's not really any of her business. I could be shacked up with all of Southampton football club including the reserves team and it would not be for you to pass judgement.'

'I would if you'd said Portsmouth,' called Barry and Cameron laughed. Ros and Amanda both glared at him.

'Despite what you may believe, Rosanna, I am interested in your welfare,' she said as she began unpacking the coffee machine. 'Now that's cleared up would anyone like a decent cup of coffee?'

'Grrr,' was all Ros could manage in response and she stomped out of the kitchen.

Ros managed to keep out of her mother's way for most of the run-up to dinner but once they were all seated with their full plates in front of them it wasn't as easy to avoid her.

'Amanda, what is it that you do for a living?' asked Cameron.

'I'm a quantitative analyst.'

'Wow, impressive.'

'I like to think so,' said Amanda.

'What is that exactly?' he asked.

'I gather key data, study and report on the mathematical and statistical components of a business. Primarily I help companies manage or avoid financial risks.'

'Oh, like Ros,' he said, pointing at her proudly.

'No, not really,' said Amanda. 'What attracted you to Rosanna?'

Barry almost choked on his roast potato but Cameron remained unfazed by the question. 'She's smart, funny, kind-hearted and she's really straightforward. What you see is what you get.'

His unexpected kind words brought a lump to Ros's throat. She couldn't remember anyone ever saying something so nice about her before. Then reality gave her a slap and she remembered she was paying him.

'Oh and she's gorgeous too,' he added quickly.

'I see. And Rosanna. What do you see as Cameron's key attributes?'

'Amanda, maybe leave the inquisition until after dinner,' said Barry, looking embarrassed.

Amanda was still waiting for a reply. Ros put down her cutlery and what she said came from the heart. 'He works really hard, with his job, his studying and volunteering but he still has time for me. He's really thoughtful. He's like human sunshine. He always sees the positive in situations and people and in me, no matter what. And I feel blessed to have met him.'

Cameron rested a hand over hers and they both glanced at each other at the same time. Was Ros imagining that they had a connection? Perhaps it was just the ridiculousness of the situation they found themselves in, but she felt connected to Cameron in a way she never had to anyone else. And in that moment she knew her feelings for him ran deep. When they'd drawn up the contract she'd never considered she might get her heart broken in the process; that definitely wasn't a risk on her list. She realised they were still looking into each other's eyes when Cameron squeezed her hand.

She broke eye contact, looking down to slosh a bit more gravy over her Yorkshire pudding. She couldn't risk him reading her face like a book and figuring out what she was thinking about him.

Chapter Twenty-Eight

Darla yawned and stretched. She'd enjoyed her lie-in. Although she wasn't as comfortable as she could be. Something tickled her nose. Her eyes snapped open to see Elliott waving a piece of straw in her face. 'Hey!' For a moment she wondered where on earth she was and why she was asleep next to Elliott.

'Hello, sleeping beauty, I made you a coffee.'

Darla realised she'd been curled up asleep on the hay bales. She quickly checked her lips for dribble and her eyes for crusty bits of sleep before sitting upright. 'I must have nodded off.'

'Sorry, that's my fault.'

'Don't be so hard on yourself. You're not that dull.'

'I meant because I got you up in the middle of the night,' said Elliott.

'In that case it is entirely your fault.'

'Peace offering?' He picked up a steaming mug of coffee and she took it.

'Ta. At least we got them all fed.' Darla looked over at the pile of lambs where they had returned to their huddle under the lamp. They looked so cute all cuddled up together and far sweeter than they were when they were demanding milk with menaces.

Elliott sat down beside her but he was pulling a face. 'Yeah, about that. They need feeding every couple of hours. So after the coffee we do it all again.'

'Blimey, it's relentless.'

'That's farming,' said Elliott.

They sipped their drinks. 'I expect you're used to it. It being in your blood and everything. The only things in my bloodline are an ancient right to graze sheep in Oxford city centre, an allergy to mustard and my mother's cleaning obsession.'

Elliott pulled in a long breath and exhaled slowly. 'I never wanted to take over the farm. I studied civil engineering at university. My dad and I frequently rowed about it but Mum understood I had to choose my own path. I loved my job. I'd always dreamed of building bridges. However, life had other plans and when faced with the choice of selling the farm or leaving my job and giving it a go as a farmer I knew I'd regret it if I didn't at least try.'

She'd not been expecting that. 'I think you're doing great.'

He snorted a laugh. 'I'm muddling along really. Horace was a godsend but now it's just me and I'm still not sure I'm cut out for it.'

'You look the part,' said Darla, taking in his robust physique.

'Yeah, dirty overalls are what all the women are into this season.'

'But it's honest work. That's a good thing. Not that being

242

a civil engineer isn't an honest job. But I guess you need to do what makes you happy. Only you know what that is.'

'That's the thing: I'm not sure. There are pros and cons with both jobs. There's more of a sense of achievement every day with farming but the pay as a civil engineer is definitely something I miss, and I really loved the whole engineering and build process. There's also the chance to travel, which I've always wanted to do.'

'Oh me too, the travel part. I long to see different cultures and immerse myself in another way of life. But if you could do it as part of a job that would be very cost-effective.'

'Don't remind me. I'm missing out on business-class travel and top hotels as well as the big salary!'

'As long as you've got food and shelter, money's only fun tokens, and I know how to get loads of free ones of those.'

Elliott looked confused. 'Now you've definitely lost me.'

'All money does is buy little moments of pleasure. But there are so many you can find for free. They might not be exactly the same but in my experience money causes a lot of problems.'

'Now I'm intrigued.' He twisted his body to look at her square on and she felt put on the spot. She studied him for a moment. Could she trust him? It wasn't likely he would bump into her parents. He seemed like a decent person and he'd just shared with her so why not?

'I went into business with my ex-boyfriend. Only it turns out all the business ventures were cons. For a short while I thought I was minted; we had money coming in all over the place and I, like a fool, didn't query it. But then all of sudden the money disappeared and so did he, leaving me with whopping debts, angry people after me and bailiffs on the doorstep.'

'Shit, Darla. I'm so sorry. What a bastard. What did you do?'

'I've not exactly finished doing it yet, which is why I'm living in someone else's house, and juggling two other jobs. Actually three now I've got a gig cleaning your mate's yacht. And that is an excellent segue into my money tokens example. I could never afford to buy a fancy yacht or even rent one for the day but I get to clean one.'

Elliott laughed but stopped when he spotted her unimpressed face. 'Oh, you're serious.'

'Yes. Because I get to spent a few hours a week in a beautiful environment and I get to have a coffee break and sit in luxury and soak it up, and I bet the people who go on it usually don't even notice the things I do. Like the softness of the cushions, the perfectly stitched leather seats and the sparkle when the sun shines on the water. And that little experience costs me nothing, in fact they pay me. I'm totally winning at life.'

Elliott laughed. 'You are the most positive person I have ever met. Most would be devastated that they had to pay all that money back. You were conned, just as much as anyone your ex owed money to.'

'I was down for a bit but I had two choices: declare myself bankrupt and disappoint my parents or find a way to pay it all back. And do you know what, I'm on track to do it.' She couldn't help feel a little bit of pride at what she had achieved.

'That's amazing.'

Darla's phone pinged and with a happy smile on her face she pulled it from her pocket. A message from her wanker ex-boyfriend had been the very last thing she'd expected to see.

***

As soon as dinner was done and the dishwasher stacked, Cameron had the good idea to suggest that he and Ros took Gazza for a walk. Of course as soon as he asked there was no going back as Gazza was already pogoing around Cameron's legs.

'He really does like you,' said Barry, watching Gazza look adoringly at Cameron while he did up his harness.

'We're best mates, aren't we, Gaz?' The little dog barked excitedly. 'See.' Cameron grinned at Barry.

'Actually,' said Barry, stepping closer to Cameron. 'I wanted to ask you something. Both of you.' He glanced at Ros who was keen to escape.

'Sure, what can we do to help?' asked Cameron, crouching down in an attempt to calm an eager Gazza.

'I'd like you to have him after I . . . you know. I had asked Peter, my brother, to take him but he's not had a dog for years, he still works and his knees are bad. And I think Gazza would be happiest with you.' There were tears in Barry's eyes.

'Barry, I'd be honoured,' said Cameron.

'Oh, um, uh,' said Ros, wrestling with a number of issues – top of the list were her curtains. It was easy for Cameron to volunteer to have the dog when it was all make-believe. The reality would be that she would end up with him. As if sensing Ros's hesitation Gazza ran to her and put his paws on her knees. His big sad eyes locked on hers.

'Only if it's okay with both of you,' said Barry, looking

at Ros, his expression not dissimilar to Gazza's.

'Um,' repeated Ros. 'I don't want to be the bad guy here but when Cameron moves out and I'm working, Gazza would be on his own for hours on end. I'm not sure that's what's best for him. At least Uncle Peter works part-time so he'd be home more.'

'I've put you both on the spot. Don't make a decision now,' said Barry. 'Have a think about it.'

Cameron squeezed Barry's shoulder. 'We'll work something out. Don't worry about Gazza. I'll make sure he's properly taken care of.'

'Thanks, lad,' said Barry, giving Cameron a manly hug and slap on the back as he fought back tears. 'Look at me being a soft old sod. Go on off with the three of you. I need a sit-down and I think Amanda is making more coffee.' He rolled his eyes and shooed them out of the front door.

'What the hell, Cameron?' said Ros when they reached the pavement, making him stop and Gazza pull hard to get going.

'What could I say? We agreed Barry's feelings come first. That was all I was doing. And I stand by what I said. I'd find a way to look after Gazza.'

'That's hardly realistic, is it? You know he'd end up with me because you will go back to your life and student digs where most landlords prohibit pets.'

'I could still do my fair share of walking him. I figured I'd still be welcome at yours. Have I got that wrong?'

'Of course you'd be welcome. It's just that the relationship contract states—' A bang above them made Ros stop talking. They both looked up to see her mother looking out of an upstairs window.

246

Chapter Twenty-Nine

That evening Ros was still dwelling on the earlier conversation with Cameron. Sometimes she hated being logical but it was hard to be anything else – it was simply how she was hard-wired. She saw things in black and white. Granted she was a little fonder of Gazza now than she had been, but she didn't feel she was his best option and having Cameron effectively volunteer her to be his owner long-term was not helpful.

However, there was now a more pressing matter as Darla had arrived in a fluster. Instead of responding to her ex with a lengthy reply containing mainly swear words, Darla was circling Ros's sofa arguing the pros and cons of contact with The Wanker.

'And what is The Wanker's actual name?' asked Ros.

'Patrick.'

'Really?' queried Ros.

Darla nodded.

Ros was surprised. 'I was expecting something more . . . I don't know, villainous.'

'If he'd been called Thanos, Loki or Doctor Doom even

I might have clocked there was something off about him.'

'I suppose.' Ros thoughtfully sipped her coffee, her calmness in complete contrast to Darla's anxious state.

'What do I do?' asked Darla, almost bumping into Ros as she paced.

'Stop walking for a start – you're making me dizzy.'

Darla halted abruptly in front of Ros. 'But seriously, what should I do?'

'Delete the message and block his number,' said Ros.

'You're right. I know you're right. But I'd quite like to give him a piece of my mind. After what he's put me through.'

'Or you could avoid him putting you through anything further by ignoring the message.'

Darla bit her lip. 'But what if he means what he said in the text, that he's sorry and he wants to put things right? Apart from the whole secretly amassed debts he was quite a nice guy. And if he's got some of the money he owes me that would be useful. I could repay things quicker and get on with my life and properly focus on my new business, although I still don't know what that would be, but that's not the point. What do you think?'

'Once a con man, always a con man,' said Ros.

'Blimey you are blunt sometimes. You don't think there's even the smallest possibility that he's realised he needs to make amends and—'

'I'm sorry, Darla, but that's very unlikely.'

'I am curious though. And before all this happened, I had really liked Patrick. We'd had fun together until it all unravelled. I find it hard to believe he is a completely bad person, and surely his message shows that he isn't.'

'I thought you wanted to, and I quote, "Batter him senseless and then batter him again to balance things up."'

Darla flopped into a chair with an oof. 'I don't know. I was angry. I guess I thought I'd never hear from him again and now he's back in touch. Shouldn't I at least hear him out?'

'Considering he ignored all the desperate messages you sent him when he left you to sort out the unholy mess he made, I don't think you owe him anything at all.'

'True. I know he doesn't deserve a second chance but—'

'I think a second chance would be extremely unwise,' said Ros.

'Don't worry, I won't let him swindle me again. How about I call him now and we both listen to what he has to say? What harm could that do?' Ros was quiet. 'Are you risk-assessing all the options and the level of harm Patrick is capable of?' asked Darla.

Ros didn't respond, she simply gave her a look. Eventually she replied, 'As long as you don't provide him with any personal details and don't agree to anything other than him returning what he owes, I think it might be okay.'

'Great, let's call him,' said Darla, whipping out her phone. She paused. 'For all the times I've had this conversation in my head I should know exactly what I want to say to him, or shout at him, but right now my mind has gone blank.'

'Have you changed your mind?' Ros was looking hopefully at her.

Darla visibly steeled herself. 'No, I need to do this.' She pressed Patrick's number and waited.

'Hello?' He sounded unsure to Ros.

Darla took a deep breath. 'Patrick, it's Darla. I got your

message. Given you have wrecked my life, how do you propose to fix it?'

'Baby, it is so good to hear your voice. These past few months I've been—'

Ros feared Darla would be easily won over so she began miming cutting her throat in the hope that Darla got the message. Darla looked slightly alarmed at the gesture.

'I don't really care what you've been doing,' said Darla into the phone. 'I'm only interested in what you're going to do now to put things right.'

Ros gave her a thumbs up.

'Baby, I get that you don't understand why I had to leave without warning but these people were—'

'Again, not interested,' said Darla. 'If you don't have anything that's going to help reduce the shitload of debt you left behind, then I'm hanging up and blocking your number.'

There was a slight pause. 'Maybe we should meet?'

Ros was frantically shaking her head.

'Why?' asked Darla.

'Because I've got some of the money and I want to make things right between us.'

This was far too hard to mime so Ros grabbed a pen and paper and hastily wrote on it: *You could pay the money into my bank account.*

Darla read it out. 'You could pay the money into my bank account.'

'I could but I would really like a chance to explain and say I'm sorry,' said Patrick, unhelpfully sounding sincere.

'Thanks, but it's only the money I'm interested in,' said Darla, looking like she was trying hard not to be swayed.

'But I really want to apologise so I guess that's a stalemate.'

There was silence from both of them. Ros waved her hands about but Darla only looked alarmed by the gesture. 'I'm away at the moment,' said Darla. 'So I couldn't meet up even if I wanted to.'

'Yeah, I heard that your mum seems to think you're travelling around Europe but according to the last entry on our joint account you paid money in at a branch in Southampton two weeks ago.'

Darla covered the phone. 'Shit! Now what do I do?' she whispered to Ros.

'Are you still there?' asked Patrick.

'Where? Southampton? No. You see what that was—'

'Oh, it's okay, I *know* you're still in Southampton,' said Patrick.

Darla gasped. This was not going well at all. 'What makes you think that?' asked Darla, her hands visibly shaking.

'Let's not get all testy with each other. I'd like to see you face to face and I'm happy to come to you. That's not such a bad thing, is it?'

'You tried to ruin my life!' snapped Darla angrily.

'No, I didn't, and that's why I want to meet, so we can sort this all out. Please let me put things straight. How about we meet somewhere of your choosing in Southampton, tomorrow?'

Ros was vehemently shaking her head. 'And then you'll leave me alone?' asked Darla.

'If that's what you decide, then of course.'

Darla covered the phone. 'He sounds like he's being

honest. This is such a dilemma,' she whispered to Ros.

'He's anything but honest. He's fooled you before. But it's your decision.'

Darla bit her lip before uncovering the phone's microphone. 'There's a café on London Road. I'll text you the details,' said Darla.

'Great. I can't wait to see you again, babe. I've been th—'

Darla ended the call and let out a huge sigh. She looked at Ros. 'Don't say it. I know I wasn't meant to meet him but I can't risk him spilling what he knows to my parents and there is a chance that he has the cash he owes me.'

'I understand,' said Ros. 'I'll take time off and I'll sit nearby in the café so you have someone to call on if needs be.'

'Thanks, Ros. You're a good friend. I knew you'd have a plan.'

'Always,' said Ros, with a smile.

***

The next morning, Darla met Ros when her cleaning shift finished so they could go over the plan one more time. Darla looked her friend up and down. Ros had on threadbare leggings and an oversized shirt that had also seen better days. 'Are you auditioning for a part in *Oliver!*?' asked Darla.

'I'm sorry, I don't follow.'

'What are you wearing?'

'Oh these? Aren't they great? I didn't have anything suitable for cleaning so I got these for ten pence each in the charity shop where Cameron works.' Ros looked thrilled with her purchase.

'Great,' said Darla, trying not to show her real feelings but Ros didn't seem to have noticed and began going through the plan they had already mapped out.

'And if you feel unsafe at all you say: *it looks like rain*,' concluded Ros.

Darla nodded and tried to keep her breathing steady. She'd not slept much thanks mainly to the prospect of having to face Patrick but also due to having to feed the lambs every two hours as Elliott was still struggling without Lee. 'What if there's an embarrassing lull in the conversation and the weather is all we have to talk about?'

'Unlikely, but then don't talk about rain. I've also put Cameron on standby in case he cuts up rough.' Ros sort of winced.

Darla laughed at Ros's turn of phrase. 'He's not violent or anything like that,' said Darla, wondering what Cameron would do in that situation.

'It's merely a precaution, and hopefully he won't be needed as he's got to hand a paper in to university so he may not be nearby. But worst case I'll call the police.'

Ros had been quite keen to call the police anyway but Darla had explained that when it had all first happened she'd cried in front of a lovely police officer in Oxford who had told her that there was little they could do because everything was in joint names. 'It won't come to that. And I'll meet you on the quay afterwards,' said Darla.

'We need to set off from here separately so we aren't associated in case there's ever a situation where we need to do this again. We can have a full debrief while we're cleaning the yacht.'

Ros had kindly offered to help Darla clean the yacht as

the meeting with Patrick was going to eat into her cleaning time. 'And then I'll buy you lunch and a glass of wine, hopefully with some of the money Patrick's going to give me.'

'This is where I'll leave you,' said Ros. 'Set a timer for ten minutes before you follow.'

'I know, and don't look at you or acknowledge you in the café. Got it.' Darla hugged her friend and watched her stride away.

The ten minutes dragged. Darla messed about on her phone and watched the minutes count down. At last she could start walking to the café. She tried to clear her mind and listen to the birds but all she could hear was the rumble of traffic and the odd screaming child. She concentrated on her steps and was soon outside the little coffee shop. She took a deep breath and went inside.

She was pretty sure she hated Patrick for everything he'd done and for how he'd betrayed her trust, but the moment she saw him she got butterflies. He didn't spot her at first, which was good because it gave her a moment to see that Ros was sitting back to back with him and that instantly reassured her – at least she wasn't alone. Patrick looked up and smiled at her. He appeared genuinely pleased to see her. She was now fighting conflicting emotions. Part of her had gone all giggling schoolgirl but the rest of her wanted to batter him with the nearest thing to hand, which was sadly nothing more substantial than the pastries currently on display.

He came forward to hug her and she stepped back. 'Hello, Patrick.'

'Darla, babe, it's so good to see you.'

Darla sat down in the seat opposite his so it was clear that she wouldn't be giving him a hug.

'What did you want to drink?' asked Patrick. 'They're on me.'

'A large mocha with cream please.' It was the most expensive thing she could think of. Maybe it was petty but he owed her.

He ordered at the till and came back to sit opposite her. 'You're looking amazing. Have you lost a few pounds?'

She had but she wasn't going to give him the satisfaction of being right. 'No, and let's cut the small talk. I have somewhere I need to be.'

He looked puzzled. 'But I've just ordered you a large mocha.'

Bugger it, she thought. 'I can always get it to go. Now, say what you came to say.'

Their drinks arrived, which gave him time to gather his thoughts. Patrick relaxed back into his seat and for a moment she feared he was going to bump his chair into Ros's. 'I was convinced you weren't going to show up,' said Patrick. 'And I wouldn't have blamed you for that. It was all a bit crazy at the end. But you have to believe me when I say I had no choice but to leave.'

'Rubbish. You could have told me rather than let me open the door to bailiffs. What the hell happened to all the money?'

'I'm glad you asked that. It's all good. I've invested it.'

She let out a derisory laugh. 'I don't believe you, Patrick.'

'Honestly. I have. Well, some of it anyway.'

Darla was losing what was left of her patience. 'In what? Stocks and shares? Premium bonds?'

255

'You've heard of cryptocurrency, right?'

'Oh for heaven's sake, you've not invested in that?'

'No, it's something like that but better,' he said. 'We just need to wait it out and we'll make a fortune.'

'I don't take risks, so I'll have my share back now please.' Darla held out her palm.

Patrick glanced at it and carried on. 'I can't I'm afraid, because that's part of the agreement that you have to leave it invested.'

'Show me proof that it's in my name.' She stared him down.

'Yeah, you don't understand. It doesn't work like that. But trust me, your money is safe.'

'No, it's not, because it wasn't even my money. It was off credit cards and maxed-out overdrafts, you moron. What money do you have to give me?' she asked, sitting up straight. Clocking Ros's raised thumbs up from behind his head spurred her on.

'Sorry, I never said I had any money for you.' Patrick winced.

'Yes you did!' Her last shred of patience was disintegrating.

'But that's the money I've invested for you. For us.'

The cheek of this guy was unbelievable. 'If you don't actually have any cash on you now, how were you proposing to fix things?'

'By explaining that I had no choice but to leave and that your money is safe. You just need to fob off the banks and credit card companies for a while longer and then it'll be sorted.'

Darla was astonished. 'Is that what you think I've been

doing all these months? Fobbing people off?'

Patrick appeared confused.

'Bloody hell, Patrick. I lost the flat and everything in it, all my personal stuff including my grandmother's clock.' She swallowed hard to keep her focus. 'Ever since then I've been paying off whatever I could so I didn't go sodding bankrupt.'

Patrick sat back. 'But you're okay now. You're settled here. Got somewhere to live?'

'I can't afford anywhere to live. And while we're on that, how the hell did you know I was staying in Southampton?'

He looked a little smug. 'As well as keeping an eye on our joint account, I can still get into one of your online shopping accounts and you've changed the address to somewhere near here. Sounded posh actually. You ordered some book about goats. I figured you were doing all right. Are you? Are you doing okay, Darla? Because I have been worried about you.'

She made a mental note to change all her passwords as soon as she got in. She'd changed most of them, but clearly she'd missed one. 'I'm fine, thanks. If that's it, I think I will get this put into a takeaway cup and get going.' Darla pointed at her large mocha where the cream was melting and dripping down the sides.

'Actually, there was one thing.' He gestured for her to stay sitting down. 'There's this amazing opportunity that came up and all I need is—'

'You are unbelievable. How can you rock up here and ask *me* for money?!'

'You've not heard how much yet.' Patrick seemed surprised when she got up and took her drink to the

257

counter. He followed her and waited while the waitress swapped her drink to a takeaway cup. 'Come on, Darla. I bet you've got a bit tucked away. I'll double your money.'

'No, apparently I've already got a large investment in something like cryptocurrency that's going to make my fortune so I'm all good thanks.' She rolled her eyes. What an idiot she'd been to think for a moment he might not be the complete wanker he'd proved himself to be.

'Ha, you're funny. So . . .' He wobbled his head. 'Will you come back to me on the cash or . . . ?'

'No, Patrick,' she said, taking her mocha in the to-go cup and mouthing her thanks at the waitress. 'It's a big fat no, and it will always be a no, so unless you have a few thousand quid for me in good old reliable cash, then please don't ever contact me again.'

She went to turn away and he grabbed her arm and leaned in. 'The thing is, I need some cash urgently.'

'Not my problem. But while you're here I would like to say that you are a total and utter wanker.' Darla wrenched her arm free and stormed out of the coffee shop. She walked for a bit, her heart thumping. She checked over her shoulder and he wasn't following her, which was a relief. She headed down to the quay where she and Ros had planned to meet. Once on the boat she went inside the saloon and sat for a moment with her large mocha to try and calm herself down. She was furious with Patrick but she was also cross with herself for daring to hope that he would pay up. With shaking hands she got her phone out, went into her online shopping account and changed the password. The last thing she needed was him ordering stuff on there.

The boat rocked slightly as someone boarded and she

gasped. 'It's me,' called out Ros.

'Down here,' called back Darla.

Ros carefully reversed into the saloon of the boat and gave her a hug. The unexpected contact made her feel emotional. 'You did so well back there. Are you okay?' she asked.

'Yeah.' Darla took a breath and thought things through. 'I might not have gained anything other than the satisfaction of telling him he's a wanker, but I've not lost anything either. I'm fine.'

'What a weasel that Patrick is.'

'He's worse than a weasel. They're actually quite cute unless you're a chicken, then not so much.'

Ros was giving her an odd look.

'Anyway, let's crack on,' Darla continued. 'The sooner we get this cleaned the quicker we can have a glass of wine.'

Darla got out the cleaning products and explained what she wanted Ros to do, when there was that slight sway in the boat. Darla froze.

'Hello again,' said Patrick, appearing above them.

Chapter Thirty

Patrick peered into the saloon below. 'This is pretty swanky. Isn't it?'

'Shit!' said Darla, her thoughts in a scramble at the unexpected sight of him.

'You're trespassing,' said Ros with authority.

'This yours, is it?' he asked.

'No, but—'

'No harm in me having a look around then,' he said, coming down the steps. He sucked in air and it whistled through his teeth. 'This is very nice. We'll probably be able to buy something like this when—'

Ros began laughing. Patrick glared at her. 'Who are you?'

'This is my friend, Ros,' said Darla, moving to stand closer to Ros. 'And we'd both like you to leave.'

Patrick sat down and seemed to relish their astonished faces. 'I wish I could but you see, I really need that money. Sort of a life-or-death thing.'

'Yours I hope,' said Ros.

'Yeah, it is actually. Have *you* got any cash?' He looked

her up and down in her charity outfit. 'Actually, you're all right.' He turned his attention back to Darla. 'Babe, you don't need to do anything. All I need is the bank card.'

'There's nothing in the joint account anyway.'

'But there's the overdraft.'

'No, there's not. I've had them reduce it each time I've paid money in, so I wasn't tempted to overspend again.' And in case Patrick came back and tried to do exactly what he was doing now.

'You stupid cow, why did you do that?' he snapped.

'So you couldn't turn up and do it all over again. You wanker,' she added to even up the insults. Darla noticed Ros was texting so leaned slightly in front of her to block Patrick's view.

Patrick no longer looked relaxed. He stood up and tried to pace but in the small space it was quite tricky and he had to keep turning abruptly every couple of steps.

'There would be more space for you to walk around looking agitated up on the quay,' said Ros.

Patrick rubbed his forehead. 'Where's your car?' he asked Darla.

She shrugged. 'I had to sell everything. Including my car,' she lied.

'Shitting hell.' He patted his hands on his head, making Ros step back a fraction. 'Come on, think,' he said. He spun around to stare at Darla and Ros. 'Where can I get my hands on money quickly?'

'No idea,' said Darla.

Ros was pouting.

'What?' said Patrick. 'Have you got a suggestion?'

Ros very slowly shook her head. 'No.'

261

Patrick paused and then he started to laugh. He splayed out his arms and banged his knuckle on the mast post in the centre of the saloon. 'Shit, that hurt. How much is this worth? This boat? What's it worth?'

'No clue,' said Darla. 'Oh no, Patrick,' she added as realisation dawned on her. 'This is my job. I'll get the sack.' She plonked herself down on the luxury leather seating. 'I'm not going anywhere. I'll not let you steal this.'

'You don't have to go anywhere. Just give me the keys.'

'No way.'

Patrick walked towards her with his palm outstretched. But something caught his eye and he reversed back. 'What's this then?' he asked, picking up the boat keys. 'Where do you start this baby up?'

'I don't know.'

'I spotted two big steering wheels up top, so probably up there,' he said, looking pleased with himself.

'You need to leave now before we start screaming and people come running,' said Darla.

'There wasn't a soul about so scream away, and I'll have your mobiles please.'

'No,' said Ros.

'Give me your bloody phones,' he snapped and Darla jumped. She'd not seen him like this before. He was an idiot for sure, but he wasn't a nasty bastard, or at least that was what she'd thought. But then if he really was in danger, that sort of pressure did strange things to people.

'Here,' she said, taking Ros's phone and handing both phones to him. 'There's no need to get nasty.'

'You're right. Just do what I say and it'll all be good. Up on deck please,' he said, ushering them up the steps.

'Now where is the ignition?' he said, partly to himself as he looked about. He found where the key went and was gleeful when the boat's engine started.

'What the hell does he think he's doing?' Darla whispered. She was furious.

'He's stealing the yacht,' said Ros. 'With us on it,' she added.

'Not on my watch,' said Darla, going after Patrick. She found him frantically trying to release the mooring ropes.

'Give us a hand will you?' he asked, sweat gleaming on his brow.

'Patrick, this is madness. I'm not going to help you steal the boat. You need to calm down and think straight.'

'Darla, this is a genius idea. One of my better ones. I need money and I need to get away. This is two birds in one bush.'

Ros called from the back of the boat. 'It's either two birds with one stone or a bird in the hand is worth two in the bush.'

'What the hell is she on?' asked Patrick, finally tugging the line free and throwing it onto the deck.

'Ros likes things to be right. And it's a good trait,' she said, following him around the yacht. 'Patrick, stealing a boat is a very bad idea. Please stop.'

'I can't!' His voice was almost a shout as he threw his arms up in exasperation. 'I owe money to lots of people and now it turns out some of them are the wrong sorts of people.' He scratched his head. 'I don't want to get you and your weird mate into trouble so why don't you get off and say I overpowered you both?' He grinned at her like it was the best idea ever.

'That makes us complicit!' yelled Ros.

'Fine,' snapped Patrick. 'Do what you like. I'm taking it anyway.' He undid the last line and the vessel was free. He went to the back of the boat where there were two large wheels. 'Which one do I use?' he asked Darla.

'You really are the worst pirate ever,' she said.

'Which one?' he shouted at her.

'I don't know!' she shouted back. 'I clean the bloody thing. I don't sail about on it sipping cocktails. That's someone else's life.'

Patrick took hold of her by both arms. 'But it could be our life. We could run away together. Be like the Bonnie and Clyde of the seas.'

'They were shot dead by the police,' said Ros.

'She is pissing me right off,' said Patrick. He took a breath and turned back to Darla. 'What do you say?'

'Stop this now.' She stared him down. She wasn't afraid and she wanted him to end the madness for his own sake as much as the bother it was going to get her into.

'Or what? There is literally nothing you can do.' Patrick stood at one of the wheels, and put his hand on the throttle. The motor upped its purring.

Darla was starting to panic. There was still nobody about. She decided to yell anyway. 'Help! Help!'

'Seriously?' Patrick shook his head at her and began to gently steer the boat away from its mooring. 'This is easy,' he said, his tongue sticking out slightly like it always did when he was concentrating. The yacht was inching backwards so he started to turn the wheel. It was a tight berth with an equally big yacht moored alongside. His inexperience quickly became apparent as a harsh scraping sound indicated something was wrong. 'What the hell?'

'Apparently it's not that easy,' said Ros, pointing to their anchor now caught on the boat next to them, which was making the rest of the boat turn into the pontoon and wedging them fast.

'Shit!' Patrick was getting cross. 'What do I do?' he yelled.

'I know but I'm not telling you,' said Ros, standing up to inspect the yacht's position.

'I can't believe this,' said Patrick, abandoning the wheel and going over to see what Ros was looking at. 'You're no help!'

'Thank you,' said Ros, blocking Patrick's way.

'Hey!' came a yell from the docks.

Darla spun around to see Cameron racing along the quay on his bike. She frantically waved back. 'Get help! He's nicking the yacht!' Cameron leapt from his bike, ran along the pontoon and jumped towards the side of the boat and grabbed hold of the guardrail wire, making the whole vessel rock. He hung there for a moment, looking at Darla. 'Not the best rescue,' she said.

'Thanks. You could give me a hand,' he said, clinging on the side of the boat.

'Who the hell is this joker?' said Patrick, making a move towards Cameron. Ros stepped in front of Patrick to block him and give Cameron a chance to climb safely on board.

Patrick pushed Ros firmly out of the way, making her topple over the back of the cockpit seat and disappear from view, landing with a thud on the deck. 'Whoops, sorry!' he called after her. As he turned around he walked straight into Cameron's fist and went down like an anchor.

'Ow, shit, that hurt,' said Cameron, shaking his hand and stepping over Patrick to get a look at where Ros had fallen. 'Bloody hell,' he said, looking shocked. Cameron handed Darla his phone. 'Call an ambulance,' he said before jumping over the seats to help Ros. Darla peered around him. Ros was lying on the deck as motionless as Patrick, but there was a pool of blood around her head. Darla gasped. The boat started to swim as her stomach churned at the sight of the blood.

'Stop! Police!' yelled someone, as a policeman pointed a taser at Cameron and Darla passed out.

Chapter Thirty-One

Ros was aware of a lot of anxious voices. 'Shhh,' she said, trying to sit up.

'Thank heavens you're awake. No, no, no, don't move,' said Cameron with abject panic in his voice.

'Whyever not?' asked Ros, shuffling herself upright so she could lean against the back of the seating. She tried to focus on the blurry faces in front of her.

'You've had an accident,' said Darla, who was rather pale and quickly looked away.

Ros mentally scanned her body. She'd likely bruised her bum, otherwise everything felt normal. 'I'm absolutely fine.'

'It looks like you hit your head on the metal cleat as you went over the back of the seat. The ambulance is on its way,' explained Cameron.

'I definitely don't need an ambulance,' said Ros.

'You do,' said Darla, still averting her eyes.

'Don't be ridiculous.' Ros put out her hand to push herself up further and felt something wet and gloopy. She looked at her palm to see it was dripping with blood. 'What on earth?' She looked to Darla for an explanation but Darla was now hiding behind a cushion.

'It's coming from your head,' said Darla. 'I'm sorry but I can't clear it up or I'll be sick.' She retched at the end of the sentence. Just the thought of it was apparently enough to unsettle her stomach.

Ros felt around her head with her clean hand until she found a wet patch. When she looked at her palm she was surprised to see that too was now covered in blood. 'Goodness. I think you're right. It's strange because it doesn't really hurt.'

'How much longer until the ambulance gets here?' called Darla.

'Almost here,' called back a police officer.

Darla told Ros that it was the nice officer who had checked that Darla was okay after she'd fainted and who had been quite keen to taser Cameron seeing as he was the only person standing whilst three other people were all strewn on the deck. Cameron had explained that it was him who had made the 999 call after receiving a text from Ros but the police officer hadn't been keen to believe him. Thankfully Darla had quickly come round and backed up Cameron's version of events.

Cameron crouched behind Ros so she could lean against him. 'You okay?' he asked.

'I feel fine. But obviously . . .' Ros waved her bloodstained hands and that was Darla's cue to make a dash for the toilets below deck.

'You had us worried there.' Cameron passed her a clean tissue.

'Sorry,' she said, wiping her hands.

Cameron scanned her with worried eyes. 'I thought that you . . . it really scared me. I'm still pretty scared,' he added, glancing at the blood.

'A little bit of blood goes a long way and the head is covered in blood vessels. What happened to Patrick?'

'I tied him up with the mooring line. He's got a worse headache than you. Well, he's complaining more.'

'You could have killed me!' Patrick shouted from the other side of the boat where police were handcuffing him.

Ros smiled over her shoulder at Cameron. 'You came to our rescue.'

'Of course I did.' The way he looked at her made her giddy or perhaps it was the head injury.

'You're lovely,' she said and then instantly wished she hadn't. 'I think maybe I've got concussion,' she added hastily in an attempt to hide her embarrassment. She was grateful for the sound of the siren that interrupted them.

Twenty minutes later the police were taking Patrick off to the station for a chat while Ros was having her head examined by a paramedic. 'Now it's stopped bleeding I could probably stitch it up here,' said the paramedic. 'But because you were unconscious we need to get you checked over at hospital anyway, so I'll let them do it as I stitch like Dr Frankenstein.' Only he laughed at his joke. 'Tough crowd,' he said with a shrug.

'Unconscious? I was out for less than a minute. That hardly needs hospitalisation. I'd be grateful if you could stitch me up here, please,' said Ros.

The paramedic winced and pointed upwards. 'The

powers that be say I need to take you in.'

'You are not employed by God,' said Ros. 'And I'm fairly certain you cannot force me to go somewhere I don't want to go, as I believe that would be kidnapping.'

'Ros, come on. He's trying to help,' said Cameron.

'And I really do appreciate his medical expertise, but with an overrun NHS I don't want to add to their problems when I'm perfectly fine.'

'I'd be happier if you went to hospital,' said Cameron.

'Me too,' said Darla, who was now out of the toilet but still rather pale.

Ros looked at the paramedic. He made an exaggerated puffing noise. 'I don't want to add abduction to my CV but there's loads of paperwork I have to fill in if you won't go. Well, it's one form but still, I could do without it.'

Ros felt defeated. 'Fine, but I still think it's unnecessary and I will be leaving as soon as possible.'

'Fair enough,' said the paramedic. 'I'll get the stretcher chair.'

'You'll do no such thing,' said Ros. 'Cameron, help me up please.'

'Independent, isn't she?' said the paramedic.

'Militantly so,' said Cameron, putting his arm around Ros and helping her to her feet.

As Ros had expected, the wait at the hospital was tedious and long but the nurses were really nice, and once she was through the waiting a lovely doctor checked her over and to her satisfaction declared that she just needed to be stitched up and sent home with a checklist of things to look out for in case she showed any signs of concussion. Thankfully she wasn't in any real pain with the exception of her bruised backside. They had given her painkillers for her head but she'd had worse headaches. Ros was sitting quietly and listening to the doctor and nurse chat whilst they stitched up her head, when she became aware of raised voices heading her way – unsettlingly familiar voices at that.

'Hold on,' said the doctor, as the curtain was pulled back to reveal her father and mother.

'They're my parents,' said Ros by way of apology. 'What are you doing here?' she asked them whilst also giving wide eyes at Cameron and Darla. Darla pointed at Cameron.

'Cabbage! What happened?' Barry looked shocked.

'We know what happened. Cameron said she'd been pushed over by a con man.' Amanda was scowling at Barry. 'Is your memory affected?'

Barry ignored her and came to stand next to Ros and hold her hand. 'Are you okay?'

'I'm absolutely fine,' said Ros.

'Is she okay?' Barry asked the doctor.

'I'm just tying off the last stitch then she's good to go. Did someone give you the concussion checklist?' he asked Ros.

'I've got it,' said Cameron. 'I'll take good care of her.'

'I know you will,' said Barry. Ros was heartened by the look that passed between the two men.

'What were you doing on a boat with a con man?' asked Amanda.

Ros replayed the whole thing in her mind. 'It's too complicated to explain. But in summary, not my con man,

271

not my boat, simply in the wrong place at the wrong time.'

'You'll need to speak to the police,' said Darla to Ros. 'Patrick could have . . .' Darla swallowed hard; the events had obviously upset her.

'Killed her?' prompted Amanda. 'I suppose that could have been the case.' She turned to Cameron. 'Was that why you called us?'

'I was worried she was not going to let them treat her and I thought if you were here . . .' he nodded at Barry '. . . she'd listen to you.'

'I doubt it,' said Barry with a warm smile at his daughter. 'But I'm glad you called us,' he added.

Ros pressed her lips together. She knew this was one of those moments when it was best that she kept her thoughts to herself. She also knew that whatever Cameron had done, however rash, he would have done it with her best interests in mind.

The nurse began removing things around them. 'All done,' said the doctor. 'You'll need to get in touch with your GP practice about getting the stitches removed in ten days.'

'Thank you,' said Ros and Barry shook the doctor's hand.

'Let's get you home,' said Cameron, sliding an arm around her to help her to her feet.

'Are we all going back to Ros's?' asked Barry.

'No,' said Ros and Cameron together.

'I think it's best that she rests,' said Cameron. 'I'll call you later to let you know how she is.'

'But I will be fine,' said Ros.

Cameron held her gently around her waist and guided

her out of the cubicle and into the corridor. 'I felt I needed backup so I called Barry. Sorry,' he whispered in her ear.

'You should be,' she whispered back with a smile.

**

After the hospital Darla went to the police station to give a statement. She knew if she didn't do it as soon as possible she'd only keep putting it off. The police officer she saw was patient and understanding, and giving a statement was a lot easier than she'd expected, but then she'd only ever seen TV programmes where police were interrogating the bad guys. Next she went to see the owner of the boat. She'd given his details to the police so she guessed if he hadn't already he'd be getting a visit from them. His house was just as she'd expected: modern, stylish and blooming huge. She knocked on his door and waited. A heavily made-up woman in her forties opened it.

'Yeah?' She was scanning Darla up and down as if expecting her to be delivering something.

'Hi, I'm here to see Mr Rogers.'

'He's out. I'm his wife. What did you want him for?'

Darla rummaged in her bag. This might be the cheat's way out but she was going to take it. 'Please can you give him these? They're the keys to his yacht. I'm Darla and I suspect he won't want me cleaning it after today so—'

'Oh hell, you're the girl who was kidnapped? Come in,' she said, taking Darla by the arm and giving her no choice as she pulled her inside.

'Actually it only drifted like a couple of feet away from the pontoon before we got wedged so I wasn't really kid—'

'Let me get you a drink. Tea, coffee, something stronger

for your nerves? Brandy!' But before Darla could choose the woman had disappeared, leaving Darla alone in the vast hallway. She reversed back and grinned at Darla. 'This way, lovey, come and sit down and you can tell me all about it.'

The living room was huge and had three very large white leather sofas. Darla perched on the edge of the nearest one and noticed the seat was covered in muddy paw prints. The woman held out a large brandy. 'Actually, I've got my car so I won't have a drink but thank you,' said Darla, keen to hand over the keys and leave.

'After the shock you've had, leave your car here and I'll pay for a taxi home. Get that down you.'

Darla stared at the glass.

'I insist,' said the woman, who didn't look like she was going to give in easily.

The stalemate got the better of her and Darla took the brandy. 'Thank you.'

'I'm forgetting my manners. My name's Margy.' She offered a limp hand, which Darla shook.

Margy came to sit next to her. She rubbed at the ingrained dirt on the seat before sitting down. 'Blooming dogs. I love them but the mess they make.'

'White vinegar and water,' said Darla almost automatically.

'That won't go with brandy.'

'No, for the stains. Mix equal parts white vinegar and water and dab it on the muddy patches, leave it for five minutes and then wipe off with a clean damp cloth.'

'I'll tell my cleaner to try that. Is it a secret formula?'

'I work a lot with animals.' Darla sipped the brandy and

274

it almost took her breath away. 'I expect Mr Rogers is quite cross, is he?'

'He was spitting feathers.'

Shit, thought Darla, was she going to get sued? Could he get her prosecuted? That was the last thing she needed. 'I'm really very sorry. You see—'

'Oh lovey, not with you.' Margy patted Darla's knee. 'With the fool who stole the yacht.'

'I thought he'd blame me and sack me.'

'Goodness, no. This isn't your fault,' said Margy.

Darla took a deep breath. 'It kind of was. The man who tried to steal the yacht was my ex-boyfriend, so it was me he followed to the boat. I wouldn't blame Mr Rogers if he didn't want me anywhere near his yacht from now on.'

'You silly thing. He'd have me to answer to if he suggested sacking you. And he wouldn't dream of it. He thinks you do a wonderful job.' Darla couldn't help but feel a little stab of pride. 'No, he doesn't blame you at all. It's all the fault of that kidnapper who almost murdered your friend. Terrible business. Is she in intensive care, your friend?'

'Err, no, she's gone home.' Darla wasn't sure if Margy looked relieved or disappointed. 'But she has lots of stitches in her head and might have concussion,' added Darla.

Margy gasped. 'The poor thing. And you witnessed it all. Now tell me everything. I mean it, don't leave anything out.' Margy fixed her with a steely gaze.

Darla took another sip of brandy and winced. She feared this was going to be a long story.

Chapter Thirty-Two

Ros wasn't used to being waited on hand and foot but she could see how a person could easily get used to it. Cameron couldn't do enough for her, and there was a regular supply of hot and cold drinks. He was also checking her vision hourly and counting down to her next lot of medication. He'd insisted on her going to bed against her better judgement, but the doctor had said she should take it easy for a couple of days so it would have been churlish to argue.

'I think you should have a snooze,' he said.

'I'm not eighty. I won't sleep tonight if I have an afternoon nap.'

'I thought I'd cook my paella tonight so I need to pop out to get the ingredients and I don't like to leave you.'

'It would still be leaving me if I was asleep,' pointed out Ros.

'True but I'd not feel as bad about it. Plus if you're asleep you're less likely to get up and injure yourself further.'

'Cameron. I'm fine. All that you're doing is really lovely but I'm fixed now so you don't need to worry.'

He flopped onto the bed, making her bounce a little. 'It

scared the life out of me seeing you and all that blood. I thought . . .' He swallowed and shook his head. 'It makes you realise how fragile life can be. How one moment everything is fine and the next it's not and you have no idea what is going to flip it.' He was looking at her with an intensity she'd not seen from him before and it held her attention. 'Sometimes it's the oddest things that give you perspective.' He took a deep breath. 'You see it made me think that maybe—' The entry buzzer sounded and interrupted him. 'I'll get that.' He jumped to his feet and left.

Ros could only hear a muffled conversation so was more than a little startled when Alastair and Sonia walked into her bedroom. 'Oh my word, your place is soooo fancy!' said Sonia with a wave of her arm.

Alastair cleared his throat. 'We heard you'd been hurt so I thought I'd better come and see how bad it was. We had a whip-round and got you these.' He awkwardly held out a large bunch of flowers.

Ros was surprised and touched by the gesture. 'You didn't need to do that, but they're beautiful and I appreciate it, thank you.'

Cameron hovered at the door. 'I'll put those in water when I get back. I just need to nip out to get the stuff for dinner. Okay?'

Ros smiled at him seizing the opportunity to not leave her alone. 'Of course.'

Alastair handed Cameron the flowers and then shoved his hands in his pockets. 'You look all right,' he said.

'Thankfully it was the back of my head.' Ros twisted around and lifted her hair.

Sonia gasped. 'Bloody hell. You proper cracked your head open. Shouldn't you be in hospital?'

'Really, I'm fine,' said Ros, putting her hair back in place. She'd noticed that it was a lot more tender now than it had been when she'd done it. The human body had a remarkable way of managing serious pain and yet a paper cut was incredibly tender – baffling.

'But you could have brain damage from something like that.'

Ros laughed and then realised Sonia was serious. 'I have my skull to protect my brain. But thank you for your concern.'

'Still, I'd be careful.' Sonia pouted and had a look about her of someone who had seen it all before.

'I expect your man is taking good care of you,' said Alastair. As if on cue the front door clicked as Cameron let himself out.

'Cameron has been great. I messaged him that someone was using threatening behaviour and that we were on the yacht and he came as fast as he could.' Even though Patrick was a completely incompetent boat thief Ros wasn't sure what they would have done if Cameron hadn't arrived when he did. If Patrick had managed to reverse out of the mooring bay and sailed off with them on board it would have been an even bigger fiasco.

'Cameron's a proper knight in shining armour,' said Sonia, although she was now paying more attention to the room than to Ros. 'Do you rent this place?'

Even Alastair rolled his eyes at Sonia. 'No, I own it,' said Ros.

'Must have cost a bit.' Sonia was looking out of the

window at the view of the harbour.

'Anyway, we're not stopping,' said Alastair. 'Just wanted to check you were all right.'

'I thought we'd at least have a cuppa,' said Sonia, looking at Ros.

'Sorry. Did you want me to put the kettle on?' asked Ros, sitting up.

Sonia nodded.

'No, thanks,' said Alastair. 'We're fine. You need to rest.' He shot another disparaging glance at Sonia who shrugged her lack of comprehension at what she might have done wrong. 'We'd best get off,' he added.

'Not before I've used the loo. Where is it?' asked Sonia, already leaving the room.

'Next door on the right,' said Ros.

Sonia disappeared and after a few moments, when Ros highly suspected Sonia was checking out the rest of the apartment, they heard the click of the bathroom door. 'Sorry about her,' said Alastair. 'She insisted on coming with me. I couldn't really say no without looking like a dick.'

'I understand. It's fine,' said Ros. 'It was very kind of you both to visit.' It was an odd thing to be having a conversation in her bedroom with someone who not long ago had been her arch nemesis.

Alastair scratched his head. 'I thought I should check you were okay what with you and me being mates now.'

Ros failed to hide her astonishment. 'Oh, right. Of course. Thank you.' She couldn't help but feel an odd sense of achievement at Alastair classing her as a mate although she didn't want to think too much about the implications.

There was an awkward silence, making Ros long for Sonia's return, something she'd not ever expected to experience. Alastair jolted as if suddenly hitting on something he could say. 'I was at the golf club a couple of nights ago trying to schmooze a head honcho from this big IT company but no dice.' Ros wasn't sure she was entirely following the conversation but she nodded along to show interest. 'Anyway, he said they needed someone to head up the risk team and I recommended you.' Alastair pulled his shoulders back, looking quite pleased with himself.

'That was good of you to think of me, but I'm not looking to change jobs right now.'

'Don't be too hasty to reject it. It had international something in the title,' he added. 'I gave him your phone number. I hope that was okay.'

'Not really,' said Ros and Alastair looked confused. 'Women don't like strange men having their contact details.'

'Oh, he's a sound fella, not a perve or anything. He's a member of the golf club.'

'That's all right then,' said Ros, trying to hide her sarcasm but Alastair was smiling so hopefully he'd not noticed.

At last they heard the toilet flush and both greeted Sonia with smiles worthy of a long-absent relative. 'Right, we're going then,' said Alastair. 'Take good care of yourself.'

'I'll update everyone in the office,' said Sonia.

'I'm sure you will,' said Ros. 'Thank you for coming,' she added quickly.

'We'll see ourselves out,' said Alastair. He gave her an awkward wave and ushered Sonia out of the bedroom. Ros breathed a sigh of relief although she was touched by the visit. Her work colleagues were definitely better people when she took the time to get to know them.

The thought of a cup of tea was now at the forefront of Ros's mind. It wasn't like she lived in a house and had stairs to tackle – she was perfectly safe to move around one level unassisted. She got out of bed and carefully made her way to the kitchen. Why was she being so cautious? Cameron was lovely but he was fussing somewhat and it was rubbing off on her and making her wary. She gave herself a metaphorical shake. She had been discharged from hospital and therefore was perfectly fit. If it had happened a few months ago she would have been living there alone and would have been more than capable of getting herself a hot drink.

Ros put the kettle on and marvelled at the influence Cameron was having on her. She knew it came from the fact he was a caring individual but she did not want to generate any level of dependency on him. She got out a mug and as she turned she noticed the flowers in the sink. He had put some water in there for them but they would be far better in a vase. Ros carefully crouched down, opened the bottom cupboard and looked inside for a suitable-size vase. Too small and not all the stems would fit, too big and they would splay out and look droopy and ridiculous.

Ros found the one she wanted and pulled it towards her. She heard the apartment door open and was straightening up with the vase held firmly in her grasp when Cameron screamed at her. 'Stop!' She froze.

Cameron strode over and slammed shut the wall cupboard door above her. 'What the hell are you doing? You almost stood up and whacked your head on the corner of that bloody cupboard!' His voice was almost a shout.

Ros slowly straightened up and put the vase down carefully on the worktop. Cameron was pacing around the small kitchen space. 'When you've stopped yelling I will explain.'

'I'm not yelling,' he said, taking his voice down a fraction, but it was still louder than his usual volume and it irked her. 'If you'd have cracked your skull on that corner in the same place as your stitches . . .' He ran his hands over his face as if trying to hide from the thought.

'But I didn't. I am fine.'

Exasperated, he threw his hands up. 'But you wouldn't have been if I'd come back a couple of minutes later.' He audibly sucked in a breath. 'I would have found you.' He pointed at the floor as if imagining a bloody scene.

'Again, that did not happen. Do you think perhaps you could think rationally?' she asked.

'Bloody hell, Ros,' he snapped and she recoiled slightly. 'You promised you would stay in bed. I blame myself. I shouldn't have left you.'

'I'm not a child.'

'No, they do as they're told,' he said, his expression almost a glare.

'I think that's evidence that you have very little experience of children.'

'Not the point. What did you get up for anyway?' he asked.

'A cup of tea.' Ros picked up the mug and he snatched it from her.

'I will get you a cup of tea and I will put the flowers in water, like I said I would. Will you please go back to bed?'

Ros pursed her lips. She could do as he asked but it wasn't in her nature to acquiesce so easily. 'I think you are overreacting. I have been discharged from hospital. I am perfectly fine.'

Cameron did not look happy. 'You are meant to be resting. Those were the instructions from the doctor.'

'Making tea isn't exactly exerting myself.'

He blinked slowly. 'You gave me a fright. I thought you were in bed. When I walked through the door I could see what you were about to do and it scared the life out of me. Can you understand that it was a shock?'

'I can. Now may I make my cup of—'

'I'd be happier if you let me do it,' he said.

There was a long pause as Ros considered whether or not to make a stand but she was feeling a little out of sorts after being upright for a while so she nodded and made her way around the kitchen counter. Somehow she managed to drag her foot where the tiles met carpet and she stumbled forward. Cameron was there in an instant and strong arms caught her. He pulled her into a hug. Ros's heart hammered in her chest and she could feel his doing the same. Maybe it was a good thing he was there. She felt so protected from everything when he held her like that.

He slowly released his hold and checked her over. They were both breathing heavily and she wasn't entirely sure that was all down to her nearly tripping over. Being in Cameron's arms stirred something intense within her. His face was close to hers, his eyes searching her face as if he was awaiting a prompt. For a second she thought he was going to kiss her.

His mobile rang and the moment was gone. Cameron kept hold of Ros with one hand and pulled out his phone with the other. 'It's Gina,' he said.

'Then you'd better take her call,' she said, unable to stop a sad sigh from escaping.

***

When the taxi finally dropped Darla back at The Brambles the sky was turning a vibrant orange. She yawned as she let herself in. The brandy and trauma of the day had taken their toll on her, but she still had the menagerie to feed.

'Darla?' Elliott rushed into the hallway. 'Thank heavens you're all right.' He scanned her up and down. 'You are all right, aren't you?' The concern on his face warmed her heart.

'Why? What's happened?'

'Marc rang to tell me about his yacht being stolen.'

'Marc?' She screwed up her face in thought. Thinking was much harder after alcohol. 'Oh, you mean Mr Rogers. His wife is really nice. She paid for a caxi tab.' There was something wrong with that sentence but she couldn't quite put her finger on what it was.

'You're drunk?' Elliott sounded confused rather than judgemental.

'Very, very long story. It took three large brandies to get to the end.'

'Shall I get you a coffee?'

She shook her head and then wished she hadn't because

284

now the hat stand was swaying – or maybe it was her. 'I need to feed the animals.'

'All done. I've been waiting for a couple of hours. Had to keep busy somehow.'

'Then maybe a coffee would be good please. And a large water. As long as I don't have to go over the story again.'

Elliott smiled. 'Not if you don't want to. As long as you're not hurt.'

She went to follow him through to the kitchen but the wall was bending round to the left. Funny, it had never done that before. Darla reached out to steady herself, missed and bumped into the kitchen doorframe.

'Steady on,' said Elliott, spinning around and grabbing hold of her. He had his arms tight around her and his face was suddenly very close to hers. He had lovely eyes. She realised they had been looking into each other's eyes for far too long. She had two choices. Pull apart and risk falling over or make the most of the opportunity and kiss him. Darla went in for the kiss.

Chapter Thirty-Three

In her mind Darla had thought it would be an incredibly romantic moment. However, in reality her gusto was ill-timed and instead of a passionate kiss she headbutted Elliott with some force. But to his credit despite the surprise attack he didn't let her go, which was good because her legs had gone a bit wobbly.

'Shit, that hurt,' said Elliott.

'Sorry,' said Darla. 'Ow,' she added somewhat belatedly as her eye socket began to throb. 'You know I didn't mean to headbutt you right?' She ran her lip through her teeth. This was embarrassing. 'Sorry.'

'It's okay. I'm flattered that you wanted to kiss me. Slightly worried about your motor skills, but flattered nonetheless.' Elliott chuckled. 'When I'd pictured that moment, it had gone differently in my mind. By differently I mean better.' He gave her a look that made her stomach flip in a good way.

'You've thought about kissing me?' she asked.

Elliott skilfully manoeuvred her onto a kitchen chair. 'I might have done.' He turned all embarrassed and bumped into the table twice as he tried to go around it. 'Ice. We need ice for head bumps.'

'Oooh, talking of head bumps. You should have seen Ros.' Darla felt her stomach lurch as she remembered all the blood, and this time it wasn't such a pleasant sensation. 'She has lots of stitches on her head.'

'Is she okay?' asked Elliott, rummaging in the freezer and then in a nearby drawer. He pulled out a carrier bag and some tea towels.

'Yeah, she is surprisingly okay. We've been messaging since it happened and Cameron is looking after her really well.'

'There you go,' said Elliott, placing something cold on her forehead. He waved a bag of peas and wrapped them in another tea towel. 'We've got half a bag each. Now to make some coffee.'

Darla watched him as he made the drinks with one hand while balancing the peas on his head with the other. She'd given him a proper whack and now her head was throbbing. He brought her coffee over first and then sat down with his.

They sat on kitchen chairs, one hand on their pea ice packs and the other on their coffee mugs, in companiable silence. 'It's not how I thought I'd be spending my evening,' he said.

'Oh goodness, shouldn't you be feeding some lambs?'

'No, thankfully they don't need feeding as often now. Apart from little um . . . there's a tiny one who is smaller than the others but she can go another hour before she needs her next bottle.'

'Did you name her?' She watched the burly man go all coy.

'I might have done.' He broke eye contact and sipped his drink.

'Go on then. What did you call her?' Darla had a feeling it was something embarrassing. 'I once had a goldfish named Sharky,' she added in the hope it would make him a little more at ease about sharing what he'd called the little lamb.

He rearranged his ice pack and looked decidedly uncomfortable. 'I called her Darla.'

'That's the nicest thing any man has done for me since Phillip Yates saved up to buy me a Barbie bedside lamp,' she said.

Elliott was looking mildly alarmed.

'I said "man" but we were both nine at the time.'

'Okay, slightly less weird.'

Darla shuffled her kitchen chair closer to his and at the risk of banging heads again she leaned in until their bags of peas touched, and then he kissed her.

***

Ros had managed one afternoon of doing very little, but anything past that was proving difficult. She'd agreed to have the rest of the week off work so that she was properly rested. Cameron was being attentive and whilst that was nice she also wanted to get back to her normal life. Thankfully Darla was coming round and Ros was looking forward to seeing her.

'Don't you need to get going?' Ros pointed at the clock. Cameron usually left before now to get to the cocktail bar for his shift.

'It's okay. I'll leave in a minute.'

'You know you don't need to hand over responsibility for me to Darla. I'm virtually back to normal. Apart from the clumpy hair that I desperately want to wash.'

'They said forty-eight hours and then only with warm water. Don't you dare do that while I'm out.' He wagged a finger at her.

'I won't. Go on, go.' She opened the door and tried to shoo him out.

He chewed the inside of his mouth and held up a finger as if he was desperately trying to think of something else to stall his departure. 'Remember, I got you that non-alcoholic cocktail mix because you can't drink right now.'

'I know. It's in the fridge. My memory is fine. Now please leave before you are late.'

He frantically looked about the apartment. 'I just need to—'

The buzzer sounded and the look of relief on Cameron's face was obvious. 'That'll be Darla. I'll let her in on my way out. Bye.'

Ros smiled after him. He really was the nicest human being she'd ever met. Gina was a very lucky woman. It was hard not to feel dispirited. At least Ros was doing her best to enjoy her time with him. Maybe a bit too much sometimes. She knew she'd have to let him go at some point soon. She felt that was likely going to be the lowest point of her life – losing her dad and Cameron simultaneously. She needed to mentally strengthen herself in readiness.

It seemed to take Darla a lot longer than usual to make it from the downstairs entry to Ros's front door. At last, she appeared. She pointed over her shoulder. 'He's like a mother hen.'

'He means well,' said Ros from the sofa.

'He gave me a list,' said Darla, brandishing a piece of paper. 'And strict instructions not to tire you out and to call if there was anything wrong. It's like pet-sitting that pug with the gammy leg. His owners were just the same. They kept video-calling and I swear even the dog started eye rolling every time the phone went off.' Darla pulled a bottle of fizz from her bag. 'Anyway, we need glasses. We have loads to talk about.'

'I can't have alcohol.' Ros pointed at the bottle.

'It's non-alcoholic. It probably tastes like shite but at least it has bubbles.'

'Are we celebrating?' Ros got the feeling she was missing something.

'You could say that.' Darla got out glasses, filled them up and brought them over to the sofa.

'Go on then. Explain,' said Ros, holding her glass and pausing, unsure if she could have a sip or if she was waiting for a toast.

'I kept my job. The yacht owner was actually really grateful that we stopped his boat being stolen and gave me extra cash to clean it up after the police and everyone had traipsed all over it. Turns out baking soda and white vinegar gets bloodstains off wood as well as loads of other substances. Teak decking is a tricky one to get clean. I was almost ill at the sight of the bucket's contents afterwards.' Darla pulled a face.

'Sorry,' said Ros tentatively, unsure as to whether she should apologise as it was her blood, even though technically it was not her fault it had been shed on the boat deck.

'No worries. It's all gone now.'

'Here's to you keeping your job?' suggested Ros, raising her glass.

'And kissing Elliott,' said Darla.

'You can't just say that without giving me more information.'

Darla took a swig of the fizz. 'Actually not bad.'

'The fizz or Elliott's kiss?' asked Ros.

'Both.' Darla grinned at her. And repositioned herself as if readying herself for an epic storytelling session. 'It was dead romantic, apart from the frozen peas.'

'You've lost me,' said Ros, taking a sip of the fizz and nodding her approval.

Darla gave her a speedy update on what had happened with Elliott. 'And then he was all gallant and wouldn't take it any further because I'd had the brandy. Since then we've been flirty texting and I'm calling in at his tonight after leaving you.'

Darla looked happy and it was lovely to see. 'I'm pleased for you. It means you're moving on from Patrick, which is a good thing. I hope you'll be very happy.'

Darla laughed. 'We're not getting married. It might not go anywhere but he's one of the good guys. I've got a few months left at The Brambles so I might as well make the most of my time there. And some fun with Elliott will be the cherry on the top.'

'Okay. Just don't get hurt.'

'It was me who headbutted him so . . .' Darla grinned.

'You know what I mean. It's far too easy to go along with

291

something thinking everything is clear and straightforward, but you can't plan for emotions. They catch you out. You think it's just a short-term agreement but before you know it, you're falling in love with someone.'

Darla stared at Ros and then threw her arms in the air in a dramatic fashion. 'Bloody hell, Ros. You're in love with Cameron. Aren't you?'

'What? Noooooo.' She could feel heat in her cheeks. 'I was talking about you and the farmer.'

'No, you weren't. You've fallen for the fake boyfriend.'

'I don't think so,' said Ros. Although she feared Darla may have found the simple explanation to how she had been feeling recently and behind her growing attachment to Cameron. She'd not felt like this before and she couldn't say it was something she'd recommend, especially when it wasn't reciprocated and was never likely to be.

Ros puffed out a sigh. 'Even if I have – and I'm not admitting it, merely pursuing your suggestion as a possibility – then it's pointless because Cameron is in love with Gina. I just need to recalibrate. Well, I would if I was in love with him, which I'm not.' She broke eye contact because it felt like lying, probably not just to Darla but also to herself.

'Oh, sweetie. You're a terrible liar. Unreciprocated loved sucks. I know, ask Phillip Yates.'

'Who?'

'Long story involving a Barbie lamp. Never mind.' Darla wrapped her in a hug. Ros would usually make such things brief but she was starting to appreciate the benefits of comforting human contact and recognised that today she needed a hug. She was feeling sorry for herself.

Darla pulled back to look at her friend. 'Are we one hundred per cent watertight on the Gina thing?'

'Yep,' said Ros flatly.

'She'd better be worth upsetting my best friend for.'

'I'm afraid she is,' said Ros.

Darla let go and wriggled back into her seat. 'What you need is an exit strategy. So that when the time comes to stop playing at boyfriend, girlfriend and flatmates, it doesn't break your heart.'

'I think a clean break might be the answer. Maybe have a change of scenery – even a new challenge perhaps.'

'Good idea. Now tell me about this Gina. She can't be that brilliant. There must be something to hate about Jaunty Gina.'

'Nope, she's annoyingly perfect.' Ros sipped her fizz and wished it had been the real deal to numb a very different pain from the one in her head.

'Perfect people are very hard to find fault with. Bitch,' said Darla with feeling and Ros laughed.

Chapter Thirty-Four

Ros had had one of her best days at work ever and was retelling it to a rapt Cameron as they made dinner together. It was her first day back at work after the incident on the yacht and it was like she had been elevated to some sort of hero status as everyone wanted to speak to her including Berlinda. Although she did have to tone down the story that was circulating because the version of events that Sonia had relayed made it sound more like a remake of *Pirates of the Caribbean* but with less rum and more bloodshed.

She'd also had a phone call from Alastair's golf club associate and she had to admit that the job he had available did sound interesting, so she had arranged to meet him after work the following week, by which time she was confident she would be using shampoo again.

'Get you being one of the cool girls,' said Cameron, giving her arm a nudge as they chopped salad vegetables side by side like synchronised chefs.

'I wouldn't go that far but work does feel different from how it used to. And now I think about it, I feel different too.' They looked at each other and she had to look away.

He stopped chopping and turned towards her. 'How so?' he asked.

She thought for a moment to consider her reply. 'It's all your fault,' she said, wagging her finger at him, pretending to tell him off. 'You've encouraged me to take risks, against my better judgement and training, and it's shown me that there are varying levels of engagement from the superficial to the significant that can deliver benefits.'

Cameron snorted a laugh. 'In other words, people are all right when you take a bit of time to get to know them.'

'Exactly what I said.'

Cameron leaned forward and Ros held her breath. He kissed the top of her head. 'You're a legend, Rosanna Foster.'

Somehow her full name didn't grate on her when he said it.

They chatted over their meal about everything and nothing. The mundane and pointless that had so often irked her before was a pleasure to exchange with Cameron. They were stacking the dishwasher when the buzzer went. Ros went to answer it. She was mildly concerned when she heard it was her dad and doubly disturbed when she realised Amanda was also with him. 'This can't be good,' she said to Cameron while she waited for them to make it to the top floor.

'It's probably nothing.'

'And that takes both of them, does it?'

'Perhaps they just want to check you're okay,' he said.

'I spoke to Dad earlier, where I confirmed that I was

completely fine. I'm not feeling fine now though.' She felt sick.

He gave her a reassuring squeeze. She was going to miss those. 'Whatever it is, we'll face it together. You've got this.'

Ros took a deep breath and opened the door. Gazza was first inside as usual and overjoyed to see them. She wished she could say the same. Barry gave her a tight hug, but her mother's embrace was considerably briefer and less effusive. Cameron made a fuss of the dog and her parents went and sat on the sofa. There was definitely something wrong.

'Can I get either of you a tea or coffee?' offered Ros.

'Or something stronger?' suggested Cameron.

'Have you got any wine?' asked Barry.

This was definitely not a good sign. She looked at Cameron and she knew that he was on her wavelength. He gave her a commiseratory smile. Even the eternally positive Cameron had sensed it. 'I'll get the drinks; you sit down,' he said to Ros.

She steeled herself and joined her parents, whereupon Gazza had a renewed bout of excitement at her close proximity. Ros had to admit there was something mollifying about the level of adoration the little canine showed her. She gave him a rub around his ears. She could wash her hands later.

'You look well,' said Barry.

'He means how's the head injury? Any lasting damage?' asked Amanda.

'That's not what I meant. But anyway, is it all okay now?' asked Barry.

'No issues at all. I went back to work today. I'm having

my stitches out on Friday. How about you?' She swallowed hard, braced herself for his response and wished Cameron would hurry up with the drinks.

Cameron had perfect timing as he handed round glasses and put down a bowl of water for Gazza. He sat down right next to Ros, so close she could feel the warmth of his thigh against hers. She was grateful for his presence. She feared this was the bad news she'd been expecting for some time. But to look at her father he appeared bright and well – it was like hope was taunting her.

'I've got something to say,' said Barry, picking up his wine glass. Ros reached for Cameron's hand and it was there. Barry noticed the gesture and smiled. 'I've not been entirely truthful with you.' Ros found she was looking to her mother for some sort of clarification but her deadpan expression gave nothing away. Barry continued. 'I mentioned to you, Ros, about a drugs trial I've been offered at the hospital, and I know you weren't keen but I signed up anyway. I figured that maybe you were right that they just wanted guinea pigs, but if by being a guinea pig I could help someone else then what did I have to lose? Turns out I had everything to gain. Now don't go getting excited because this is definitely not a cure but I've been on the medication for a few weeks now and the tests show that the cancer is currently under control. I don't know how much time it will buy me but there's a bloke in Australia who was the first to use it and he's still here two years later, so let's keep our fingers crossed.'

Ros went down on her knees, so she was the right level to give him the biggest hug and she held on tight to her dad. She'd never dared to hope for a miracle but here it was. She wasn't one for tears but the ones now coursing down her face she couldn't control. Happiness and immense relief came over her in waves. She wasn't losing her dad, well, not just yet anyway. She had no idea what the future held but for now she was going to enjoy this moment of respite and be thankful that he'd not listened to her advice.

'Brilliant news, Barry,' said Cameron, shaking him warmly by the hand. 'I'm made up for you.'

'Thanks, lad. I didn't like keeping if from you both but I didn't want to give you any false hope.' Barry pulled back a little from Ros's tight embrace. 'Cabbage, you okay?'

Ros sniffed back more tears. 'Oh, Dad. I love you so much.'

'I love you too, Cabbage. Now let's raise a glass.'

Ros went back to her seat, blew her nose, and Cameron handed her her wine.

'To the future, however long it may last,' said Barry and they all clinked glasses.

* * *

Darla rolled over and for a moment wondered where she was, but Elliott's warm naked body filled in the gaps. She grinned to herself at the memory of the previous night's antics. She checked the clock, another hour before she had to get up. She turned over and an alarm went off. Elliott stirred, whacked the alarm and rolled over to face her. It was nice to see him smile for a change. 'Good morning,' he said.

'It's a bit early.'

'Yeah, sorry about that. Farming is relentless. It doesn't stop for anything, not even birthdays or Christmas.'

'How about a quickie before work?' she suggested.

'Oh absolutely. Everything stops for that,' he said, reaching out and kissing her.

Mid-kiss her phone started going off. At this time in the morning it was either a crisis or more hopefully her boss ringing to say the building had been demolished and she didn't need to go in. Through the kiss she said, 'I best see who it is.'

She reached for the phone whilst still trying to kiss Elliott, and must have inadvertently answered a video call from her parents because when she looked at the screen their confused faces were staring back at her while in the tiny box was the image of Elliott kissing her ear. 'Oh sh . . . shalom, good morning, Mum. Dad. Just a second.' She angled the phone down so hopefully all they could see now was the bed covers. She turned to Elliott. 'I don't suppose you can speak French,' she whispered.

'*Mais oui, bien sur, ma cherie.*'

'That's perfect. Strong on the accent.'

'Oh, you like that?'

'Shhhh. French only while I speak to my parents.'

'What?' She gave him a look. '*Quoi?*'

She flipped her phone back over. 'Hi.' She gave an awkward wave. 'Sorry about that. I'm just here with—'

'*Bonjour, je m'appelle* Elliott.'

Maybe this was a bad idea. 'Anyway, what's up?'

'Elliott it would seem,' said her dad with thunderous eyes. If he hadn't looked so cross it would have been funny.

'Oh no, he's just popped by. He's going now.' She shooed a very confused Elliott with a wave of her hand. He responded by throwing back the covers and getting out of bed, and she had to bring the phone closer to her face to avoid him flashing her parents, although they seemed almost as alarmed by her early morning close-up. 'Are you both okay?' she asked while watching Elliott leave the room. He had a gorgeous bum.

'We're sorry to call so early,' said her mum. She had a troubled expression, which Darla assumed was not solely down to seeing her daughter being kissed by a random stranger. 'It is early where you are, isn't it?' asked her mum.

'Yes, very. But that's okay. What's wrong?'

Her mum looked to her dad. Darla felt uneasy. 'There's no easy way to say this but we thought you ought to hear it from us rather than someone else—'

'Or on the internet,' chipped in her mum. 'I got a message from a friend of Barbara's who'd had a Facebook thingy from a friend of his mum.'

She loved them but, boy, sometimes they were frustrating. 'Hear what?' she asked.

'Patrick has been arrested,' said her dad.

His statement threw her. She should probably seem surprised so belatedly she gasped. 'Oh dear. But he's nothing to do with me anymore. We split up a long time ago.' She feared her very bad acting would give her away.

'He tried to kidnap someone,' blurted out her mum, her hand rushing to her mouth.

'No, he . . . I'm sure he didn't mean to,' said Darla.

'How do you accidentally kidnap someone?' asked her dad, still looking cross.

'I don't know. But it's nothing to do with me so that's good.' What was she saying?

'We thought we should warn you in case he got in

300

touch,' said her father.

'He might go on the run,' said her mum, who had possibly been watching too many ITV dramas.

'No, he's . . .' It was hard not to correct the mistakes in the story and fill in the blanks when she knew that the police hadn't charged him with anything more serious than attempted theft and criminal damage so he was likely only looking at a fine. 'I'm sure Patrick will apologise and sort everything out.'

'The man's a criminal, Darla. He could be capable of anything.' Her mum leaned in with wide eyes. 'He could hold you hostage!'

Yep, far too many ITV dramas. 'Okay. Well, I'll be sure to keep away from him. If he were to get in touch. Which he won't. Because why would he?' She was gabbling so she stopped and pulled the covers up a little higher.

'Anyway, we thought you should know so we'll leave you to . . . whoever.'

'Okay, thanks. Love you both. Bye.' Darla had never been so glad to end a call with her parents.

Chapter Thirty-Five

Ros slept the best she had for a long while and for the first time in many months when she woke up the sense of impending doom wasn't weighing upon her. She'd not realised how much her father's condition had been a dark shadow over her life. Thankfully now that shadow had lifted. Her father had taken a risk and it had paid off. It was an odd sense of elation even though her dad had advised caution and had gone over all the expected caveats that it was still early days on the treatment and it did not mean he was in remission or that his battle with cancer was over. But his future looked decidedly brighter, which was definitely cause for celebration.

'Good morning,' said Cameron, walking from the bathroom to his bedroom with a bath towel slung low on his hips and his usually bouncy hair in wet curls. Seeing him reminded her that whilst her biggest concern had been resolved it had now created another one.

'Morning. Actually when you're dried and dressed do you think we could have a chat?' she asked, trying hard not to stare at his naked torso.

'Sure, what about?' he said, coming over. His glistening body was somewhat of a distraction.

'It's about the contract. Or more precisely the impact of Dad's announcement on said contract.'

'Okay.' He sat down and the towel gaped open.

'Naked!' she squeaked. Ros quickly averted her eyes. 'You'd best get less exposed under there with no clothes. Some clothes. Anything to cover things up.' Apparently she'd lost the ability to form proper sentences.

'I don't think we should make any snap decisions but—'

There was no way Ros was going to be able to concentrate while he was wearing just a damp towel, especially one that was no longer providing proper coverage. 'I'm sure you'd be more comfortable with clothes on. You get dressed and I'll make us both a coffee.'

'Okay. I'll be back in a jiffy.'

Ros made the coffees and Cameron returned in a Cookie Monster T-shirt and flowery board shorts. She was getting used to his childish attire and now found it endearing. Perspective was an interesting thing. A little like looking at the world through a kaleidoscope so that you only saw the pretty things.

'Thanks,' he said, sitting down and moving his mug onto a nearby coaster. It was an added bonus that he was house-trained. 'It's brilliant news about your dad. I'm really stoked about it. And it explains why he's not needed me to walk Gazza lately. He obviously has the energy to do it himself, which is a great sign.'

'I know. I feel the same but we do need to discuss the contract. And basically it is now null and void so you are free to go, but I will of course pay you up to the original

303

anticipated end date so you won't be out of pocket. And thank you. You did the job beyond my expectations.'

'Oh right.' Cameron seemed shocked. 'I was hoping I'd be able to stay here until the new house share is sorted.'

Ros almost slipped off the arm of the sofa in her haste to answer him. 'Of course you can stay. Stay as long as you like. I'm not chucking you out. I just didn't want you thinking you were stuck with the um . . . situation and with me. But we can stop this silly sham now, which will be a relief, won't it?' She nodded more times than was necessary to a sentence that she didn't agree with. In the end she'd thoroughly enjoyed being in a fake relationship with Cameron.

'Right. Because I don't think we can just call a halt to it without letting on that it was a set-up and that would upset Barry, which I definitely don't want to do.'

'Nor do I. Good point. We need a credible way to end it.'

'We do and one that won't upset your dad.'

'Right.' They both thought for a moment. It was a lot harder to end a fake relationship than she'd imagined it would be. Of course she'd not had to think about how it would end because they'd envisaged that her poor dad's demise would be the end point on a number of levels. 'I don't have the answer,' she said at last.

'Nor me.' He sipped his coffee. 'If you agree, how about we carry on as we are and have a think about some options for ending this in a way that doesn't upset anyone?'

'Excellent idea,' said Ros, feeling slightly guilty because it meant she got to spend more time with Cameron. The thought made her happy. It also took away the pressure of having to come up with an immediate exit strategy.

'Cool. I'm going for a run before lectures and I thought teriyaki beef salad for dinner?'

'Sounds lovely. I'll see you after work.' They had settled into a routine and she was going to miss it. Coming home to an empty apartment would be a hard thing to readjust to, but readjust she would have to. At least she had Cameron in her life for a little while longer.

An impromptu lunch with Darla was a lot more appealing than it once would have been. She was starting to realise that she had lived her life to a far too rigid schedule. The early June sunshine was gentle and an added bonus as they sat in the park, ate their sandwiches and updated each other on their lives.

'Ros, I am over the blooming moon for you and your dad. That really is the best news ever.'

'I agree. I can't quite believe it.' It had felt like she had dreamed it up and yet it was real.

'Oh, but what happens with you and Cameron now?' asked Darla.

'I'm afraid Cameron and I come to an end.'

'Or . . .' Darla looked serious for a moment. 'We bump off Gina and you two date for real.'

'Nice idea.' Ros shook her head good-humouredly at her friend. 'If not somewhat murderous. I told him this morning that he's free from the contract but Cameron said we can't just finish things; we need to think through a plausible and non-traumatic end to the relationship.'

'If only life was like that,' said Darla with a sigh.

'Oh don't tell me there are problems between you and Elliott.'

'The complete opposite. It's great. Apart from his ridiculously early starts. He's good fun and I even like mucking out when I'm with him. And the sex. If it was an Olympic sport he would be getting gold medals all the way.'

'So what's the problem?'

It was unlike Darla but Ros could see that she was less bubbly than usual. 'Like you and Cameron, at some point it has to end and I'm already feeling a bit sad about that.'

'I understand about my situation because mine is entirely fabricated but you and Elliott, why do you need to split up?'

'In a few months I will be kicked out of The Brambles. By then I will be debt-free and hopefully in a position to set up my own company, but in order to do that I'll have to move back in with my parents in Oxford and, as Elliott lives here and is working virtually 24/7 on the farm, that makes it a bit too difficult to see each other.' She looked glum but only for a moment. 'But that's assuming we last that long. Who knows? I'm going to stop grumbling and focus on enjoying myself. I need to live in the moment.'

'Good idea.' Ros finished her sandwich. 'Have you got any further with ideas for your own company?'

'Nope. I can't think of anything unique and original. I guess I'm not cut out to be an entrepreneur. But I've not given up – I'm still hoping something completely genius will pop into my head.'

'Does it have to be unique and original?' asked Ros, thinking that perfectly ordinary businesses were set up all the time.

'If it's not then I'd be in competition with long-established businesses and it's hard enough getting a new company off the ground anyway. Loads fail every year. I thought about setting up my own little cleaning business, but there are literally hundreds in the Oxford area. Why would mine stand out? It's a shame because I think Dusting Darla has a ring to it.'

Ros held her hand up. 'I might have an idea.'

Darla shuffled her bum forward. 'Go on.'

'How about if you specialised? You could stay in Southampton and set up a cleaning company specifically for boats. Mr Rogers was pleased with what you were doing and thrilled at how well you removed the bloodstains from his floor, so that could be something unique and original.' Ros was pleased with her suggestion.

'Boats with bloodstains might be a little too niche and slightly worrying if I ended up with a large regular customer base. But I do like your thinking.'

'You have lots of good concepts for cleaning. Like your suggestion for getting rid of the Gazza urine smell on my curtains. It really did work.'

'I've got loads of tried and tested hacks for cleaning. Especially where animals are concerned.' That was the moment when they both had the same idea at the exact same time, pointed at each other and gasped.

***

Darla was buzzing since her lunch with Ros. Not only did she think they had come up with a pretty original idea, she already had a ready-made client base locally from all her pet-sitting clients. Her plan was to set up Dusting

Darla and focus on two sets of clients: boat owners and pet owners, and when they overlapped like Mr and Mrs Rogers she'd offer them a discount.

Her excitement was unfortunately matched by her fear that setting up and running a business was beyond her. After the mess she'd got into thanks to Patrick she was particularly afraid of making a total hash of it and either ending up in even more debt or, worse still, going bankrupt. Thankfully Ros had allayed her fears on that front by promising to be there for her every step of the way.

She relayed her ideas to Cameron as it was a very quiet night at the bar. A nearby pub was having a tequila night.

'It sounds amazing,' he said when she'd finished explaining her idea. 'And Ros will make the best business adviser.'

'I know. I'm lucky to have her. I'll need to find some new lodgings when my gig at The Brambles ends. I don't think I'll be able to do the house-sitting and run a business as moving every few days won't really work.'

'I'm sure you could move in with Ros when I move out,' he said.

'Have you two got a splitting-up date yet?'

'Nope. I think we're both avoiding it.'

For a moment Darla was hopeful he was having second thoughts. 'Why's that?'

'It's quite a big thing to unpick, and it needs to be believable because it would be awful if Barry found out that we've been acting all this time.'

'You've grown quite fond of Barry and Ros, haven't you?'

'Yeah. Barry's a mate, and Ros . . . well, she's Ros.' What did that mean?

308

'I might be shooting my mouth off but I think you and Ros would make a great real-life couple.'

'Ahh well you see the thing is—'

'I know what the thing is. The thing is Gina, right?'

Cameron stared at his toes and let out a long slow breath. 'Yep. That's the th . . . I mean she's the thing.'

'Are you and Gina a big thing then?' asked Darla, watching him closely for his reaction. His contorted facial expression was something to behold.

'Me and Gina . . . it's a very long story,' said Cameron.

Darla glanced around the quiet bar. 'I have time.'

Cameron leaned back against the bar top. 'We've been going out off and on since we were kids and then we had a break when she went to uni.'

'And now?' Darla was keen to get things crystal clear.

Cameron scratched his head. 'We're not actually seeing each other but we're not seeing other people either.'

'Does that mean you're single?' Darla felt a spark of hope for Ros.

He looked sheepish. 'At Christmas a couple of years ago I had a bit too much to drink and I went around to Gina's parents' place and did this whole big speech thing about me wanting to better myself and that I was going to ask her to marry me when I had got my degree.'

Darla spluttered out a laugh. 'You're not really going to do that are you?'

He ran his hands down his face, momentarily warping his features and reminding her of the Edvard Munch painting entitled *The Scream*. 'I meant it when I said it. I really did . . .'

'And now?' she asked, feeling apprehensive.

A tiny frown darted across his forehead. 'I can't go back on my word.'

'You can. She'll think you're a bit of a shit but you can change your mind. That's assuming you don't love her anymore.'

'That's the thing. I do love Gina. I've always loved Gina. It's just . . .'

Darla wasn't the most patient person. 'It's just what?' She waved a hand for him to finish the sentence.

'No, it's definitely Gina. It's like it was mapped out for us long ago.'

'Sure?'

Cameron scratched his head and sighed. 'Yeah.'

Darla couldn't help but feel disappointed for Ros, but she put on her best smile for Cameron because he was her friend too. 'Then that's grand and I'm very happy for you.'

'Cheers,' he said, giving her a brief hug.

'I'm really sorry,' repeated Darla for the umpteenth time. They were sitting on Ros's sofa clutching empty mugs. She'd felt compelled to tell Ros about the Cameron and Gina situation because she didn't want her harbouring any false hope, especially as she felt Ros had been putting off the break-up and enjoying playing house with Cameron a fraction too much.

'It's not your fault,' said Ros looking sanguine. 'It's fine. I'm fine. It was always only a business arrangement and it would, quite frankly, be weird if we strayed outside of those boundaries.'

'That's a good way to look at it,' said Darla. 'Are you any

closer to working out how you and Cameron are going to end things?'

'No, it's a bit of a tricky subject.'

'Right,' said Darla, rolling her sleeves up. 'Get that flip chart out. I'll break you two up.'

'Thanks, I think,' said Ros, drifting off to her bedroom.

When Cameron came home thirty minutes later they had quite a list.

'Hiya,' he said. 'What have we got here?' he asked, putting down his satchel and joining them both at the flip chart.

'Fifty ways to leave your lover,' sang Darla. When that got no response she pointed to the header on the chart. 'Fifty reasons to split up,' said Darla, feeling quite proud of herself.

'But we've not reached fifty yet. It's quite hard,' said Ros.

Cameron scanned the list. 'They're good and everything, but for each of these one of us has to take the blame.' He pointed to the list and read aloud. 'Cameron is cheating on Ros. Ros is too busy at work and has no time for Cameron. Cameron has got an infectious disease and Ros doesn't want to catch it. They're all like that.'

'Apart from these two.' Darla tapped the board near the bottom.

'Either Ros and Cameron are incompatible sexually or they're allergic to each other,' he read out. 'I'm not sure we'd be telling anyone the first one even if it was the reason. And allergic to each other? Not very likely. Is it even a real thing?' he asked and looked between the two women. Darla nodded as Ros firmly shook her head.

'Cameron's right,' said Ros. 'I don't think there's a way to do this without one of us taking the blame. I guess as this was my idea it should be me.'

'Actually it was my idea,' said Darla.

'Then I definitely blame you,' said Cameron with a smile. 'Could we say we were in a threesome but we both wanted Darla so we agreed that nobody would have anybody?'

'No,' said Darla and Ros together.

There was a lull while they all perused the board. Cameron held up a finger as if he'd had a flash of inspiration. 'Whilst I would have liked to have kept in touch with Barry, I think you should blame me for the break-up. Nothing too awful though, please,' he said.

'Why?' asked Ros.

'Because you're his daughter and I don't like the thought of him thinking you did something wrong. And you don't want him to badger you to fix it. So it has to be me.'

Ros squeezed his shoulder. 'Thanks, that's a gallant thing to do.'

'You know me,' said Cameron with a shrug.

'I do,' said Ros.

'Great,' said Darla, feeling pleased that they'd found a way forward but the other two looked rather glum considering she'd solved their issue. 'I'm going to put a star by all the ones where Cameron initiates the split, then I'll leave you two to work out the details. I think that deserves—' But she was interrupted by the entry buzzer.

Ros answered it. 'Dad! Hello, how lovely it's you.' She waved frantically at Darla and Cameron who were already manhandling the flip chart out of the room.

Darla and Cameron hid it in Cameron's wardrobe. Darla caught sight of a Ken and Barbie T-shirt. 'Seriously?'

'Yeah. They're the original perfect couple,' he replied.

'If you like out-of-proportion boobs and no penis,' she said, coming back into the living area. 'Barry, hi, how are you? I've heard the good news.' And she pulled the slightly bemused man into a hug.

'We were talking about Ken and Barbie,' explained Cameron, looking embarrassed. 'Nice to see you, Barry. Drink?'

'No, I'm not stopping. Amanda is downstairs with Gazza.' He pulled a face.

'Is she still here?' asked Ros.

'Yes, your mum's still here. But she's leaving soon. I'd really like you to sit down with her before she goes. Please.'

'I'll need to check my diary,' said Ros.

Cameron cleared his throat and gave her a look. 'I'm sure we can sort something out.'

'Great,' said Barry brightly. 'Anyway, the thing I came round to tell you was I'm having a party!' He waved his hands in the air and grinned at them all.

There was no response for a beat too long so Darla felt she should say something. 'Who doesn't love a party? Great idea, Barry. What's the occasion?'

'No reason other than I am happy to be alive and I thought you only get all your family and friends together when there's either a wedding or a funeral and if it's the latter I'll miss it so I thought, sod it let's just have a party. You're invited, Darla.'

'Ace. Thanks, Barry. Do I need to RSVP or can I say yes now?'

'No formal reply needed. So that's one definite. How about you two?' He looked at Cameron and Ros.

'When is it?' asked Ros.

'I still need to finalise a few things but it's next Saturday and I'm hiring one of those fancy floating gin palaces for the night. I'm really going to push the boat out. Get it?'

'No,' said Ros.

'That sounds like a great night,' said Cameron, with a glance at Ros. 'I just need to see if I can get the time off work.'

'Oh.' Barry had a look of disappointment on his face. 'Of course. Fingers crossed. It wouldn't be the same without you.'

'Thanks,' said Cameron, appearing touched.

'Anyway. I'd better dash before someone gets bitten.' Barry pointed down the stairs.

'Most likely Gazza,' muttered Ros. 'Bye, Dad. Take care.' She gave him a kiss and he left looking at least ten years younger than he had done only weeks before. The door closed behind him.

'I guess we need to split up before the party,' said Cameron, looking disappointed.

'No, you saw Dad's face. He wants you there. You're like family now. We'll have to wait until afterwards.'

'Cool,' said Cameron, instantly brightening up. 'Because I'd hate to miss it.'

'And I might be able to get some leads for my new business from whoever owns the boat,' said Darla and she put up her hand for a high five, but there were no takers.

Chapter Thirty-Six

Darla stood back to admire her handiwork. Ever since she'd brought the escapee hen back from Elliott's farm in a string bag, she'd been toying with an idea and thanks to a few spare bits of timber, some dowelling and a length of rope it was now a reality.

'What is that exactly?' asked Elliott, surprising her by wrapping her in a hug.

'It's a swing,' she said proudly, leaning back against him.

'For the chickens?'

'Duh! It's in the chicken coop.'

'But they're poultry. There's a reason for the phrase "bird brain" you know. How will they ever work out how to— Well knock me down with a feather.'

They both watched as the most dominant of the hens flapped her wings and hopped onto the swing. Admittedly it only swung once before she came straight off looking more than a little startled by the experience. But she had definitely been interested enough to give it a go.

'I figured it's not the most exciting life being a chicken so I made them a swing. Ooh look – The Captain is having a go.' The cockerel pecked at the bar of the swing until it swung back and bumped him on the head, making him squawk his frustration and stalk off.

'It's inspired.'

'I know,' said Darla happily. 'I'm making a slide for the goats next. She held her cordless screwdriver aloft and revved it while pretending to roar like a lion.

'Steady on, you'll be taking over from Nick Knowles on *DIY SOS*.'

Darla stuck her tongue out. 'How's little Darla?'

'She's thriving but she still races to the gate when she sees me just in case I've got a bottle for her.'

'Aww I think she likes to snuggle with you. I mean who wouldn't?' She leaned back into his embrace as they watched the chickens stalking cautiously around their new swing. 'How's everything else?'

That was the moment it looked like a barn had landed on his shoulders and his whole demeanour changed. 'Manic. I don't really have time to come up here, but you, Big Darla, are irresistible.'

Darla pouted. 'Not sure about the Big Darla thing.'

He shook his head. 'No, me neither. Sorry.' He kissed her and she had hopes of some afternoon delight. She was about to lead him off to the bedroom when he pulled away. 'Sorry, I need to get back to work.'

'What if I come and help with whatever it is that needs doing? I'm pretty handy, you know.' She held the screwdriver aloft but this time she almost dropped it.

'This afternoon I plan to be scraping rot out of sheep hooves,' he said with a wince.

That didn't sound like fun at all. She pulled a face. 'Err,

is there blood involved?'

'Sometimes.'

'That's a no from me,' she said.

'I suspected it would be. I might catch you later?' He looked forlorn as he turned to leave.

'There's a gammon and veg in the slow cooker, so come up here when you're finished.'

Elliott puffed out a defeated sigh. 'It'll probably be late.'

'That's okay. I want to talk to you about my plans to dominate the cleaning world. Well, Southampton anyway.'

'Sounds good.'

'You know, you don't have to be a farmer. You have one life but you'll not get the most out of it if you don't live it the way you want to. It's your life, not your parents'.'

'That's deep for a Tuesday,' he said.

'I'm serious. If it's not making you happy, it's a whole lot of hours over a lifetime to be doing something you don't enjoy.'

'And you like cleaning, do you?' he asked with a chuckle.

'I blooming love it,' she said.

He raised an eyebrow.

'I'm serious. There's a real satisfaction of taking something grubby and making it pristine. I love my job. Jobs,' she corrected. 'And I'm excited about the new business.'

He frowned a little. 'I guess you've found your thing.'

'I think I have.' She gave him a kiss. 'See you later, when I'll bore you silly about it.'

'Can't wait,' he said at last, raising a smile before trudging off.

Ros had an enjoyable lunch with Alastair's business associate from the golf club. The gentleman had a refreshing attitude to risk management in that he valued it highly. They discussed the role he was trying to fill in detail including the necessity for extensive travel as he wanted his risk director to be hands-on with all the global offices. They chatted about Ros's CV and previous roles and also about sailing as he was in the process of upgrading his yacht, so Ros may have secured another client for Darla. Ros had no idea if she'd be called in for a formal interview but she was definitely interested in the role he'd described. It was quite a jump in terms of responsibility and salary, but she thrived on a challenge so she very much hoped she would hear from him in due course.

She got home to find Barry had messaged to say that as the party was on a fancy superyacht he thought it might be nice if people dressed up to make it extra special. Ros appreciated the sentiment but her wardrobe didn't. She and Cameron stared at the mass of black and grey.

'I see what you mean,' said Cameron, rubbing his chin. 'I always thought it was a cliché when women said, "I've got nothing to wear," but you definitely don't have anything to wear that fits Barry's brief.'

'I thought maybe I could wear this,' she said, pulling out a classic little black dress.

'When did you wear it last?' he asked.

'A funeral.'

'I rest my case,' said Cameron, shutting the wardrobe door. 'This is the best excuse ever for a shopping trip.'

'I'm not a big shopper,' said Ros. The truth was more that she actively avoided it.

'Well, you are today.' He linked his arm through hers and towed her out of her bedroom.

Forty minutes later they were browsing in Westquay shopping centre. It was an unfamiliar place to Ros. Unlike most she'd not spent her formative teenage years shopping with her mum or trawling the aisles with friends for the latest fashions. There had been brief shopping trips with her father, which had always been pre-planned and targeted, and that was the approach she now applied for herself. If she needed new clothes then she ordered them online; it was a simple transaction that was straightforward and time-efficient.

'Hey, look at these.' Cameron was already inside a shop trying on sunglasses. 'Try some,' he suggested, passing her a pair.

'I have a pair of sunglasses,' said Ros, returning them to the stand.

'But these are cool, right?' He struck a pose and she had to laugh.

'Yes, they suit you.'

'You have a go.' He passed her a pair. Reluctantly she tried them on and faced him. 'Now that's what I mean. Super cool. Look.' He pointed at the mirror. Ros considered her reflection. It seemed odd to her that basically obliterating key features of the face, namely the eyes, somehow improved it. 'You have to get those,' he said.

'I don't think so. I rarely wear sunglasses and anyway we came for outfits.' She put them back on the stand.

'Okay. Outfits first but then we should come back and get those.'

'We'll see,' she said, heading out of the store.

The first clothes shop they went into didn't feel like her thing at all. The music was particularly loud and intrusive and the shop itself a bit of a maze and badly labelled. She was looking at a pretty floral item that was either a long top or an incredibly short dress when she got a tap on the shoulder. She turned around to see Cameron wearing a bright pink bucket hat and loud shirt covered in pineapples as he pulled a pose worthy of a superstar rapper. 'How about this? I know, I need to get a couple of gold teeth but then I'll be sweet.'

'I'm not sure that's what Dad had in mind.'

'Fair enough. How are you getting on?' He came to look at what she was holding. 'That minidress would look amazing on you. You should try it on.'

'I'm not sure I'm ready for something like that. I'll keep looking.'

After two more shops they still hadn't made any purchases. They left Westquay in search of some inspiration. The next shop had even more hats for Cameron to try, each with accompanying dramatic poses.

Whilst Ros found him entertaining she was conscious that they had veered off track. 'We're not really getting anywhere, are we?'

'As usual, you are right.' He removed the strange deerstalker affair from his head. 'Let's go on a mission to find at least one outfit from this store and meet back here in fifteen minutes. Deal?'

'I don't know—'

'Fifteen minutes,' he said, tapping his watch, and he darted off. With a shrug Ros began perusing the rails.

Fifteen minutes later, Ros was waiting back where Cameron had left her when what looked like a mobile jumble sale approached her. 'Cameron?'

'Thank heavens I'm in the right place. I can't see a thing,' he said from behind the mound of clothes he was carrying.

'That's more than one outfit and quite a few dresses. Are they your thing?'

'The dresses are for you. Actually most of it is for you. You're the priority. They're quite unstable. I think putting the satin dress in the middle was a mistake so if you could lead me to the changing rooms I'd be very grateful.'

There was a pause as Ros shook her head at him, even though he couldn't see her.

'Er, Ros. Are you still there?' he asked.

'Yes. Come on then.' She took hold of his arm and guided him through the store.

The first thing she tried on was a mid-calf-length black dress, the single outfit she had picked. When she stepped out of the changing room Cameron was already shaking his head. 'No black. You have black. You don't need black,' he said gently, shooing her back inside.

She perused the items she had in the changing room, which were only a fraction of the vast clothes mountain

Cameron had picked up because she was only allowed to take a few items at a time in with her. She wasn't sure about any of them. Cameron's voice called through to her. 'Just pick one to try. Any one. It doesn't matter.' Was he some sort of mind reader?

'Okay. Thanks, Gok Wan!' she called back and she heard the fitting room attendant giggle.

By about the fifth outfit she was losing the will to live. She strode out in an orange dress with a heavy, swooshy skirt. 'That's the one!' said Cameron, throwing his hands up in a hallelujah gesture.

She had to admit it fitted her well and felt good on but there was one overwhelming issue. 'But bright orange?'

'I love it,' said Cameron.

She scratched her head. 'I'll put it in the maybe pile. I can't try on much more.'

'Okay.' Cameron held up a hand. 'There is one you need to try. I think it's a good compromise.' He went off to sweet-talk the assistant and root through the large pile of stuff they had left with her.

Ros tried not to get huffy as she got changed once again, but even she had to admit that the woman looking back at her from the mirror did look rather stylish. The dress was navy and cream, in a similar style to the orange one, but it went in and out in all the right places. It did make her feel a little special as she swished from side to side. She walked out of the fitting area and a few heads turned. She cleared her throat and Cameron spun around. He pointed at her. 'Now you look stunning – *that* is stunning. Do you agree?' He looked tentative.

'I think I do,' she said, feeling a little shy.

'We have a winner! Get in!' He made the same gestures he did when he was watching the football. She couldn't help but feel a little special at his reaction. 'Get that and then we do it all again but for my outfit.' He grinned at her and she groaned. 'Only joking, I ordered mine online while you were browsing in the first shop.' She went to give him a playful whack and he ducked, so she chased him a little across the store.

'Madam!' called the alarmed fitting room assistant who appeared moments away from calling security.

'Sorry,' said Ros sheepishly as she skulked back into the changing room feeling as light as air. She'd never imagined that she would have such a good time shopping. Had she been missing out all these years or was it yet again simply the Cameron factor? That whatever she did with him she enjoyed disproportionally more than she would have done with anyone else or, as was frequently the case, on her own?

Chapter Thirty-Seven

On the day of Barry's party there were too many things to co-ordinate so Ros had agreed to go from her dad's house and meet Cameron at the docks. Barry was uncharacteristically jittery as he seemed to have visions of everyone being late and the boat going without them.

'Dad, it'll be fine. There's only a dozen of us and everyone knows what time they need to be ready. I have messaged in the group chat with a reminder that they need to be there at least twenty minutes before departure time or we will leave them behind.'

'See, that's exactly what I'm worried about.' He began pacing with a concerned-looking Gazza at his heels. It was a little like the obedience trials at Crufts although most of those canines wouldn't have been as easily distracted by the sound of a cupboard door opening.

'Stop fretting,' said Ros. 'We won't leave anyone behind.'

'And what about the caterers? Are you sure we've ordered enough? It's not like they can pop to the cash and carry if we get low on something.'

'Goodness,' said Amanda, appearing in the doorway

wearing a long dark green dress and looking very elegant. 'I hope it's not coming from the cash and carry given what you're paying them.'

They both looked at Ros. 'I'm sure it's all top quality. Now please can we trust that everything is in hand and try and enjoy the evening?'

'I take it you're not wearing that.' Her mother nodded disapprovingly at her white shirt and black trouser combination.

'No . . . I'm getting changed now.'

'Where's Cameron?' Amanda pressed her lips into a hard line. 'Or should I not ask?'

'Cameron is meeting us at *Chuckles*,' said Ros.

'Chuckles? Please don't tell me there's a clown?' Amanda appeared horrified.

'It's the name of the superyacht.'

'I see.' Amanda's face told a different story. 'Let's hope Cameron turns up,' she added.

Ros wasn't someone who put their hands on their hips but she was sorely tempted. 'And why wouldn't he be there?'

'No reason.' She sipped her coffee. 'He doesn't seem like the dressing-up sort. More dishevelled and casual. No offence.'

'He is a man of many talents,' said Ros. 'And whatever he wears he'll look perfect to me.' She meant it and the thought made her feel a little sad. She'd overcome her own prejudice about how he looked and dressed. 'It's the man inside that matters. And Cameron is someone special.'

'Hmm,' said her mother.

'Amanda, you really don't help sometimes do you?' said Barry.

'Why is everyone so touchy?' she said. 'Goodness, Barry, your bow tie looks like it's been tied by a chimpanzee. Joke!' she added quickly as she put her drink down and went to adjust his tie. Ros saw an opportunity to escape and get herself ready. She'd not be up to Amanda's standard but she was the last person she wanted to impress. As long as her dad had a good time, that was all that mattered.

Ros had washed her hair earlier so only needed to wet it and have a bit of a play with the hot brush. It wasn't a tool she had mastered. It was something her dad had bought her a couple of Christmases ago but it seemed like the perfect night to see if she could make her hair a little more special than her usual straight affair. Especially as Barry had hired a photographer to capture moments through the night so he had something to look back on.

When Ros came downstairs she was expecting a sarcastic comment from Amanda but her stunned expression made her very happy and a little bit smug.

'Someone scrubs up well,' said Amanda.

'You look amazing, Cabbage.' Barry had a tear in his eye as he hugged her.

The taxi arrived soon afterwards. Barry reluctantly left Gazza with a carrot, a large bone and a promise that he'd return with a doggy bag as Ros ushered him out of the door.

It was quite a scene on the quayside: people had heeded her mild threat of going without them and had arrived early and were now milling around in their finery. *Chuckles* the superyacht was ready and waiting and looked even bigger than the photographs Ros had been shown. More than twenty metres long, gleaming white and over three levels – it was certainly an impressive vessel. Uncle Pete greeted them warmly wearing a white tuxedo and a vibrant red bow tie, which Amanda curled her lip at, and Ros was pleased to see Uncle Pete looked buoyed by her response. 'I wanted to stand out in the photos. I thought dark colours were a bit bland.' He eyed Amanda's dark green dress up and down. It was going to be an interesting night.

Ros scanned the quayside for Cameron but there was no sign of him. Once Barry had made his way to the front, they were all handed glasses of fizz and ushered onto the boat. Barry looked pleased as punch as he greeted everyone and Ros could understand how happy it made him to see old friends again. Uncle Pete gave him a bear hug and when they finally pulled apart both the men had tears in their eyes but no words were exchanged. She was pleased to see the photographer had captured the moment.

'Hey, Ros. How are you?' asked Uncle Pete, giving her a hug.

'I'm good thanks. How are you and your ailments?'

Pete chuckled. 'I'm very well. Now where's this fella of yours?' He scanned the people nearby.

'I'm not entirely sure, but he'll be here and I'll introduce you.'

'He is real then? Not like Tilly?' Ros had no idea what he was talking about although something was stirring at the back of her mind. 'Your imaginary friend, Tilly. You remember. They used to steal biscuits and wee in the garden.'

'Oh heavens. I must have been about three or four.'

The memories filled her with embarrassment. 'Cameron is definitely real.' The thought of him brought a smile to her face.

'Glad to hear it,' said Pete, taking a glass from a proffered tray. 'Don't forget to introduce me.'

'I won't,' she said, having another scan of faces. There were now more people on the boat than on the quay. But there on the pontoon was a face she recognised. Not one she was fond of but definitely one she recognised: Cyril was waiting to come on board. Ros couldn't help but grin. She had no idea what Cameron was doing but she was learning to go with it and that it would invariably turn out well.

Darla appeared. 'Hi, Barry. Happy party day,' she said, giving him a hug. 'Thanks for inviting me,' she added.

'Thanks for coming,' said Barry. 'I thought you could keep Ros and Cameron company, as the rest of the guests are from a different generation. I hope you don't feel like a gooseberry.'

'Oh no, I won't. I've got a boyfriend. He's called Elliott and he'll be up when I get home. When I say up, I mean with the sheep.' Barry's eyebrows were rising. 'Actually not sheep because they're young ones – lambs. He'll be feeding lambs because he's a farmer.' Barry seemed relieved when she finally reached the end of the explanation.

'That's nice. Have a good evening,' said Barry, looking thankful to move on to the next guest.

'Hiya.' Darla launched herself at Ros. 'Elliott said I looked good enough to eat.'

'You do – you look fabulous. Have a glass of Prosecco,' she said, pleased to see Darla positively glowing with happiness. It made Ros feel a little bewildered as she was beginning to sense she was missing out on something. She'd never felt like this before. It had always been the downside of relationships that she had been most aware of – the niggles, the annoying habits and the compromises. Perhaps they had simply been indicators that she was with the wrong person. This was all Cameron's doing. He'd made her look at things differently. Opened her eyes to new possibilities and in so doing had made her a little restless and yearning for a close relationship. The sight of him manhandling Cyril on board only made her feelings for him stronger. But it was all a big waste of time, effort and energy. What she needed to do was refocus.

'Hey,' said Cameron, setting Cyril down and embracing Barry warmly. 'Looking good, Barry.'

The older man adjusted his bow tie with a wobble of his head. 'You too, Cameron. Help yourself to a drink.'

'Hey, you,' said Cameron, placing a now familiar kiss on Ros's cheek. 'You look amazing. That dress is perfect on you. Your stylist must be very special,' he said with a cheeky wink.

'Oh, he is.' Ros looked Cameron over. Wild hair under control, freshly shaved, purple velvet bow tie and very well fitted dinner suit. He looked divine.

'I'm sure Cyril is having a lovely time but I don't remember him being on the guest list.'

'It was a last-minute idea. Your dad called and asked me to bring him. He thought it might be fun for photo ops.'

Once everyone was on board the crew began scurrying about and someone gave Barry a microphone. 'Is this on?' he asked as it screeched into life, sending someone's hearing aid haywire. 'That's a yes then. Welcome, everyone.

I'll do a long boring speech later but for now grab a glass, make merry and watch us set sail . . . well, there's no sails but you know what I mean.' He raised his glass. 'Cheers!'

Cameron squeezed Ros's arm. 'You can relax. Everyone is here and on board. Your dad looks happy and healthy. It's all good.'

'Thanks, Cameron.' He had a way of putting her at ease.

'Before I forget,' he said. 'Two messages on the answer machine. One from Great-Aunt Ursula. Saying again that she's sorry she couldn't make it but she's off to the Shetland Isles tomorrow so the logistics were too tricky. And either a scam or a wrong number because it was some guy after information to confirm you have a passport so they can secure flights to Dubai. I mean, do people really fall for tricksters like . . . that . . . ?' Cameron trailed off; she suspected it was her own guilty expression that had made him freeze the way he had. 'He was a fraudster, right?'

'Err.' Ros was starting to think that she'd not thought this through. A cheer went up as the boat pulled away from the dock and the photographer snapped away. 'He's not a fraudster.'

Cameron's expression changed. 'Was he a travel agent? Are you off on holiday?'

'Err.' Ros was struggling to come up with a suitable response.

'Ros, what's going on?'

'I've been offered a job that is international, starting in Dubai, and the flight is one way.'

The shock on Cameron's face was clear. 'What the hell?'

'It would be a new start.'

'Am I meant to say congratulations? Hang on, does

everyone else know? Is it just me who's been kept in the dark?' He appeared to be getting agitated.

'I've not told anyone.' She was still waiting to see a contract before she made a final decision.

'How was this going to work? You were just going to pack your stuff and leave and not say anything?' His voice was rising.

'No.' She'd not actually thought about it in any detail. 'I was offered the job unexpectedly.'

'Unexpectedly. You didn't have an interview?' People were beginning to stop their conversations and tune in to the argument.

Ros thought back to the nice chat over lunch. 'It was quite informal.'

'So you *did* have an interview but you didn't say anything. You kept it a secret.' Cameron pushed his hand through his thick hair, unsettling it. 'Jeez, have you been planning this for ages? I thought we . . .' There was a look from him that she wished she could interpret. 'But then, it's nothing to you is it? All this. You and me.' He pointed between the two of them.

'Cameron. Am I missing something? Because I understand you have plans to get engaged.' There was a whoop of joy nearby. 'Not to me,' she clarified for whoever had got excited and also for the photographer who was zooming in for a close-up. She realised everyone was now silent and all eyes were on them. This was very bad indeed.

'What's going on?' Darla marched up.

'Ros is going to Dubai indefinitely,' said Cameron.

'It's not indefinitely; it's undecided until I've assessed the level of work involved there before I'll likely move

331

on . . .' she was now acutely aware of the attention '. . . to um, Saudi Arabia.'

'Arabia?!' Darla was almost shouting. 'I don't even know where that is. You promised me you'd help me to get my business off the ground. You said you'd be my business adviser. What the hell, Ros?'

'I'm sorry. I was going to speak to both of you.' She looked at the assembled faces. Including her father and mother whose attention was also firmly fixed on her. 'All of you,' she corrected.

'I guess you leaving neatly draws this relationship to a close then,' said Cameron. 'No discussion. No working things out so it's best for everyone. You went for the unilateral decision and as usual went for what suits Ros and sod everyone else.' His jaw was tense. She'd not seen him this cross before.

'I didn't know what the best thing to do was,' she said, aware that her voice was little more than a whisper.

A hearing aid nearby whistled. 'Can you speak up?' someone called.

'You think this is for the best? Running away to Dubai without a word. No discussion. Not even a Post-it Note on the counter. Bloody hell, Ros. I guess that makes this easy then. We're done!'

Someone gasped as Cameron awkwardly tried to exit through the mass of people. Only to get to the exit and discover that they were now some hundred metres offshore and surrounded by sea.

Chapter Thirty-Eight

Ros was shaken and her pulse was thumping in her ears. She watched Cameron pace up and down and for a moment feared he was going to launch himself overboard in his desire to get away from her. But instead he went below deck and Ros took a deep breath. She needed to think.

Darla came over and steered her off to one side. 'That was excellent, but I wish you'd tipped me off. For a moment I thought it was real.'

'What?'

'The big public row,' whispered Darla, checking over her shoulders like a rubbish spy. 'The whole staged break-up. Genius.'

'That wasn't staged,' said Ros. 'That was a real argument.'

Darla took a moment to process what Ros was telling her. 'Then you are actually taking a job halfway across the world?'

Ros wobbled her head. 'It's not signed and sealed yet but—'

'What the actual—' Thankfully Darla's next word was

drowned out by the boat's horn, which also drew people's attention back to them leaving the marina and got them waving to any random person walking by, which Ros was hugely grateful for. 'I said what did you think you were doing not telling me?' snapped Darla.

She'd not seen her angry before. It seemed to be the night for annoying agreeable people.

'I was going to tell you. It's all moved very fast and I think quite a few assumptions have been made, because I've not signed—'

'Assumptions! You clearly assumed we'd all be okay with you buggering off. You promised you'd be here for me and my business. I don't know what I'm doing but I thought it would be okay because you were going to help me. I'm really scared of messing this up and ending up bankrupt.' Tears were welling in Darla's eyes and her voice was getting squeaky with emotion.

'I'm really sorry. I didn't mean to upset anyone. I thought it was for the best. A clean break. Get away from the whole thing.'

'So it was all about what was best for you. No thought for anyone else. Not even for your dad who maybe would like to spend some time with you now he knows he has some time left?' She shook her head, her jaw tight. 'I thought you'd changed. But that's never going to happen.'

Darla dashed across the flybridge, down the staircase and then came to the same conclusion as Cameron. 'How the hell do you get off this thing?'

'You can't, not for another three hours,' said one of the crew as he skirted past.

Ros managed to take a breath before her dad came

over. She held up her hands. 'I know. I get it. I've done the wrong thing.'

Barry shook his head. 'I've not come to have a go at you.'

'Thank you.' It was a huge relief.

'Only you're a fool if you're going to let Cameron go. He's the best thing to happen to you in years.'

Ros opened her mouth but before she could say anything Uncle Pete was waving Barry over for a photograph. Ros was left standing on one side of the flybridge with the wind in her hair and the ocean ahead of her. The promise of a beautiful sunset tickled the horizon. She'd never felt so dejected and alone in her life.

What was meant to be a happy evening had quickly turned into the night from hell, for her at least, but thankfully Barry seemed to be enjoying himself. Everyone was giving Ros the cold shoulder. Ironically as the breeze picked up people left the flybridge for the more sheltered deck below, leaving Ros alone with her thoughts and chilly shoulders.

She heard footsteps behind her and turned to see her mother ascending the staircase. That was all she needed. She returned to looking out to sea and the twinkling lights of the Isle of Wight in the hope Amanda would get the message.

'I know I'm probably not who you want to talk to, but seeing as nobody else was offering I thought I should,' said her mother.

'It's fine. Don't feel obliged.'

'Oh I don't. I can see both sides of the issue. And I believe you have been treated somewhat harshly.'

'Thank you,' said Ros tentatively. Amanda was the last person who she would have expected to be on her side.

Her mother leaned her back against the rail and looked at Ros. 'I did what you're doing.'

'Getting cold?'

Amanda ignored the quip. 'I put my career before everything. I thought it defined me and if I took my foot off the pedal for a moment I would slip quickly down the corporate ladder and be lost in the sea of forgotten part-time mothers.'

She really painted a picture. 'Are you admitting it was wrong to leave me and Dad?'

'I'm saying I felt it was too much of a compromise to be a mother and a quantitative analyst. I feared trying to do both to a high standard would ultimately mean I would fail at one or both of them. Making a choice seemed like the only sensible option.'

'Great. That does not make me feel any better.'

'Your father and I discussed it before we had you. He was desperate for a child but I had a number of concerns. The whole mothering thing somewhat baffled me and still does. I knew I could do the basics and keep you alive—'

'Goodness, I wasn't a Tamagotchi, Mother.'

'Indeed. Perhaps I should have practised with one of those first. You see, your father said he would pick up the majority share of the parenting duties. However, when it came to it he didn't keep his side of the deal.'

Ros was stunned for a moment. 'You're blaming Dad?'

'Not entirely. I understand that it wasn't feasible for him to undertake that amount of childcare and if he had, his business would have suffered significantly. I think he wrongly assumed my maternal instinct would kick in and I would become your main carer but that didn't happen. And he didn't want you in nursery and childcare all the time.'

'But that's where I ended up because he couldn't manage me and the business.'

'Ironic really,' said Amanda. 'I think some people are not natural parents. Barry was far more at ease with you than I was. We never connected. I don't know why. I waited until you were settled in school then I turned to the role I knew I could do well and that was being an analyst. I spent less time at home and more time at work until the relationship broke down irretrievably.'

Ros shook her head. 'I'm sorry but if this little chat was meant to make me feel better I need to report that it's not.'

'I was simply explaining what happened. How the decisions I made took me down a particular path.'

'And our relationship was just collateral damage?' Ros shook her head at her mother's lack of tact.

'I continued to pay towards your upkeep, and we spoke every week.' Amanda turned around and watched the lights with Ros. 'Then your father asked me to stop calling because it was too upsetting for you. So I did. That was when I understood how much my job had cost me, because for the first time I realised that I did care a great deal about you. But it was too late to turn back. It seemed like it would be best for everyone if I just kept away.'

Ros wasn't sure how to respond so instead they carried on watching the dying sunset together. Tonight it wasn't having quite the calming effect it usually had on Ros.

At last Amanda spoke. 'There's the last ferry,' she

said, pointing at the vessel a little way off and following a straight course.

Ros turned her head although she had no idea why, it wasn't exactly something unusual.

'You used to love watching the ferries come in and out when you were young,' said Amanda.

'Did I?' Ros had no specific recollection of this.

'Yes. We used to go to a tiny strip of beach near the ferry terminal and sit on the bench there. Sometimes we'd stay until the sun went down. I don't expect you to remember. It was a very long time ago,' said Amanda as they both watched the ferry go by.

***

Darla was hopping mad and trapped on a boat with no escape other than to jump overboard, but worse than that she was hurt. Ros's announcement had been a shock but it had been the realisation that Ros could simply move to another country without mentioning it to her and without any thought of the impact it would have. Impact was the right word – Darla felt like she'd been barrelled into by an out-of-control St Bernard and she knew exactly what that felt like.

When she left Oxford she'd left family and friends behind and Ros had been a lifeline. Someone cool-headed and calm who had helped her plan her way out of the mess she was in. They'd grown close or at least that was what Darla had believed until tonight. She knew Ros had her quirky ways but she'd always felt that deep down Ros cared and wouldn't let her down – how wrong she had been. When she really needed her she was buggering off somewhere hot and sunny with no return ticket. Darla felt adrift. She watched the fading sunlight sparkle on the surface of the water like phones at a concert when the slow song is played.

The older partygoers had gone inside and were lounging on the plush leather seating, sipping drinks as their laughter drifted outside. Darla didn't feel much like partying anymore. She looked around and saw Cameron sitting on the sun pad at the bow of the yacht. She wandered down to join him.

'Mind if I sit here?'

'Be my guest,' he said, staring out at the sunset's burnished colours.

'Can I just double-check that that wasn't some big stunt upstairs?' Darla knew she was grasping at flimsy straws but was still hoping it was a misunderstanding.

'Not a stunt,' he said. He snorted out a breath. 'To think we spent ages trying to work out how best to split up and then we end up doing it in the absolutely worst way possible. I feel awful. Poor Barry.' Cameron looked into the cabin behind him where Barry and Pete were roaring with laughter at something.

'I think he's okay,' said Darla.

'Thank goodness he is. That man has been through enough.'

'You're fond of him aren't you?'

'Yep.' He leaned back and puffed out a deep sigh. 'This whole thing hasn't been anything like I thought it would be. It was meant to be just an additional gig to earn me some extra money. But it's turned into . . .' He looked up to where Ros was standing on the flybridge gazing into the night. 'It's ended up becoming such a mess.'

'If it's any consolation, I feel shat on too,' she said.

Cameron laughed. 'I'm not sure it is, but thanks anyway.'

'At least I've got Elliott and you've got Gina,' said Darla.

'I guess,' said Cameron as a chorus of 'For he's a jolly good fellow' broke out inside.

Chapter Thirty-Nine

After Ros finally escaped the boat and had made sure Barry was home safely, she returned home to a silent apartment. Cyril was lying on the sofa and all was quiet so she assumed Cameron had gone to bed. Perhaps that was for the best. Another confrontation would likely not solve the problem.

After little sleep she stirred to the sound of a door closing. She dragged herself fully awake. How could she be wide-awake half the night and yet come morning she was in a deep sleep? She pulled on her dressing gown and left the bedroom. Straightaway she realised Cyril had gone from the sofa, as had the throw and Cameron's cactus. His bedroom door was ajar. She took a deep breath and tapped on the door. There was no response.

'Cameron. Do you want a coffee?' she asked, stepping tentatively inside. The room was empty and anything of Cameron's was missing. She walked over to the kitchen area where a sticky note was stuck on the worktop, which read: *I'm sorry things ended the way they did. Having slept on it I think you're probably right that a clean break is for the best. So I've cleared all my stuff out. Wishing you all the best for the future – Cameron. PTO*

She picked up the note and turned it over. *PS. For the record I don't regret the relationship contract, only how it ended.*

Ros went to check his room again. The bed was stripped, the cupboards empty apart from his Cookie Monster T-shirt abandoned on the topmost shelf. She pulled it down. She still didn't understand why he wore T-shirts featuring children's characters but it was oddly one of many things she was going to miss about him. In a bit of a daze she went to get washed and dressed.

Ros put the kettle on and had to stop herself from automatically getting two mugs out of the cupboard. He'd gone and it was going to take some getting used to. Despite what everyone seemed to have assumed she'd not confirmed that she was taking the new job. She looked around her apartment; with the plants and Cameron's things gone it had a sparse feel to it that she'd not noticed before. Or maybe it had not bothered her until now. There was nothing else here for her apart from her dad. She had genuinely believed her taking the new job would be best for everyone, not just her.

She had been upfront about her father's condition with her potential new boss so would have been able to return to the UK when needed and had planned to come back once a month. But now she was unsure if that was enough and not just from Barry's perspective but also from her own. She had a dilemma and as she'd upset all her friends she had nobody to talk it over with.

She'd not realised how long she'd been staring into her

drink until the entry door buzzed and she put the cold mug down and went to answer the door.

'Hey, Cabbage, can I come up?'

'Sure,' she said and she buzzed Barry in.

When she opened the door, Gazza was first inside pulling the lead free from Barry's hand. The little dog did a lap of the apartment, clearly looking for someone. He returned to Barry with his lead bumping along sadly behind him and he flopped down with an audible huff.

'That yours?' asked Barry, pointing at the Cookie Monster T-shirt she was wearing.

She scratched her neck self-consciously. 'It's Cameron's.'

'And he's not here,' said Barry, scanning the place.

'No, he moved out first thing. I don't know where he is.' She'd been wondering most of the morning where he would have gone. 'Can I get you a drink?' she asked, tipping her cold coffee away.

'Err, a cuppa would be nice thanks.' Barry got out his mobile. 'Cameron is in Matlock.'

Ros cocked her head at him. 'What makes you think he's gone home?'

'Pete likes his social media and he's not following many people so if someone posts he usually sees it.'

'Who posted?'

'Cameron posted a picture of the Heights of Abraham and said, "Home sooner than planned."'

She was relieved to know where Cameron was, although that only lasted a moment. If he'd gone home, he'd likely be with Gina. She made the drinks. 'Did you want a biscuit or anything?'

'No, the tea is fine,' said Barry.

Ros checked the cupboard. Cameron had left something behind: one last bag of Hula Hoops. She took them and the drinks over to the sofa. 'Did you enjoy the party?' she asked.

'I had a terrific time. Don't know why we haven't done something sooner. We're all hoping to meet up every couple of months either for a coffee or lunch or maybe even a barbecue.'

'Nice.' Ros stuck her hand in the crisp packet and pulled out her finger with a Hula Hoop on the end. She considered it briefly before eating it off her finger. It wasn't a miracle cure but Cameron was right: it was more fun to eat them like that. She had a few more, then became aware that her dad was watching her. 'Sorry, did you say something?' she asked.

He smiled. 'No, I was remembering you doing that as a child.'

'Did I?' Ros was surprised. If she had eaten them like this, it was long forgotten.

'Yep.' He sipped his tea but he was still eyeing her closely. 'I know it's none of my business but I'm going to stick my oar in anyway. You and Cameron, you had the makings of a great relationship there. Surely you're not going to leave things as they are?'

Ros's shoulders sagged with the weight of her guilt. Now was the time to come clean. 'Dad, please don't judge me for what I'm about to tell you. But me and Cameron wasn't the big love affair you thought it was. You see . . .' It was so hard to tell him; she felt awful. The best thing she could do was spit it all out quickly and hope he didn't have a heart attack with the shock. 'I'm really sorry but I overheard you tell Uncle Pete that you wanted to see me settled in a relationship, so I paid Cameron to pretend to be my boyfriend.' She waited.

Barry was nodding and took ages before he spoke. 'I thought as much.'

'What?' Ros was instantly affronted that he'd seen through their intricately planned charade. 'How?'

'There were a few things that didn't add up at the start. And your mother thought she overheard something.'

'If you knew, why didn't you challenge us?'

'Because I guessed why you had done it. And thank you for that. It was an incredibly kind thing to do.' He reached out to squeeze her hand and she had to pop the two Hula Hoops that were on her fingers into her mouth quickly.

'At least you know the truth now. And everything is back to normal, so that's a relief,' she said.

'Is it?' He looked at her over his mug.

'Yes. It was exhausting keeping up the pretence.'

Barry pursed his lips. 'You see, I didn't see it like that. What I saw was two people who cared for each other, had each other's backs and enjoyed sharing time together. That was what I witnessed with my own eyes and I don't think either of you are that good at acting or that it was all make-believe. There was genuine friendship between you. You both had a laugh together but everyone could see there was also so much love and care for each other. There is no more solid base for a relationship than that.'

Ros wanted what he was saying to be true but that would just be a fantasy and she didn't need to torture herself with that. 'It's a lovely notion but I fear you are seeing things through rose-tinted spectacles.' She finished the last Hula

Hoop and scrunched up the packet. Gazza jumped to attention even though he'd seemed to be sound asleep.

'They're prescription varifocals and I can see perfectly well through them. Anyway, I'll not dwell on it.'

'Please don't, Dad. Cameron is very likely about to propose to someone else so . . .' The thought made her sadder than she cared to admit.

'Oh.' Barry seemed surprised. 'Is that why you've decided to work abroad?'

'It's not definite yet. I'm still thinking it over. But a fresh start was appealing. Although I did want to talk it over with you. I'd never go if you needed me here.'

'I understand.' He nodded. 'I think you should go. In life you usually only regret the things you don't do. Everything comes into sharp focus, either with or without varifocals, when someone stamps an end date on things. You need to do what's best for *you* now, nobody else.' He gave her a hug.

'Thanks, Dad. You'll be first to know when I decide.'

***

The day after the party Darla was still smarting that Ros was leaving for a new life and hadn't even told her. And she was having doubts about her ability to get a business off the ground without her friend to support and guide her. She swapped her livestock library books for business-related ones, which scared and bored her in equal measure. There was far more involved in setting up a new company and she didn't know where to start. Darla was busying herself with trying to work out how best to make a slide for the goats when she heard a familiar sound. She turned around to see Winston sitting on the garden wall.

'Winston, you're alive!' Emotion caught in her throat. She immediately called Elliott.

'Hiya, I was just thinking about you. How was the party?'

'Horrendous. Barry had a great time. Anyway, I have news. Winston has just rocked up. It's like yin and yang. A bad thing happens and then a good thing happens to balance it out.'

'Right. I'm not entirely sure I know what you're talking about but I'll be over in about half an hour. Please keep him occupied with tuna if necessary.'

They said their goodbyes and Darla ended the call. The whole time not daring to take her eyes off the elusive Winston. 'Goats, your play area will have to wait.' Nibbles bleated her annoyance at the delay, or at least it sounded like she was. Darla exited the goat pen and went to make a fuss of Winston. He seemed pleased to see her and happy to have his head scratched. From the cursory check she gave him he seemed fine, which was a relief. Now all she had to do was to lure him inside. Or easier still she could just pick him up and carry him in.

He was purring flat out when Darla gently lifted him into her arms. 'Good boy. You're going to get some tuna while we wait for Elliott.' The cat rubbed around her chin. It was all going well until she had to loosen her hold so that she could open the back door and that was when Winston took off. With a quick wriggle he was out of Darla's one-arm hold and away. 'Noooooo!'

Darla was inside waiting for the kettle to boil when Elliott let himself in. 'Hiya. Where's the wanderer?' he asked, looking about the kitchen.

'I'm really sorry. I had him in my arms but then I couldn't hold him properly when I was opening the door and he just jumped down and ran off. I can't find him. Even the tuna didn't work.' She pointed at the open tin on the table.

'Oh, never mind. I'm sure he'll come back,' said Elliott, not looking convinced by his own words.

Darla's phone rang. It was the house-sitting agency. 'I'd better get this,' she said to Elliott before answering the call.

Darla listened as the person on the other end made her already crappy day much worse. She thanked them – for what, she wasn't sure – and ended the call.

'Everything all right?' asked Elliott, filling the waiting mugs now the kettle had boiled.

'No,' said Darla. 'I can't believe it. I'm being evicted. I knew this wasn't forever but now someone is buying the place so they were telling me I'm not needed anymore, but they don't know exactly when my last day here will be. I'm going to be homeless again,' said Darla with a sob.

Elliott was quick to wrap her in a hug. 'It's okay. Everything is going to be fine because—'

'No, it's not! I love it here. I even love the goats and the chickens. Except for The Captain,' she said as more tears dripped off her chin. 'He's still a vicious little bugger.'

'Here,' said Elliott, handing her a clean tissue.

She dried her eyes to see he was smiling. That wasn't really the reaction she was expecting. Mutual dismay felt more appropriate. 'This is serious you know. I'll have to leave. I won't be just up the road anymore.'

348

'Slow down,' said Elliott. 'I was waiting to tell you something.'

'Tell me what?'

'I'm not going to be a farmer anymore.' He looked very pleased when he said it. 'It's because of you and what you said about me having to do what makes me happy. I'm going to go back to being a civil engineer. I start in a few weeks.'

'Right. Congratulations,' said Darla, feeling that she probably didn't sound as enthusiastic for his news as she should have, but it was hard when her world was imploding.

'I'm keeping the farm. Lee is going to be a tenant farmer so I can dabble if I want to, but it won't be my full-time job.'

'Great.' Darla tried hard to find a smile.

'Oh, and I've missed the really important bit. I'm buying The Brambles.'

It took a moment for what he said to register. 'It's you who's kicking me out?'

'Or you could stay . . .'

Darla was very confused. 'You want me to house-sit for you?'

'No, I want you to move in with me.' He wobbled his head. 'I guess technically I'd be moving in with you but you get what I mean. Sorry I didn't tell you before; it's taken a while to work all the finances out and then it all happened quite fast and I hadn't factored on word getting through to you so quickly.'

Darla blew her nose. 'Then I'm not homeless. And you want us to live together?'

'Beautifully summarised. Assuming you want to do that too?' He suddenly looked unsure, which was odd because right at that moment Darla had never been more certain of anything in her life. She threw her arms around his neck and kissed him.

They were interrupted by mewing outside and the sound of paws on the back door. They sprung apart. 'Winston!' they both said together as they leapt to their feet. They dashed for the back door. Darla got there first but she was surprised by what she saw as she opened it.

Winston was there but he wasn't alone. There was also a very pretty pale ginger striped cat and four kittens. Two with the same pretty pale ginger colouring as the new feline and two mini versions of Winston. Darla started to cry all over again.

Chapter Forty

It was a couple of days after the party and Ros was feeling apprehensive. The paella was almost ready but her guests hadn't arrived. When the entry buzzer sounded she was relieved and let them in. First to arrive was her dad and Gazza. As she hugged Barry, Gazza did his now usual lap of the apartment in search of Cameron. Ros put some water down for him and offered him a chew stick she'd bought specially. Gazza grabbed the treat and trotted off to eat it under the table. The buzzer went again and she let in her second guest. Darla tentatively put her head around the door before coming inside.

'Darla, hello. I didn't know you'd been summoned too,' said Barry.

'Hi, Barry.' Darla gave him a hug.

Ros waited until they parted and both looked at her expectantly. 'I asked you here because I thought it best to explain that—'

'Is this a farewell dinner?' asked Darla, putting her hands on her hips.

Barry's expression was tense.

Ros shook her head. 'No, I'm not taking the overseas job.'

'Thank heavens for that!' Darla wrapped her in a big hug and squeezed her tight. 'I'm over the flipping moon. I've tried to stay mad at you but it's really hard. And I proper missed you.'

'It's only been two days.'

'Still two days too long,' said Darla, giving her friend another hug. 'And now you can help me with my business and it won't fail. Hurray!'

'I'll do my best.' Ros was already feeling that she'd definitely made the right choice.

Barry waited his turn. 'I'm pleased you're staying. But only if you're sure it's what you want to do.' He watched closely for her response. The parallel to her mother's life choices had not passed Ros by. The thought that she was about to repeat her mother's mistake had been the cold hard reality check she'd needed.

'I decided I wanted to be around both of you more than I wanted to get away from . . . everything else. You are the most important things in my life and I'm sorry it took all of this for me to see that.'

'Don't beat yourself up,' said Barry.

'The universe works in mysterious ways,' added Darla with a wise nod.

'I've already contacted the other company who were lovely about it and said if things change I should get in touch. And then my boss called me in, said he'd heard rumours that I'd been head-hunted. I confirmed that was true and he offered me a pay rise and a bigger remit.'

'So it's all worked out for the best,' said Barry. 'I am pleased.'

'Yes,' said Ros. Although it didn't feel that way. She missed Cameron. There was a big Cameron-shaped hole in her life – he was going to take a lot to get over.

'Brilliant, what's for dinner?' asked Darla.

'I'm making paella. And there's fizz chilling in the fridge.'

'Lovely,' said Barry.

'Hang on. Is this Cameron's famous recipe?' asked Darla.

Ros nodded.

Darla smiled at her. 'Then we're in for a treat.'

***

Barry popped the cork of the champagne, which made Gazza bark and while Ros was serving up Darla tried to encourage Barry onto the balcony. 'Come and look at the view,' she said.

'I know. I have been here before,' he said with a laugh.

'Barry,' she hissed as she grabbed his arm. 'Come outside.' Sometimes men needed the unsubtle approach.

'Oh, okay.' Barry followed her onto the balcony and Darla pulled the door to. As soon as she had done that Gazza came to paw on the other side. 'For goodness' sake,' she said, letting him join them.

'Is everything all right?' asked Barry.

'I don't think so but I don't know how to fix it,' she said in hushed tones. 'I was hoping you could help.'

'What's wrong?' he asked.

'I think Ros and Cameron like each other for real but he's gone home to ask some girl he's not dated for years to marry him. And Ros is here, moping.'

'I know,' said Barry. 'Those two were made for each other. They need their heads banging together.' Darla and Barry both peered through the glass door to see Ros watching them with a furrowed brow. They both grinned at her and turned away quickly.

Darla pointed excitedly at the boats in the marina so that Ros wouldn't be too suspicious. 'I just think maybe there's something we can do.'

'Great. Then we should do it,' said Barry.

'Okay. What is it that we're doing?' asked Darla.

'Getting those two together.'

'Yes, but how? He's in Matlock and she's here.' She bit her lip.

'Hmm, that's a good point. But I'm sure we can work something out.'

'Are you gossiping?' asked Ros, whipping open the patio doors and making them both jump.

'Admiring the view, and the big boats,' said Darla, pointing at them with her glass.

'I expect you're enjoying having the place back to yourself. Not having to share with a messy student,' said Barry and out of sight Darla mimed: *What the hell are you doing?* Barry waved away her protest.

'Er, not exactly,' said Ros. 'He wasn't messy. And strangely I'd got used to having him around.'

'Right.' Barry pouted. 'Would you say you're missing him then?'

Ros swallowed hard. 'It was a business arrangement that always had a finite duration.'

'Admit it, you liked Cameron, didn't you?' said Darla.

'It's all academic now and not something I want to dwell

354

on. And dinner's ready,' said Ros, going back inside.

'Lovely,' said Barry. As Darla went to walk inside, he caught her arm and held her back for a moment. 'They've done so much for me, I think trying to get them to realise how good they are for each other is the least we can do. Failing that we'll bang their heads together.'

'Agreed,' whispered Darla. Now all she had to do was come up with a foolproof plan that Ros wouldn't see straight through. She had a feeling that wasn't going to be easy.

A few days later Darla had invited Ros to meet her for dinner at the little Italian restaurant in town and was sipping her water while she waited. She and Barry had dreamed up a plan, but it was far from foolproof and certainly not up to Ros's planning standard. As Darla sat there she went over all the things that could go wrong. She checked the time on her phone. Three minutes until Ros was due. Darla bit the inside of her lip and watched people go by out of the window. Her phone pinged with a text message and she almost leapt out of her chair; she was that jittery because there was a lot riding on this. The message was from Barry.

How's it going?

Darla replied:

Nothing to report. Will update when or if anything happens.

Barry replied:

OK. On tenterhooks here.

Darla:

You and me both.

Darla took a deep breath and tried to calm herself down. She was pleased to see Ros walking towards the restaurant. Darla could mentally tick off one thing that was going to plan. But that was only a small part of what needed to happen if this was going to work. Ros came inside although she was frowning hard as she approached.

'Hiya,' said Darla, trying possibly too hard to sound breezy. 'You okay?' she asked as they hugged. 'You look well.'

Ros pursed her lips. 'Do you remember the last time we came here?'

Darla was instantly delighted. She had picked this restaurant for a very specific reason. 'Err, I'm not sure. We came here a few months back. I liked the linguine. The wine was chilled. Am I missing something?' Darla retook her seat and pretended to peruse the menu.

'I was coming here when I got a pie in the face from a bunch of students. And one of them was Cameron.' Ros was staring out of the window as if rewatching the scene.

'Oh yeah. Bloody students,' said Darla, hiding behind the menu.

'Anyway. How are you?' asked Ros, sitting down.

'Good. Elliott has already started handing over responsibility at the farm. Before he starts his new job as a civil engineer we're having a bit of a staycation with some added decorating. I've invited my parents down, which is both terrifying and exciting, and Nibbles might be pregnant.'

'That's quite a lot going on,' said Ros, although she was distracted by something outside. 'What on earth?'

Darla turned around and saw her cue to leave. 'I wonder what that's all about,' she said before grabbing her bag and dashing off.

＊

It took Ros a moment to realise she had been set up. Cameron was standing outside the restaurant window wearing a tutu. He waved tentatively and pointed at Darla's now vacated seat. Ros nodded and Cameron grinned back at her. Oh how she'd missed that smile.

All heads turned as he walked confidently through the restaurant. 'Hiya,' he said, seeming shy as he reached the table. 'Can I join you?'

'If you want to, I'd like that.' He slid into the seat opposite. Ros tried to ignore the bright orange tutu that was sticking up above the table. 'It's lovely to see you but I'm wondering what's going on.'

'I heard you're not taking the job and that you're sticking around,' he said.

'And that warranted dashing back to Southampton in a tutu?'

He laughed. 'Not exactly. I think I might have been a bit hasty and I'm sorry for the way I reacted on the boat. I'd just heard that message on the answerphone and I felt you were making decisions for both of us. Ending things. It felt like a real break-up and I guess I was more invested in us than I wanted to admit.'

'I think we both were. So how have you been?' she asked.

'Miserable.'

'Oh.' That wasn't what she'd expected him to say. 'Why?'

'I missed you.'

Ros's stomach clenched. Did that mean what she hoped it did? 'What about Gina?'

Cameron pulled a face. 'Turns out she was also very drunk the night I promised to marry her and has absolutely no recollection of it whatsoever. She thought it was hilarious that I felt I had to honour that commitment. She laughed so hard I feared she was going to rupture something. She'll be dining out on this forever.'

'That was a little hurtful,' said Ros, feeling for Cameron's ego at being rejected and laughed at.

'No, she's cool. We'll always be the best of mates, but there's nothing else there.'

Ros swallowed. 'I see. That's a shame.' She felt that was probably the right thing to say.

'Is it?' He leaned forward. 'I was hoping you and I could start again.'

As if Ros wasn't confused enough a waiter appeared and placed a paper plate piled high with shaving foam in between them.

'I didn't order that?' she said.

'I did,' said Cameron. 'I think that day I met you – and you took a pie to the face for me – was a key moment. And I'd like to even things up. So if you want to get your revenge . . .' He tilted his head at the custard pie.

'I don't think so,' said Ros. She didn't like mess.

'Please.' Cameron was giving her one of his looks that made her insides feel like they were full of jelly.

'You want me to squish this in your face. And make us quits?'

'Exactly.' He closed his eyes and leaned forward.

'Okay.' She picked up the plate and stuck it in his face. The other diners in the restaurant broke into a mix of laughter, gasps and a round of applause. As Cameron wiped foam from his face Ros noticed there was something written on the bottom of the paper plate. She put it down so she could read it properly. *You took a risk. Congratulations – you have won a date with Cameron DeFelice.*

'What is this?' asked Ros, laughing.

'You won a prize!' he said. 'A proper for real date with me.'

'Will you be wearing the tutu?' she asked.

'Only if you want me to,' he said with a grin.

'I think perhaps we can lose that.'

'Is that a yes to going on a date?' he asked, seeming unsure.

'It is.'

'That's good, because otherwise I'd feel like a fool when you saw the other side of the plate.'

Ros picked it up, turned it over and wiped off the remaining foam. Underneath it said – *Ros Foster, I love you, signed Cameron DeFelice.*

'I know you like things to be official,' he said. 'Can I kiss you?'

Ros didn't have to do a risk assessment for that one. 'Definitely.'

He leaned across the table and their lips met. The restaurant diners burst into applause. When they pulled apart, Ros was distracted by someone tapping on the glass window behind them. There was Darla and Barry both giving her the thumbs up, while Gazza pawed at the glass in a desperate attempt to get to Cameron.

'I'm guessing you had help with this,' she said.

'Yeah, just a bit,' said Cameron as he waved them away and went in for another kiss.

Epilogue

One week later

The smell of the barbecue was filling the air at The Brambles and Darla was on tenterhooks waiting for her parents to arrive. It was a warm sunny day with enough breeze to ruffle the leaves in the trees and to make the goats slightly skittish. They loved their new activity centre; there was usually at least one of them on it unless there was food about, then that always took priority.

It was a little gathering of the friends Darla had amassed since she'd moved to Southampton and even she was quite surprised with how many people she knew and could now call her friends. There were lots of people from both her jobs, plus Ros, who was more like family now, so she'd invited her mum, dad and Gazza too. Gazza was busy tailing Elliott, like a little furry bodyguard, as he ferried food from the kitchen. Darla watched Elliott carrying the tray of meat. His muscles were showing nicely under his polo shirt. He was such a lovely man and she was so lucky to have him in her life.

If she could just explain everything to her parents without them wanting to disown her then it would all be perfect. Darla had set up the grill at the side of the house and now the charcoal was lit there were plumes of smoke coming off it and straight into Elliott's face.

'It's a bit windy here so I'm going to move around to the back of the house,' said Elliott.

'No, you can't,' said Darla. 'I've done kebabs.'

Elliott looked confused. 'There's space for everything.'

She pulled him a bit further around the side of the house. 'They're *chicken* kebabs,' she whispered with a theatrical nod towards the back of the property.

Elliott grinned as realisation struck. 'You're worried about upsetting the hens?'

'I'd be a bit traumatised if you slapped a human toe on there.'

'I think everyone would be disturbed by that. Including the chickens,' said Elliott. 'Okay, how about I turn the barbecue so the smoke blows in the other direction?'

'Great solution,' she said, giving him a kiss. They were interrupted by the sound of car wheels on gravel and her stomach felt like it was full of stones.

Ros appeared. 'I'll keep an eye on everything here while you speak to them,' she said, giving Darla a much-needed hug. 'You've got this. And I've got you,' she added.

Darla swallowed hard. 'Thanks.' She turned around, slapped on a smile and went to face the reckoning.

***

Ros went on tiptoes to look over the wall and watch Darla greet her parents who seemed impressed by the faded grandeur of The Brambles. She wished she could do more to help but this was something Darla had to do alone. All she could do was be there to support her whatever the outcome. She was fast learning that was what friends were for, and what an important lifeline they were. She felt familiar hands slide around her waist as Cameron hugged her from behind, his hair and then his face appearing at her shoulder. 'Has the firing squad arrived?' he asked.

'Don't say that! I hope she's okay. And them too to be fair. It'll be a bit of a shock. They think she's been sailing the seven seas trying exotic cuisine when she's been here living off discounted food from the 7-Eleven.'

'Come on, get a sausage while they're hot,' he said, taking her hand. 'Elliott is also a *Doctor Who* fan. Seems like a top bloke to me.'

'He's making Darla happy so that's all that matters.'

'I hope I can do the same,' he said.

Ros raised her eyebrows.

'With you I mean. Not Darla,' he clarified.

'Well recovered.' They joined the small queue for food behind Barry and Amanda. Ros had queried Darla's suggestion to invite her mother, but Darla argued that there was safety in numbers and that Ros should make a bigger effort to spend time with Amanda. The tides were changing and Ros was starting to feel differently about her mother. Their chat on the yacht and Ros's own dilemma over the job opportunity had helped her to at least understand a little better the situation her mother had been faced with. They were very different people but they were slowly getting to know each other.

'I like your top,' said Amanda.

'Thank you. Cameron has a better eye for casual attire than I do,' said Ros.

'Should the dog not be on a lead?' Amanda asked Barry.

'No, he's fine. He can't get out of the garden,' said Barry.

Gazza was busy patrolling the line. He barked when he reached Cameron, even though he'd already greeted him a number of times already. Unfortunately his bark was quite sharp and a lady who had just had a selection of barbecue food added to her plate jumped and lost her sausage. Gazza was on it like a seagull after a chip. Despite its temperature the sausage disappeared in a matter of seconds and Gazza was already looking around for the next one.

'Whoops,' said Barry quietly to Ros and Cameron as if trying not to out himself as Gazza's owner. He spotted them holding hands. 'Hey, look at you two back together.'

'Well—' began Ros but Barry waved her words away.

'I know what you're going to say. But you've always been great together in my book.'

'Thanks, Dad.' It meant the world to her that he was so happy that they were properly in a relationship now. It was early days but as a lot of the groundwork had been done it was all feeling pretty wonderful from her perspective, and the fact that no flip charts had been required was a revelation and also a slight disappointment but she'd get over that.

'How are you, Barry?' asked Cameron.

'So far so good,' he said. 'I'm the model patient apparently. Everything is going well. And long may it last.'

Gazza barked at the same lady who promptly dropped her replacement sausage. 'Not again,' said Barry in hushed tones as Gazza wolfed down the ill-gotten gains.

Darla came out of the back door with her parents right behind her. Ros really wanted everything to be okay. She'd not expected it but setting things straight with her own mother had been a huge relief. It was going to take some time to build trust between them but they now had regular meet-ups in the diary. They had even been for a takeaway coffee together and made a stop at the bench at Sunset Shore.

'Please just grab me a hot dog,' said Ros to Cameron. 'I need to check on Darla.'

'Sure,' said Cameron, giving her a brief kiss, as if he would miss her while she was away from him.

Ros walked over to her friend. 'How'd it go?'

'Okay. A little bumpy. They were a bit upset that I felt I couldn't tell them the truth. And amazed that I made all those trips up.' Darla pulled a face. 'But they like The Brambles, they want to meet Elliott and they're really supportive of my new business. And the best bit was I got loads of hugs.' She wiped away a tear. 'I've really missed them.'

'I know you have. But it sounds like it went brilliantly. Well done.' She gave her a hug. 'Does it feel like a weight has been lifted?'

Darla took a deep breath. 'More like all the little chickens that have been roosting in my mind have been let out into the run.'

Ros wasn't sure what that meant. But rather than challenge her friend she said, 'I'm glad they've gone.'

'I guess they've made room for all the trials running my own business is going to throw at me.'

'I know you're going to be just fine on that front.

Remember who did the risk assessment?' she said with a smile. 'Come on, let's get some food.' Ros linked her arm in Darla's and they walked back to the barbecue.

Cameron turned around and smiled at them both. He was the happiest person Ros had ever met and it was infectious. He went to hand her a hot dog just as Gazza barked. Cameron tightened his grip and the sausage flew out the end of the bun.

'Gazza!' The little dog grabbed his prize and ran off at speed, making everyone laugh, even Amanda.

THE END

Acknowledgements

Firstly a big thank you to everyone at Team Avon. It has been my home for ten books and I am hugely thankful for everything they've done for me. Special thanks to my editor Rachel Hart for her support and for loving the character of Ros as much as I did! Thank you to Enya Todd for the illustration for the fabulous cover, and to Emily Langford for designing it.

Thanks to my long-suffering agent, Kate Nash, who is always there with support and wise words. Sometimes they make me sit and rock in a corner for a while, as I did when she said the original second thread of this book needed to be swapped out. It was a mammoth task but she was absolutely right and this is a much better book for it. So thank you for being there for the tough conversations as well as the lovely lunches!

Big thank yous to my technical experts – Heather Guppy and Anne Boffey – for all things nautical. Thanks especially to Heather for going above and beyond with a visit to her yacht, being a beta reader and for providing a demonstration of how to put on a life jacket in the garden centre café. Thanks to Andy Hobbs from Solent Superyacht Charters who I met at the Royal Southampton Yacht Club where he answered all my questions about superyachts.

Thanks to Sarah Bennett, Donna Ashcroft, Pernille Hughes, Anita Chapman and Jules Wake for an exciting writing retreat ;-) which was where this novel was born and the planning began.

Thanks to Christie Barlow and Paula Fleming for brainstorming, great food and laughs in Norfolk which helped to get this book written.

Love and thanks, as always, to my family for their ongoing support. I couldn't do this without you.

Big shout out to all the book bloggers, booksellers and library staff for reviewing and recommending my novels. And, of course, a huge thank you to you my lovely readers for choosing my book – happy reading!

One ambitious businesswoman.
One irresponsible heir. A deal that will turn
both their lives upside down . . .

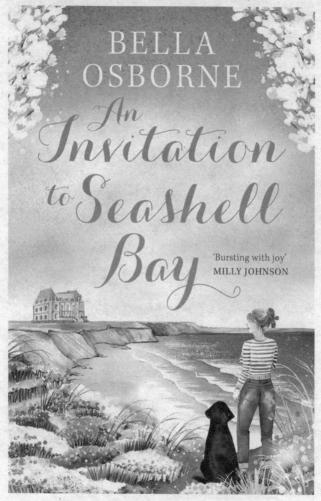

BELLA
OSBORNE

An
Invitation
to Seashell
Bay

'Bursting with joy'
MILLY JOHNSON

Available in all good bookshops now.

**One blind date. One chance encounter.
One life-changing moment.**

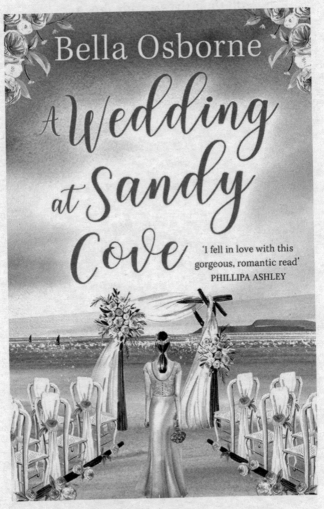

Available in all good bookshops now.

Ruby's life is about to change for ever . . .

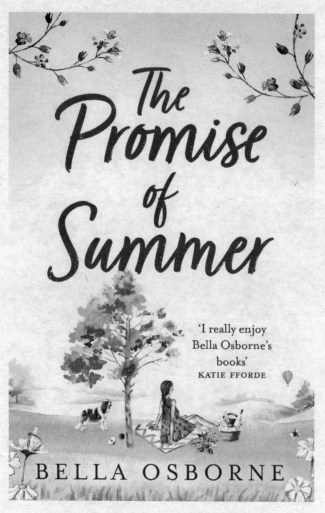

The
Promise
of
Summer

'I really enjoy
Bella Osborne's
books'
KATIE FFORDE

BELLA OSBORNE

Available in all good bookshops now.

A big family. A whole lot of secrets.
A Christmas to remember . . .

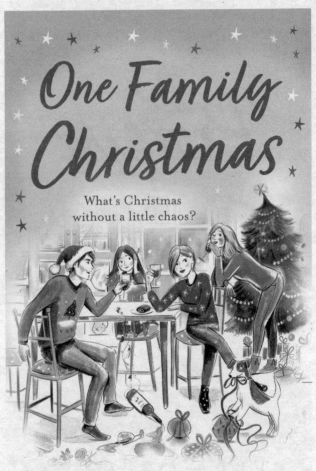

One Family

Christmas

What's Christmas
without a little chaos?

BELLA OSBORNE

Available in all good bookshops now.

Regan is holding a winning lottery ticket.
Goodbye to the boyfriend who never had her back, and
so long to the job she can't stand!
Except it's all a bit too good to be true . . .

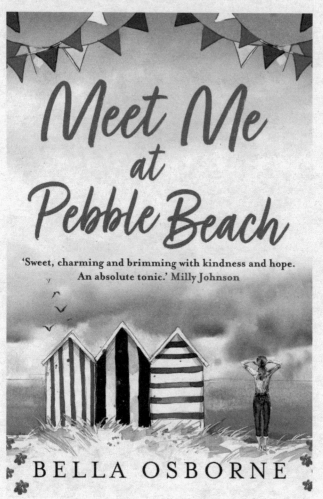

Meet Me
at
Pebble Beach

'Sweet, charming and brimming with kindness and hope.
An absolute tonic.' Milly Johnson

BELLA OSBORNE

Available in all good bookshops now.

Life's not always a walk
in the park . . .

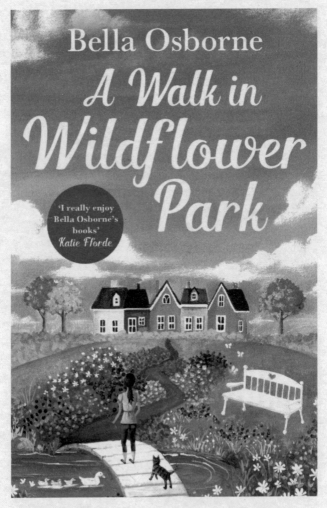

Available in all good bookshops now.

Join Daisy Wickens as she returns to
Ottercombe Bay . . .

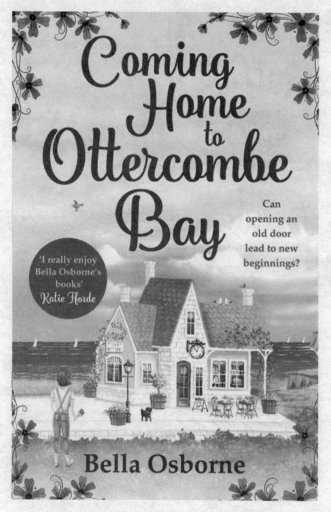

Coming
Home
to
Ottercombe
Bay

Can
opening an
old door
lead to new
beginnings?

'I really enjoy
Bella Osborne's
books'
Katie Fforde

Bella Osborne

Available in all good bookshops now.

**Don't miss these delightful
cottage adventures . . .**

Available in all good bookshops now.

EXCLUSIVE ADDITIONAL CONTENT

Includes an exclusive, previously cut scene and
details of how to get involved in *Fern's Picks*

Dear lovely readers,

I'm delighted to introduce you to our next pick,
Finding Love at Sunset Shore – a gorgeous,
emotionalbut ultimately heartwarming read set
in sunny Southampton.

In *Finding Love at Sunset Shore*, we are introduced to Ros,
who is left with a serious predicament after she overhears
that her father's dying wish is for her to find love. That's
where Cameron, a struggling mature student, comes
in. The pair concoct a plan which could just help solve
both of their problems, but it's not long before
their differences drive each other crazy.

Full of humour, warmth and irresistible charm, *Finding
Love at Sunset Shore* will make for perfect reading in
the sunshine. I hope you love this feel-good novel!

with love
Fern x

Look out for more books, coming soon!

For more information on the book club,
exclusive Q&As with the authors and
reading group questions, visit Fern's website
www.fern-britton.com/ferns-picks

We'd love you to join in the conversation,
so don't forget to share your thoughts using
#FernsPicks

An exclusive, previously cut scene:
A date at the theatre

Warning: contains spoilers

As they walked by the theatre, Cameron stopped abruptly and stepped in front of her. 'You like classic musicals so I took a punt on *My Fair Lady*,' he said, producing a pair of tickets. He looked at her over the tickets. 'I don't know anything about musicals so this may have been a very bad idea.' He scrunched up his features as he waited for her response. Ros was taken aback. She generally despised surprises, but she had to concede that on this occasion she impact was pleasant.

'Excellent choice,' she said.

'Have you seen it before?' asked Cameron.

'I have.'

He looked disappointed and she was quick to try to change his expression.

'But it was a very long time ago.' Memories flooded Ros's mind. 'My mother took me to London to see it as a child. I was enthralled. Loved every minute of it. She did too. She overanalysed the story and the characters afterwards but then that's what she always did. Turned everything into a study.'

'Right. But you don't mind seeing it again?'

'I'd love to see it again. I think I may view it differently as an adult,' said Ros, already looking forward to the experience.

'Great, let's get some cola and ice-cream,' Cameron said,

holding the door open and standing back.

'Here I think it's more Prosecco and scones, I'm afraid.'

'Oh, that's cool too,' said Cameron, regaining his confident exuberance as they went inside.

Cameron was over the moon to find that they did do ice-cream as well as cake and a number of other options so they went into the auditorium with a small picnic of unhealthy food and drinks. Inside, it was like stepping back in time to a golden age. The little theatre had received a grant some years before and, after a lengthy programme of work, had been restored to its former glory. The space had almost a glow about it thanks to the matching crimson walls, giant stage curtains and seating.

Cameron lead the way and they got themselves settled. The seats were good, he'd gone for second row balcony on the end to enable him to stretch out his long limbs. But the view of the stage was excellent. It had been a while since Ros had been to the theatre. She had to have a long think about when it might have been. It wasn't something she did now and she wondered how many things had left her life in a similar manner. Pastimes that she had once enjoyed simply deleted. Perhaps it wasn't wise to dwell on such things. If she had cast aside frivolous theatre visits then it was for good reason. Work was all-encompassing and it was often difficult to fit other things around it. And there was no tangible benefit to a trip to the theatre. However, despite her thoughts Ros still enjoyed a little frisson of excitement as the lights went down and hush descended.

Cameron leaned into her space and she paused. 'Are you okay? Do you have everything you need?' he whispered.

'Yes, Cameron. I believe I do.'

Questions for your Book Club

Warning: contains spoilers

- Which of the characters in the story did you most relate to? Why do you think that was the case?

- Ros was presented with a way to put her father's mind at rest. What would you have done in this situation?

- Ros was risk averse. Why do you think she was like this?

- Why do you think Ros felt so strongly about her mother having left the family home?

- Darla took on a lot at The Brambles thanks to a miscommunication. What would you have done in her situation?

- What do you think Ros learned from Cameron and vice versa?

- How do you feel Ros's relationships changed throughout the story? (Relationships with her father, mother, Darla, Cameron, Gazza and her work colleagues.)

- What was your favourite part of the story? Why?

- What do you think the future holds for Ros and Cameron?

- How did the book make you feel? Did it evoke any emotions?

Fern's
Picks

An exclusive extract from Fern's new novel

The Good Servant

March 1932

Marion Crawford was not able to sleep on the train, or to eat the carefully packed sandwiches her mother had insisted on giving her. Anxiety, and a sudden bout of homesickness, prohibited both.

What on earth was she doing? Leaving Scotland, leaving everything she knew? And all on the whim of the Duchess of York, who had decided that her two girls needed a governess exactly like Miss Crawford.

Marion couldn't quite remember how or when she had agreed to the sudden change. Before she knew it, it was all arranged. The Duchess of York was hardly a woman you said no to.

Once her mother came round to the idea, she was in a state of high excitement and condemnation. 'Why would they want *you*?' she had asked, 'A girl from a good, working class family? What do you know about how these people live?' She had stared at Marion, almost in reverence. 'Working for the royal family . . . They must have seen something in you. My daughter.'

On arrival at King's Cross, Marion took the underground to Paddington. She found the right platform for the Windsor train and, as she had a little time to wait, ordered a cup of tea, a scone and a magazine from the station café.

She tried to imagine what her mother and stepfather were doing right now. They'd have eaten their tea and have the wireless on, tuned to news most likely. Her mother would have her mending basket by her side, telling her husband all about Marion's send off. She imagined her mother rambling on as the fire in the grate hissed and burned.

The train was rather full, but Marion found a seat and settled down to flick through her magazine. Her mind couldn't settle. Through the dusk she watched the alien landscape and houses spool out beside her. Dear God, what was she doing here, so far away from family and home? What was she walking into?

When the conductor walked through the carriage announcing that Windsor would be the next stop, she began to breathe deeply and calmly, as she had been taught to do before her exams. She took from her bag, for the umpteenth time, the letter from her new employers. The instructions were clear: she was to leave the station and look for a uniformed driver with a dark car.

She gazed out of the window as the train began to slow. She took a deep breath, stood up and collected her case and coat. *Come on, Marion. It's only for a few months. You can do this.*

Available now!

Fern's Picks

The No.1 Sunday Times bestselling author returns

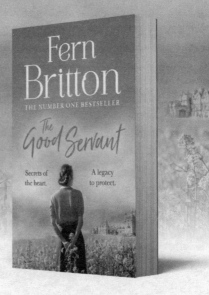

Balmoral, 1932

Marion Crawford, an ordinary but determined young woman,
is given a chance to work at the big house as governess
to two children, Lilibet and Margaret Rose.

Windsor Castle, 1936

As dramatic events sweep through the country and change all their lives
in an extraordinary way, Marion loyally devotes herself to the family.
But when love enters her life, she is faced with an unthinkable choice…

Available now!

Femi's Picks

Our next book club title

In a quiet village in Ireland, a mysterious local myth is about to change everything…

One hundred years ago, Anna, a young farm girl, volunteers to help an intriguing American visitor translate fairy stories from Irish to English. But all is not as it seems and Anna soon finds herself at the heart of a mystery that threatens her very way of life.

In present day New York, Sarah Harper boards a plane bound for the West Coast of Ireland. But once there, she unearths dark secrets that could change the course of her life…

With a taste for the magical in everyday life, Evie Woods's latest novel is full of ordinary characters with extraordinary tales to tell.